Pamela Evans was born and brought up in Ealing, London. She now lives in Surrey, near to her family and five beautiful grandchildren.

Her previous novels, which include THE TIDEWAY GIRLS, UNDER AN AMBER SKY, WHEN THE BOYS COME HOME, IN THE DARK STREETS SHINING and THE SPARROWS OF SYCAMORE ROAD, are also available from Headline.

HARVEST NIGHTS

Pamela Evans

headline

First published in 2010
by HEADLINE PUBLISHING GROUP

First published in paperback in 2010
by HEADLINE PUBLISHING GROUP

4

Cataloguing in Publication Data is available from the British Library

ISBN 978 0 7553 4545 8

Typeset in Bembo by Palimpsest Book Production Limited,
Falkirk, Stirlingshire

Printed and bound in Great Britain by
Clays Ltd, St Ives plc

Headline's policy is to use papers that are natural, renewable and
recyclable products and made from wood grown in sustainable forests.
The logging and manufacturing processes are expected to conform
to the environmental regulations of the country of origin.

HEADLINE PUBLISHING GROUP
An Hachette UK Company
338 Euston Road
London NW1 3BH

www.headline.co.uk

To my lovely family

Acknowledgements

Many thanks to Sherise Hobbs, Celine Kelly and the rest of the team at Headline, including the designers who produced such a gorgeous jacket. Thanks also to my agent Barbara Levy, and historical researcher Ruth Boreham who helped me to find out about apple growing in the 1920s.

Chapter One

1920

'You've spilled the milk, you clumsy girl,' the woman at the table by the potted palm complained. 'Look at the mess you've made. It's all over the tablecloth.'

It was an exaggeration of ludicrous proportions, since the tiny spot on the cloth was barely visible, but Clara Tripp said, 'I'm very sorry, madam. I'll go and get something to clear it up with at once.'

'No, that simply won't do,' declared the customer. 'I need a clean tablecloth.'

Clara inhaled a deep, calming breath, observing the woman's dark, hostile eyes peering at her from beneath the upturned brim of her black, flower-trimmed hat, and suppressed the urge to slap her for the sheer wastefulness of her demand. But the customer was always right here at Taylor's Tea rooms and staff courtesy was of the essence, so she said, 'Yes, of course, madam. I'll see to it right away.'

'I should think so too, and be quick about it or my tea and toast will go cold,' the woman commanded. 'I'm not going to eat or drink anything until the table is cleaned up.'

Bracing herself for a trouncing from the supervisor for adding to the laundry bills of the establishment, Clara weaved her way through the damask-topped tables, a slim, dark-eyed brunette of twenty-one, smartly accoutred in a black dress with a white pinafore and cap, black stockings and black shoes.

September sunlight filtered through the lace-curtained windows into the elegant interior of the popular West End tea room. The warm air was infused with the cinnamon scent of toasted teacakes, and a hubbub of refined conversation mingled with the clink of crockery. Clara was counting the minutes until her dinner break when she would go for a walk in nearby Hyde Park. But now she was being hailed by an impatient man who claimed, aggressively, that he'd been waiting far too long for his crumpets and if they didn't arrive soon he would go elsewhere for refreshment. Suitably apologetic, she assured him that she would chase his order up, received a sympathetic look from a passing waitress and went to the supervisor to report the man's complaint and ask for permission to get a clean tablecloth.

'You are trained not to spill so much as a smidgen of anything or act in any way that might be annoying to the customer,' lectured the supervisor, a warship of a woman of around forty in a black dress without the pinafore to illustrate her seniority. She didn't wait at table herself unless they were short-staffed or excessively busy but stood at the back of the room keeping a watchful eye on her team of waitresses. 'So why has this spillage happened?'

'I must have jogged the milk jug when I put it down on the table, but the drop was so small you could hardly see it,' Clara replied. 'The woman is being unreasonable.'

'Why would the customer make a fuss if there is no need?'

'For attention, perhaps,' suggested Clara.

'Mm. Maybe so, but people spend their money to come here and have us wait on them, and their patronage pays our wages,' the older woman pointed out sharply. 'So if they want a bit of extra fuss, that's what we will give them.'

'A clean tablecloth to replace one with hardly a mark on it seems a bit extravagant to me.'

'It isn't your place to comment,' snapped the supervisor. 'The customer claims you spilled enough milk to warrant a clean cloth so you did as far as I'm concerned. It is pure carelessness and not good for our reputation or for restaurant expenses. You're lucky it isn't policy here at Taylor's to deduct extra laundry costs caused by lack of care from a waitress's wages.'

'Sorry, miss.'

'So I should hope, and don't let it happen again.' She put her signature to an order form and handed it to Clara. 'Go along to the linen store and get a clean tablecloth and make sure you apologise wholeheartedly to the customer. Grovel if necessary to regain her favour. There are a great many establishments similar to ours in London at the moment and the competition for custom is fierce, so we have to keep on our toes and offer only the best quality service. Off you go now.'

Clara changed the tablecloth and carried on with her work. After the two complainants, it was a relief to receive courteous thanks and a generous tip from a satisfied customer. The latter usually outweighed the former because Taylor's was well known for the high quality of its food and service.

'Coming for a look round the shops?' asked one of the other waitresses who was eating her sandwiches in the staffroom when Clara went in for her dinner break.

'No, I'm going for a walk in the park. I'll eat my lunch on a bench in the fresh air.'

'We shouldn't have to bring our own sandwiches,' grumbled the girl. 'I've heard that Lyons waitresses are given free food when they're on duty. If Taylor's weren't so stingy they'd do that for us.'

'They might lower our wages to cover the cost, though, and I'd rather have the extra dosh,' said Clara.

'Mm. There is that, I suppose,' agreed the girl, munching into a fish paste sandwich.

'I'm off then,' Clara announced, slipping into her coat and removing her white starched cap. 'See you later.'

Oxford Street was choked with open-topped motor buses, cars and delivery vans as well as horse-drawn carts, barrows and bicycles. Clara hurried towards the park, the noise and fumes fading as she went through the gates and walked along the leafy paths, feeling invigorated by the crisp autumn air.

The trees were gloriously seasonal in varying shades of russet and yellow, dappled sunshine shining through them as she walked on a carpet of fallen leaves towards the Serpentine. By the lake she sat down on a bench to eat her lunch, observing people as they passed by. There were mothers and working nannies pushing high black perambulators, and shop girls on their breaks walking arm in arm. Office workers in their dark clothes were out making the most of the weather, too, before the onset of colder days. But what interested Clara most was a gardener working on one of the flower beds nearby, preparing it for winter.

Seeing him handling the soil reminded her of her time in the Land Army during the Great War, when she'd worked on an arable farm in Wiltshire. The land girls had put in long hours and the work had been so crippling that they'd ached right through to the bone when they'd crawled into bed at night. During winter months they'd been numb with cold during their outside labours and had had to scrape the ice off the inside of the bedroom windows every morning. To call the farmer a slave driver was a lenient description, but what laughs they'd had when he wasn't around; what camaraderie there had been between her and the women she was billeted with. Those Saturday night dances at the village hall had been terrific fun and there had been the long walks into town in search of civilisation, singing as they'd struggled to find their way along the country lanes.

She became reflective, recalling one particular village dance when she'd met a young soldier who'd been stationed at a camp nearby and had been soon to depart for the battlefields of France. He was from Kent, she remembered him telling her. His family had had an orchard there. They'd danced together all evening but she'd never seen him again, or ever forgotten him.

Most of her Land Army friends had been relieved when the war ended and they could return to less gruelling employment, but not Clara. The experience had given her a taste for something she felt completely in tune with. Unfortunately there wasn't any call for female agricultural workers nearly two years after the armistice. That sort of work was out of the question for a London-based woman like her.

Still, the war was over; that was the important thing

and she had nothing to complain about. The Tripps had been spared having anyone at the front; her father had been too old and her brothers too young. At least now-adays there were a few alternatives to domestic service for women, in restaurants and shops in the London area. Some that she knew had even found work in offices and factories.

She herself had a job with a modest but regular wage, and a family she adored even though they were infuriat-ingly different from other families of their ilk and had been a source of great embarrassment to her when she was younger and sensitive to such things. And, of course, there was Arnold, her betrothed. Sometimes, though, their courtship felt more like a habit than a love affair. But what else did she expect? A palpitating heart every time they met? That wasn't realistic. She'd been courting him for a year and he was a part of her life; a good man. It was only natural for the excitement to have worn off.

Finishing her last cheese sandwich, she rolled the paper bag into a ball and put it in the litter basket, then strode out around the park before she made her way back to work.

'Where's Mum, Cuddy?' Clara asked her eleven-year-old brother Cuthbert when she got home from work that evening.

'She's gone next door,' he replied. 'Someone's having a baby in there or somethin'.'

'You'll have to cook us a meal, Clara,' demanded her brother Sydney, a lean, dark-eyed, swarthy lad of sixteen. 'I'm starvin'.'

'There are some meat pies in the larder,' mentioned Cuddy helpfully. 'We could have those with mashed potato.'

Clara took a pinafore from the hook on the back of the door, looked in the larder for potatoes and started to peel them. This scenario was not unusual. Many a time Clara came home from work and had to get the family a meal because Mum had forgotten the time or gone to visit a sick neighbour, or had simply got talking in the local shop.

She heard someone come in the front door, and turned to greet her father.

'Your mother not in, then?' Frank observed as he came into the kitchen.

'She's gone next door,' Clara informed him. 'It sounds as though the baby's on its way.'

'Oh. Well, I don't suppose she'll be long,' he said vaguely. He was used to his wife's lack of organisation.

'Do you want me to lay the table, Clara?' offered Cuddy, who was the sweetest-natured boy.

'Yes please, love, if you wouldn't mind.'

'Are you a girl or somethin'?' asked Sydney, his dark eyes gleaming mockingly.

'No, o' course not.' Cuddy was fair-haired with blue eyes and his pale skin turned crimson at his brother's remarks as he got the knives and forks out of the kitchen drawer. 'There's nothing wrong with helpin'. I don't see why Clara has to do it all when Mum isn't here.'

'You're just crawlin' round her,' accused Sydney, who had a cruel streak in him lately, especially when it came to the treatment of his younger brother.

'No I'm not.'

'Leave him alone, Sydney,' said Clara. 'You're always picking on him.'

'The lad's only joking,' put in her father. 'Cuddy's got to be able to take a bit of teasing.'

7

'And he can, Dad, believe me,' Clara came back at him, fiercely defensive of her kid brother. 'Heaven knows he has to, the amount of it he gets from you and Sydney.'

The conversation was interrupted by the sound of the key being pulled through the letter box and the front door opening, heralding the arrival of Clara's mother.

'Sorry I'm late, my little chickens,' came her cheerful apology. 'I got held up. Her next door thought she was going into labour so I stayed with her till her husband got home from work. It turned out to be a false alarm in the end but I couldn't very well leave her while she was in a state and on her own, could I?'

'Course you couldn't, love, so don't worry about it,' said her husband, a dark-complexioned, handsome man, his near-black hair now tinged with grey. It was from him that Clara and Sydney had inherited their deep brunette looks. Frank was a labourer on the railways but subsidised his income from that with occasional wheeler-dealing through a contact in the local pub. 'Clara's taking care of everything.'

'What would we do without you, Clara?' trilled Flo, a dumpling of a woman with a mop of fair curly hair and round blue eyes. 'Give us the potato peeler. I'll take over now.'

'You've timed it right because I've just about finished,' said Clara with a grin.

'Oh, you,' Flo laughed, tapping her daughter's arm in a jocular fashion. 'I'll have the meal on the table when you get in tomorrow night. I promise.'

'Yeah, yeah, we'll see,' said Clara patiently.

What her mother lacked in domestic efficiency she made up for in heart, which meant that she was an easy person to forgive. It wasn't that she was lazy or uncaring. Clara remembered how she would sit up all night with any of her children when they were sick, and when Dad couldn't find work she went out at the crack of dawn cleaning shops and offices to put food on the table. It was just that her priorities were different from those of the other, more conventional women in the street and she seemed incapable of sticking to a routine. If she wanted to go and visit a neighbour, or bake some special cake that took ages and was usually a failure, she would do it and to hell with polishing the front step or cleaning the windows.

It could be annoying, especially when there was ironing to be done and Clara had to set to and do the job. For all that, she was a brilliant mother and Clara knew that she would give her life for her family if it was ever necessary. Of course, some people didn't see it that way. The less friendly residents of Green Street thought she was a bit of a fly-by-night who didn't look after her home properly. But their views weren't worth bothering with, in Clara's opinion.

The Tripps' reputation wasn't exactly top drawer in this working-class back street of Shepherd's Bush, what with Mum being thought of as slipshod, Dad doing the odd bit of business on the side with no questions asked, and Sydney's determination not to walk the straight and narrow.

Making a nuisance of himself was Sydney's speciality at the moment; he and a group of mates he hung around with. They gathered on street corners talking and laughing noisily, whistled and called out after girls, insulted all and sundry and pilfered from shops in what they thought of as a very clever lark. Her parents had no end of complaints about him. Clara loved him as a brother but didn't like him as a person these days, and hated the way he was with Cuddy.

Dear Cuddy, who sang like an angel and was constantly tormented by his brother and father for it. Whereas Clara and her mother recognised his lovely voice as a God-given talent and encouraged his musical ability, the other two judged it to be effeminate and never let him forget it. Unfortunately, Cuddy's admiration for his brother was unconditional and he wanted nothing more than to be like him, tough and streetwise. Over Clara's dead body! She hoped that Sydney was just going through a phase, because his bad behaviour was only recent. If it didn't pass soon he was going to end up in prison and break their mother's heart.

But now her mother was saying, 'You'd better turn the gas up under those spuds, love, or we'll have the others claiming starvation.'

Eventually they served up hot meat pies and mashed potato and the family sat round the table in the cosy, gas-lit parlour, a well-used room at the back of the house.

'We had a really good laugh today at work.' Sydney worked as an assistant and delivery boy for one of the grocery shops near Shepherd's Bush Green. 'This woman comes in the shop, a youngish piece, really smart, and well stacked up top, if you know what I mean. A pair of lovely porkers.'

'Enough of that sort of talk, Sydney,' Flo said sharply, while Cuddy erupted into giggles. 'I won't have it in this house.'

'I was only saying—'

'I heard what you were saying and I don't like it. You

were being vulgar and it isn't the sort of thing you should be talking about in front of your young brother.'

'I'm sure Cuddy knows about women's bosoms, dear,' said Frank mildly.

'Very probably, but I don't want him encouraged to speak of them in those sorts of terms. Anyway, you should be discouraging Sydney's disrespectful turn of phrase, not egging him on.'

'He's sixteen, for Gawd's sake. He's not a kid.'

'He still lives in this house—'

'Anyway,' interrupted Sydney, determined to say his piece. 'This bit o' stuff starts making eyes at the boss. She must have wanted something on the cheap.' He emitted a guffaw of mocking laughter. 'It wasn't him she wanted, that's for sure: he must be fifty if he's a day, the silly old duffer. But the joke is that his wife is standing next to him behind the counter. He goes all soppy over this bit of skirt and me and Marge were in stitches.'

Cuddy was mesmerised by the story, and even Frank was grinning, but Flo wasn't amused. 'You're mocking the man who pays your wages and it isn't right,' she admonished her son.

'Oh, give over, Flo,' said Frank. 'It's only a bit of fun.'

'So what happened then?' asked Cuddy, eager to know the rest of the tale. His brother could make an errand list seem riveting to the young boy.

'Well, the boss's missus takes over from him and sends him off to the stockroom to get something. She wasn't taking any chances with her ol' man. Laugh, we nearly died. You should have seen the young piece's face. She was hoping for a few slices of boiled ham for nothing and all

11

she got was a black look from an old bag with a face like a rotten apple.'

'That's quite enough,' intervened Clara firmly. 'That's no way to speak about people. Don't set your brother a bad example.'

'Mind your own business.'

'It is my business,' she informed him. 'You let this family down on a regular basis and I don't want my little brother copying your behaviour.'

'What's it got to do with you, you miserable cow,' he demanded. 'You're my sister, not my mother.'

'That's enough, Sydney,' said Flo. 'Don't talk to your sister like that.'

'Why not?'

'Because I say so,' she told him, almost shouting. 'You keep your gutter talk for the street and not this house.'

Sydney's eyes were hot with rage as he focused them menacingly on his mother and sister. Then he pushed his half-eaten meal away from him with such force that the contents of the plate spilled over on to the table-cloth. Before anyone had a chance to react, he scraped his chair back and stood up. 'I've had enough of this. You can stick your rotten food where the monkey stuffs his nuts.'

'Oi, oi . . . that's enough,' his father intervened, rising to his feet angrily. 'There's no call for that.'

As Frank took a step towards him Sydney was gone, out of the room and the house, slamming the front door after him.

Cuddy's eyes filled with tears.

'Don't upset yourself,' said Clara, putting a comforting hand on his arm.

'Sydney is always getting into trouble,' he wept, tears rolling down his cheeks. 'You lot are always telling him off.'

'Only because he's forever behaving badly,' Clara pointed out, thinking how peculiar human nature was in that the meaner Sydney was to Cuddy the more the younger boy admired him.

'Come on now, Cuddy,' urged his mother, clearing up the mess Sydney had made on the tablecloth. 'Finish your food and forget all about it.'

The boy pushed his plate away. 'I don't want any more,' he said thickly.

'Don't be silly, now,' Flo began.

'Stop fussing over him, for goodness' sake,' bellowed Frank irritably. 'And you, Cuddy, stop that ridiculous blub-bing and eat your meal properly. This family can't afford to waste food.' He turned to his wife. 'We need to main-tain some sort of discipline in this house, Flo.'

Especially in Sydney's case, thought Clara. It wasn't Cuddy who needed to be taken in hand. It was his brother. But she gave Cuddy an encouraging look and said gently, 'Eat what you can manage, kiddo.'

The air was fraught with tension caused entirely by Sydney but felt by Cuddy while his brother went off without a care, observed Clara. Sydney's moods ruled the household at the moment. Almost every day there was some sort of altercation with him. Why was he being like this? What had happened to the younger brother she had so adored when they were children?

She had been brought up to respect her parents and wouldn't normally voice her opinions on the way they raised their family. But when Cuddy had gone out into the street to play and she and her mother were alone in the kitchen washing the dishes, she said, 'I think Sydney is completely out of control, Mum. Something needs to be done about it before he gets into real trouble.'

Flo emitted an anxious sigh. 'I know. I've tried talking to him, but will he listen? It's these new mates of his. He's never been the same since he got in with them.'

'Perhaps Dad needs to come down a bit harder on him,' Clara suggested.

'What can your father do? He can't raise his hand to him. Not now that Sydney's almost a man and taller than his father. It would turn into a brawl and I won't have fighting in the house.'

'Dad could get tougher with him verbally. He could tell him to behave himself or get out.'

Flo swung round to look at her daughter in outrage, her hands dripping with washing-up water. 'Oh, Clara. I could never turn a child of mine out.'

'Only temporarily, of course. Just long enough to make him count his blessings.'

'But where would he go?'

'A bit of hard living for a short time might be exactly what he needs. Maybe it would bring him to his senses and make him realise just what he's got here and how much you and Dad do for him.'

'Absolutely not,' Flo stated. 'That isn't the answer.'

'Maybe it is a bit extreme,' Clara conceded. 'But his behaviour makes me so angry because he upsets all of us and he couldn't care less. You see all these poor ex-servicemen on the streets selling matches because there are no jobs for them when they've been out in France fighting for their country, while Sydney treats decent people like dirt and he's in paid employment and not a bit grateful for it.'

'They only pay him a pittance at the shop,' Flo pointed out, rubbing a plate with the dishcloth.

'It's still a job, Mum.'

'You can't blame Sydney for not being old enough to go to war.'

'No, of course not, but a bit of respect and gratitude for what he has wouldn't go amiss.'

'Mm,' murmured Flo. Her daughter had yet to experience the intense emotions of motherhood. Naturally she couldn't be expected to understand that every one of these quarrels with Sydney was like a knife in his mother's heart because she loved him and felt protective towards him no matter what. Those feelings hadn't lessened because he was grown up and badly behaved. He was still her child, but she no longer had control and didn't know what to do about it. She fully accepted that she was flawed as a house-keeper although she'd always tried her best to be a good mother, but the way things were at the moment she seemed to have failed dismally as far as Sydney was concerned.

'Don't worry about it, Mum,' Clara said in a gentler tone, sensing her mother's distress. She put her arm round her shoulder. 'It will all work out. Things usually do in the end. We'll get it sorted, you, me and Dad.'

'So just another ordinary evening at the Tripps' then,' Arnold remarked ironically that same night when Clara confided in him about the argument earlier. The couple were having a rare few moments alone on the sofa in the parlour, her parents and Cuddy having gone to bed, and Sydney not being home yet.

'You've said it,' she responded. 'The number of quarrels in this house lately is sky high; a night without some sort of row is the exception. And it's all Sydney's fault.'

'He'll grow out of it,' said Arnold, a well-built man of twenty-three with mid-brown hair, shandy-coloured eyes and a stubby moustache. 'He's just trying to prove what a big man he is. Most lads go through that.'

'You weren't all that much older than he is now when you went away to war,' she reminded him.

'I was a couple of years older and I was probably a right horror before I went,' he said. 'Anyway, thank God the war is over and he doesn't have to go.'

'Yes, of course.'

'Maybe that has something to do with it,' suggested Arnold thoughtfully. 'He can't go and prove he's a real hero so he throws his weight around at home.'

'What's being rude and generally obnoxious got to do with being a hero?'

'Nothing at all, but hanging around with a crowd of ruffians and getting into mischief makes him feel like a hard man. Round here that counts for a lot when you're his age. It'll pass.'

'I hope so, for all our sakes. I still believe he's a good lad at heart and has just got in with the wrong crowd,' she sighed. 'Poor Mum is at her wits' end.'

'Would you like me to have a quiet word with him?' he offered. 'I'm nearer to his age than your mum and dad and boys never listen to their sisters. I'm not saying it's the answer, but anything is worth a try.'

She looked at him gratefully, filled with fresh hope. Arnold was one person Sydney did seem to respect, maybe because he was strong, self-confident and never lost for words. 'What a good idea. He might listen to you. He's always looked up to you.'

'I wouldn't say that, but I've always got on well with him. I'll do it as soon as the opportunity arises.'

'Thanks, Arnold,' she said, squeezing his hand and looking into his deep-set eyes. 'You're a good sort.'

Arnold had already been back in Civvy Street when Clara had first met him, one of the thousands of men who had come back from the trenches to face the misery of unemployment. Initially he'd done a stint of street selling but he had eventually got a job as a van driver for a pie-making company and now went all over London delivering to shops. Sometimes the job took him further afield and he stayed away overnight. Arnold was a survivor, his positive attitude and likeable ways making him popular around these parts. Something of a rough diamond, he had a swagger about him which had appealed to Clara when she'd first met him at a local dance. He'd asked her out, they'd got on well and it had developed from there.

'That's all right, sweetheart,' he said now. 'So give us a kiss and I'll be on my way.'

She did as he asked and saw him to the front door. He picked up his cap from the hallstand and opened the door just as Sydney came strolling down the street.

'Ah. The man himself,' Arnold said to Clara in a low tone. 'You go inside and shut the door. I'll see you tomorrow.'

She closed the door quietly and went upstairs to get ready for bed, confident that Arnold would do his very best to make her brother see sense.

'Wotcha, mate,' said Arnold. 'Had a good night?'

'Yeah, not bad.'

'A little bird has told me that you've been misbehaving at home.'

'My big-mouthed sister has been opening her gob, I suppose.'

'Don't you dare speak about her like that.'

'Oh yeah, and who's gonna stop me?'

'I think you know the answer to that.' Arnold looked at him with a grave expression. 'When are you gonna grow up and start behaving like a human being?'

'What's it got to do with you?'

'A lot, as it happens. You're upsetting your sister and that upsets me.'

'Too bad.'

'Look, son,' Arnold began in a quieter, more persuasive manner. 'I know you want to be cock of the walk among your mates. I did the same thing myself when I was your age. But there's no call to give your family a hard time. They don't deserve it.'

'*Me* give *them* a hard time,' he exploded. 'That's a good one. It's them who are always on at me.'

'That isn't the way I've heard it.'

'Miserable lot. They never want me to have a laugh.'

'There's having a laugh and there's being downright ignorant,' said Arnold, his attitude becoming suddenly aggressive as he grabbed Sydney by the arms and pinned him against a wall. 'And you, most definitely, come in the second category.'

'Oi! Take your hands off me,' gasped Sydney, who hadn't realised just how tough Arnold was.

'When I'm good and ready,' responded Arnold, increasing the pressure of his hold on him. 'But not before you've listened to what I have to say to you.'

'You've no right to—'

'And you've no right to put your family through hell every time you set foot inside the door,' interrupted Arnold. 'So start acting your age and stop upsetting your family or you'll have me to deal with. If you must misbehave don't do it on your own doorstep and don't bring it home with you. It isn't clever and your mates won't think any more of you because you give 'em a hard time at home.'

'How would they know what I do indoors?'

'You probably boast about it.'

'You don't know what I talk to my mates about. You know nothing about them.'

'I know the type well enough to know that they won't be there for you when you get into real trouble,' Arnold told him, 'which you will if you carry on as you are. Oh yes, I've heard about what you get up to outside, making a nuisance of yourself on the streets.'

'We're mates; we look out for each other.'

'Don't make me laugh. The sorts of blokes you're knocking about with are only out for themselves, so do yourself a favour and get rid. Get yourself some decent friends or a girlfriend or a hobby or something.'

'No thanks.'

'I can't force you to change your habits but there is something you *will* do or you'll find that I'm not such a nice bloke as you thought,' said Arnold, his manner becoming seriously threatening. 'You *will* go into the house and apologise to your sister for upsetting them all earlier and you will *not* tell her how I got you to agree.'

'You've got a hope.'

Arnold was no weakling, and when he pulled the boy forward then practically threw him against the wall, indicating what he was capable of if necessary, and moved his face closer to his, he became extremely frightening. 'Just do it.'

'There's no need to get violent.'

'I can get a lot nastier than this, believe me, and so just tell me that you'll do it.'

'All right, all right, I'll do it, so get off me.'

'You're sure?'

'Yeah, yeah.'

'Good boy,' said Arnold, moving back. 'I think we understand each other now.'

Sydney rubbed his arms and walked off huffily.

'I shall know if you've done it and God help you if you haven't,' was Arnold's parting shot. He received a grunt in reply, and swaggered on down the street with a satisfied smile on his face.

Clara was feeling a lot more optimistic about Sydney's behaviour since his apology a few nights ago. Her brother had been, if not his old self, at least a little more civil around the house. Good old Arnold. He seemed to have succeeded where the rest of them had failed. He must have given Sydney a thorough talking to and it hadn't fallen on deaf ears as it did when she or her parents tried it.

She was having a good day at work too. No complaints so far; just nice polite customers and a few decent tips. There was enough trade to keep the staff busy but, being early afternoon, there wasn't the frantic crush there would be around teatime when customers had to queue to get a table.

'Good afternoon, sir. Are you ready to order?' she asked

with her notebook and pencil ready, smiling at the next customer who was studying the menu.

'Yes, I am,' the young man replied, without looking up. 'I'll have tea and sandwiches and some fancy cakes, please.'

'A full tea, very good, sir.'

He lifted his gaze and his eyes widened.

'Clara?' he said questioningly.

'Charlie,' she gasped, turning pink with pleasure as she recognised the soldier she had met when she was a land girl four years ago. 'Is it really you?'

'Yes, it's me,' he said, beaming, and she noticed the very slight Kentish accent she remembered. 'What a stroke of luck seeing you again. You look wonderful. How are you?'

'I'm fine. Yourself?'

'Pretty good.'

She could feel the supervisor's eyes on her. 'I shall have to go and get your order or I'll be in trouble. We're not encouraged to linger for too long when we're serving.'

'Oh, I see,' he said, showing concern. 'You get on with your work then. I don't want you to get into trouble on my account.'

'Don't worry about it,' she said quickly. 'I'll be back with your tea as soon as I can.'

Well that was a turn-up for the books, she thought, as she walked back to the kitchens with the order, then went to another table with her pad, feeling Charlie's eyes on her the whole time and enjoying the sensation. She'd met him at a village dance and they'd danced every dance together and shared one brief goodnight kiss after which they had gone their separate ways, he with his soldier mates, she with her Land Army pals. She didn't even know his surname.

There had been no mention of keeping in touch. He'd told her he was going away to France in a few days, which could have been the reason why. The war years had been strange times. Some soldiers hadn't wanted to get involved when they were going into the front line. She'd been disappointed that he hadn't even suggested that they write to each other, but had soon got it into perspective. He had just been a soldier she had met at a dance and he would have had more important things on his mind than some girl he had danced with.

After that she went to more village dances and met a lot more soldiers. But she'd never forgotten Charlie with his sparkling blue eyes and ready smile.

'Here we are, sir,' she said, arriving with a tray. She set the teapot down on his table along with a two-tiered cake stand with dainty sandwiches on the bottom and fancy cakes on the top.

'You can drop the sir.'

'All part of the job, sir,' she said, grinning at him. 'My boss doesn't miss a thing that goes on in this restaurant. I sometimes think she can lip-read from the back of a waitress's head.'

'That sounds bit grim,' he remarked. 'Perhaps we can meet after you finish work? Just for a chat?'

'I finish at six o'clock.' She glanced at the clock. 'I could see you then if you like.'

'Lovely.'

'I'll meet you outside then, shall I?'

'I look forward to it.'

'Enjoy your tea,' she said and continued with her duties with a spring in her step, trying not to smile too widely.

*   *   *

22

They went to a Lyons tea shop and laughed about it being a busman's holiday for her. They talked about that night at the village dance and how much fun they'd had. He said it was the last time he'd been happy for a long time and he'd never forgotten it.

'It was my last night off before I went to France,' he told her. 'Not much fun around then.'

'You came back all in one piece, though,' she observed. She had changed into her own clothes after her shift and was wearing a crisp white blouse and grey skirt.

'Yeah, I was lucky. I got away lightly, just a bullet wound in my shoulder.'

'So you didn't get off scot-free then.'

'Not quite, but it could have been a lot worse,' he said. 'It doesn't bother me much.' He paused, and she noticed that he'd lost the youthful bloom she remembered, though he had an outdoor look about him and a light tan. He still had the clean-cut features, the shock of fair curly hair and the gorgeous blue eyes but there was sadness about him somehow. Was it a new harshness around his mouth? Or something in his eyes that had been put there by his experiences on the front line? 'Anyway, what have you been doing with yourself since we last saw each other?'

'After the war, I came home from the country and got a job here as a waitress,' she told him. 'Then I met a boy and got engaged; all very predictable for a girl like me.'

There was a brief hiatus; then, 'I went one better,' he said. 'I got married.'

'Oh, I see.'

It was a defining moment; as though they both knew they had to make their positions clear and lay down the ground rules. At least that would stop any fanciful notions from developing, she thought. Of course they would both be attached. Why wouldn't they? It was four years ago and it wasn't as though anything you could put a name to had happened between them.

'I married a girl from my local village,' he continued.

'I seem to remember you telling me that you lived in Kent,' she remarked. 'A family orchard, wasn't it?'

'That's right.'

'What brings you to London then?'

'I'm here on business.'

'That sounds very grand.'

'Not at all. I'm trying to get my foot in the door with some of the hotels here; to get them to agree to let us supply them direct. We do use a selling agent for most of our sales but I try to find the time to do some marketing myself because it saves on commission. Unfortunately I hardly ever get round to it because of my workload in the orchard. But I must try to do more because agents don't come cheap.'

'Are you in London for long?'

'Just for the day. I'm going back to Kent tonight.'

'A flying visit, then.'

He nodded. 'No time for anything longer. It's our busy time of year at home, coming up to the apple harvest. So it's all hands to the wheel.'

'I expect you employ extra people to help at harvest time, don't you?' she said, remembering from her time in the country. 'I've heard of town people going fruit picking.'

'Oh yes, we couldn't do without our temporary pickers. The same people come year after year. In some cases whole families turn up. They treat it as a working holiday and have a great time. The men do the really hard graft but there's plenty for the women to do. Even the kids help out; they're usually from London or other big cities so they think it's great fun to sleep in a tent in the middle of a field.' He paused, frowning. 'Mind you, we're down on numbers signing up this year for some reason. Still, not to worry. I expect we'll have enough when picking actually starts. If not we'll all have to work that bit harder.'

'I would love to do something like that,' she told him with a wistful look.

He looked surprised. 'Really? A townie like you? I should have thought the Land Army would have put you off tending the land for good and all.'

'Quite the opposite,' she told him. 'It gave me an appetite for it. I loved my time as a land girl.'

'Well, we need temporary staff if you fancy a fortnight in the country in a couple of weeks' time,' he said lightly. 'We pay well, even though it is classed as unskilled labour, and all food is provided. Our rates of pay are higher than many other orchards.'

Her dark eyes lit with pleasure at the prospect but she knew it wasn't possible. 'And what's my employer going to say when I ask for two weeks off?'

'You could say you're taking a holiday. As long as they don't have to pay you maybe they wouldn't mind,' he suggested.

'It isn't as simple as that,' she told him. 'It's a question of finding someone to cover for me.'

'Overtime for one of the other waitresses, perhaps? But don't put your regular job in jeopardy because of something so short term.'

'No, I couldn't do that. I have to pay my way at home.'

'You'd probably make as much money or more per week as you do as a waitress, so you wouldn't lose out over the time you would take off from the tea rooms,' he said. 'With us, the earnings are related to how hard you work, and you seem like a grafter to me.'

'Oh, there'd be no problem with that; I've never been afraid of hard work,' she said with confidence. 'But even apart from the job, I couldn't just go away and leave Arnold.'

He frowned. 'Not even for just two weeks? Surely he wouldn't mind, especially as you wouldn't be out of pocket.'

'No . . . It just isn't done for an engaged girl to go away without her fiancé,' she explained. 'Anyway, it wouldn't be fair to him.'

'Oh well, if you change your mind, here's the address,' he told her, digging into his pocket for a card and handing it to her. 'We start at the end of the month. Accommodation is under canvas and everything you need is provided. If you decide to give it a try, telephone me just to make sure we still have places available. There are public call boxes in London, I've noticed.'

She nodded. 'It's a nice idea, but I won't be able to make it,' she told him. 'Much as I'd like to.'

'You may as well take the card anyway,' he offered.

She put the card into her handbag. 'Well, I'd better be getting off home,' she said. 'My mother will be wondering where I am.'

'Yes, and I must go back to the station,' he told her. 'I'll just pay the bill and be on my way.' He looked at her with real warmth in his eyes. 'It's been lovely meeting you again, Clara. Thank you for making me such a happy soldier that night at the dance.'

'It worked both ways,' she said, rising. She hesitated.
'And thank you for the tea.'

'A pleasure.'

She walked across the café to the door and out into
the street, her sense of elation draining away and leaving
her feeling oddly depressed.

Chapter Two

'A couple of weeks in the country would do you the world of good,' her mother told her over their meal that evening when Clara casually mentioned the fruit-picking opportunity, referring to Charlie as an old friend from her Land Army days who'd happened to come into the tea rooms. 'You really enjoy that sort of thing.'

'Yes, I know I do, but I have a job to go to here, Mum,' she reminded her. 'I can't just disappear for a fortnight.'

'That's easily solved,' announced Flo. 'I'll go in to Taylor's and tell 'em you've had to stay home on family business or something. A little fib now and then doesn't do any harm so long as no one gets hurt by it. It isn't as though they'd pay you if you weren't there.'

'I wouldn't let you do that anyway, Mum,' Clara insisted. 'If I were to go to Kent, which I won't, I would tell them the truth at work in advance so that they could get my shifts covered.'

'Cor, I'd jump at the chance if it was me,' put in Cuddy. 'I wish I could go.'

'You could take him with you, couldn't you, Clara?' suggested Flo excitedly, ignoring the fact that her daughter had made it clear she wasn't going. 'He could do with some country air.'

'I'm not going to the country, Mum,' Clara told her again in a firmer tone. 'So please stop going on about it.'

'It would put some colour in Cuddy's cheeks as well as yours.' Flo's enthusiasm refused to be dimmed. 'It would be worth keeping him off school and risking a visit from the school board man for an opportunity like that, don't you think, Frank?'

'Yes, love. Not half.'

'Do you really think that's a good idea?' said Clara. 'Cuddy needs to go to school.'

'It doesn't hurt to break the rules occasionally,' Flo retorted. 'It isn't as though we ever normally keep him off school, except when he's poorly.'

'I think you should go to Kent, sis,' Sydney cut in with a wry grin. 'If only to give me a break from your efforts to keep me on the straight and narrow.'

'Will you stop keeping on about it, all of you,' Clara said crossly. 'Even apart from my job here, there's Arnold to consider. I'm sure he wouldn't like the idea of my swanning off to Kent without him.'

'Mm, there is that,' her mother mused, shaking the pepper pot over her meal of steak and kidney pudding and vegetables. 'I'd forgotten about him.'

'Well now that you've remembered him, can we drop the subject, please?'

'Yeah, all right, love,' her mother agreed.

The subject didn't remain dropped for long, though. When Arnold called later on, he hadn't been in the house for more than a minute before Sydney said to him, 'Clara's got the chance to go to Kent on a working holiday and she won't go because she thinks she can't leave you.'

'Right, that's it. Come on, Arnold,' Clara intervened, taking him by the arm. 'Let's get out of here before this lot drive us both mad.' And she steered him towards the front door.

'Where are we going?' Arnold enquired as they headed down Green Street towards the town, arm in arm.

'To the flicks, the Empire or just for a walk; anywhere as long as we're out of that madhouse.'

He laughed. 'Getting you down, are they? What's all this about a working holiday in Kent anyway?'

'Nothing. That's just Sydney shooting his mouth off as usual.'

'There must be some talk of it or he wouldn't have said anything,' Arnold persisted.

'Oh, I just happened to mention that I'd met an old acquaintance who told me they were looking for temporary fruit pickers in an orchard in Kent and the family think I should do it,' she explained. 'There's no question of my going.'

'What old acquaintance?'

'Just some bloke; name of Charlie Fenner. His family have an orchard.'

'Ooh, very impressive. How do you know an orchard-owning type from Kent?'

'From my Land Army days. He was stationed at a camp near where I was billeted.'

'And?'

'And nothing,' she said. 'I met him at a village dance one night and I haven't seen him since then until today. He's married, so don't start getting any daft ideas.'

'You know me better than that.' She did too; he really wasn't the jealous type. He was too confident in himself for that. 'So how did you meet up with him again?'

She explained, adding, 'I hardly knew him back then. It was just a dance we were at together one night. Anyway, today I had a cup of tea with him after work just to be polite. During the course of the conversation he told me that they use temporary labour for fruit picking on his family orchard. I made the mistake of mentioning it to my lot indoors and they were ready to pack me off with no thought whatsoever of my responsibilities here.'

'Sydney seems to think it's me who's stopping you from going.'

'I'm hardly likely to go off and leave you for a fort-night, am I?'

'Do you want to go?'

'Well . . . I wouldn't mind,' she admitted. 'I do enjoy that sort of work.'

'Then you must go. Don't worry about me,' he assured her. 'I'll be all right. I'll miss you, of course, but it isn't as if you'll be going away for ever.'

She halted in her step and turned to him. 'You mean, you *really* wouldn't mind?'

'I'd be lost without you, of course,' he was quick to point out. 'But if it's something you really want to do, it wouldn't be right for me to stand in your way.'

'Oh, you are so good to me,' she said, reaching up and kissing him lightly on the lips. 'But I can't go anyway because of my job at the tea rooms.'

'I can see that could be a problem. But there must be ways round it,' was his thoughtful response. 'If they won't keep the job open for you while you have a couple of weeks off without pay when you've helped them out so many times in the past, filling in for girls when they've been away and doing more than your fair share of Sundays and evenings, then you can get another job when you get back. Good waitresses are always in demand in London.'

'I don't know so much about that, Arnold,' she said. 'They say unemployment is rising to crisis point.'

'Not in your line of work,' he disagreed. 'A girl like you can do anything, Clara. You're bright, pretty and capable. You have to take your chances while you can.'

'It's only a couple of weeks of fruit picking, Arnold,' she reminded him. 'Not a job promotion. It isn't going to lead to anything.'

'No. But it will be an experience, and something you'll enjoy, so I think you should do it.'

'The way you're trying to talk me into it, anyone would think you want me to go.'

'Don't be daft. It's just that I don't want you to look back after we're married and blame me for stopping you from doing something that you would have enjoyed when you had the chance. I don't want that on my conscience.'

'Just teasing,' she said lightly. 'Anyway, as everyone seems so keen for me to go, I'll give it some more thought.' She paused, remembering something. 'What if Sydney gives Mum and Dad a load of trouble while I'm away?'

'They'll deal with it,' he replied. 'He's their responsibility, not yours.'

'It isn't like that in our family, Arnold. We all pull together.'

'I know you do,' he said in a softer tone. 'But he's been better since I had that chat with him; you told me so yourself, and you can't live your life according to your brother's moods. Anyway, I'll keep my beady eye on things.'

'In that case, I'd better start working out a way to get a couple of weeks off from the tea rooms.'

'Remind that supervisor of yours of all the times you've put yourself out for them,' he told her.

She squeezed his hand as they continued walking. 'Are you sure you don't mind?'

'I'm quite sure,' he assured her. He didn't mind in the least, as it happened. In fact, it was very convenient for him to have Clara out of the way for a while.

'Thanks, Arnold.'

'You're welcome. We might as well go to the flicks if you fancy it,' he suggested as they reached Shepherd's Bush Green and saw the queues snaking out of the cinemas, the waiting crowds being amused by street entertainers while a uniformed commissionaire walked along the lines calling out seat prices.

'That would be lovely,' she said and they joined the queue, enjoying the acrobat performing amazing feats in front of them. Queuing was all part of the fun of an evening at the pictures.

'You need some proper entertainment before you go to the back of beyond, away from civilisation,' he grinned.

'I'm only going for two weeks,' she reminded him. 'I'm sure I can survive for that long without a night out at the flicks.'

'I'm not so sure about that,' he said, teasing her. He was in good spirits because it looked like things would work out very nicely for him indeed.

*　　*　　*

'Remember to be very careful how you handle the apples, Cuddy,' Clara reminded her brother as he helped her to carry her picking basket to the sorting tables. 'Bruising can cost the grower a lot of money. It can cause rotting before the fruit even reaches the point of sale.'

'I am being careful, sis.'

'And when you're picking, are you making sure you lift the fruit first and twist it slightly to avoid pulling the stem from the fruit? If it has to be forced it isn't ready.'

'I'm doing everything the foreman told us to do on our first day,' he assured her.

'That's the stuff.'

'It's good here,' he enthused. 'Especially at night after work. When we all sing round the campfire.'

'Yeah, I enjoy that too.' They reached the sorting tables and put their basket with the others waiting for attention.

'Will we be going up the trees again before tea break?' Cuddy enquired.

'It's almost time for our break now, I think,' she said. 'You can go off and play for a few minutes if you like.'

Watching him run back to the campsite, she felt a surge of satisfaction in her decision to bring him to Brierley Orchard with her. The country life suited him well and he was in his element here. Not normally a very robust child, now his cheeks were glowing from all the fresh air and he seemed to be more confident in himself without the constant teasing from his brother and father. There was a limit to what he could do in the way of work because he was still only small, which meant he couldn't take the weight of too much fruit in the picking bag at one time, but he was a good little picker for all that and very nimble up and down the ladders. He also made himself useful by helping to carry the loaded baskets for other workers and running errands for the foreman.

With the pressing persuasion of everyone at home – who had only her interests at heart – she'd finally decided to grab this opportunity with both hands. She'd been honest with the supervisor at the tea rooms and the management, recognising her previous dedication to the job, had agreed to let her have the time off without pay.

So here she was in sunlit Brierley Orchard in the heart of the fruit-growing area of Kent near Tunbridge Wells, and the weather had been glorious ever since they arrived. An area of grassland behind the Fenner family home – a large rambling farmhouse with stone outbuildings that were used for storage – was spread with tents for the temporary workers. Most of the families here for the fruit picking were poor; many were from the East End of London. Some of the men, most of whom had fought in the war, were skilled in their own trade but currently out of work, so fruit picking was a way of earning some money and giving the family a change of scenery at the same time.

Clara was enjoying every moment. It wasn't in her nature to labour blindly at a task; she preferred to learn while she earned so asked questions whenever the opportunity arose. Brierley was a beautiful place: acres of apple trees laden with fruit surrounded by miles of countryside, much of it orchard land, and currently bathed in autumn sunshine.

'Everything all right?' enquired Charlie, appearing at her side looking tanned with his shirt sleeves rolled up, his much loved golden Labrador Rex by his side. 'Not working you too hard, I hope.'

'No. I thrive on hard work.'

'A glutton for punishment, eh?'

'I think I must be,' she said, smiling and brushing the back of her hand across her damp brow and pushing her hair back from her face. 'Though, of course, I don't see it as punishment. It's a novelty, I suppose.'

She was even lovelier than he remembered and he had thought about her often over the years. She had been a light in the dark recesses of his mind during those black days on the battlefields of France. That night at the dance he had been feeling bleak at the thought of another stint in action, having already had his fill of it. He'd been sent back to England for special training, and when he'd escaped into Clara's arms at the dance he'd savoured the moment but not seen any point in arranging to stay in touch. At that time it hadn't seemed possible that he could stay alive during a second spell on the front line. He'd seen too much. He knew the reality; the things that were never printed in the newspapers. Acts of inhumanity beyond his comprehension that tormented him still, even though he did his best to forget them.

When he'd finally got back to Brierley after the war, he'd been hungry for love and had fallen straight into the arms of Hester the barmaid at the local pub. She'd been eager for marriage so their courtship hadn't been a long one. He'd known he was being manipulated but it hadn't seemed to matter. Looking back on it, he thought he must have been still in a state of trauma after the war and trying to find comfort in any way he could.

Now Clara had slipped back into his life and he couldn't help wondering what might have been if things had been different when they'd first met.

He was recalled to the present by Clara, who was saying, 'Penny for them.'

'Actually, I was just thinking how lucky it is that we've met again,' he told her.

'Yes; a real coincidence.' She smiled. 'Our meetings are destined to be brief though, it seems, because at the end of next week I'll be back in London.'

'Are you glad you came?'

'You bet,' she enthused, her eyes shining. 'In another life maybe I'll get to be a fruit grower's daughter.'

'The foreman speaks very highly of you,' he said. 'He's been telling me that you've been asking a lot of questions about the business.'

'It's just the way I am,' she explained. 'I think of it as an enquiring mind, though some might call it nosiness. Because I enjoy the work I want to know more about it.'

'You're in a minority,' he told her lightly. 'Most of our temporary workers aren't interested in anything beyond how much they are going to get paid.'

'That's understandable for the men with families to support. I'm one of the lucky ones; I have a job back at home. I would never have come here if I'd thought I was taking a job from someone who really needed it.'

What a worker she was. Picking, sorting, lugging great baskets about; she took it all in her stride.

There was a sound of a bell being rung from the house. Rex barked and was calmed by Charlie. 'It's all right, boy, it's only the tea bell,' he said, stroking the dog's head.

'It's a welcome sound. I was thinking it must be getting close to tea break,' she said. 'So my trip back up the ladder is postponed for ten minutes.'

'It's not so long ago we didn't allow women to go

up the trees,' he told her. 'It used to be all men and boys.'

'That's one thing the war did for us women,' she laughed, glancing down at her slacks. 'Gave us the chance to wear the trousers.'

'I suspect we'd have had a job stopping *you* from going up the trees picking, even if it hadn't been the done thing.'

'You do know me a little then.'

'I'm beginning to,' he said slowly, looking at her and becoming serious. 'Back then when we met, Clara, it wasn't the time . . .'

'I know.'

They fell into an odd silence, which was broken by Cuddy rushing up and saying, 'Come on, Clara; it's teatime. They've got lemonade too.' He looked at Charlie and added politely, 'Hello, Mr Fenner.'

'Hello, Cuddy.'

As the boy ran off seeking sustenance, Clara experienced a moment of pride in him. Charlie said, 'He's a good kid.'

'Yes, he's the light of my life,' she told him. 'But I must go or I won't have time to drink my tea or eat the lovely cake your mother makes for us.'

'Don't let me hold you up, then.'

As she walked towards the house along with the other pickers, while he went on his way with his dog by his side, she reflected upon how well the Fenner family treated their workers. They expected a hard day's graft from the casual labour but, unlike some orchard owners she had heard about from the other pickers, they made sure their workers were properly fed and had regular breaks. The food was basic but wholesome and every afternoon they had cake.

Charlie always found time to come round checking that all was well. His less amiable brother Vincent sometimes made an appearance but Clara hadn't seen much of the rest of the Fenner family. She'd noticed a striking redhead with a kind of spurious glamour about her and been told that she was Charlie's wife Hester. She had also briefly met his parents when she and Cuddy had first arrived. But the one she had most to do with was Charlie's younger sister Eva who was sixteen and seemed to have taken a shine to Clara and Cuddy. She usually came over to the campsite of an evening and enjoyed the revelry with them.

As Clara joined the queue, she saw that Eva was behind the trestle table pouring the tea from a huge enamel pot with Charlie's wife by her side giving out slices of cake.

'Hello, Clara,' said Eva, a slim, fair-haired girl with a pronounced Kentish accent. 'How are you today?'

'Fine, and I'll be even better when I've had a cup of tea and a slice of your mother's delicious cake. Tell her from me that her cakes are so good she could win prizes for them.'

'I'll tell her.'

'And of course she'll be *so* interested,' said Charlie's wife sarcastically.

Eva flushed and glared accusingly at the other woman.

'What's the matter?' Hester asked innocently.

'You know very well what.' Embarrassed, Eva looked at Clara. 'I'll see you later.'

'I'll look forward to it.' Clara nodded.

She took her tea and cake and sat down on a low garden wall to eat it, feeling the sun warm on her face. Charlie's wife seemed a bit of a madam, she thought, and suspected that it wouldn't be wise to make an enemy of her.

The Fenner family was seated round the big wooden table in the huge farmhouse kitchen, finishing off their evening meal.

'If everyone's finished can we get on with the clearing up?' asked Eva, looking fidgety.

'Give us a chance to digest our food, for goodness' sake, Eva,' snapped her mother Mabel, a large, red-cheeked woman with arms like young trees, her grey hair scraped back off her face.

'She wants to get off out mixing with the hoi polloi,' suggested Hester. 'That's why she's in such a hurry.'

'I'm not sure it's a good idea for you to be getting familiar with the workers, Eva,' said her mother.

'Why not?' asked Charlie.

'Isn't it obvious?'

'No.'

'Because they're the hired help, of course.'

'They're just people, Ma, and very nice too, most of them,' Charlie pointed out. 'It's good for Eva to have someone besides us to talk to. She's a young girl; she needs company.'

'We are on a different level from them and they know it as well as we do,' declared the fearsome Mabel Fenner. 'They need their privacy as much as us. It just i'n't right for family to socialise with them.'

'At least they know how to have fun,' declared Eva. 'There's precious little of that in this dead and alive hole when they're not around. Why do we have to live in the middle of nowhere?'

'Because we're fruit growers and this is where we earn our living,' said her mother in her broad Kentish accent. 'Why do you always have to be so danged difficult about everything? You keep on the whole time.'

'All she wants is a bit of fun, Ma,' Charlie said in defence of his sister. 'I can see no harm in her going down to the campsite of an evening.'

'You want to watch yourself down there of a night,' warned Vincent. 'Some of the men have a drop too much cider. A young girl like you isn't safe with drunks around.'

'It's Clara and Cuddy I go to see,' Eva told him. 'Anyway, the men are entitled to have a drink or two when they've been working hard all day. And they don't get drunk while I'm there.'

'You shouldn't be there anyway,' Vincent went on. 'You probably make 'em feel awkward. They'll think they can't let their hair down with the boss's daughter among their ranks.'

'Leave her be,' put in their father John, a large, quiet man with a look of the country about him, his face leathery and traversed with small blue veins from years in the open air. 'The strangers will be finished and gone from here soon.'

'Anyway, Clara doesn't feel awkward 'cause I'm there,' Eva informed them. 'She likes me. I know she does.'

'Oh, stop keeping on, for pity's sake,' said Mabel, who had no patience with her daughter at all. 'Do what you like. I don't care what you do as long as you shut up. I can't abide the sound of your whining voice.'

Eva's face all but crumpled. After a lifetime at the sharp end of her mother's tongue she ought to be used to it. But Mabel's callous treatment still had the power to crush her.

41

'Give her a break, Ma,' said Charlie, as always his sister's champion. 'She's just a young girl, wanting a bit of life, and company outside this house.'

'She's a danged nuisance with her moods and craving for attention,' Mabel rasped, turning to her daughter. 'As you've ruined the atmosphere as usual, we might as well get started on the clearing up. So get a move on, and if you want to mix with the riffraff I'm sure none of us care.'

'Hear, hear,' said Vincent.

Charlie watched the cruel remarks hit home He saw his sister's eyes grow wet with tears but she said in a spirited manner, 'And I'm sure I don't care what any of you do either.'

'Good,' put in Hester.

Eva scraped her chair forcefully back from the table and ran from the room.

'Come back here,' shouted her mother. 'You've got to help with the dishes and you're not getting out of it because you're sulking, so don't try it.'

Charlie found his sister outside in the yard.

'I'm sure Mum doesn't mean it, Eva,' he said in an effort to comfort her. 'It's just her way.'

'She does mean it and you know it,' she came back at him fiercely. 'She hates the sight of me and always has done as far back as I can remember. And we all know why. Well, I can't change what happened but I can get away from her constant sniping. I can't wait to leave here and as soon as I get the chance I'll be off.'

'Come here,' he said, holding out his arms to her.

'They all hate me,' she wept into his chest.

'That just isn't true,' he told her. 'You know that I'm always here for you.'

'You're the only one,' she said. 'Victor is horrid and Hester can't stand the sight of me.'

'I'm sure Hester doesn't dislike you in particular,' he said, trying to spare his sister's feelings. 'She likes to have a go at people for some reason and you seem to be in the firing line.'

'She's so full of herself.'

Charlie couldn't deny it but at the moment his mind wasn't on his wife's failings. He was thinking about Eva and the vicious circle in which she was trapped. Her mother had no time for her at all and had brought her up to believe that she was to blame for a family tragedy that happened when she was just four years old. As a result of a lack of mother love Eva craved attention, which made her frequently difficult to deal with. She was so full of insecurity she could be overly talkative, aggressive and hypersensitive, which was irritating for everyone and caused them to be unkind.

He'd tried to talk to their mother about it on several occasions; had said he thought she was unfair to Eva, but she refused to discuss it. He suspected that she didn't even realise how much she hurt her daughter, it had become such a habit. So he could see no way out for his damaged sister and was beginning to think she would be better off away from Brierley.

'I know it isn't easy for you, but try not to overreact to everything that's said to you,' he advised. 'People don't always think before they speak.'

'I try not to, but it hurts so much when Mum is nasty,' she sobbed. 'I don't know how much more I can stand.'

'I tell you what,' he said gently, 'you dry your eyes and go and help with the washing up to keep Mum sweet, then go and see your friends at the campsite. I'll take your side against any opposition.'

'Thanks, Charlie,' she said thickly, wiping her eyes with a handkerchief. 'I don't know what I'd do without you.'

If he was brutally honest, neither did he. Without him there to support her, her mother could destroy her completely.

'I don't know why you always have to quarrel with your mother over that blinkin' sister of yours,' said Hester later on, when she and Charlie were back in the cottage where they lived in the grounds of Brierley quite near to the big house. 'The girl is a spoiled brat and a pain in the neck and she isn't worth bothering with.'

'Spoiled? Eva? That's a good one,' he retorted. 'The only members of the family who treat her with any kindness at all are me and occasionally my father.'

'She works you like a danged puppet,' said Hester, her green eyes flashing, her mouth set in a hard and resentful line. 'She knows she can cause as much trouble as she likes and you'll always take her side. Every single time!'

'Someone has to.'

'I don't see why,' she came back at him. 'The more you fuss over her, the less likely she is to behave herself.'

'I don't fuss over her. I merely try to give her some support.'

'You fuss over her—'

'Leave it, will you, Hester,' he cut in wearily. 'There's no point in us arguing about it because we'll never agree on the subject.'

There was a silence, then Hester launched a new topic. 'You say you already knew this girl Eva has palled up with before she came here to work.' Charlie had mentioned their previous acquaintance to Hester when Clara and Cuddy had arrived, since he saw no reason to hide it. 'How well did you know her?'

'Hardly at all, I've told you.'

'That's all right then.'

'Good.'

Hester was far more interested in getting at him about his family than in some common foreigner from London who stood no chance with him against herself. 'Your sister is always talking about wanting to leave home,' she said. 'Let her go, I say, and give us all a bit of peace.'

He sat down and opened the newspaper to hide his emotions. Hester was so utterly heartless at times, it was hard to take. But he couldn't face another argument with her at the moment. There had been too many recently. Pick, pick, snipe, snipe; she was like an angry cat. He didn't want to discuss his feelings on the matter of his mother's relationship with her daughter because, despite her many faults, he didn't want to be disloyal to Mabel. That was something Hester would never understand.

'What a family, I dunno,' Hester goaded him. 'A mother who can't abide her daughter, a father who hardly says a word all year, a selfish little cow as a sister. The only one who's got any sense of humour round here is Vincent.'

He slammed the paper down on to his lap. 'You were keen enough to marry into my family, weren't you?' he reminded her through gritted teeth.

'I didn't know what a flawed lot they were then, did I?'

'Probably because you rushed me into marriage before you had a chance to get to know them.'

'That isn't how I remember it.'

'Well, that's how it was,' he growled, rising to his feet in anger. 'And if I'd known it was going to be like this, you'd have never got me up that aisle.'

'Why, you pig . . .' She lunged towards him, punching her fists into his chest. He didn't retaliate. No matter how much he was provoked he would never hit a woman. He did move back from her spiteful jabs, though.

'Feel better now that you've finally made me feel I can't stay in my own home again tonight?' he asked in a weary tone. 'Now that you've driven me out to the pub?'

'I'm sure you'll find it no hardship going there,' she scowled.

'Where else can I go? I wouldn't want to go over to the house and let them know that you're making it impossible for me to stay at home of an evening because you never stop getting at me.'

Hester suddenly wondered if she might have pushed him too far. She didn't want to lose her place at Brierley. Not until she was ready, anyway. But she soon recovered from her doubt. 'Do what you like,' she said, shrugging. 'I don't care what anyone thinks.'

'You don't care about anything or anyone except yourself.'

'Oh, bugger off and leave me in peace.'

He grabbed his coat from a hook on the door and left the cottage with Rex at his heels, instantly aware of the distant sound of music and laughter drifting through the air in the gathering dusk. As he got closer to the main house, he could see the campsite lit with lamps and smell the campfires burning. How he wished he was a part of it. No wonder Eva liked to go over there of an evening so much. But there was no point in his going over and giving his wife another stick to beat him with.

He walked on past the big house and headed for the village, thinking that life with Hester was becoming more miserable by the day.

Watching from the window until he was out of sight, Hester moved across the room and brushed her long red hair in front of the mirror over the fireplace, her eyes full of admiration. As soon as it was fully dark, she donned a coat and left the house.

'It must be really good to live in London,' Eva said to Clara as they sat together on a blanket on the grass in the glow of the fire. Cuddy was with some other boys across the field.

'Like most things it has its good and bad points,' Clara responded, thinking how pretty Eva was in a childish sort of way. She was thin and small for her age and had fair hair and blue eyes like Charlie. 'It's very different from here, that's for sure.'

'Do you go out dancing much?'

'Now and again. We have a dance hall near us called the Hammersmith Palais. Arnold and I go along there sometimes.'

'Sounds exciting.'

'It is good fun,' she said, 'especially with all the new modern dances. You see them all at the Palais. They have jazz too.'

'I wish I lived in London.'

'But it's lovely here, Eva,' Clara exclaimed. 'All this open space, beautiful countryside and a great big house to live in. Cuddy and I live in a small house in a row of others just like it in a road where kids play in the street and women stand on the steps gossiping.'

'Sounds good to me,' Eva enthused. 'At least there are plenty of people about.'

'You're right about that,' said Clara. 'It feels like too many at times. Sometimes on our street it seems as though you have no privacy at all. You go out in a new coat and the neighbours are all speculating about where you bought it.'

'Who cares about privacy?'

'You would if you didn't have it,' Clara said wryly. 'Anyway, London isn't all fun and excitement. There's a lot of poverty and men out of work. Many people can't afford to go out and have fun at the picture houses and dance halls. And some parts are very run down. It's very busy everywhere. You can't move for the crowds some-times where I work in the West End.'

'I'd like to do what you do,' Eva said wistfully. Clara had already told her how she earned her living. 'It must be fun meeting all the different people.'

Clara laughed. 'Not always, I can assure you. Anyway, you don't meet them as such; you serve them, and there is a big difference. By the very nature of the job you're never allowed to forget that you are a member of the lower classes. Some of the customers are downright rude.'

'I'd still like it.'

'The grass is always greener,' Clara pointed out. 'I'd love to have your way of life. Being in the country, working on the land, yet all you want is town life.'

'It's more than just that for me,' Eva confided, her mood becoming more serious. 'I want to get away from home; away from my mother in particular.'

'Oh, Eva, you don't mean that.' Clara was shocked. 'Your mother would be very hurt to hear you say that.'

'No she wouldn't. She'd be glad to be rid of me,' Eva stated categorically. 'She can't abide the sight of me.'

'I'm sure we all feel like that about our mothers at some point or other when we're growing up,' suggested Clara tactfully. 'They have to discipline us so that we know how to behave, and it makes us resentful. But you'll grow out of it.'

'Oh no, it isn't just that,' Eva said seriously. 'My mother really doesn't like me because of something very bad that I did when I was little. She would put out the flags if I left home, honestly. She's always telling me how she can't stand the sight of me.'

Clara was distressed to hear this but was sensitive enough not to probe into the dark hinterland of Fenner family history. 'Oh, Eva. You really shouldn't say such things.'

'I'm only saying what's true.'

This sort of talk was beyond the comprehension of someone from a close family like Clara's. 'Perhaps your mother gets frustrated sometimes and says things she doesn't mean,' she suggested hopefully. 'We all do that at times.'

'She means every word, believe me,' Eva told her. 'There's only Charlie who gives a fig about me in our family. My dad, bless him, sometimes sticks up for me but he doesn't often say much. He's probably scared stiff of Mum. She's very domineering. Ask Charlie how she feels about me if you don't believe me.'

'I wouldn't dream of poking my nose into your private affairs,' Clara told her.

Eva shrugged. 'When I do come to London, can I come and see you?' she asked. 'I really am going there one of these days. I'm determined.'

'Of course you can come and see us,' she agreed without hesitation. 'I'll give you our address before I leave. But I expect you'll forget all about Cuddy and me once we've gone.'

'I'll never forget you and Cuddy,' Eva said with passion in her voice. 'I really love having you here and I'll miss you both like mad when you leave.'

'Well, we've still got a few days left. So don't let's spoil it by being sad.' Clara looked towards the others. 'Oh, good, the man from the tent next to ours has started playing on his mouth organ. Let's join in the singing.'

Clara joined in heartily with the others in a rendition of 'Keep the Home Fires Burning', a song that had been popular during the war. Eva joined her after a while and they swayed in time to the music. Clara found herself feeling sad at the thought of going back to London. Still, all good things had to come to an end. Didn't they?

The next few days flew past and it seemed no time at all before it was the last night around the campfire. People were drinking and talking and exchanging addresses. It had been a warm humid day, exceptionally mild for October, and the evening air was balmy, though there was the smell of rain in the air.

'Whatever will I do of an evening next week after you've gone?' Eva asked Clara.

'The same as you did before we came,' Clara replied.

'Sitting in with Mum and Dad,' she said woefully. 'Even Charlie isn't there after supper. He and Hester go home to the cottage. Vincent usually goes out too.'

'I'm sure you'll manage,' said Clara, who was feeling a little emotional herself because she knew she would never do anything like this again. Marriage to Arnold and raising a family would be the next stage in her life.

'Can I write to you?' Eva asked.

'Of course you can. I'd be disappointed if you didn't. You've got the address.'

Eva looked towards the revellers, who were forming a line and moving, dancing and jigging around in the light from the fire.

The two of them joined in along with Cuddy and his friends, and they kept going until everyone was out of breath. As they came to a ragged halt, someone struck up a riotous 'Knees Up Mother Brown'.

It was as they flopped down on the grass afterwards that they saw the first flash of lightning, which was followed immediately by a deafening clap of thunder.

'That sounded close,' said Clara. 'Storms usually start further away and build up.'

'And here comes the rain,' said Eva as a sudden downpour hammered down. Everyone was drenched in an instant and started hurrying for shelter.

'You'd better go indoors, Eva,' called Clara. 'Cuddy, come on, let's get inside the tent.'

Cuddy did as he was bid but Eva seemed reluctant to go anywhere. 'You're leaving tomorrow,' she said.

'Never mind that, Eva, just get inside. Your family will be worried if you stay out here with us,' said Clara. 'Go before you get even more soaked.'

'G'night then,' Eva said and hurried off towards the house, a small dejected figure.

Inside the tent Clara said to Cuddy, 'Put your wellies and waterproofs on, love, because the rain is coming in. Let's hope it passes over quickly. We'll be sleeping in a puddle otherwise.'

But the storm showed no sign of letting up. The thunder seemed to grow even louder if that was possible, the lightning so bright it was like daylight. The rain fell so heavily on to the canvas it was almost deafening. A gale seemed to have blown up, too, and was howling around the tent, threatening to collapse it.

'Exciting, isn't it,' said Cuddy, peering out of the flap.

'Not really, no.' Clara was cold and damp. 'Don't keep the flap open, love; the rain will come in and it's already getting very wet in here.'

'It's like a flippin' lake out there,' he said, breathless with awe. 'Some of the tents have given way by the look of it. People are trying to save their belongings from blowing away.'

'I'd better go and see if I can help,' she told him. 'You stay in the tent and try to keep dry.'

'Not likely,' he said. 'I want to help too. Wait till we tell Sydney about this. I bet he's never been out in a storm like this.'

'I don't think any of us have ever seen a storm like this,' she said, 'let alone been out in it.'

'Him and Dad will have to be impressed when I tell 'em about it, won't they?'

'Never mind about them,' said Clara, wishing that their approval wasn't so vital to him. 'Let's go and see if we can help the people out there. Make sure your waterproof is done up properly. We'll take the oil lamp so that we can see where we're going.'

Outside they found total chaos, many of the tents having collapsed completely under the strain of the wind and the heavy rain. Underfoot all was mud now and campers were falling over and finding it hard to get up because it was so slippery. People were trying to re-erect the tents but the wind was too strong; it just lifted some of the tents off the ground completely. Clara and Cuddy's tent collapsed almost as soon as they were out of it. And still the lightning and thunder raged. They could also hear the creak and crumble of damage to farm buildings, and the dog was barking.

There was a hush as a streak of lightning crackled over the orchard.

'Look at that tent over there,' said Cuddy, the rain dripping from his oilskins. 'It looks as though there're people trapped underneath it. I'm going to see if I can help.'

No one knew what to do. There seemed nowhere to go to find shelter. People were shouting; children were crying.

Then the calm, reassuring voice of Charlie Fenner could be heard above the noise of the storm.

'Everyone over to the barn,' he said, sounding comfortingly in control. 'We'll do what we can to fix you all up with something to sleep on and get you dried off. My brother has a lamp. Follow him while I make sure everyone is safe.'

Now that her eyes were accustomed to the dark outside the range of the oil lamp, Clara could just make out what was going on in the dimness. 'Cuddy,' she called, realising her brother wasn't with her. 'Cuddy, come on; we're going to the barn to take shelter.'

There was no reply.

'Cuddy, where are you?'

'I'm over here,' he shouted back. 'But I'm stuck in the mud and I can't see where you are. It's so dark.'

'Keep calling and I'll follow the sound of your voice.'

'Here, I'm here . . . here . . . here.'

Blindly she tramped along, slipping and sliding, the rain beating down on her, running down her face and blurring her vision. Then there was a crackle of lightning and a crash and she couldn't hear Cuddy any more.

'Cuddy, Cuddy,' she called, tears streaming down her cheeks and mingling with the rain, her throat aching from the violence of her calls. 'Cuddee . . .'

But there was no answer except for the storm, the crashing thunder, the ferocious lightning. She shrieked her brother's name over and over again, but all to no avail.

'Is your brother in trouble?' asked Charlie, appearing at her side.

'He was calling out to me then I heard a crash. Oh, Charlie, what am I going to do?' she sobbed.

'Don't worry, Clara, we'll find him.'

They shrieked and shouted but the only sound was the noise of the weather and the distant barking of frightened dogs. Walking was made nigh on impossible by the mud.

'Here, hang on to me,' Charlie suggested. 'I'm accustomed to the lie of the land.'

She grabbed his arm gratefully and they trudged on in the light from the lanterns. Then they saw it close by: a large tree lying flat on the ground.

'It must have been struck by lightning,' Charlie said. With the wind still howling and the rain lashing at them, they walked in the light of the lantern, treading carefully because of all the scattered broken branches.

Then she saw them poking out of the debris. Two wellington boots . . .

Chapter Three

Clara had always thought the expression 'paralysed with fear' was just a figure of speech; until now. She simply couldn't move.

'Try not to think the worst, Clara. We have to stay positive, both of us. I know this won't be easy for you, but I really need you to stay calm and do everything I say.' Charlie's voice registered as though from afar although he was standing right next to her. 'If you can do that we'll have young Cuddy out of there in no time.'

As her body began to function again and the numbness abated, she shook from top to toe. 'Of course I will,' she agreed in a trembling voice. 'What do you want me to do?'

'I need you to go and get help for me,' he told her, managing to sound reassuring despite everything. 'I'll have to have some men to help me lift the tree. I can't do it on my own.'

'I'm not going anywhere while my brother is under there,' she declared. 'I'll help you lift it.'

'Don't be foolish,' he told her. 'Two men couldn't lift that. I need as many as you can get.'

His strength calmed her and she knew she must do as he asked. 'Of course. I'll go,' she said through her tears.

'Quick as you can, then, and mind you don't slip over in the mud,' he warned.

How she made her shaky legs work she never knew but somehow she found herself stumbling towards the house.

There was no shortage of male volunteers to assist Charlie, and despite cries for her to stay with the women, Clara went with them. Eva appeared by her side with a lantern.

'I thought you might need some company,' she said, putting her arm round her.

They stood aside from the area where the men were working so as not to be in the way, and they couldn't see exactly what was happening. They could hear the men calling out to each other, though, as they worked together to remove the tree.

After what seemed like an agonising age, they heard Charlie say, 'That's it, boys. I've got him.'

Then some men appeared carrying lanterns to light the way for Charlie and another man who were carrying Cuddy between them on what looked like a makeshift stretcher.

'Is he . . . ?' began Clara in a shaky voice.

'He's alive,' said Charlie.

'Oh, thank God.'

'He's unconscious though,' he told her grimly. 'We need to get medical help right away.'

Clara went with Charlie to the hospital in his father's open-topped car. They laid Cuddy on the back seat with a blanket over him and his head on her lap. Eva gave her a coat, scarf and goggles to help protect her from the dust, dirt and wind – though the storm had finally moved away and it had stopped raining. With her hand protectively on Cuddy's arm, she imagined she could feel his every heartbeat, and prayed for them not to stop. She was also dreading that the vehicle would break down as motor cars were prone to do; she'd seen enough frustrated drivers in London coaxing their engines into life with a starting handle to know that. With tension drawing tight, the journey to Tunbridge Wells seemed endless as the car made its way slowly along the bumpy, partly flooded country lanes.

'We've got a telegram,' announced Flo shakily the following evening, having just been to answer a knock at the door. 'Oh, Gawd help us, Frank. It's a bleedin' telegram.'

'Don't panic,' said her husband, getting up and taking the telegram from her, his own hands trembling slightly. He looked at it but made no move to open it.

'How can I not panic?' she asked. 'No good news ever came in a yellow envelope.'

'Let's open it, shall we, and see what it's about instead of dithering around getting into a state,' suggested Sydney. 'Give it here. I'll do it.'

As his parents looked on fearfully, he tore open the envelope and read the contents,

'Relax, it's nothing to worry about,' he informed them. 'Clara and Cuddy are staying on in Kent for an extra week, that's all. She says she'll explain when she gets home.'

'Phew, that's a relief,' said Flo, mopping her damp brow with the back of her hand. 'I'll be glad when they're home safe and sound, though. Something must have happened to make her stay there longer because she only booked two weeks off work and she's much too sensible to push her luck with her job.'

'It can't be anything serious, or she would have told us,' Frank pointed out.

'We'll just have to wait and see, won't we?' said Flo, who wasn't quite so sure of that.

Clara had deliberately omitted the reason for their extended stay at Brierley to avoid her mother's flying into a panic and getting on the first train to Kent. There was no point in her doing that since the drama was now over and Cuddy was out of hospital, after staying one night there under observation. He'd had a very narrow escape, though; his life had only been saved by some branches of the tree which had kept the full weight of the trunk away from him. He'd been knocked out by a blow to his head and had sustained a great deal of painful bruising.

The Fenners had insisted that he and Clara stay on in the house as their guests for an extra week to give Cuddy some time to recover before travelling; naturally the boy was very shaken up. Maybe they were feeling guilty because the accident had happened on their property, Clara thought. But it was kind of them anyway and she appreciated it.

It was a beautiful old house furnished in antique style and kept spotlessly clean, the scent of polish and soap permeating all the rooms apart from an outer lobby where the men took off their muddy boots. Eva had told Clara that her mother was a fanatical housewife and ran the home with the same efficiency as the men of the family managed the orchard. But for all their property and land, the Fenners were not a happy family, Clara observed after just one mealtime with them. There seemed to be animosity between them all except for the father of the family, John Fenner, who was a quiet, unobtrusive soul. Hester sniped at Charlie and Eva, Vincent mocked Charlie at every opportunity and Mabel was so hateful to Eva that Clara was stunned. She could see now why the girl wanted to leave home.

Discussions got heated in the Tripp household from time to time, just as in any other family, but these people didn't simply have a row to clear the air; they seemed to loathe the sight of each other. Apart from John Fenner, only Charlie appeared to let it all go over his head, except when Eva was being picked on and then he leapt to her defence.

The atmosphere wasn't pleasant for the visitors, though everyone was very cordial to them, except perhaps for Hester who didn't say anything at all to Clara and treated her with a kind of deliberate indifference.

'More pie, Clara?' offered Mabel Fenner who, as well as being an expert with the cleaning and laundry, was an outstanding cook. Her pastry melted in the mouth, and her cakes were heavenly.

'If there is enough for everyone else, yes, I'd love a little piece, please,' she said.

'Mum always makes enough to feed an army,' remarked Charlie, looking at his mother affectionately. 'I'm sure Cuddy could manage a little more too.'

The boy responded in the affirmative and the seconds were served.

'I'll be going home looking like the side of a mountain if I carry on eating so much,' Clara said with a smile.

'It wouldn't matter,' said Vincent unexpectedly. 'You'd still look nice.'

She flushed at the compliment.

'Take no notice of him,' put in Hester, and Clara was surprised to see real hostility in her eyes. 'He flatters all the girls.'

'And of course there are thousands of girls around here for him to flatter,' said Eva with irony. 'He said it to Clara because it happens to be true.'

'Oh, shut up, you silly child,' snapped Hester.

'Yes, don't start acting up again, Eva,' said Mabel, much to Clara's astonishment. Why had she not supported her own child against Hester, especially when Eva was only being complimentary towards a visitor?

'My fault again then,' Eva retorted.

'Whose else would it be?' Hester came back at her. 'It's always you. You started it.'

'No I didn't.'

'Now now, you lot,' said Charlie. 'Can't you behave decently just for once? We don't want to embarrass our visitors.'

'Yes, sorry, Clara,' Mabel apologised. 'You'll have to excuse my daughter. She's a bit highly strung.'

Excuse her daughter? But Hester had clearly been the instigator of that battle.

'She's a monster,' Hester was quick to concur.

'Always has been a troublemaker,' agreed Vincent.

'Leave her alone, for pity's sake, all of you,' said Charlie angrily. 'You'll have the poor girl in tears in a minute.'

'Anyway,' began Clara, in a deliberate attempt to take the attention away from poor Eva, 'now that you've had the chance to have a proper look round, did the orchard sustain very much serious damage in the storm?'

'Enough, but it wasn't a complete disaster,' replied

Charlie. 'We lost several of our good trees and some of the barns took a hammering. But fortunately our storage buildings weren't damaged. That really is a blessing, especially at this time of the year, because good storage is money in the bank in this business. The better we can keep the fruit, the higher the price at the end of the season and beyond.'

'And I suppose you're not so much at the mercy of the buyers if they know that you're not in a desperate hurry to sell the whole of the harvest at once.'

'Exactly,' said Charlie. 'What's more, your reputation depends on producing good quality fruit, even when it's been stored. Then the buyers will trust you.'

'So the sorting is really important too,' she commented. 'You wouldn't want any bruised fruit getting put into store with the others, because the rot will spread over time.'

'That's right.' He smiled at her, then looked around the table. 'I think we've got a potential fruit grower here, folks.' His gaze returned to Clara. 'I reckon if you worked here permanently you'd be running the place in no time.'

'Perhaps we ought to hire her,' joshed Vincent and Clara noticed Hester give him a furious look, which struck her as extremely odd.

'I have a job waiting for me at home,' she said, adding lightly, 'That is, if they still want to employ me after my taking another week off without notice.'

'You can't help it if your brother has been injured. Surely they'll understand that,' said Charlie. Turning his attention to Cuddy, he asked, 'How are you feeling now, young man?'

'All right, thanks,' said Cuddy politely.

He'd been very quiet throughout the meal, Clara had

noticed, and guessed he was feeling awkward because of the bad atmosphere here. It was uncomfortable enough for her and he was ultra-sensitive to that sort of thing.

'Do you fancy a song or two at the piano after supper?' asked Charlie, obviously trying to put Cuddy at his ease. The two of them had already discovered that they shared a love of music. 'Just for a bit of fun.'

A beam lit the boy's face and he said, 'Cor, yes please.' Clara gave Charlie a grateful smile.

Hester said, 'You and that damned piano, Charlie. Anyone would think you could play the danged thing the way you're always banging about on it.'

'Anyone who's heard him would know that he hasn't got a clue,' Vincent chipped in.

'It's my way of relaxing,' Charlie told them, 'and it doesn't do anyone any harm.'

'It doesn't do much for our eardrums,' his brother came back at him.

'You don't even hear me,' Charlie reminded him. 'I always make sure that I keep the door closed when I'm playing. Anyway, I play well enough to hold a tune, which is more than you can do, Vincent.'

'I had better things to do with my time when we were kids than sit at a piano practising scales.'

'Like going down the village and making a nuisance of yourself.'

'Now you're being unfair, Charlie,' their mother rebuked him. 'Vincent was never a bad child; a bit headstrong at times, maybe, but always a good boy.'

Surely never had a mother been so obvious in her favouritism, thought Clara.

'I can imagine Vincent being a right little horror,' said

Hester as though the idea pleased her. 'But at least he has a bit of go in him. I like that in a person.'

'Oh yeah,' responded Vincent arrogantly. 'I've always had plenty of go in me.'

Hester laughed.

There was an interruption from Cuddy. 'May I leave the table, please?'

'Not until we've all finished, dear,' said Mabel in a polite but firm manner. 'It would be bad manners.'

Seeing the boy flush at her sharp tone, Charlie said, 'Surely we can break the rules for once, Ma, especially as the boy's covered in bruises. They must be painful.'

'Yes, all right then, I suppose so,' said Mabel, sounding aggrieved as she looked at Cuddy. 'You can go.'

'Have you had enough to eat, Cuddy?' asked Charlie in his usual considerate manner.

'Yes, thank you.'

'Then off you go and I'll see you later in the sitting room for a tune or two at the piano.'

'Thank you for the lovely food, Mrs Fenner,' said Cuddy, pleasing his sister with his good manners.

'You're welcome,' Mabel acknowledged.

Although she managed to achieve something that vaguely resembled a smile, there was something resentful and grudging about Mabel Fenner, observed Clara. There didn't seem to be one iota of warmth in her, except perhaps when she was speaking to Vincent. Clara got the impression that their extended stay here had been brought about by Charlie rather than his mother.

Oh well, it wasn't for Clara to judge her. This time next week she would be back home in London, and Brierley and the Fenner family would be just a memory.

They were the strangest group of people she had ever come across, though. Charlie and his father seemed to be the only ones who weren't trying to score points over the others; only Charlie seemed to have any heart. Even Eva was so troubled that she tended to be on the defensive and stroppy with her family. Still, was it any wonder with Mabel Fenner for a mother?

Later that evening, Clara thought there was something enormously touching about a strong man like Charlie Fenner sitting at the piano with a small boy at his side. She was standing nearby watching as the two of them made music together.

It almost brought tears to her eyes to see this big man produce such a lovely sound from the keyboard with his large stubby fingers while Cuddy had fun singing the popular music hall song 'Oh Mr Porter' to his accompaniment.

'Bravo,' she said when the song came to an end.

'We're just mucking about; having a laugh with some music hall songs,' explained Charlie. 'Nothing serious tonight.'

'The two of you are naturals. You should go on the stage as a double act.'

Charlie laughed, looking relaxed and happy, a different person altogether from the strained man he was in the company of his family. 'I have very limited musical talent, I'm afraid; just enough to enjoy playing the piano for pleasure.' His smile melted Clara's heart. 'But it's nice to have someone to enjoy it with me. We have some fun together, don't we, lad?'

'I'll say,' Cuddy enthused.

'I'm so pleased,' Clara said. 'My brother doesn't get much encouragement from the male side of the family at home.'

'Well, he'll get plenty of encouragement from me,' said Charlie. 'Shall we have another half-hour tomorrow night? Perhaps we'll do something more serious, if you like.'

'I don't mind what we do as long as it's musical.'

'Bedtime now,' said Clara. 'Off you go, Cuddy. I'll be up in a minute to tuck you in.'

'Clara,' he frowned, his countenance suffused with pink. 'I am eleven, you know.'

'And I'm twenty-one but I wouldn't mind someone tucking me in now and again.'

'If you weren't already spoken for I'd offer to do the job myself,' joshed Charlie with a wicked grin.

'I'll pretend I didn't hear that,' Clara returned, taking the joke in good part.

Cheeks aflame, Cuddy fled from the room, limping slightly from his injuries.

'He wants to seem grown up in front of me,' remarked Charlie, closing the lid of the piano and gathering the music up and putting it away in the top of the piano stool. 'I suspect he really does want you to tuck him in.'

She nodded in agreement. 'He's always embarrassed about his singing at home because of the men of the family,' she explained, 'so he's forever trying to act the big man and it's become a habit. It's the environment we live in. In our street, boys of his age are out fighting not singing in the school choir.'

'I understand,' he said. 'I'll encourage him all I can while you're here. It gives me a chance to accompany someone. No one else in the family ever touches the piano, and

66

you've heard how they take the mickey out of me because I like to play.'

'Yes, I did notice that.' She paused thoughtfully. 'No one plays the piano in our house at all.'

'Not even Cuddy?'

'No. We just have it because a piano in the front room is traditional,' she explained. 'Cuddy probably thinks he'd get teased even more if he started having piano lessons.'

'It seems a shame.'

'Still, he's enjoying himself here with you,' she told him. 'If the storm hadn't happened we wouldn't have stayed on and he wouldn't have had the chance of some like-minded company. So some good has come out of it.'

'Am I right in thinking it's been no hardship for you either?' he enquired.

'You are spot on.'

'Not pining for your intended too much then?'

'I miss him, of course,' she said quickly, experiencing a stab of conscience for not thinking about Arnold very much at all since she'd been here. 'But as I enjoy country life so much I'm making the most of it.'

'I suppose it's a nice change in the short term,' he remarked.

'I would enjoy it in the long term too,' she said. 'I have some sort of affinity with the country which I first discovered in the Land Army.'

'Our sort of life is usually something people are born into,' he told her. 'I'm not sure if you would like it so much in winter when we still have to work outside, digging, planting, cutting down old trees and a host of other jobs.'

'I think I would. The cold weather didn't bother me too much in the Land Army.'

'You're unusual.'

She shrugged. 'Maybe,' she said lightly. 'I don't know where I get it from, but I know that working on the land is the right thing for me. Obviously it can't happen and I shall go back to London and settle down quite happily to my normal life, but in a perfect world I would live and work in the country.'

'You'll have to take plenty of walks in the park,' he smiled. 'And maybe you could grow things in the garden.'

'We have a concrete backyard with a very small patch of shabby earth.'

'Well, wait until next year and you can come and help us again at harvest time.'

'I'll be married by then and I can't imagine Arnold agreeing to my going off after that.'

'Bring him with you.'

She burst out laughing. 'Arnold would sooner eat rusty barbed wire than spend so much as an hour in the country. He's a London boy through and through, bless him.'

'I'm running out of ideas,' he said lightly.

'That's because there aren't any more,' she told him, smiling. 'A lot of people have an impossible dream and that's mine. But I recognise it for what it is and don't waste time hankering after it.'

'I hope not,' he said. 'I wouldn't want to be responsible for making you discontented with your lot. After all, it was me who suggested that you come to Brierley.'

'It isn't in my nature to be discontented with my lot, as you call it. London is where I belong. The rest is just wishful thinking.' She could feel the atmosphere becoming highly charged with emotion for some reason she couldn't quite identify. 'Well, I must go and make sure Cuddy is settled. Thanks for being so good to him.'

'A pleasure.'

'Goodnight then.'

'Goodnight, Clara.'

As she left the room, she was imbued with a sensation of glorious warmth and excitement. I'm only feeling like this because he was so kind to Cuddy, she told herself; it won't last, but I'll enjoy it while it does.

Charlie found himself in low spirits after Clara left him. She was such uplifting company and he knew he wanted more of it; much more. Instead he had to go home to the cottage and listen to more of Hester's fault finding. Sometimes it seemed as though there was nothing he could do to please his wife.

But he was married to her for better or worse and that meant taking the bad with the good. Unfortunately the good had been extremely brief and things had gone downhill soon after the honeymoon eighteen months ago. They said that to marry in haste was to repent at leisure, and that was certainly true in his case. These past few months Hester had been unbearable. She criticised the way he looked, the way he spoke and the way he ate his food; even the way he sat in the chair of an evening annoyed her.

He could only take so much, so he would eventually retaliate and it would end in another row. Sadly that was the pattern of their life together now. She would never admit it and it was painful for him to face up to the truth, but he was almost certain that he had merely been her way out of spinsterhood and the job she loathed at the pub. She was as hard as nails. And the way she treated his sister really upset him. He wouldn't put up with it and it caused even more disagreements between them. He couldn't remember the last time Hester had brought so much as an iota of joy to his life. And he obviously didn't make her happy no matter how hard he tried. It was demoralising to know that he hadn't come up to her expectations as a husband. Maybe he hadn't tried hard enough.

Whatever the truth of the matter, he had been brought up to believe that marriage was for life so he had to keep doing his best to try to make it work. And that meant going home to the cottage and attempting some sort of civilised cohabitation. Maybe tonight Hester would take one of her nocturnal walks around the orchard. That always seemed to improve her temper.

Bidding his parents a falsely cheerful goodnight, he left the house and headed towards the cottage.

It was Clara and Cuddy's last night at Brierley. Their suitcase was packed, Cuddy was in bed and Clara was staring rather wistfully out of the window into the moonlit yard.

'What are you looking at, sis?' asked Cuddy. 'Anythin' going on out there?'

'No. Nothing at all,' she replied. 'I'm just having a last look and feeling a little bit sad to be leaving.'

'Me too.'

'Still, it will be nice to be back home and to see everyone again, won't it?'

'Oh, yeah, I can't wait to see Mum and the others and my mates,' he said. 'It's just that it's so different here . . . you can't help liking it somehow.'

'It's a lovely night out there,' she observed. 'The moon is really bright.'

'What are you going to do with yourself until it's time for you to go to bed?' he enquired. 'Will you go downstairs to sit with the family?'

'I don't think I can face it tonight,' she confessed. It was always a strain but she had felt obliged to put in an appearance downstairs for the sake of courtesy after Cuddy had gone to bed. Usually just Eva and her parents were in evidence by that time but the atmosphere was generally fraught with tension and there was almost always some sort of altercation between Eva and her mother which upset Clara, especially as she was powerless to intervene. 'But it's a bit too early to stay in the bedroom. I don't want to seem rude.'

'Why not go for a walk?' he suggested brightly. 'You don't have to stay in with me. You'll be able to find your way in the moonlight, and they won't be offended because you're not sitting with them if you're doing something else.'

'Good idea, Cuds,' she agreed. 'A walk is just what I need. And there'll be someone in downstairs if you need anything.'

'I'm not a kid,' was his predictable response.

Having explained her plan to her hosts, she set off across the yard and into the orchard, where the moon cast a translucent glow over everything. Sticking to the paths between the fruit fields and heading for the gate and the lane beyond, she managed to maintain a steady pace, keeping her eye on the ground for any potential pitfalls. The scent of the night was ambrosial, moist and earthy with a hint of woodsmoke. It was wonderfully uplifting.

She found herself looking ahead to tomorrow and experienced a surge of pleasure at the thought of seeing the family and Arnold again. It would be nice to have some normal company. Not that the Tripps could ever be described as an average family, but they were warm-hearted and direct and the house wasn't filled with threatening undertones as this one was. But for now she would savour this last breath of nocturnal country air.

Opening the gate and walking along the deserted lane she heard the distant sound of voices, but there didn't seem to be anyone about. A courting couple in the fields somewhere, she thought, hearing laughter, high pitched and low. The voices grew nearer. The pair were obviously heading towards the lane. Feeling rather uncomfortable, as though she might be invading their privacy by being there, she stepped out of sight behind a tree.

Presently she saw two figures, shadowy in the moonlight, climb over the fence into the lane and head towards her. Having begun something that felt like a subterfuge, it now seemed impossible to step out of hiding. They really would think she was a voyeur then, so she moved well back out of sight.

'Oh, I don't know what I'd do without you, darling,' she heard a woman say as the couple grew closer. 'Our meetings are the only thing that makes it worthwhile getting up in the morning. I spend all day just longing to see you.'

'It's the same for me.' A man's voice.

'I think we should go away as soon as possible,' said the woman. 'We can be together all the time then.'

'We have too much to lose by doing that,' the man responded.

72

'Yeah, there is that, but I can't stand the way things are at the moment, I really can't,' she told him. 'It's you I want to be with. Not him.'

'We have to be realistic,' he pointed out. 'I'd lose my share in the business if this ever came to light. The old folks are very strict about this sort of thing. They'd throw me out of the family and bang would go my inheritance. The old man would write me out of his will altogether.'

'You might have to wait a long time for your inheritance anyway,' she said. 'In any case, we can't hang around until you have that safely in your pocket before we make a life together. We'll be too old to enjoy it by then.'

'Not necessarily. Besides, I can't see you being happy without the comfortable standard of living you've got now. And if I left the family business I wouldn't be able to support you to the same standard that he does.'

'Surely you could get a decent job as an orchard manager, couldn't you?'

'That can't be guaranteed. And I wouldn't get as much money as I do now, even if I were lucky enough to find something suitable.'

'I wouldn't mind that.'

'You say that now.'

'I mean it.'

'You'll feel differently when you're living on bread and cheese, I can guarantee it,' he said. 'I wouldn't like it either. Let's be honest. We both enjoy the good things of life.'

'I'm not denying it, but a man of your experience could earn a good living on the land anywhere.'

'Not as good as I do now,' he told her again. He was starting to sound irritable.

'I'm beginning to think you are just toying with my

73

affections,' she said in a girlish tone, but making it obvious that she meant it. 'You're all over me to start with, but as soon as it comes to serious intentions you always put obstacles in the way.'

'Only because they are facts. I want us to be together as much as you do.'

'Do something definite to prove it then,' she challenged him. 'There must be a way.'

'Yeah, there must be,' he agreed but Clara detected an edge to his voice. 'I'll see if I can find out what jobs are around in my line of business.'

'Do you mean it?'

'Of course I do,' he said, not sounding in the least convincing. 'We'll go somewhere as far away from here as possible.'

'That's better,' said the woman. 'As long as I know you are doing something positive about it I can just about bear the way things are at the moment.'

'That's my girl,' he said. 'Now, how about I show you again how much I want you.'

She giggled. 'You are insatiable.'

'And you love it.'

There was giggling interspersed with talking and running footsteps and then their voices faded; obviously they had gone back into the field.

Clara was shattered. Hester and Vincent cheating on Charlie! No wonder Hester hated it if Vincent gave Clara so much as a second glance. Poor Charlie. Betrayed by the two people whose loyalty he should be able to rely on: his wife and his brother.

Clara's only concern in this was Charlie. Should she tell him? Surely he had a right to know what was going on. Her insides twisted at the thought of the pain it would cause him. Maybe he already knew, or suspected. You could never tell what went on inside someone else's marriage. She didn't know Charlie well but guessed he wasn't the sort to turn a blind eye to a thing like that.

She questioned her own violent reaction to the shameful discovery. After all, Charlie was nothing to her; just a young man she had met once at a dance several years ago and had worked for temporarily in the present. What right did she have to interfere in his personal affairs? None at all. It pained her to think of anyone being deceived so heartlessly. But she also knew that it hurt that bit more because it was Charlie and he was special to her.

With a heavy heart she wondered if she should stay silent on the subject. Maybe this thing with Hester and Vincent was just a fling and would run its course and Charlie need never know. Vincent certainly hadn't seemed keen to make a commitment to Hester. In which case Clara would have destroyed a marriage needlessly if she spilled the beans.

No longer enjoying her walk, she made her way back up the lane towards Brierley, knowing she must make a decision before she went back to London tomorrow.

'I'll miss you both ever so much,' Eva said to Clara and Cuddy the next morning in the yard at Brierley as Charlie put their suitcase into the car.

'We'll miss you lots too, won't we, Cuddy?' said Clara.

'Yeah. Course we will,' he agreed. 'You should come to London to see us. You said you've always wanted to.'

'Maybe I will get there one day,' said Eva wistfully.

'Ta-ta then,' he said, shaking her hand politely then moving away with haste for fear she might kiss him.

'Cheerio,' she said.

Clara wrapped her arms around her. 'Keep in touch,' she said. 'You've got our address. Don't forget to write. I'll want to know how you're getting along.'

'Come on, Clara, make it snappy,' Charlie urged, 'or you'll miss the train.'

'Coming.' She gave Eva one last hug and hopped on board, waving as the open-topped car rolled jerkily out of the gate into the lane.

'So it's back to civilisation and the bright lights for you then,' remarked Charlie.

'That's right,' said Clara who had been awake most of the night agonising over whether she should tell him about Hester and Vincent or not. She still hadn't made up her mind. It was all so complicated. 'Out every night of the week, living the high life.'

'Really?'

'No, of course not. Just joking,' she told him lightly. 'Arnold and I are saving up to get married, remember, so we can only afford to go out occasionally.'

'Saving up for your own pots and pans, that sort of thing,' he suggested.

'The odd bit of furniture would be nice too.'

'Of course. These things all have to be paid for.'

'Exactly.'

Cuddy said something and she was able to be silent with her thoughts while the two of them chatted. Her turmoil was reaching such a point as to make her feel physically ill. In a few minutes they would be at the railway station and she would probably never see Charlie again.

Should she tell him or should she go home with the betrayal unspoken? Which would be best for him?

She was recalled to the present with a start. 'Come on, sis,' Cuddy was saying. 'We're there.'

Charlie was already out of the car and walking towards the station entrance with the suitcase. He turned and waved them on.

'The train is just coming in so you'd better get your skates on,' he called.

On the platform, with Cuddy on board the train, Charlie said, 'You take good care of yourself, Clara.'

'Yes, I will. You too.'

'You did a really good job at Brierley with the picking and it's been lovely seeing you again.'

'Charlie . . .'

'Yes.'

'I have something to tell you.'

'You'd better say it quick then,' he urged her. 'The train will be going in a minute.'

She looked into his face and his lovely warm blue eyes.

'What is it?' he asked, looking concerned. 'Whatever is the matter? Are you ill?'

'No, no, I'm fine.'

'Whatever it is you'd better spit it out,' he said as the doors slammed all along the train and the guard lifted his whistle to his lips.

'It's nothing,' she heard herself utter. 'Just . . . well, thanks for making our stay so special.'

'My pleasure,' he said, smiling. 'I've enjoyed having you both around.'

'Ta-ta then.'

'Cheerio, Clara.'

She clambered on to the train and sat down without looking out of the window because she didn't want him to see the tears in her eyes. She felt as though she had let him down as surely as Hester and his brother had and she hated herself for it. But she just couldn't bring herself to tell him what she'd seen. He would be devastated.

Chapter Four

'Well, the country air has certainly put some roses in your cheeks,' Flo said approvingly to Clara and Cuddy over their evening meal on their first night back. 'You look the picture of health, the pair of you, even though Cuddy has been in the wars.'

'Brown as berries,' added her husband. 'You look as though you've had a fortnight in the sun at Brighton.'

'I don't think the sun ever shines for a fortnight at a stretch there, Dad,' said Clara with a wry grin. 'It's working outside in the fresh air that's done it; the weather was lovely apart from the storm.'

'The storm that injured my boy,' said Flo, turning to Cuddy, her expression becoming serious. 'You should have let me know he'd been hurt, Clara.'

'You'd only have upset yourself and come tearing down to Kent when it wasn't necessary,' she told her. 'If it had been serious, as we thought at first, of course I would have let you know.'

'A boy of that age needs his mum when there's anything wrong with him, isn't that right, darlin'?'

'I was fine, Mum, honest,' Cuddy assured her, colouring up.

'Stop babying him, for goodness' sake, Flo,' her husband said predictably. 'He's come through the accident with no harm done so he doesn't need a lot of fuss. He's got enough sissy tendencies as it is. You'll make him worse with your pampering.'

'You wouldn't be talking about sissy tendencies if you'd seen how he behaved in the storm.' Clara defended her brother hotly. 'He was a proper little hero and he only got hurt because he was trying to help other people. You should be proud of him, Dad. Not finding fault.'

'I am proud of him, o' course I am,' said her father defensively.

'It doesn't sound much like it.'

'I don't like to see your mother fussing over him too much, that's all. It isn't good for any boy, hero or not!'

'If I want to make a fuss of him I will,' retorted Flo. 'I'm the boy's mother and I know what I'm doing.'

'You're too soft.'

'Boys have feelings as well as girls, you know,' she came back at him indignantly.

'Yes, and they learn not to show them by the time they're men,' he said. 'That's how the system works. A man needs to survive in the outside world, which means staying strong and maintaining control.'

'What a load of rubbish you come out with some-times,' Flo exploded. 'Showing your feelings is nothing to be ashamed of. You men don't half get some daft ideas.'

'It's the way of the world, Flo.'

'All right, you two,' said Clara. 'Let's have no arguments on our first night back.'

'Sorry, love,' Flo said apologetically.

'Yeah, me an' all,' added Frank. 'You know that me and

your mum are the best of friends really.' He paused, then changed the subject. 'So what were these people you were staying with like?'

'Weird,' replied Cuddy without hesitation.

'Oh? Really? In what way?' enquired his mother.

'Charlie and Eva were lovely but the others always seemed to be angry and getting at each other. There were awful silences and looks like daggers at mealtimes. I couldn't wait to get away from the table.'

'I thought you said they looked after you very well, Clara,' said Flo, frowning.

'They did. They were nice to us but not to each other,' she explained. 'There was plenty of food and drink for the workers, but when Cuddy and I moved into the house we ate with the family and felt awkward because they were so horrible to each other.'

'Mrs Fenner was awful to Eva all the time,' said Cuddy. 'It made me feel sick to hear her. If I was Eva, I'd leave home.'

'Sounds like a bit of a dragon to me,' Flo decided. 'What was the food like?'

'Lovely,' replied Cuddy at once. 'Mrs Fenner is a really good cook.'

'She does have some redeeming features then.'

'Oh yeah, she's brilliant at cooking and cleaning and stuff like that,' he told her. 'The dinners were smashing and we had gorgeous cakes every afternoon for tea.'

'Her cooking is better than mine, then,' said Flo.

'Couldn't be worse, could it, Mum?' said Sydney, looking down at his plate and chortling. 'I was just wondering if you'd put cement powder instead of flour in the pastry for this meat pie.'

'I'll box your ears for you, you cheeky young toerag,' she warned him.

'Yes, don't be rude,' added her husband supportively, though he was unable to stifle a chuckle.

'You can say what you like about my cooking but you lot all seem to thrive on it. Anyway, I do my best,' she told them. 'I haven't got the right sort of hands for pastry making. As I've told you before, good pastry hands have to be cold and mine must be warm or something.'

'How does that account for the rock cakes that really do live up to their name then, since you mix them with a spoon?' asked Frank, teasing her.

'How would I know? I make them the same way as everyone else but for some reason they never come out like other people's. Gawd only knows why.'

'Don't worry, Mum. You have plenty of other virtues and we love you just the way you are. We'd sooner have you any day than Mrs Fenner or anyone else at all,' said Clara.

'I'll say,' added Cuddy.

'You speak for yourself,' joked their father. 'I wouldn't mind having this Mrs Fenner woman around if it meant we were going to get some decent meals.'

Clara and Cuddy both found the idea of their father being at the mercy of Mrs Fenner hilarious and roared with laughter.

'You *would* mind having her around the place, believe me, Dad,' declared Clara. 'One day of her and you'd be a broken man. Her husband rarely says a word. He's probably too frightened of her, the poor thing. I had a few little chats with him and he seemed nice. I felt sorry for him.'

Frank winked at Clara. 'Perhaps I'd better stick with the woman I've got then, and put up with the indigestion.'

'You'll have an aching jaw as well as indigestion if you don't put a sock in it,' said Flo good-humouredly. 'Anyway, you don't look too bad on it so I must be doing something right.'

'You, my little flower, don't do a thing wrong in my book,' he said. 'So Mr Fenner can keep his missus.'

'Ugh, listen to the soft soap,' Sydney put in. 'He's just trying to get round you, Mum, in case you make him have second helpings.'

'There's never much left for second helpings because you all want such a lot the first time round,' Flo pointed out. 'Peculiar, really, when you think of how bad the food is supposed to be.'

'We're all so hungry we'll eat anything,' persisted Sydney, enjoying the fun.

'All right; joke over. You've taken it far enough.' That was Clara, ever the peacemaker. 'You'll really upset Mum in a minute.'

'It'll take more than a bit of ribbing from them to upset me, love,' said Flo cheerily. 'I'm far too used to it.'

'Anyway,' began Clara in a much-needed change of subject. 'What's been happening here while we've been away?'

'Nothin' much,' said Sydney.

'Has Arnold been round a lot?'

'He popped in a couple of times,' Flo replied. 'Just to see how we were.'

'He didn't stay long,' put in Sydney. 'Probably had a date with some good-looking woman.'

'This is Arnold you're talking about,' Flo reminded him. 'He doesn't do things like that.'

'He might. I would if my girlfriend went off and left me,' declared Sydney with youthful arrogance.

'You'd have to find a girlfriend first as well as someone to go off with,' Clara chuckled.

'I can have any girl I want,' he boasted, though his cheeks were suffused with pink.

'Prove it by going out and finding one then,' his sister teased him.

'I'd rather be with my mates.'

'Not still that awful gang, I hope,' said Clara.

'A man's mates are his own business and nothing to do with his sister.'

'So it is still them.' She paused and took a breath. 'But I'm not going to spoil our first night back by nagging you about it.'

'Thank goodness for that. I've had a break from it these past few weeks,' he told her. 'It's been lovely without you, sister dear.'

'You just watch yourself with those yobs,' persisted Clara. 'That's all I'm saying . . . for now.'

'I can look after myself,' he said with a nonchalant shrug.

There were times, Clara thought, when Sydney seemed almost as vulnerable as his younger brother. For all his swagger, he was desperate to impress. Unfortunately, the people he wanted to make an impression on weren't the sort who were admired by those who really cared for him. Paradoxically, she had a sneaking feeling that he would miss the family's attempts to keep him on the straight and narrow if they stopped doing it. For all that he was a young man, there was still something of the boy in him.

As everyone started talking at once, the others clamouring to know more about their stay in the country, Clara found herself trying to define the difference between her family and the Fenners. It wasn't as though the Tripps didn't have ferocious disagreements and plenty of them. But their love for each other filled the house even though it didn't come in the form of soft, sentimental talk. They teased, bantered and argued noisily but despite it all, each one of them would go to the ends of the earth for the others if needs be. She was almost certain the same couldn't be said of the Fenners, except of course for Charlie who was the saving grace of that family. Her heart twisted at the thought of the disloyalty surrounding him. He really didn't deserve it.

'I was rather sorry to see Clara and her young brother leave,' said the normally silent John Fenner over supper at Brierley that evening.

They all looked at him in surprise because he was usually so quiet at mealtimes.

'Why is that exactly, dear?' Mabel enquired.

'No particular reason; it's just that they were such nice company I enjoyed having them around.'

'I was sorry to see them go too,' said Eva mournfully. 'It isn't the same without them.'

'How ridiculous,' snorted Hester, who couldn't bear to hear praise for anyone except herself. 'They were hardly here long enough for anyone to get used to them, and as far as I could see there was nothing special about either of them.'

'I think you're wrong there, Hester,' said John.

Disagreeing with anyone was rare for him. 'The boy coped wonderfully well with his accident, which must have been a very frightening experience, and the girl made a real contribution to this place. She took an intelligent interest in the orchard. We could do with more people like her.'

'I agree with you, Dad,' added Charlie, who had been very sad to see her go. 'She didn't have to work that last week as she was here as our guest, but she was outside helping whenever she could.'

'She had to do something to pay for her keep, I suppose,' Hester agreed with reluctance.

'No she didn't,' corrected Charlie. 'The accident happened on our land so I told her that they would stay with us free of charge until young Cuddy was well enough to travel. It was the very least we could have done.'

His wife shot a look at him. 'Don't tell me you paid her for the last week as well as feeding them for nothing,' she said.

'Of course we did,' he said. 'She wasn't asked to work but what she did was very useful so she was entitled to get paid. She was out there helping clear the debris left by the storm; up and down the trees removing leafless wood and any other jobs that needed doing after the harvest. Besides, she would have been back at work had it not been for the accident, and I don't suppose she can afford to lose a week's pay.'

'Honestly, they were just a couple of common strangers and they seem to have taken you all in,' Hester said disapprovingly. 'The accident wasn't our responsibility. We can't be blamed for the storm.'

'No, but we can help the victims of it,' said her father-in-law mildly. 'Anyway, in what way exactly have we been taken in?'

'They've given you some sort of sob story and you've fallen for it,' she told him.

'I heard no sob story from them; they seemed very happy with their life. They asked for nothing from us at all.'

'Just because their manners weren't as bad as you'd expect from rough London riff-raff, you all seem to think that they're some sort of saints.' She turned to Vincent for support. 'What about you, Vincent? What did you think of them?'

'I can't say that I found anything wrong with them,' he admitted casually. 'The girl was an excellent worker and the boy seemed a nice enough kid.'

Charlie could have reminded his wife that she didn't come from a particularly salubrious background herself. She was from a poor family and had been living hand to mouth as a barmaid when he'd met her. But he let it pass and said, 'Clara did more than just work. She was eager to learn too. She asked me so many questions she probably knows as much as we do about the fruit-growing industry by now.'

'Now you really are being ridiculous,' snorted Hester.

'Well, perhaps that was a bit of an exaggeration,' he conceded. 'But it is very unusual to get a temporary worker so interested in the running of the orchard. They usually get on with the job, take their money and go.'

'What did you think of them, Mabel?' Hester asked, almost beside herself with jealousy. 'Are you a member of the Tripps' fan club?'

'I haven't given them a great deal of thought,' replied

Mabel, who took no part in the business side of things at all. For her the Tripps' stay had merely meant two extra people to cater for. 'They both seemed harmless enough to me.'

'Well, I seem to be the only one in this family not to have had my head turned by a couple of interlopers.'

'A bit too pretty for you, was she, Hester?' suggested Eva. 'Did she make you envious?'

A withering look was sent in Eva's direction; her suggestion was far too near the truth for Hester's liking. 'I didn't even notice what she looked like.'

'Oh, don't make me laugh,' said Eva. 'No one could help noticing what she looked like.'

'Well I didn't.'

'Don't believe you.'

'Now now, you two,' Charlie put in. 'Don't let's have another cat fight.'

'Yes, behave yourself, Eva,' said Mabel predictably.

There were times when Charlie could cheerfully throttle his mother and now was one of them. He gave his sister an affectionate wink and some of the hurt went out of her eyes. Then he changed the subject, and engaged his father and Vincent in orchard talk for the rest of the meal.

'Well, have you missed me?' Clara asked Arnold when he came to the house later that evening and they managed to escape from the family into the front room. It was cold and musty because it was only heated at Christmas and on special occasions, but at least they could have a few minutes on their own.

'Does Big Ben chime?' he responded, smiling at her. 'I've been like a lost soul without you.'

'Don't overdo it, Arnold,' she joshed.

He grinned in acknowledgement of his overstatement. 'I did miss you, though,' he told her.

'How did you pass the time?' she enquired. 'You didn't come round here much.'

'I was working mostly; did a lot of overtime which will boost my savings for our future,' he replied. 'There were a lot of late deliveries to be done and the money was good. I stayed home of an evening if I wasn't working, o' course.'

Up went Clara's brows.

'Well, all right, I went down the pub for a few pints a couple of times,' he admitted sheepishly. 'But only once or twice for an hour or so with my mates. It wouldn't be fair for me to go out spending money while you're away working.'

'You're entitled to some relaxation,' she said, smiling. 'You know I don't mind. I'd sooner that than have you moping at home because I'm not around. That would make me feel really guilty.'

'I must be the luckiest bloke alive to have you,' he said, brushing her lips with his.

'Even though I went off and left you?'

'Yeah, even then. Anyway, how did you get on in the great empty countryside?'

'A dedicated city dweller like you will probably find this impossible to believe but I loved every moment,' she told him, adding diplomatically, 'Of course, that isn't to say that I didn't miss you.'

'I believe you,' he said casually. 'I'm glad you weren't disappointed, because I know how much you wanted to go.' He gave her one of his wicked grins. 'I reckon you must be stark raving mad to want to go and work in the country, though.'

'You can't beat it,' she told him. 'In the last week when we stayed on I helped out with the more general orchard work as the harvest was over and learned even more about the job.' She took a deep breath and patted her upper chest to illustrate her point. 'Think of all that lovely fresh air.'

'And the mud and the dirt and the wind and the rain and the lack of any sort of entertainment,' he added, teasing her. 'Just the thought of it makes me nervous.' He lit a cigarette and pretended to be shaking. 'I reckon I'd pass out if someone gave me a shovel and told me to start digging.'

'Don't give me that,' she said, laughing. 'You've been through the war. I reckon you did plenty of shovelling and saw more than your fair share of mud.'

'Exactly,' he responded. 'And I never want to do anything like that ever again.' He looked serious for a moment, then grinned. 'Even Shepherd's Bush Green is a bit too rural for me.'

'Knowing you, that's probably true!'

'Still, it wouldn't do for us all to be the same, would it?' he said. 'Though I never thought I'd have a country bumpkin for my future wife, hardened townsman that I am.' He looked at her with a glint in his eye. 'Shouldn't you have straw in your hair or something?'

'I've been to an orchard, not an arable farm,' she said with a smile.

'It's all the same to me,' he said. 'They're all great stretches of nothingness full of bad smells. Give me the grey and dirty town streets any day and the pubs and the picture houses.' He puffed on his cigarette and created a cloud of smoke. 'Anyway, how have things been here at the Tripp residence? Has Sydney been behaving himself?'

'As far as I know,' she answered. 'That talk you had with him must still be having an effect.'

'I called round here a couple of times and everything seemed all right so I guessed he wasn't giving your folks too much trouble. I know I said I'd keep an eye on him but I didn't want to breathe down the boy's neck.'

'It would only have antagonised him anyway, if you made it too obvious.'

'That's what I thought,' he told her. 'But if he gets troublesome again you just let me know.'

'Will do. He's still hanging around with that rough gang so I might have to,' she said.

'You can't expect too much too soon. If he's behaving himself at home, it's a start.' He put his arm round her and drew her close. 'But let's forget about Sydney for the moment. It's time we did some catching up.' He gave her a squeeze. 'Oh, I've really missed you. It's so good to have you back.'

The door burst open.

'Ugh, are you two at it again?' said Cuddy.

'What do you want, love?' asked Clara.

'I wanted to play the piano.'

'But you don't play,' Clara pointed out. 'No one in this house ever touches the piano.'

'I was just going to have a go because I'm thinking of learning if Mum and Dad will let me have lessons,' the boy explained. Clara guessed that he had been influenced by Charlie Fenner and for some reason this pleased her. 'But it doesn't matter. I can do it another time.'

'Shouldn't you be in bed?' suggested Arnold.

'No. It's Saturday and I can stay up late on Saturdays.'

'In that case, perhaps it's time you and I went for a walk, Clara,' he said co-operatively.

'No, no, it's all right, honestly,' insisted the ever considerate Cuddy, edging out of the room. 'I'll have a go another time.'

'Good lad,' said Arnold, and as soon as the door closed behind him he took Clara in his arms.

It was true he had missed her, even though he had welcomed her absence with open arms. She was a wonderful girl and he loved her from the bottom of his heart, but she was much too good for him; there was absolutely no doubt about that. Fortunately for him, she didn't know it, and if he boxed clever she never would, so things could continue as they were.

'What shall we do tonight?' asked Shoulders, so called for the exceptional width of his upper body, swathed tonight in a dark overcoat with the collar up to create effect. He was the unelected leader of the group of mates Sydney spent most of his spare time with. Half a dozen of them were gathered on Shepherd's Bush Green.

'We need to find some girls,' suggested Tub, a young man with a glandular imbalance which caused him to be permanently overweight. He was regularly tormented by Shoulders and his acolytes because of it.

'Yeah, I think so too,' agreed one of the others.

'So what about Hammersmith Palais then?' suggested Tub.

'Don't talk daft. Since when did we go to poncy places like that?' demanded Shoulders, pushing Tub roughly.

'I just thought . . . well, that's where girls go, ain't it? If we wanna find some—'

'But it ain't where we go, you thickhead,' said Shoulders in a bullying manner. 'It's much too posh. Anyway, it costs a lot to get in and they'll all be older than us at a place like that so we wouldn't get a look in with the women.'

'We might,' said Tub. 'I've heard the girls who go there are smart and good looking.'

Shoulders put his hand on Tub's flabby chest and pushed him so hard he staggered backwards. 'You wouldn't get a girl if there were thousands of 'em on this green begging for it. No girl would want a fatso like you.'

'I just thought it might be a laugh,' said Tub meekly.

'I do the thinking round here, not you,' Shoulders reminded him, squaring up to him in a menacing manner.

'He was only saying it might be an idea,' Sydney pointed out. 'There's no need to get rough with him.'

Shoulders swung round, his beady eyes hot with rage. 'Are you disagreeing with me, Trippo?' he snapped, moving towards Sydney, a couple of his dedicated supporters by his side. 'Are you?'

'I'm just saying that Tub didn't mean any harm, that's all.'

'Tub has a great big belly but he doesn't have much of a brain so don't make the mistake of taking any notice of anything he says,' said Shoulders.

'He isn't thick,' Sydney dared to point out.

Sydney's lapels were grabbed and he was pulled towards Shoulders until he could feel the gang leader's revolting nicotine breath on his face.

'What's that you said?' he asked, his minders closing in and gripping Sydney's arms. 'What did you say?'

Sydney felt the pressure increase and as Shoulders moved back he could see his rough features in the light from the gas lamp, his square jaw, flat nose and mean eyes, and the dark hair slicked to his head. Sydney was inwardly trembling but he said, 'You heard. I said Tub isn't thick.'

There was a hush among the others because someone had dared to speak out against the leader. 'Right, you know what to do, boys,' said Shoulders.

Sydney felt a fist in his chest, one punch then another and another until he was groaning with pain.

'All right, lads, don't get carried away,' Shoulders snapped suddenly. 'He's one of us, remember.'

The boys moved away.

'That was just to remind you who's in charge around here, Trippo,' Shoulders informed him. 'If you disagree with me again you'll get worse. Understood?'

Sydney wanted to put up a fight. More than anything he would like to give Shoulders a dose of his own medicine. But he heard himself say, 'Yeah, I understand.'

'Good. So let's get on with the evening's entertainment then, shall we?'

There was an enthusiastic roar of approval from the others. Sydney stood back and said nothing. He hated himself for not standing up to Shoulders. The thing he most dreaded in life was to be a coward and he'd always tried his hardest not to be, so why had he allowed himself to stand back and take it? Probably because the whole lot of them would have turned on him if he'd fought back, they were so in thrall to the powerful figure of Shoulders. But that was no excuse for not sticking to his guns for a friend. He was very disappointed in himself.

At the beginning Sydney had been thrilled to have Shoulders and the boys as mates. They were tough and well known in the area among the younger generation of their ilk. Being one of them had made him feel special; something better than just a shop boy kowtowing to customers all day long. Seeing them at night gave him something to look forward to after being with the boring old people at work all day. He liked the camaraderie; the feeling of belonging.

But lately he'd found himself bored with the whole thing; had been irritated by Shoulders and found him rather stupid. Sydney had wanted to suggest that they do something civilised tonight like going to the pictures rather than hanging around the streets terrorising people. But somehow he was still here. He couldn't bring himself to make the break. Even apart from the fact that Shoulders would have him beaten up if he stopped appearing, he'd have no mates of his own age. All his old friends had dropped him since he'd got in with Shoulders and his cronies.

His pals from school were all mad on football and girls. They didn't go in for rough stuff. He'd mocked them at first for being scared of the tough company he kept but now he could see that they were just bored by it. He was always in trouble at home since he'd been in this gang, too. It had been glamorous at first and had made the family seem dull and boring in comparison, and he supposed he must have shown it. They were always going on at him about his bad behaviour, anyway.

'Booze, that's what we need,' Shoulders was saying.

'They won't serve us in the pubs around here,' said someone. 'They know we're not old enough.'

'So we go to the Bottle and Jug,' said Shoulders. 'And if they don't serve us we'll make whoever's behind the counter understand that we mean business. You know how it's done.'

The others were all fired up. Despite himself Sydney felt the adrenalin flowing. He followed the rest and they walked across the Green towards the nearest pub and went in a door at the side of the main entrances. It opened into a small, dimly lit room with bottles and barrels on the shelves behind the wooden counter where a middle-aged woman they knew to be the landlord's wife was on duty. She looked frightened when they burst in, filling the place with their presence, and demanded to be served.

'A bottle of brown ale, please, missus,' said one of Shoulders' minders, the leader himself standing back, 'and the same for all my mates. We'll all pay for our own.'

The woman looked uncertain. 'How old are you?' she asked, casting her eye over them.

'None of your business,' said Shoulders' second in charge.

'You're just kids and I'm not serving you.'

'If you don't we'll come over there and help ourselves,' the boy said menacingly. 'And we might take more than we pay for, so get on and serve us or you'll regret it. You could end up with a couple of black eyes.'

She looked terrified now, Sydney observed, and it made him feel sick inside. At that moment he wanted out of it, and he turned towards the door ready to leave.

'You going somewhere, Trippo?' demanded Shoulders, gripping his arm tightly.

Sydney looked at the other boy's acne-ridden face and saw the evil in his deep-set eyes. 'I . . .' he began.

'I don't think so,' Shoulders cut in, 'so don't even let it cross your mind.'

'There's no need to get rough with the lady,' Sydney objected. 'She's only doing her job. You needn't be so rude to her, either. She deserves some respect.'

'Don't be such a big girl and get up to the counter and pay your money and get your beer,' he ordered.

Sydney did as he was told, full of self-loathing, especially when the woman looked so scared of him. Was this what he wanted from life, to see fear in the eyes of a woman who could be his own mother? He wanted to reassure her; to tell her that he meant no harm and would protect her from the rougher element of the gang. But instead he said curtly, 'A bottle of brown ale, missus, and look sharp about it if you please.'

'You arrogant young thug,' said the woman.

'That's more like it, Trippo,' said Shoulders as Sydney walked away from the counter with his beer. 'I thought for a minute you might be going soft on us.'

'Nah, not a chance,' said Sydney, unscrewing the top of the beer bottle and taking a swig.

'Come on then, lads,' said Shoulders as they all piled out of the pub leaving the landlord's wife looking relieved. 'Let's go and find some excitement.'

Sydney trailed along with them, some of the old thrill returning with the effect of the beer. Deliberately blotting out the troubling voice of his conscience, he swaggered towards the Green.

'Thanks for sticking up for me, Trippo,' said Tub, appearing beside him and speaking in a low voice. 'I appreciate that.'

'It was no trouble, mate.'

'I'm sorry you got hurt.'

'It'll take more than those two to hurt me,' said Sydney, full of bravado.

'Don't get into trouble on my account,' Tub said anxiously. 'Shoulders' boys can get very nasty.'

'Don't worry about me,' he said, the spirit of gang culture returning. 'I can look after myself.'

Indeed, walking along with the other boys, everyone laughing and joshing, he felt invincible.

Chapter Five

1921

Taylor's Tea rooms were full to capacity and there was a long queue of people waiting for tables, most of them carrying store bags. The January sales were in full swing and it was always a busy time for the catering establishments around here as people flocked to the West End from the suburbs and beyond in search of bargains. Clara thrived on bustle. The buzz when the place was crowded energised her.

'Have you been lucky at the sales today, ladies?' she enquired politely, judging that the two ordinary-looking women who had come in laden with bags would appreciate her interest.

'We've had a whale of a time, dear,' said the one in the red hat. 'We got plenty of bargains and I got a very nice winter coat for less than half price. I had to fight tooth and nail for it, though. Some other woman was after it. She swore she got there before me.'

'They nearly came to blows over it,' added her companion. 'I thought there was going to be fisticuffs.'

99

'Oh dear,' said Clara with a half-smile. 'You'll be ready for your tea then.'

'Ready for bed more like. I'm absolutely exhausted,' said Red Hat. 'My poor feet are killing me too. Walking about all day has played hell with my corns. Heaven only knows how I'm going to make it to the station.'

'I'd give you a piggy back but your weight would probably crush me to death,' chortled her friend.

Red Hat tutted but she was smiling in the way that close friends did with each other. 'See how she treats me,' she said to Clara. 'No respect at all.'

'Our fine refreshments will put new life into you both, and you'll be rested by the time you go,' said Clara pleasantly. 'What can I get for you?'

'Tea and scones, please,' said Red Hat.

'Same for me, please, dear,' said her companion.

Clara wrote the order on her pad. 'Tea and scones for two coming up,' she said.

She turned away, took another order and delivered it to the kitchens, dealt with a couple of bills, then cleared some tables for the people at the front of the queue.

'Ooh, it's bitter out there,' remarked a woman as she sat down heavily at one of the tables.

'The cold weather doesn't seem to deter people from going to the sales,' said Clara conversationally.

'Ten foot of snow wouldn't keep me away,' declared the woman. 'The January sales are the highlight of my year. It wouldn't be the same without the crowds, and the weather can't be helped, given the time of year.'

Clara continued with her work, entering into conversation when the customer appeared to want it, and never thrusting it on them when they didn't. She considered herself extremely lucky not to have lost her position here despite the extra week she had taken off without prior notice. Initially, after her return, she'd been unsettled, having discovered the depth of her love for country life whilst at Brierley, but, knowing she had no choice, she'd put her heart and soul into her work at Taylor's and soon got back into the swing.

Christmas had seemed to be upon them quickly after she got back. It had been the customary jolly affair at home with games, sing-songs and all the usual festive food and drink. Dad had a little too much of the latter on Christmas night, as did Sydney, who wasn't used to it so had to be helped to bed.

Things hadn't changed between herself and Arnold. That extra special something between them was still missing but he was the one she had chosen to marry so she accepted him for what he was: a good man. He had been working a lot of evenings lately so she didn't see much of him during the week. It didn't particularly worry her; she didn't feel the need for them to live in each other's pockets.

Brierley was often on her mind, and especially Charlie, and she wondered how things were with his marriage now. She'd had a few letters from Eva which mentioned everyday happenings at the orchard but never Charlie specifically. But why would they? Eva didn't know that Clara had a special interest or that Charlie's wife was having an affair with Vincent.

Clara constantly reminded herself that neither the Fenner family nor Charlie's marriage was any of her concern. She had quite enough to worry about here at home.

The main problem since she'd been back was Sydney. It wasn't so much that he was rude and ill behaved as he had been in the past. It was more that he seemed depressed and moody and tended to be snappy with everyone. She was certain it had something to do with those awful friends of his but she couldn't persuade him to talk about it.

'There's nothin' wrong with me at all so give over askin', will you, Clara?' he'd say when she got him on his own and tried to coax him into confiding in her. 'It's like being at flippin' school, living here with all these questions; just leave me alone.'

But now a blast of cold air blew around Clara's legs as someone came in when she was standing at a table near the door. As she shivered she found herself imagining how cold it must be for Charlie if he was working outside. He'd said the job was tough in winter. She admonished herself. It was Arnold she should be concerned for; not Charlie. But Arnold was inside a van most of the time and protected from the weather.

She was recalled to the present with a jolt when she realised that her customers had made up their minds and were giving her their order. Deeply engrossed in her own thoughts, she hadn't heard a word and had to ask them to repeat it.

'We'd like tea and fancies, please, miss,' said an elderly gentleman who was with a woman of about the same age. 'And be sure to take the order this time?'

'Yes, sir. Of course,' she said, writing it down on her pad. 'Anything else I can get you this afternoon? Any sandwiches?'

'No, that will be all, thank you.'

As she walked across the room towards the kitchens, the supervisor waylaid her.

'I notice the customer had to ask twice for his order because you were daydreaming,' she said. 'That isn't the way a Taylor's waitress has been trained to behave.'

'Sorry, miss,' said Clara.

'Don't let it happen again, Miss Tripp,' she warned her. 'I shall know if it does.'

I bet you will, thought Clara, as she went on her way wondering how the supervisor had spotted her lapse in concentration. She had been on the other side of the room at the time. She came to the conclusion that her superior must be in possession of a sixth sense.

Still, it was a warning to Clara. In future she must make sure she kept her mind on the job or she would lose it. Personal matters must be mulled over in her own time!

It was a bitterly cold Saturday night in January and the town was white with frost, the stars diamond bright in the velvet-dark sky. But still Sydney and his friends roamed the streets, their breath turning to steam every time they opened their mouths. The weather was immaterial to these boys. It was the company that mattered. Indoors, to their way of thinking, was for old people, pansy boys and people who had no friends. They had managed to get served with some beer at the Bottle and Jug again and were gathered on Shepherd's Bush Green drinking it.

Shoulders wasn't in a good mood. Sydney guessed that the cold weather was making him grumpy, because it really was bitter, especially standing about. Although Sydney's feet felt numb, they were aching too somehow, and his fingers were freezing inside his gloves. But naturally he didn't admit it. As well as feeling miserable with the cold, he was on edge because Shoulders was in the frame of mind to pick on someone, and, as usual, it was Tub.

'Your mother must be a hell of a big woman to have given birth to you, Tub,' he taunted. 'In fact she must be about the size of an elephant.'

'No. My mum is just an ordinary build,' said Tub hotly.

'How come you're like you are then?' asked Shoulders cruelly.

'It's me glands,' replied the other boy dismally. 'You already know that, because I've told you before.'

'I bet his mother is the size of an 'ouse, don't you, lads?' Shoulders continued loudly.

'Yeah, she must be 'uge,' the others chorused.

'Don't you dare say things about my mother,' Tub warned them with an unprecedented show of courage.

'Well, well,' said Shoulders. 'Hark at him, boys. I'm sure you didn't mean that, did you, Tub?'

There was a brief hiatus, then Tub said, 'Yeah, I did, as it happens. You can say what you like about me but I won't have you saying things about my mum.'

'*You* won't have *me* saying things about your mum,' said the other boy in a tone of scathing mockery. 'Cor, that's the funniest thing I've heard in ages; that really is comical.' He moved closer to Tub. 'In case you haven't noticed, fatso, I say what goes around here, not you. So you will apologise to me right now for speaking out of turn.'

'You're the one who should apologise to me for speaking out of turn about my mother,' said Tub after a moment. Sydney held his breath, dreading what was to come.

'Oh, you're getting funnier by the second,' snorted Shoulders, swigging his beer and laughing. 'I think he needs teaching a lesson, don't you, lads?' He looked at his two favourite cronies. 'Go on; do your stuff and make a good job of it.'

Sydney winced as the two boys set about Tub. 'Oi, leave him alone,' he shouted, darting forward and trying to pull them away, only to have the other members of the group drag him back, landing a few punches on him at the same time. 'Two on to one ain't fair.'

'You're getting above yourself, Trippo. We'll deal with you later, so you can look forward to some of what Tub's getting,' growled Shoulders, standing aside so as not to get involved in any violence himself. 'Keep hold of him, boys. Do your worst. Make him realise who's boss around here.'

Sydney struggled hard and finally managed to free himself by biting one of his captors on the hand. 'You're killing him,' he gasped, forcing his way forward and seeing his friend lying on the ground while his attackers punched and kicked relentlessly. 'Leave him alone, for pity's sake; can't you see what you're doing to him?' His voice was ragged with emotion; there were tears streaming down his face. 'He's got his eyes closed. You've killed him, you bastards. You've bloody well killed him.'

'Rubbish,' said Shoulders, moving forward as his pals continued the beating.

'Stop it, will you,' Sydney shouted, his voice distorted by fear and concern for the injured boy. 'No more. For God's sake stop.'

'Blimey, you have taken it a bit far,' said Shoulders, seeing the bruised and battered boy lying motionless on the rime-covered grass. 'Come on, let's get out of here.'

There was the sound of running footsteps as all the boys, except Sydney, left their mate for dead.

Sydney was terrified. 'It's all right, Tub,' he said shakily, leaning over his unconscious friend. He took off his coat and laid it gently over the boy. 'Don't worry. You're gonna be fine. I'll get you some help as quick as I can. Just hang on. Please hang on.'

'What's going on 'ere, then?'

Swinging round, Sydney saw a police constable.

'We need help, and fast. He's hurt bad. I think he might be dead.' Sydney was pale with fright, trembling all over and feeling sick.

'What happened?'

'He got beat up, but never mind about that now, please. He's in a bad way.'

'I'll say he is,' said the constable, getting down on his knees to find out if the boy was still alive.

'Listen to me, Sydney. If you don't tell the police who beat your friend up, you're likely to get the blame,' said Clara in the early hours of the next morning as she and her brother sat together in the cold living room, the fire having turned to ashes long ago. 'So do the sensible thing and give them what they want: some names.'

'I'm not a grass.'

'Oh, for goodness' sake! You could be on a murder charge if that boy dies,' she pointed out in exasperation. 'And from what we've heard from the police that seems like a distinct possibility. He might never regain consciousness.'

'If they charge me that's my hard luck,' he said miserably. 'I was with the group so that makes me partly to blame. Anyway, Tub is the one you should be worrying about, not me. He didn't deserve any of it.'

'And I am worried about him, of course I am. But I'm also concerned about you getting blamed for something you didn't do. You tried to help him,' she reminded him. 'You tried to stop them, so how can you be to blame?'

'I should have done more before he got into that state,' he said, leaning forward with his head in his hands.

'How could you if the others were holding you back?' she asked, desperate to make him see sense. 'At least you managed to stop them eventually.'

'Yeah, I suppose so,' he admitted with reluctance, 'but the damage was already done.'

Sydney looked terrible. He was deathly white with dark shadows under his eyes, his face and neck suffused with nervous blotches and bruises sustained in the affray. Clara recalled the terrible few hours since two policemen had knocked at the door to inform them that Sydney was at the police station being questioned about an incident on Shepherd's Bush Green. Poor Flo had been so distraught, Clara had gone to the police station with her parents to give them some support. Because he was under age, the police had eventually let them bring Sydney home pending further inquiries but had made it clear that they hadn't heard the last of the matter. The Tripps had had to agree to take him back to the police station the next day.

After much persuasion from Clara and her parents, Sydney had told them what had happened but had refused to give the names of the offending boys. Clara had finally coaxed her anguished parents into going to bed, to rest even if they couldn't sleep, and sheer exhaustion had eventually forced them to agree.

'Honestly, Syd, I'm not exaggerating when I say that you'll be in serious trouble if you don't tell the police who the other boys are,' she said now. 'When the constable arrived on the scene, you were the only one there. The police have to get results and you're right there in the frame.'

'The bobby must have seen the others as they ran off,' said Sydney.

'Yes, but they can't do anything unless you tell them who they are, which leaves you right in the cart as you were at the scene of the crime,' she told him. 'Your poor friend is in no state to tell them what really happened.'

He shrugged but didn't say anything.

'Why do you want to protect these boys anyway?' she wanted to know. 'Is it because you think they'll come after you?'

'They'll do that anyway for going against them and helping Tub,' he told her. 'So it makes no difference.'

'Why protect them then?'

'It's like telling tales at school,' he explained. 'It's one of those things you just don't do.'

'It's very different from that, and a whole lot more serious,' she pointed out. 'Do you like these people?'

'No.'

'Why go around with them then?'

'I liked them at first. I thought they were the best mates a bloke could have; they were tough and sure of themselves and I was honoured to be with them,' he said. 'But I've been fed up with them for a while now.'

'Why didn't you stop seeing them, then?'

'You can't just walk away from people like that,' he tried to explain. 'Look what happened to Tub and he didn't do anything, just told them not to be rude about his mum.'

'So this is why you've been so miserable lately?'

'I suppose so. I wanted to break away . . .'

'But you were afraid?'

'A bit, I suppose,' he admitted. 'But it wasn't only that. I didn't want to be on my own; to have no mates to go around with.'

'And now?'

'I want nothing more to do with them, *ever*,' he stated categorically. 'But if I'm gonna be done for murder I won't be around anyway.'

'Sydney, please don't say that,' she begged him. 'You didn't do this awful thing, so tell the police who did. If you won't do it for yourself, do it for Mum and Dad.'

'That isn't fair, Clara,' he objected. 'That's blackmail.'

'Well, neither is your attitude fair. Think what it would do to them if you had to take the consequences of a murder charge. It's a hanging offence. They'd never get over it. Not ever! Anyway, surely you don't want these thugs to go unpunished, and be free to go around beating people up whenever they feel like it?'

Sydney sat up, looking at her. 'Lay off, sis,' he urged her in a weary voice. 'Just leave it for now, will you? We're both tired; we should go to bed.'

Clara could see his despair; could understand his youthful sense of loyalty even though it was misplaced. She got up and went over to him, putting her hands on his shoulders. 'I can see that you're in a dilemma and I'll be behind you whatever happens.'

He reached up and touched her hand. 'Thanks, sis. You're a pal,' he said thickly.

'Night, Syd.'

'Night, Clara.'

She was close to tears as she made her way upstairs.

Her brother wasn't an angel but he did have a heart and he was really suffering over this.

Clara thrashed around wakefully in the sheets for what was left of the night and was thoroughly glad when it was time to get up. She had just got out of bed when there was a gentle tap on her door, followed by the appearance of Sydney.

'Just to let you know that I've made up my mind and I am going to tell the police the truth about what happened,' he told her.

'Oh, thank God for that,' she said, relieved. 'I knew you'd do the right thing in the end.'

'But I have something to do first so will you make some excuse to Mum and Dad if I'm not back for breakfast? Tell 'em I've gone for a walk or something. I'm going to slip out the front door while they're in the kitchen.'

Clara's brow furrowed. 'Where are you going?'

'I'll tell you when I get back.'

'Sydney, please don't do anything reckless.'

But he was gone, closing the door carefully behind him.

It still wasn't properly light as Sydney walked through the gaslit streets to the other side of Shepherd's Bush and knocked on the door of a terraced house in a back road similar to the one the Tripps lived in.

'Sorry to disturb you,' he said to the woman who answered the door, whom he presumed to be Shoulders' mother, a stout woman in a wrapover apron. 'Can I see Jack, please?' Jack was Shoulders' real name.

'It's a bit early to come callin', innit?' she said disapprovingly. 'Too damned early for my liking. So bugger off.'

'Please, I'm sorry to disturb you but it's really important and I won't keep him long,' he persisted.

'He's 'avin' his breakfast and then he's goin' to work,'
she told him. 'So come back at a decent hour.'

'Please,' begged Sydney as she was about to close the
door. 'I promise I won't keep him long.'

She clicked her tongue against her teeth, then turned
her head and shouted into the house. 'Jack. There's someone
to see you. So get out 'ere quick and don't be long or
you'll be late for work.'

As she went inside, Shoulders emerged in a pair of
rough trousers and a thick shirt suitable for his work as a
labourer at a local factory. He looked entirely different
without the flashy suit and overcoat he wore when he
was out with his mates.

He didn't look at all pleased to see Sydney. 'What are
you doing here?' he growled, stepping outside and bringing
the door to behind him.

'I want to be straight with you rather than doing
anything behind your back . . .'

'Oh yeah? Straight about what?'

Sydney paused for a moment while he mustered his
courage. 'I've come to tell you that I'm going to tell the
police exactly what happened last night and who was
responsible,' he said determinedly. 'I'm buggered if I'm
going to take the rap for something I didn't do. Anyway,
you and your minders want stopping.'

'Dunno what you're talking about, mate,' said Shoulders with an air of feigned nonchalance.

'Oh yes you do. Beating the life out of Tub was all
your doing.'

'I didn't touch a hair of his head.'

'No. You're too crafty for that and far too much of a coward,' said Sydney with feeling. 'You make other people do your dirty work. But you were to blame for the assault on Tub and if he dies you'll be his murderer as sure as if you beat him yourself. It was all your fault and I shall tell the police that.'

'You bloody well won't, you know,' Shoulders said, taking a step towards Sydney.

Sydney stood his ground. 'So what are you going to do to stop me?' he asked.

For once the other boy seemed lost for words. He just stood there looking at Sydney with contempt.

'Not so much of a big man when you haven't got your lackeys with you, are you?'

'I knew you were going soft on us,' Shoulders said, ignoring the question. 'I could tell by the way you've been acting lately.'

'I hadn't gone soft,' Sydney told him. 'I'd come to my senses, that's all, and begun to see you for what you really are, a miserable bully without any guts.'

'You go near that police station and you won't live to stand up in court,' Shoulders threatened.

'I'll take my chances,' Sydney responded, feeling stronger than he ever had before, his mettle growing with every second of this confrontation. 'I'd sooner take a thrashing than let you carry on bullying people and having them beaten up.'

'You dare,' said Shoulders. 'You just bloody dare, I'm warning you.'

'Stop me then,' Sydney challenged him. 'It's just the two of us; you against me. So come on, stop me.'

The other boy didn't move.

'I thought you wouldn't,' said Sydney. 'You haven't got the bottle. You're a strong man when you've got people around you who are daft enough to do what you want. You're not so confident when you're on your own.' Sydney put his hand on Shoulders' chest and pushed him. 'You are pathetic and I don't know why I ever wasted my time hanging around with you.'

'I'll have you done over good and proper for this,' Shoulders warned him. 'You won't have a bone left in your body that ain't broken, I can promise you that.'

Just then his mother's resonant voice came from the back of the house. 'Get back in here this minute, Jack,' she ordered loudly. 'Your breakfast is getting cold.'

'You'd better do as your mother says, hadn't you?' said Sydney in the same mocking tones Shoulders used on other people. 'Or Mummy will put you to bed early tonight with no supper.'

'You're going to regret this, Trippo.'

'Not half as much as you're going to regret what you did to my mate Tub.' He looked at the other boy and wondered how he could ever have thought that he was worth bothering with for even so much as a second. 'Ta-ta. See you in court.'

As he turned to go he could hear Shoulders' mother shrieking at him. 'Get in here and finish this food. I didn't cook it to have to put it in the bin. We can't afford to waste food so get on and eat it then clear off to work.'

As Sydney turned the corner out of Shoulders' street, he saw two policemen walking towards him. Instinctively he stiffened, his insides turning to water even though he fully intended to tell the truth. Wondering how they had known he was here, he slowed his step as they approached, preparing himself for a possible arrest. But they just walked past him without a second glance and turned the corner into the street where Shoulders lived. Must be just out on the beat, he thought, and carried on home to put his parents' minds at rest by telling them of his intentions.

'The police have been here, Sydney,' said his mother, coming out of the kitchen into the hall as soon as he came in the front door.

'Oh, no. Sorry that you've been put through that, Mum,' he told her. 'But you've no need to worry because I'm gonna do it. I'm going to the police station to give them the names they want, so they needn't have come chasing after me.'

'They didn't come after you. There was no need, because your friend has beaten you to it and told them the truth about what happened.'

He looked at her, puzzled. It couldn't be Shoulders, as he'd just left him. One of the others must have decided to do the right thing, although it didn't seem very likely. 'Who was it?' he asked.

'The one who was beaten up.'

'Tub?' he said, astonished. 'You mean Tub is alive?'

She nodded. 'He's regained consciousness and told the police everything. So you're in the clear, son. That's why they came to the house. To let us know.'

The relief was so intense it physically weakened him; for himself but even more for his injured friend. 'Did they say if Tub is going to be all right?' he asked.

'No. They only told us that he'd come round,' she said. 'But that in itself is promising.'

'Good news, eh, Syd?' said Clara, coming into the hall on her way upstairs to get ready for work.

'Where have you been at this time of the morning anyway?' asked Flo.

Knowing that his mother would be worried about him if she knew what he'd just been up to, he said, 'I just went out for some fresh air to clear my head.'

A look passed between himself and his sister and he knew she had guessed where he had been. She winked at him, then made her way upstairs.

'That will have given you an appetite for your breakfast then,' Flo said.

'It certainly has,' he told her. 'I could eat a horse.'

'It's ever so good of you to come to see me,' said Tub, whose real name was Percy. 'It's nice to have some company of my own age while I'm stuck here in hospital.'

'I won't be able to stay long because I'm taking your mum and dad's time on the ward and the staff here are very strict about no more than two visitors at a time,' he explained. 'Your mum said I could have a few minutes with you but she and your dad will want to come back in soon. How are you feeling, anyway?'

'There ain't much of me that doesn't hurt, to tell you the truth, but they say I'm gonna be all right eventually,' he said. Eventually was certainly the word, Sydney thought, looking at his friend's bandaged head, bruised face, and arm in a plaster cast. 'Thanks for trying to help me, mate.'

'Thanks for telling the police what happened,' Sydney said gratefully. 'It took some bottle and it's taken me right out of the frame. I'm with you all the way on this one; we'll stand up to them together.'

'I've had a gutful of 'em, mate,' Tub told him. 'I don't care what they do to me now as long as they get their comeuppance. Nothing could be worse than the treatment I've had for months.'

'Whatever you get I'll get too for going against them, but with a bit of luck they won't do anything to either of us because they'll be sent away to Borstal or some-where like that. I shall stand up in court if it will help get them put away.' Sydney went on to tell Tub about his visit to Shoulders' house.

'Blimey, that was brave of you,' said Tub in admiration.

'I felt I had to as I was planning on giving the police his name. I didn't want to be sneaky about it; wanted to tell him to his face. Anyway, he's nothing when he's on his own,' Sydney told him. 'He was full of threats but too scared to lay a finger on me.'

'I don't know why I got mixed up with them in the first place,' Tub confessed. 'I was a bit lonely, I think; didn't seem to have any mates. Shoulders and the others started taking the mickey out of me one day on the street. Then he came over all nice and asked me if I wanted to go around with them. I was flattered, I suppose. Of course, all they wanted was someone to pick on but I didn't want to admit that to myself. I put up with it because I liked being part of a group. It was awful but somehow better than being on my own. But they went too far the other night.'

'That goes for me too,' Sydney told him. 'I'm sorry I wasn't able to get them off you in time to prevent you getting hurt so badly.'

'You did your best,' he said. 'You're the only one who ever stood up for me and I appreciate it. You stuck your neck out for me several times and I'm grateful. You're a good bloke.'

Sydney coloured up. He wasn't comfortable with flattery. 'It was nothing,' he said.

He realised at that moment that he didn't really know Tub at all as a person; he didn't know any of the boys in the gang. There was always a lot of shouting and joking but no one ever said anything of any consequence about themselves.

'It was something to me,' said Tub.

'I think I'd better be going now,' said Sydney, embarrassed. The other boy looked disappointed. 'I'll come again though,' he added with sincerity. 'And when you're back at home I'll call in.' He smiled. 'Perhaps we can have our own two-man gang, without any rough stuff.'

'That would be really good.' Tub smiled.

Sydney left the hospital with a warm feeling of having begun a new friendship.

'At least it seems to have cured Sydney of his love affair with those yobbos,' said Arnold a week or so later when he and Clara were sitting on the sofa in the front room. 'So some good has come out of it all.'

'What a price, though,' said Clara with feeling. 'A boy has to get beaten half to death to make him see sense. I think the whole thing is shocking.'

'How is the injured boy coming along?' Arnold asked. 'Have you heard how he is?'

'Yeah, he's home from hospital and recovering, apparently,' she told him. 'Sydney seems to be quite friendly with him.'

Arnold didn't look too pleased to hear that. 'I was hoping he'd finished with that crowd altogether,' he said.

'This lad isn't one of them, apparently,' she explained. 'He was just the whipping boy. So the two of them seem to have palled up, which I think is rather nice.'

'What's going to happen to the ones who beat the boy up? Do you know?'

'They're being sent to one of these places for boys of sixteen to twenty-one. They've been in trouble before, apparently, and have had several warnings. Sydney knew nothing about that, he says, but I doubt if it would have stopped him seeing them if he had. In fact, it might have made them seem even more glamorous to him. You know what boys of that age are like. Fortunately, he seems to be well and truly over them now.'

'From what I've heard, they're very harsh places, those Borstal institutions, and a good job too. Perhaps that will knock some sense into them.'

'That's a bit brutal, Arnold.'

'They'll only be getting a dose of their own medicine, the little sods,' he said with venom.

Arnold showed a very hard side at times, which Clara put down to the fact that the male attitude towards these things was different from a woman's. But she didn't like it, all the same. 'Even so, violence isn't always the answer.'

'You women are too soft,' he said, smiling at her. 'But I wouldn't have you any other way.'

'Anyway, how have you been?' she asked, in an effort to erase a growing feeling of irritation with him and his attitudes. 'I haven't seen you for a few days.'

'Sorry about that, love. I've been doing a lot of over-time again,' he explained. 'I told you I might be.'

'You see more of that delivery van than you do of me,' she said jokingly. 'I reckon you're besotted with it. It's the power of being behind the wheel, I reckon. Some men are half in love with their motor cars, so they say.'

'I might be if it was a flash saloon, but it's difficult to get romantic about a delivery van,' he smiled. 'I just think I should grab the overtime while I can.'

'Of course you should,' she said encouragingly. 'The way you're carrying on we'll be able to afford to set up home sooner than we thought.'

'That's the whole idea,' he said. 'What else would I be working for? You and me, sweetheart, that's all that matters to me; our future together means everything.'

'Oh, Arnold. You're such an old romantic at times,' she said, squeezing his hand. 'I wish I could save more money, but by the time I've paid Mum for my keep and my fares to work and other bits and pieces, there isn't much left for saving.'

'Don't you worry about that,' he told her. 'You let me take care of that side of things.'

'I like to do my bit.'

'I'll be doing it anyway after we're married when you're at home looking after the kids, so don't worry about it.'

Clara felt suddenly stifled and longed for escape. She was rather taken aback by the strength of her feelings.

'Slow down, Arnold,' she said sharply. 'Let me have my wedding day before you start talking about children.'

'I was just trying to reassure you about the financial side of things,' he said.

She was immediately filled with compunction. He was doing his best for them and all she could do was want to run away at the thought of domestic bliss with him. 'I was only joking,' she fibbed.

'That's all right, love,' he said pleasantly, making her

feel even worse. She really didn't deserve him. As she wanted children anyway when she got married, why did she feel so trapped? Her emotions were a mystery to her lately.

Chapter Six

Charlie Fenner was taking his frustration out on the piano at the big house following yet another heated argument with Hester after which she had stormed out in a fury. Life was a living hell at the cottage; the two of them seemed to become increasingly incompatible with every day that passed. It wasn't all Hester's fault. There were two people in the marriage so he must take his share of the blame. Hester wasn't a bad person; it was more that she didn't seem to know what she wanted from life. She'd wanted him until she had his wedding ring on her finger, then she'd quickly become discontented.

Experience had taught him that there were two ways of keeping his sanity: one was a few beers at the pub, the other was some Mozart. This evening, music had won hands down because his brother had gone to the pub to play darts and his overbearing company was almost as irritating as Hester's.

As it happened, the piano proved to be a bad choice because he could hear the muffled tones of an altercation between his mother and sister in the kitchen which he found impossible to ignore, because he knew how much these quarrels upset Eva. Hoping that his father might intervene he carried on playing, raising the volume to drown out the noise. But as their voices rose to shrieking point, he could finally stand it no longer. He banged his hands on the keys in rage then got up and headed towards the sounds of battle, followed by Rex, who had been sitting contentedly by the piano but was beginning to growl and sniff at the door because of the raised voices.

'How many more times must I tell you to put the things away proper, Eva, instead of throwing them in the cupboards any old how,' Mabel was shouting, washing the dishes while Eva dried them. 'You're so danged slip-shod in the way you do things. I've never known anyone like it. Lord knows where you get it from; it certainly i'n't me.'

'It doesn't matter how I do them, you'd still complain,' retorted Eva. 'Nothing I do is ever good enough for you.'

'Try harder then, for goodness' sake, and stop whining,' Mabel snapped. 'That's all you ever do and I can't abide it.'

'Lay off her, Mum,' Charlie cut in, entering the room. 'You've been going on at her for ages and it just isn't fair. You really shouldn't be so hard on the poor girl.'

Mabel turned on him. 'Who asked your opinion?'

'It isn't so much an opinion as a fact. This has got to stop.'

'Don't interfere between mother and daughter.'

'Someone has to.'

'Anyway, why aren't you at home with your wife?'

'Because we don't happen to have a piano at the cottage

and I'm in the mood to play,' he told her. 'Not that it's possible with this terrible racket going on.'

'Tell your sister that, not me,' said his mother. 'She's the cause of all the trouble in this house. She's enough to make a saint shout. Always has been.'

'Mum,' said Charlie in a tone of scathing admonition. 'That isn't the way to speak to your daughter.'

'It's her own fault that I go on at her, and we all know why that is, don't we?'

Charlie was about to speak but stopped in his tracks when he saw his sister's face. It had become bloodless and there was something in her eyes that went beyond despair. It was a look of deep and crippling agony.

'I didn't mean to do it, Mum. I was four years old and I don't even remember it,' she said, her voice distorted with anguish. 'Am I to be punished for the rest of my life?'

'At least you have a life,' Mabel said pointedly.

'What can I do to make you forgive me?' Eva said, spreading her hands in a gesture of helplessness. 'You've punished me every day of my life since then. Isn't that enough?'

Mabel swung round, her large hands dripping water on to the stone-tiled floor. 'It could never be enough for what you did.' Her voice was full of rage and pain and she was trembling. 'Never, ever, ever. Do you understand?'

'Mum, stop it,' Charlie said quickly as his mother started towards Eva with her hands outstretched as though to inflict physical harm. 'That's quite enough. Now calm down, for goodness' sake.' He got a tea towel for his mother's wet hands and handed it to her, standing between the two women and facing Mabel. 'You have to let this go. Can't you see how much you're hurting Eva? You can't keep on treating her this way. It's too cruel. You'll make her ill if you carry on like this.'

'It's all right, Charlie,' Eva intervened, seeming in control suddenly. 'It isn't worth your trying because she'll never change. I don't think she can help herself. She's got a warped mind.'

'You're the one with the warped mind, my gel,' Mabel accused her.

'*Shut up, Mum,*' Charlie yelled, desperate to make her stop. 'Just leave her be.'

'Don't speak to your mother like that,' said Mabel, her voice shaking, her face blotched with red patches.

'What else can I do to stop you being so wicked to her?' he asked wildly. 'It's become such a habit, I don't think you even know you're doing it.'

'Oh, do what you like,' she said angrily, and went back to the washing up. 'Gang up on me, I don't care.'

'Thanks for trying, Charlie,' said Eva gratefully, seeming unusually calm. 'But I'll be all right, don't worry.'

He looked at his sister's pale face, the youth crushed out of it by years of mental cruelty. But there was a spark of determination about her that he hadn't seen before and didn't quite understand. 'Sis, what is it?'

She put her arms round him and spoke close to his ear so that their mother couldn't hear. 'I'll be all right. Don't worry. Everything is going to be fine from now on. You go back to the piano. I shall be going to my room when I've finished here. Mum will run out of steam eventually. She always does in the end. Not even she can go on shouting for ever.'

'Come over to the cottage if you need me after I've

gone home,' he suggested. 'Hester has gone out so I'll be on my own.'

'Thanks. I'll bear it in mind,' she said.

She moved away, and as Charlie left the room with the dog trotting along beside him Mabel was saying, 'Get on with the drying up or we'll be here all night. And let's have less of the whispering, madam, if you please.'

'Yes, Mum,' said Eva obediently. It didn't matter what her mother said any more. Eva could bear it now that she had made a decision that had given her fresh hope.

The nearest thing Eva had to a suitcase was a small holdall that she had used once when she was about twelve and had gone away to Herne Bay for a few days at the seaside with the Sunday school.

Now she got it out of the wardrobe, put it on her bed and packed some clothes into it. Then she opened the tin she kept her money in – saved from a small allowance her father paid to her for her help around the orchard – and put it into her purse. The bag was put back in the wardrobe out of sight of anyone who might happen to come in, and then she wrote a note and got into bed fully dressed to wait for the first light of dawn.

Alighting from the train at Charing Cross station, Eva felt her legs turn to jelly with fright at the sheer volume of people and noise. Everyone looked purposeful, as though they knew exactly where they were going. The contrast to the environment she was used to was so striking she was overwhelmed by it. She had never seen anything like it before, this great sea of people surging towards the barrier. Following them and handing in her ticket, somewhat shakily, she was even more bewildered on the main concourse where the masses split up and hurried in different directions.

She had known it would be busy, of course, but for a country girl who had never been further than a quiet stretch of the Kent coast it was awesome indeed. Steam floated around the building, stinging her eyes and throat; there was the hiss of engines and a roar of human voices. Feeling very small and alone she was completely at a loss to know what she should do next.

'Excuse me, please,' she said to a station worker nervously. 'Can you tell me how to get to Oxford Street?'

'The Tube is your best bet, miss,' he said, pointing his finger. 'Go that way and you'll see a sign for the Underground. Oxford Circus station will put you right in the middle of it.'

'Thank you very much,' she said, not having the first idea what he meant, especially as he spoke at high speed compared to the more leisurely dialogue of the Kentish people. This was all much more frightening than she'd expected, she thought, as she headed for this thing Londoners called the Tube.

Being rendered helpless by a fit of the giggles when you were on duty in a select tea room was not to be recommended, and Clara and a fellow waitress were trying to recover after two seemingly refined female customers of a certain age had had a loud disagreement which had come to blows and resulted in their being escorted from the premises. The very rarity of the scenario here had set the two waitresses off and they were still infected long after the women had left. They daren't even look at each other in passing.

Aware of the fact that the supervisor had eyes like binoculars, Clara took a deep breath and approached a table where, out of the side of her eye, she had noticed a young woman come in and sit down with her back towards Clara. Praying that she didn't disgrace herself while taking the order, Clara said, 'Good morning. Are you ready to order yet?'

'Hello, Clara.'

She was so taken aback to see Eva sitting there, the urge to giggle disappeared in an instant. 'Eva,' she gasped, smiling. 'How lovely to see you.'

'And you.'

'Are you here on a day trip?' she asked.

'No . . . I've, er . . . I've left home,' she blurted out, looking pale, nervous and exhausted. 'I hope you don't mind my coming here but you were the only person I could think of to turn to.'

'Of course I don't mind,' she assured her, immediately concerned for Eva, who was clearly in a state of distress. 'But can you give me an order so I don't get in trouble with my supervisor, and I'll meet you later on in my dinner hour and we can talk. I'm not allowed to linger for too long with any one customer.'

Eva looked at the menu. 'I'll have hot buttered toast and tea, please,' she said.

'Coming up,' Clara said for the benefit of her nemesis, writing it down and walking briskly towards the kitchens.

'Do your family know where you are?'

They were in Lyons having tea and a bun, as it was too cold for the park. Clara had said she would eat her sandwiches in the staffroom later when she had a break; the bun would keep her going until then.

Eva nodded. 'I left a note saying that I was going to London and wouldn't be coming back.'

'As long as you didn't just disappear,' said Clara. 'That would have been really worrying for them.'

'You did say I would be welcome at your house if ever I came to London and I'm afraid I've taken you at your word,' Eva explained. 'But I couldn't very well turn up at the door out of the blue and I remembered you telling me where you worked so here I am, though how I found it I'll never know. How does anyone find their way around in London?'

'You'll soon get used to it,' Clara assured her.

'I don't have anywhere to stay,' Eva admitted bleakly.

'You must stay with us, of course,' Clara assured her warmly. 'As long as you don't mind taking us as you find us and sharing a bedroom with me.'

'Of course I don't. But what about your parents?' she asked. 'How will they feel about having me thrust upon them?'

'I shall have to ask them, of course, but I shouldn't think they'll mind. They're very easy-going. But I must warn you that our place is a whole lot different from what you're used to. We don't have a big house like yours or a great deal of money.'

'I've got some cash to pay for my keep until I get a job,' Eva said quickly. 'So I'll pay my way. I intend to get a job even if I have to go out cleaning.'

Clara remembered something. 'Oh, and I have to warn you that my mother's cooking is not always top notch. Your ma is such a brilliant cook you may not find it easy.'

'Food is the last thing on my mind,' Eva said.

'Yes, I can imagine. Why didn't you write to let me

know you were coming? We could have got everything ready if we'd been expecting you.'

'Although this has been brewing for a long time, it was a spur of the moment decision. I knew last night that I couldn't stand any more; that I *wouldn't* stand any more.'

'Of living in the country?'

'Of my mother. She hates me, you know.'

'I'm sure that isn't true, Eva,' Clara said tactfully, though having seen Mabel Fenner in action she knew there was bad feeling there.

'No, she really does,' Eva told her. 'I was to blame for something terrible.' She paused, then burst out emotionally, 'I might as well tell you the truth. I killed my little sister, you see, and Mum can't forgive me for it.'

Clara was shocked. 'Killed your little sister,' she echoed. 'Oh, Eva, I can't imagine you doing a thing like that.'

'I didn't mean to do it, but I was to blame for her death so I killed her.'

'How were you to blame?'

'I was supposed to be looking after her while my mother was busy doing something and she wandered off across the fields and fell into a ditch. She must have hit her head or something, because by the time they found her she was dead.'

'Oh, how terrible!' Clara felt sick at the thought. 'How old was your sister?'

'Two.'

'And how old were you?'

'Four.'

'Four years old and you were responsible for a younger child?' Clara was outraged.

'It was only while my mother was doing something

indoors and my sister and I were in the garden,' she explained. 'I don't know why I let her wander off because the whole thing is so vague in my memory. I just know what I've been told. Something else must have attracted my attention, I suppose, and I didn't notice what she was doing.'

So that explained Mabel Fenner's hostility towards her daughter, thought Clara. It seemed even more callous now that she knew what was behind it. Eva's mother should have helped her daughter to cope with such a tragedy; given her reassurance, not castigated her for it for all this time, especially as it wasn't her fault.

'You can't be held responsible for something like that when you were only four years old,' she said. 'If anyone was to blame it was your mother. She shouldn't have left the two of you unsupervised at such a young age.'

'It wasn't for very long,' said Eva, even now feeling the need to defend her mother against outsiders. 'And what happened was an accident.'

'Yes. But if blame is being handed out, it shouldn't be aimed in your direction.'

Eva stirred her tea slowly, looking down into the cup. 'Well, I suppose it must be very hard for a mother to lose a child,' she said. 'I don't suppose she'll ever get over it.'

Such was the contradiction of human nature, Clara suspected that it would hurt Eva even more if she spoke the truth and said that Mabel Fenner was just a hateful and cruel woman, so she simply said, 'Yes, very hard. I doubt if any mother could. But I still say it wasn't your fault.'

'Maybe not.'

'*Definitely* not!'

'Anyway, I want to put the past behind me and look forward to the future now that I've made the break from home.' Eva cast her eye around the busy tea shop where people were waiting for tables. 'Though I do feel like a fish out of water here. It's so noisy and crowded everywhere.'

'Give it a week or two and you'll feel like one of us,' said Clara in an encouraging manner. 'In fact, you seem different already.' She looked at the tweed coat that reached Eva's ankles, and the long hair scraped back into a bun. 'We'll have to do something about your clothes though, eventually, if you decide to stay here. Get you looking a bit more up to date if you're going to be a London girl.'

'I'd like to look like you,' said Eva. Clara was wearing a red coat and beret, and her dark hair was cut in a medium-length bob.

'There's nothing special about the way I look because I can't afford much, but I do like to keep up with what women of my age are wearing,' said Clara. 'So we'll smarten you up without breaking the bank. But there's plenty of time for that. Let's get you settled in first.'

'Thank you, Clara.'

'Look, I'd like to stay here with you but in a few minutes I have to go back to work, I'm afraid, so you'll have to find something to do to amuse yourself until I finish, then you can come home with me. Perhaps you can look round the shops.'

'I'll be brave and do some exploring to fill the time, though I don't expect I'll stray far from here while it's all still so new.' She paused, then reached over and touched

Clara's hand. 'Thanks, Clara,' she said. 'I haven't known you for very long but I feel as though you're a true friend.'

'See how you feel about that when you've been sharing a bedroom with me for a while,' said Clara, smiling.

'I've always thought that shepherd's pie was supposed to have mashed potato on top,' said Frank Tripp that night over the evening meal. 'But this potato has more hard lumps in it than Brighton beach has pebbles.'

'Squash them out with your fork then,' instructed his wife, without taking offence. 'Mine's all right, anyway.'

'It isn't so bad if you mash it all up really well, Eva,' advised Cuddy helpfully. 'It tastes fine.'

'It's very nice, Mrs Tripp,' said Eva, who couldn't believe the way they all teased poor Mrs Tripp without upsetting her. If anyone spoke that way to her own mother all hell would break loose. Apart from Sydney, who seemed to be a very quiet boy, they had all been so warm and welcoming to her she didn't feel out of place at all, though naturally she was still a little shy. The family repartee was a joy to listen to. There was banter but no bickering of the sort that went on at Brierley during mealtimes.

Eva's compliment to Flo caused a roar of laughter.

'I dread to think what you've been used to if you think this is nice, love,' said Frank. 'And yet we've heard from Clara and Cuddy that your ma makes lovely meals.'

'She's just being polite, Dad,' Clara pointed out. 'Her mother is an excellent cook.'

'You'll notice the difference here then, love,' quipped Frank, grinning. 'But there's no need to stand on cere- mony. Flo knows she isn't the world's best cook. You wait till you taste her pastry. You need a hammer and chisel rather than a knife and fork when we have pie.'

'Not true, Eva,' put in Clara. 'It's sometimes a bit hard, that's all.'

'I'll make you cook your own meals one of these days, you ungrateful lot,' Flo threatened. 'It's bloomin' hard work, cooking. I don't have the patience to fiddle about with it. It's all good nourishing food even if the pastry does have the texture of boot leather.'

'I could do some cooking for you sometime to give you a break if you like, Mrs Tripp,' Eva offered with a cautious smile, her blond hair now falling loosely beyond her shoulders, her face flushed from the warmth of the fire. 'I've always had to help my mother in the kitchen since I was little so I've had plenty of practice.'

'I might take you up on that one day,' said Flo, smiling at her. Clara had explained Eva's circumstances when she'd asked her parents if she could stay with them. And she seemed like a very nice girl. However, Flo was a great believer in there being two sides to every argument so she had made no judgements about her mother. 'You'll be sorry you offered after a while.'

'We won't though, not if it means we get decent grub,' said Frank, chuckling and adding quickly, 'Just joking, Flo.'

'You'd better be.'

'You're very quiet tonight, Sydney,' said Clara. 'Have you had a bad day at work?'

'No.'

'What's the matter then?'

'Nothin'.'

'Don't believe you.'

'Can't a bloke be quiet in his own home without getting

133

the third degree?' he objected. 'Honestly, there's no privacy at all in this flippin' house.'

'Oo-er,' said Clara. 'Someone's got the hump.'

'I will have if you don't stop keeping on.'

'All right, don't start throwing your toys out of the pram.'

'Anyway, Eva,' interrupted Flo in a timely diversion, 'what do you think of our beloved city so far? Do you think you're going to like it here?'

Eva found her eyes swimming with tears at the sheer warmth of the atmosphere around her. 'Yes,' she replied. 'I think I'm going to like it very much indeed.'

'We can't have a girl living in this house,' Sydney told Clara in hushed tones, having got her on her own in the kitchen after Eva had gone upstairs to bed.

'Why ever not?'

'Because she's a girl, o' course, a grown up one.'

'So am I, and you don't have a problem with that.'

He heaved an eloquent sigh. 'That's different and you know it,' he said. 'You're my sister.'

'Eva won't bite, you know.'

He rolled his eyes. 'You know very well what I'm talking about. Washing and bathing and that.'

'Oh, I see. I'm sure Eva won't be upset by the sight of you in your vest at the kitchen sink. But she might be if your pyjama flies flap open.'

'Oh, Clara, as if I would let that happen,' he said, so offended at the suggestion he was unable to see the joke. 'But what about if she strips off to wash? I won't know where to put myself.'

'If anyone is embarrassed it will be her, especially as

she's used to having her own room in a house big enough to get lost in,' she said, thinking about it. 'We'll all have to help her to adjust. And you'll have to steer clear when anything ablutionary is going on.'

He scratched his head. 'Isn't there anyone else she can stay with in London?'

'No. No one.'

'Well, I don't like it and as a member of this family I have the right to object.'

'Look, Sydney, I can understand that you might be a bit shy with a girl of your own age, a stranger, around the place,' she told him. 'But she's been given a terrible time by her mother down in Kent for years and she really does need a break; somewhere to stay where the people are kind to her will be a godsend to her at the moment. So please try to make her feel welcome.' She gave him a pleading look. 'Do it for me if you can't do it for her.'

'Oh, all right, I suppose I'll have to try,' he said miserably, 'but I'm not at all happy about it.'

'Shall I sew your pyjama flies up for you?' she teased him. 'Will that help?'

He threw a tea towel at her.

'I've always known the girl was selfish, Charlie, but I didn't think she would go so far as to clear off and leave us all worrying about her. Is there no limit to what she'll do to get attention?' Mabel Fenner raged that night after the evening meal, when Eva's departure had been discussed in mixed opinions. Hester had said good riddance, Vincent hadn't cared one way or the other, John Fenner had said rather worriedly that he did hope she would be all right, Mabel had been furious and Charlie hadn't said very much at all.

'She hasn't gone because she wants attention, Mum,' he pointed out now. 'She's gone because she's unhappy here, and who can blame her?'

'You'll just have to go and fetch her back,' declared Mabel, ignoring the last part of his speech. 'She will have gone to that Tripp family. They're the only people she knows in London.'

'Clara will look after her,' Charlie assured her. 'I'm certain of that.'

'She's not going to get the chance because you are going to get Eva back,' his mother stated categorically. 'You know where the Tripps live, don't you?'

'Yeah, but I'm not going to bring Eva back,' he told her in a definite tone. 'I will go to London to make sure she's all right but I won't force her to come back here against her will.'

'So you are prepared to go against me, then?'

'On this issue, yes, I am.' He was adamant. 'Frankly, I'm surprised she hasn't left before now.'

Mabel frowned. 'What do you mean?'

'You've driven her out and I think she'll be happier away from here,' he told her. 'For a while at least.'

'That's a nice thing to say to your mother, I must say.'

'I'm sorry if it upsets you, Mum, but it needed saying,' he said. 'I've been telling you for years that you're too hard on her and trying to persuade you to go easy.' He gave her a searching look. 'Anyway, why do you want me to bring her back here? She obviously makes you miserable and you do the same to her. So if she isn't around you'll be happier, surely.'

'My feelings don't come into it. Her place is here and this is where she should be.'

'So that you can use her as a verbal punch bag as you've done for most of her life.'

'I don't know what you mean.'

He looked at her, observing the harshness in her cold grey eyes, the resentful downturn of her mouth. 'No, I don't believe you do,' he said sadly. 'You've been making her life a misery for so long you don't even know you're doing it.'

'She's wilful; she needs discipline.'

'She doesn't need to be told that she's useless every single day of her life.'

'Are you saying that you won't even try to bring her back?' Mabel asked, as though she hadn't heard what he'd said.

'I'll go to London and make sure she's settled in and that the Tripps are happy for her to stay with them,' he said. 'I will also make sure that the Tripps are not out of pocket by her being there. I will tell her that you want her to come back but I won't force her to return with me if she doesn't want to. As I just said, I think she'll be better off away from here.'

'I'll send Vincent, then.'

'There's no need for that,' he said. 'If Eva has left just to make a point, to pay you back for all the hurt you've caused her, I might consider trying to persuade her to come back. If she genuinely wants to give it a try in London, then I will leave her where she is and wish her the best of luck.'

'Fat lot of good as an eldest son you are.'

'That's the best I can do,' he told her in a tone that defied argument. 'But if Eva does come back here at any time, I shall keep a very close eye on the way you treat her. I won't let you give her such a hard time ever again. She must have been feeling desperate to just up and leave like that.'

'You know what Eva is like.'

'Yes, I do, but do *you*?' he asked. 'I know that she's a high-spirited and loving young girl, whereas you seem to think she's some sort of hell child.'

Mabel stared at the floor and was unusually silent. He knew that she was still grieving for the child she had lost. It was almost like an illness with her.

'I'll go to London tomorrow,' he announced. 'I'll get a train first thing in the morning.'

'I knew you'd come,' Clara said to Charlie when he treated her to Welsh rarebit for lunch in Lyons. He'd come into Taylor's earlier and arranged to see her in her dinner break. 'I knew the Fenner clan wouldn't leave Eva alone.'

'We couldn't just ignore the fact that she's left home, could we?'

'She's a very troubled girl, and having seen the way your mother treats her I'm not surprised.'

'I agree with you.'

Up went her brows. 'What, no outpouring of defence for your mother?' she said.

'Not in this case, no. My mother is also very troubled, though I realise it must seem to you as though she is simply heartless in the way she deals with Eva.'

She considered her next words carefully. 'Eva has told me all about your baby sister's death.'

'Oh, I see.'

'Sad.'

'Very. I was only eleven at the time but I was old enough to notice that everything changed in our family after that. Mum has never got over it and she still takes her grief out on Eva. I've talked to her about it on many occasions, and begged her to lay off, but all to no avail.'

'It isn't for me to give an opinion on your family matters, of course, but I'm going to stick my neck out in this instance and ask you, plead with you if necessary, not to force Eva to go back with you if she doesn't want to.'

'I wouldn't dream of doing so; she isn't a child and she knew what she was doing when she left,' he assured her. 'That isn't why I'm here at all.'

'No?'

'Absolutely not.' He went on to explain the reason for his trip. 'Mum wants me to take her back, kicking and screaming if necessary, but not me. That won't achieve anything.'

'I'm glad about that, because at this early stage, when London is still so new to her, she's probably feeling vulnerable and might be persuaded to go back when I don't think it would be right for her at this point.' She paused thoughtfully. 'Even apart from the way things are with her and her mother, she's got this hankering to live in London that she needs to get out of her system one way or the other. But, personally, I think she's got the gumption to make a go of things here if that is what she really wants. She seemed to fit in with us right away.'

'A change of scene certainly won't do her any harm, I must admit,' he said. 'She never meets anyone new at Brierley.'

'She's got the right attitude in that she's keen to pay her

own way,' she told him. 'In fact, she's going out to look for a job today. It must be quite frightening for a country girl new to the metropolis. I think this is something she needs to do for her own sake, even apart from the bad state of affairs with her mother. If she doesn't settle after giving it a really good try then maybe she'll go back home a stronger person for the experience and more able to cope with her mother's attitude towards her. Being away from Brierley and constant reminders, maybe she can put the past behind her and stop blaming herself for something that wasn't her fault.'

'I need to make sure your parents aren't out of pocket by putting her up.' He reached into the inside pocket of his jacket and took out his wallet, removing some notes and handing them to her.

She shook her head and waved them away. 'I think you should let her find the money herself,' she suggested. 'She has some savings and has already given Mum enough for her keep for a few weeks. Why not let her earn what she needs in future? A degree of independence will be good for her. We all pay our own way in our family.'

'She might not be able to get a job,' he pointed out. 'Unemployment is high, according to the papers.'

'It's a lot tougher for men who need a decent wage to support a family, I think,' she suggested. 'There are more of the menial, low-paid jobs that we girls will do, especially as she doesn't mind what she does, which will help. If she doesn't have any luck, I'll get in touch and you can send us some cash; meanwhile take your money back to Kent with you.'

'That's all very well, but your parents mustn't suffer financially because my sister has decided to leave home,' he said. 'It wouldn't be fair.'

'They won't, I promise you; they can't afford it, so I

shall contact you well ahead if Eva's job prospects aren't looking good.'

He shrugged and smiled. 'What can I do but agree when you put it like that?'

'Nothing.' Her own smile stirred something deep inside him, despite all his intentions to steel himself against feeling anything for her.

'In that case I'll do as you say.'

She nodded. 'Are you intending to see Eva while you're here?' she asked.

'Of course.'

Her brow furrowed. 'I'm not so sure that's such a good idea, you know,' she said thoughtfully.

'Oh?' He frowned. 'Why is that?'

'Because, at this early stage, she might be feeling home-sick with everything being so strange to her, and apart from your father you are the only member of your family who has any time for her, according to her. She adores you, and if she sees you she might be tempted to go back before she's given it a fair chance.'

'That's a good point, but she'll be hurt if you tell her that I've been to London and not come to see her.'

'Not if I also tell her that you only came to make sure she's all right and you're thinking of her and you'll come and see her again when she's settled,' she suggested. 'She can write to you in the meanwhile.'

'Sounds like a good idea to me, although I would have liked to see her, of course.'

'Don't let me stop you,' she said. 'It was only an idea. I could be wrong.'

'No, I don't think you are. As long as you explain why I didn't come to see her,' he said.

'I'll make sure she knows.'

'What a wise woman you are for such a young person.' He was reminded of those dark days in the trenches when the memory of her had been so comforting. He was in a similar position now, though his current trap was a war zone without bullets.

She found herself looking around the crowded café, the Nippy waitresses in their well-known black and white uniforms weaving their way daintily through the cast-iron-framed and marble-topped tables. People were queuing out of the door for seating. 'I wish it was as busy as this at our place,' she remarked wistfully. 'Things have been very quiet since the end of the sales. Business just dropped off after that.'

'Yes, I noticed that Taylor's wasn't as crowded as last time I was there.'

'The customers are all here at Lyons, that's why,' she told him. 'Their tea shop chain is very popular and our strongest competition. Some of the independent catering establishments find it hard to compete. Despite drastic price cuts to tempt customers, people seem to prefer to go to Lyons.'

'Is Taylor's in trouble then?' he enquired with interest.

'We haven't been told anything, but I think the firm is struggling. February is never a good month anyway, but you only have to look at the crowds in here to know that there is plenty of custom about.'

'So you must be worried for your job?'

'Not yet, but if things don't soon pick up I will be,' she admitted. 'Obviously they'll have to get rid of some of the staff if the turnover is down for any length of time. Some of the smaller places are going out of business altogether.'

She looked at the clock on the wall. 'I shall have to keep my eye on the time.'

'Do you have to go quite so soon?' He was ridiculously disappointed at the thought of her leaving.

'I'm afraid so. I can't afford to put a foot wrong with the management while business isn't too good.'

'I understand.'

Seeing how wistful he looked suddenly and misunderstanding the reason for it, she said, 'Look, don't worry about your sister. I'll take very good care of her, so please don't fret about her. If there is any problem at all I will contact you, I promise. But Eva is probably stronger than you think. She needs to spread her wings a little.'

'I know, and I trust you.'

'Good.' As they looked into each other's eyes, the chemistry between them was almost unbearable in its intensity.

'Do you have time for another cup of tea?' he asked.

She smiled. 'I've got about another ten minutes, so yes please,' she said. 'If you can get a waitress to serve you, that is. They're all rushed off their feet in here.'

He managed to find a Nippy to take his order for two more teas and he was so grateful for this little extra time with Clara that he couldn't help blurting out, 'It's so nice being here with you.'

'Likewise,' she said, meeting his eyes and recognising her own feelings mirrored there. With difficulty she averted her gaze and asked how Hester was.

'She's all right,' he replied, stifling the urge to bare his soul to her about the appalling state of his marriage. 'How's Arnold?'

'He's fine,' she said.

Those few words had put the rules firmly back in place. Although nothing was said, she sensed that they both knew that they were in great danger of breaking them if they didn't stay on their guard.

Chapter Seven

Eva didn't just embrace life in London; she grabbed it with both hands and revelled in it. Realising that opportunity wasn't going to come knocking on the door without any effort on her part, she went out looking for it. The only employment she could find was in a local laundry so she took that and from then on was out of the house before anyone else in the mornings.

It was common knowledge that work in the lower echelons of a laundry was gruelling but she didn't complain. In fact, she seemed to rather enjoy it; the company anyway, as some of her workmates were girls of about her own age.

As it was her first visit to London, Clara and Cuddy took her to see the famous sights in any spare time they had at the weekends. She was enthralled by such landmarks as Big Ben, Buckingham Palace and many other favourites. At home she was the answer to everyone's prayers because she was a willing helper with the chores and was very happy to give Flo a hand with the cooking. Some nights she made the meal on her own, to great appreciation from the whole family.

The garrulous, often aggressive young woman who irritated the life out of most of her own family with her tendency to argue and overreact had been replaced by a calmer and more likeable young woman. Clara could hardly believe the difference, though she had seen evidence of Eva's good side at Brierley when she'd been away from the Fenner family in the orchard with herself and Cuddy.

The Tripps, apart from Sydney who still wasn't comfortable around her, enjoyed having her there and treated her like one of their own.

'Go easy with those scissors, Clara,' warned Flo one evening in March when Eva had been with them for over a month. 'You don't want to chop all Eva's hair off.'

'I want her to cut it, Mrs Tripp.' Eva was sitting on a chair in the kitchen with a towel around her. Flo was making a pot of tea and Cuddy was watching the haircut with interest.

'Yes, I know you do, dear, but my daughter is getting very scissor-happy lately. She's hacked great lumps off all her hemlines as well as her hair.'

'Shorter skirts and hair are fashionable, and as I can't afford a new wardrobe I've altered the one I've already got,' explained Clara. 'Anyway, I only raised the hemlines a little.'

'You had beautiful long hair and now it's all gone,' mourned Flo.

'Oh, Mum, you don't half exaggerate,' claimed Clara, whose lustrous dark hair was just above shoulder length. 'I only took an inch or two off and you must admit it looks all right.'

'Yeah, well, maybe it doesn't look bad, but I liked it the way it was before.'

'That's because you're my mum and mothers always want their daughters to stay the same as they were when they were little,' she said. 'Anyway, it will soon grow.'

'I've seen lots of women in London with bobbed hair and want mine cut just the same,' declared Eva.

'I'll do yours too if you like, Mum,' Clara offered jokingly, brandishing the scissors in her direction. 'A bob would suit you a treat.'

'I'm far too old for that sort of caper,' laughed Flo, whose greying fair hair was dragged back into a knot at the back, springy wisps poking out round her face.

'Clara and Arnold are taking me out dancing on Saturday night, Mrs Tripp,' announced Eva excitedly. 'So I need to look a bit more up to date or no one will ask me to dance.'

'You'd better get on with it then, Clara,' Flo conceded. 'We can't have Eva being a wallflower.'

'She wouldn't be anyway, whatever the length of her hair; she's far too pretty.'

'Yes, you're right.'

Studying Eva's hair and mulling things over, Clara made a suggestion. 'How about I just cut the front and sides and leave the back long until you get used to the sides being shorter? That's what I did with mine. A lot of people do that. You can have the back done later if you still want to.'

'Good idea,' said Flo, looking relieved as she poured the tea. 'That's much less risky.'

'Whatever you think best,' Eva agreed.

'Your tea is on the table, girls. I'm going into the other room for a sit down,' Flo told them.

'Right then, here goes,' said Clara, wielding the scissors. 'Fingers crossed and say a prayer.'

★　★　★

'What on earth is going on out there?' asked Frank as gales of laughter drifted into the parlour from the kitchen.

'Clara's cutting Eva's hair,' replied Flo, sipping her tea.

'What on earth for?'

'It's more fashionable, apparently, to have it shorter and Eva wants to follow the herd,' she explained.

'There's nothing wrong with her hair as it is, is there?'

'That's what I think, but that's the way the girls are these days. The war changed things for women, even working class ones like us.'

'Women have always had long hair; it's traditional,' remarked Frank. 'I don't like the idea of them without it. It won't be feminine.'

'It's a question of fashion, dear,' Flo told him. 'Clara and Arnold are taking Eva out dancing on Saturday night and she wants to make sure that she gets plenty of partners.'

'Dancing?' repeated Sydney, who had been sitting quietly listening.

'That's right,' his mother confirmed.

'Where?'

'That place they call the Palais de Danse in Hammer-smith, I think.'

'Oh, no.'

'What's wrong with that?' she asked.

'Nothing,' he said in a manner to suggest the opposite, and rose quickly with a purposeful air. 'I'm going over to Tub's place.'

'What's the matter with him, I wonder?' remarked Frank after Sydney had left.

'It'll be something and nothing, I expect. You know

what the young 'uns are like,' said Flo. 'He's staying out of trouble, that's the important thing.'

It had become nigh on impossible for Sydney to speak to his sister alone since Eva had moved in. The two of them were nearly always together when they were at home; either talking and giggling in their bedroom, doing their hair in the kitchen or sitting in the living room together altering their clothes or knitting. Eva was omnipresent in the house; every time he went into a room she was there and it was driving him crazy.

When he got back from Tub's that night he was determined to get his sister on her own. He finally managed it after Arnold had gone home, by which time everyone else was in bed. Clara was in the kitchen washing some cocoa cups at the sink.

'What do you think you're playing at, taking Eva out dancing?' he demanded.

'Just giving her an introduction to what most other young people are doing.' She threw him a look. 'Why do you sound as though you disapprove?'

'Because you're taking her to the Hammersmith Palais,' he said accusingly.

'What's wrong with that?'

'A lot of bad types go there, especially on a Saturday night.'

'How do you know? You've never been there.'

'I've heard about it. Blokes go there just looking for girls.'

'And vice versa,' she pointed out. 'That's the general idea at a dance.'

'Eva's a country girl,' he reminded her. 'She's naïve; she

could get in with the wrong type. I've heard they have jazz music there.'

'And that makes it a den of iniquity, does it?'

'It does have a reputation for attracting dodgy types, yeah,' he told her.

'Ooh, good. I can't wait to get there,' she said, teasing him. 'It will be fun to meet a few hardened villains.'

But Sydney's sense of humour had deserted him over this. 'It isn't funny, Clara,' he admonished her.

She grinned. 'I think it's extremely funny. Anyone would think we were taking her to Piccadilly to put her on the streets, the way you're carrying on. We're only taking her to a dance.'

'If you must take her dancing why don't you go somewhere more respectable; to a local hop in a church hall or somethin'?'

'Because there aren't any on that I know of, and anyway dance halls are a lot more fun,' she said. 'Honestly, Sydney, you're acting like an old woman. For a boy who was a rebel not so long ago, I find it most peculiar.'

'So I'm peculiar then,' he came back at her heatedly. 'But I'm still entitled to my opinion.'

'Arnold and I will be with her,' she told him, realising that he was genuinely concerned. 'We'll look out for her.' She paused, smiling. 'But if you're that worried you can come along as her chaperon.'

He gave her a withering look. 'There's no need to take the mick. It's a serious matter.'

'There is nothing serious about a night out at a dance,' she said. 'Why are you so worried about her, anyway? I thought you hated the idea of her being here.'

'I do, but since she is here we have to look out for her,' he said. 'She doesn't know London ways.'

'She'll have got a pretty good idea after being here for more than a month and working at the laundry,' Clara pointed out. 'The girls she works with aren't exactly shrinking violets by the sound of what she says about them. They will have opened her eyes to a thing or two.'

He shrugged. 'Oh well, it seems what I say counts for nothing around here.'

'That isn't true at all and you know it,' Clara disagreed. 'Look, it's kind of you to worry about her but if she is going to make London her home she needs to experience it. We can't protect her from life here; she needs to be a part of it and that means exposing herself to what goes on outside the front door. She's long overdue some fun anyway after the miserable life she's had. But I promise you, she'll be quite safe with Arnold and me.'

'I'll just have to take your word for it then,' he said quickly. 'G'night.'

'G'night, Sydney,' she said, looking after him thoughtfully as he left the room and headed for the stairs.

Why he was giving himself such a hard time over some bloomin' country girl who had done nothing for him except make him feel uncomfortable in his own home, Sydney had no idea. He couldn't even sit in the parlour without feeling clumsy, and everything he said at mealtimes came out wrong. If he ever found himself in a room alone with her he didn't know where to put himself so made a hasty exit. None of the others had a problem. They all loved having her around.

It wasn't that he fancied her or anything like that.

But for some reason that he didn't understand he felt protective towards her, probably because she was so vulnerable being from the sticks. He didn't want to worry about her; it was a flaming nuisance. He was young and single; he wanted to be carefree. He'd had enough trouble in the time leading up to Tub's beating and all the stress that came with it, and here he was tormenting himself about some girl from a distant fruit orchard.

Oh well, perhaps she'd get fed up with it here soon and go back to Kent, he thought hopefully as he got into bed, then life could revert to normal. Meanwhile his sister was going to thrust her in the path of any number of dangers on Saturday night and there wasn't a damned thing he could do about it!

'Well, Eva isn't having any shortage of partners, is she?' said Arnold as he and Clara foxtrotted around the floor. 'She seems to be having a high old time.'

'Isn't it lovely for her?' responded Clara, pleased that her new friend was enjoying herself. 'I'm glad I taught her some basic steps, though she would have soon picked them up anyway.'

'Just as I did,' he said with a wry grin. He wasn't exactly nimble-footed on the dance floor.

'Better than you did, I would hope.'

He laughed. 'Anyone's better than me.'

'You said it.' She grinned.

Clara was enjoying herself immensely. It didn't matter that Arnold wasn't a good dancer. He moved in time with the music and they got round. It was the lavish surroundings and the atmosphere that was so captivating.

Coloured lights and cheery music, the smell of scent and cigarettes, crowds of young people standing and sitting around the dance floor. The magic of it always hit Clara as soon as she walked into the carpeted foyer and heard the strains of the band drifting out from the ballroom. The Palais had brought something really special to the area when it opened two years ago, drawing people from all over London and beyond. Clara had heard it said that it was the most luxurious dancing place in all of Europe, and it was within walking distance of her home.

The music ended and they made their way to the side of the floor. Eva bounced over excitedly. 'Oh, isn't it fun,' she whooped. 'I am having such a good time.'

'So we've noticed. I'm really pleased for you.' Clara smiled.

'Can we come again soon, please? Like next week?'

'I'm not sure about coming again as soon as that. Arnold and I are saving up and it works out a bit expensive to come every week.'

'Maybe someone from work will come with me,' Eva suggested. 'I just love it and can't wait to come again.'

'Someone seems to like you,' remarked Clara, noticing a young man Eva had just danced with heading in their direction. 'He's coming for you again.'

'Oh joy,' she said and sailed on to the floor with the young man, who had dark hair and was rather good looking.

'She's clicked then,' said Arnold.

'Looks like it,' agreed Clara.

After dancing all the dances in the second half, including the last waltz, with the young man, whose name was

Wilfred, Eva surprised no one by announcing that he had asked to see her home. Clara wasn't sure about it.

'You're not her mother,' Arnold pointed out while Eva was out of earshot. 'She's sixteen going on seventeen and not six, so I don't see that you can stop her.'

'You make sure you take her straight home then, Wilfred,' she said, realising that she sounded like her own mother.

'Of course I will,' agreed Wilfred, who had nice smiling eyes. 'I'm just going to get my coat.' He turned to Eva. 'I'll meet you in the foyer in a few minutes.'

'I'll be waiting,' she said dreamily as they headed for the cloakroom to join the queue for coats.

Having once sampled the nightlife Eva couldn't get enough of it and went out dancing every weekend with her friends from work. She went to the pictures a few times with Wilfred, then George, then someone called Tom. She socialised as though it might all end tomorrow. Whether she was making up for lost time or needed to escape into fun to forget her past, Clara wasn't sure. But she was pleased to see Eva enjoying herself after such an awful childhood. It was natural for a young woman to flirt a little. Anyway, enjoyment was a fashionable activity after the misery of the war years and many young people were making the most of the new dance halls. It wasn't unusual either for people of all ages to go to the flicks several times a week.

Eva was still a joy to have around at home. On Sundays she usually cooked the roast, to a great deal of praise. Sydney still worried about her, especially when a new boyfriend appeared on the scene. 'She'll get herself a bad name, going out with all these different blokes,' he could be heard to wail when she wasn't around.

'She's just enjoying her new freedom. It's harmless fun,' his sister assured him.

'She wants to watch her step, though,' he said, sounding about fifty.

'Tell her that, not me.'

'Oh, no, I wouldn't dream of it.'

'Stop going on about it to me then.'

In May something happened to Clara that took the focus away from Eva and turned it on to herself. She'd known that business hadn't been good at Taylor's for a while because of the fierce competition in the area, so she should have been prepared, but when she and some of the other waitresses were given a week's notice it came as a shock.

'You'll soon find another job, love,' said Arnold supportively when they were out for a walk that evening.

'I'll have to, because Mum needs money for my keep,' she told him. 'If I can't get work as a waitress I'll have to do something else; anything as long as I can earn enough to pay my way.' She looked at him. 'Sorry, Arnold, but I might have to use some of my savings if it takes a while to find a job.'

'Don't worry about that, sweetheart,' he said warmly. 'I'm earning good money at the moment with all the overtime that's coming my way and as long as one of us is putting something away our fund will still build up. If you need dosh you know where to come.'

'You're such a good man,' she said.

He took off his hat and brushed his hand over the top of his head, grinning. 'Ah there it is. My halo is still in place.'

She couldn't help laughing. 'You twerp,' she giggled.

'That's the stuff, Clara. Keep smiling,' he said.

'I'll try,' she told him.

The Fenner family were gathered round the big kitchen table for the evening meal when Charlie made an announcement. 'I had a letter from Eva this morning,' he said.

'Oh, good. How is she?' asked his father warmly.

'She's fine. More than just fine, actually,' he told them. 'She's having a whale of a time. She loves it in London. She's been going out dancing and to the pictures.'

'Disgraceful.' Mabel sniffed.

Charlie gave her a look. 'That's why she writes to me and not you, Mum. She knows you don't wish her well, though she does send her love to all of you.'

'How is she getting on in her job?' enquired John.

'She doesn't say much about the job as such; it's mostly about her workmates. They all go out together of an evening, apparently.'

'Sounds as though she's turning into a right little trollop,' said Hester.

'Hey, steady on, Hester,' Vincent admonished, frowning at her. 'She is my sister, if you don't mind.'

'Just making an observation.'

'That sort of remark isn't welcome,' he said sharply. 'She is family, remember.'

Hester flushed angrily and fell silent.

'Her friend Clara has had a bit of bad luck though,' Charlie went on. 'She's lost her job and isn't finding it easy to get another in the same line of work.'

'That must be a worry for her,' said his father. 'How is she managing without a wage coming in?'

'She goes out cleaning shops and offices at the crack of dawn to pay her way until she can find another position as a waitress,' replied Charlie.

'She should come and work here for a few months,' suggested his father casually. 'We could do with someone with her interest and dedication around the place for the next few months. If we had someone to help with the checking and spraying to keep the trees free of insects, and a host of other jobs that have to be done at this time of year, it would make our lives a whole lot easier.'

'I know you're not serious, but that's not a bad idea, Dad,' enthused Charlie. 'Though I doubt if she would come, seeing she's engaged to be married.'

'It would be a lot better for her than going out cleaning early in the mornings, and if we pay her decent money she might be persuaded,' suggested John, interest rising. 'I've never known anyone as keen on the job as she was, so she might welcome the opportunity to do something she really enjoys on a temporary basis. Say we offered her four months' work with plenty of weekends off to go home. Might that coax her into it?'

'She might well want to come, but the boyfriend might not be too pleased about it.'

'You could get experienced local workers to do all those jobs, couldn't you?' said Hester, blatantly critical and causing a tense silence because the women of the family didn't normally enter into discussions about the business. 'Why on earth would you want to take on someone like her from miles away who knows next to nothing about the apple-growing business?'

'Because enthusiastic, dedicated people like her don't come along very often and she would be very useful to us,' explained her mild-mannered father-in-law when he'd recovered from the shock of Hester's audacity in asking. 'Clara has a keen interest, and is a great little worker.'

'Oh, really.' Hester made it clear from the way she looked that she wasn't impressed.

'What do you think, Vincent?'

'Sounds all right to me,' he replied, seeming disinterested. 'Yeah, it might not be a bad idea.'

'Let's have a chat about it later on, Dad,' suggested Charlie, who didn't want to get into a discussion with his wife over the issue.

'All right, son.'

Mabel knew her place and stayed silent, but Hester's eyes burned with fury.

'Is something the matter, Hester?' asked Vincent later on when he and his brother's wife met in their usual place on the edge of the orchard after dark. 'You seem a bit peeved.'

'I should danged well think I am,' she said furiously. 'You went against me on two occasions over dinner.'

'Oh? Did I?'

'You know very well you did, so don't play the innocent,' she fumed.

'I'm not. I honestly don't know what you mean,' he said.

'First you shot me down in flames over your sister,' she informed him, 'and then you opposed me about employing that wretched Tripp woman.'

He was becoming increasingly irritated by her possessive attitude towards him. His affair with her was supposed to be a thing of pleasure, not misery, and he didn't want to have to account to her for every word he said. 'Eva is my sister,' he pointed out. 'You can't expect me to sit back while you call her a trollop.'

'She's a pain in the backside and you're not slow to tell her so when she's here,' she reminded him.

'When she's around, maybe so, but she isn't here to defend herself, is she?' he pointed out. 'Anyway, Eva might be a bit irritating at times but I won't stand by and have that sort of thing said about her.'

'All right, maybe I was a bit out of order,' she admitted, afraid of losing him if she pushed him too far. 'Perhaps I shouldn't have said that. But you did go against me about Clara Tripp.'

'I didn't deliberately go against you,' he sighed wearily. 'I agreed with the others because they were right when they said she's a good worker. It doesn't matter to me one way or the other if the woman comes to work for us or not. I was just having a conversation with my father and brother about work. It was business, Hester, and none of your concern.'

'You didn't have to take their side against me so obviously. It was really hurtful,' she complained.

'I didn't even realise that I had,' he said, angered by her accusations and the frequency of them. 'It was a matter of no real importance to me.'

'It didn't sound like that to me.'

'In that case you must have misinterpreted what I said. Anyway, I don't know what you've got against Clara Tripp. She wouldn't interfere with you. You live at the cottage and only eat with the family in the evening because it's a tradition. So you'd hardly see her. It isn't as though you're out in the fields working, is it? So her being here wouldn't make any difference to you.'

'I thought she was a bit common,' Hester said.

'She seemed all right to me, but it would make no difference to her work if she was,' he said casually. 'In any case, she probably wouldn't take the job if it was offered to her as she's engaged to be married. The boyfriend would almost certainly forbid it. I would if any fiancée of mine wanted to go away for a few months.'

'That isn't the point; you went against me and that's what upset me,' she complained. 'I mean, we are supposed to be special to each other, aren't we?'

'The others don't know that, do they, and the last thing we want is for anyone to suspect it by my taking your side every time there's a discussion.'

'I still think it was mean of you—'

'Hester, you are being really boring lately,' he interrupted with exasperation. 'We don't have very long together so why waste time going on at me about something so trivial? You are actually married to my brother, remember, and I don't get on at you about that, do I?'

'You know I would leave him tomorrow if you were to say the word,' she reminded him.

'And you know that we have to wait for the right time for that or we'll both suffer,' he came back at her.

'I s'pose so,' she said with reluctance.

'Good. So now that that's sorted, be a good girl and do what you do best. Come here and give me a kiss.'

She knew she was annoying him with her attitude but couldn't seem to stop herself. She wanted total commitment from him which he didn't seem willing to give. Possessiveness was in her nature. Maybe that was why she had become so disenchanted with Charlie: because he simply wouldn't allow himself to be bullied. Though in rare moments of honesty she would admit to herself that the need to embark on an affair with his brother was more to do with always wanting something other than what she already had. It was inherent in her; she'd always been the same for as far back as she could remember.

But for now she needed to concentrate on getting back into Vincent's favour or he might not want to continue seeing her at all. She must try to please him and remind him of what he would miss if he ended their relationship. So she put her arms round him and prepared to make it up to him in the only way she knew how.

'So are you telling me, Charlie, that you came all the way to London to offer me a job you are almost certain I won't take?' said Clara, a few days later.

'Well, yes, but this way I get to see Eva. It'll be nice to see Cuddy too.'

It was the middle of the afternoon and he had turned up at the Tripps' front door unannounced in the hope of finding someone in. Because Clara's cleaning work started in the small hours and finished early, he had been in luck and found her at home alone. Flo was visiting a neighbour, Cuddy was at school and the others were out at work. Charlie came straight to the point and offered her a job at the orchard until the autumn. She was enormously flattered and thrilled at the thought of such an opportunity but knew there was no way she could accept it.

'Surely there must be plenty of experienced people closer at hand who would be more useful to you,' she suggested now.

'I expect there are and if we were to put the word out

we would probably have a string of applicants,' he told her candidly. 'But we weren't actually thinking of hiring anyone new. Dad just happened to suggest it when we heard from Eva that you'd lost your job in the tea rooms and it seemed like a good idea.'

'So it's a charitable gesture.'

'Absolutely not.' He could hear his voice rising because it was so far from the truth. 'We were impressed with your work when you were with us last year and we could do with some extra help over the summer season, you've lost your job, so this is something that will benefit us all.'

'I'm very flattered, of course . . .'

'But you've Arnold to consider.'

'Exactly.'

'Surely he would want you to do work you enjoy, rather than what you are doing now, and it would only be for a few months.'

'I'm sure he would, but I don't think it would be fair to him,' she insisted.

'Yes, I can see that you might feel like that, but we'd pay you a decent wage.' He was ridiculously disappointed at her negative reaction even though he'd known she wasn't free to take the job. His instinct was to get down on his knees and beg her to come to Brierley, married man or not. He had no intention of behaving in any inappropriate way; just to have her around would brighten up his life. 'Of course you would need to discuss it with Arnold, we understand that. The offer is there if you want to think about it but we'll understand if you can't accept.'

'Hello, I'm home,' came a cheery voice from the hall and in swept Flo. 'Oh, a visitor. How lovely!'

Clara made the introductions.

'Have you not made the man a cup of tea, Clara?' Flo said in a tone of mild admonition.

'I haven't got round to it yet.'

'Forgive my daughter's bad manners, Charlie,' Flo apologised. 'I don't know what she's thinking of.' She waved her hand towards the sofa. 'Sit down and make yourself comfortable while I put the kettle on. Tea won't be long.'

'Thank you very much, Mrs Tripp,' he said.

'Call me Flo, dear,' she invited warmly. 'We don't stand on ceremony here.'

He smiled, now knowing where Clara got her warm heart from and why his sister loved living here.

'Oh, what a lovely opportunity for you, Clara,' said Flo effusively when Charlie explained the purpose of his visit over tea and seed cake. 'A whole lot better for you than going out scrubbing floors for a living at some unearthly hour; especially as you enjoyed it so much at the orchard last year.'

'It isn't that easy, Mum,' Clara reminded her. 'I can't just go away and leave Arnold for four months.'

'Mm, I understand that. But Charlie has said that you can come home some weekends if they don't need you,' Flo pointed out. 'Anyway, most of the time you don't see Arnold during the week when he's working overtime and I don't hear you complaining about that so I can't see a problem, especially if there's a decent wage involved.'

'I think we'll have to let Clara make up her own mind,' suggested Charlie, giving Flo a surreptitious wink.

'Yes, of course,' she said, smiling and changing the subject. 'You'll stay for a meal with us, won't you, Charlie?'

'Well, it's very nice of you to offer, but I don't want to impose,' he told her.

'Impose? You wouldn't know how,' she said, having taken an instant liking to him. 'You'll want to stay to see your sister when she gets in from work so let's have no arguments. I know you've a train to catch, but we don't eat late.'

'That would be lovely then. Thank you very much indeed,' he said.

'A pleasure,' Flo beamed.

Over the meal everyone had their say about the job at Brierley.

'You must be mad to even consider burying yourself alive in the country for four minutes, let alone four months,' declared Sydney. 'Phew, just the thought scares the living daylights out of me.'

'It isn't that bad, Sydney,' said Eva defensively. 'But I must admit that I prefer town life.'

'We're all made different and Clara loves the country,' put in Flo. 'So I think she'd be very silly to refuse a one-off opportunity like this.'

'I'd go like a shot if it was me,' declared Cuddy, who had given Charlie an ecstatic welcome, as had Eva. 'We had a smashing time there even if I did get hurt.'

'I'd help your mum out here, Clara,' offered Eva. 'So you could have an easy mind about that.'

'It should be very nice in Kent at this time of the year too,' put in Frank. 'The country life wouldn't suit me, and I don't mind admitting it, but as you like it, Clara, and it's only temporary, why not? You might not get another chance like this.'

'She won't once she's married, that's for sure,' Flo added.

'When you've all finished telling me what to do,' began

Clara, deeply disappointed that she wasn't in a position to take the job, 'can I say that I'll speak to Arnold about it. If he doesn't want me to go, and I am fairly sure he won't, then I won't go.' She turned to Charlie. 'Sorry I can't be more definite than that.'

'Don't worry about it,' he said. 'It was only an idea and we knew it was a long shot.'

'I'm not sure when I'll be seeing Arnold next, to discuss it with him,' she said thoughtfully. 'It might not be until the weekend.'

'Don't worry,' he told her. 'Just let us know by letter or telephone when you've decided.'

Flo and her husband exchanged a look. 'Are you for real, Charlie?' asked Flo lightly. 'It all seems too good to be true.'

He laughed. 'I'm only offering her a temporary job,' he pointed out. 'Not giving her a pot of money. And she'll have to work hard for every penny, she knows that.'

'Even so,' said Flo. 'You're very patient.'

'Let's wait and see what Arnold has to say,' he said, embarrassed by the praise.

'Yes, we'll have to do that,' agreed Flo. 'Meanwhile, would you like another piece of meat pie, Charlie?'

'Yes, please.'

'Brave man,' Frank laughed.

'Come off it, Dad. Mum's pastry has improved a lot since Eva has been here and giving her a few tips.'

'Yeah, yeah, just teasing,' he said.

And the conversation moved on to other things, the family showing a friendly interest in Charlie's way of life. By the time he left to catch his train, he was warmed through to his heart, though more than a little disappointed by the fact that Clara was almost certainly going to refuse his job offer.

Arnold listened to what Clara had to say when she saw him at the weekend. She had taken him into the front room so she could speak to him in private.

'You'd be away for about four months, you say?'

She nodded. 'But I could come home some weekends,' she pointed out.

'And I'm supposed to be happy about it, am I?' he said, sounding peeved.

'No, of course not. I'm telling you that I've been offered a job. I haven't said that I'm going to take it.'

'I should damned well hope not,' he exploded. 'We are engaged, remember.'

'I haven't forgotten, though it wouldn't be too difficult since I very rarely see you during the week.'

'You know why that is,' he said heatedly. 'I'm busy earning money for our future. I always see you at weekends.'

'All right, keep your hair on. I was only defending myself by pointing out the reality,' she said.

'I don't know what I'm supposed to do at the weekends if you're away picking apples in some godforsaken place in the country,' he complained.

'I told you, I'd be able to come home some weekends. And I wouldn't be picking apples, not until later in the year anyway,' she pointed out. 'The job will involve much more than that. I'd learn a lot about horticulture.'

'And what good will that be to you?' he demanded.

'We're given a brain to use,' she reminded him, feeling stifled by his narrow view of the matter. 'As I have been offered the opportunity to learn something new, it seems like a good idea to take it, especially as it's a subject that interests me and work I enjoy. But as you are so opposed to the whole thing I won't take the job, so you can take that sulky look off your face and forget the whole thing.'

'So I have to feel guilty for stopping you doing something you really want to do,' he challenged her.

'Of course not,' she told him. 'You know that isn't the way my mind works. I told Charlie that I have commitments here and it was very unlikely that I would be able to accept his offer. I know where my priorities lie.'

'And you must know me well enough to know that I would never stop you doing anything you really wanted to do,' he said with a sudden change of attitude.

'Sounds like it,' she said with irony.

'Well, maybe I was being a bit hard just now when you first told me about it. If you really want to go, then you go ahead, with my blessing,' he said. 'It will be better for you than going out cleaning early mornings.'

She threw him a shrewd look. 'Why the sudden change of heart, Arnold?' she enquired.

There was a brief silence. 'Maybe I've realised it would be selfish of me to try to keep you here in London,' he replied at last. 'Personally, I think you must be mad to want to go away to the country, but if that's what you'd really like to do, I'll be here waiting for you when you come back.' He smiled at her. 'So when I've gone home you'd better start packing a bag.'

'Oh, Arnold, I don't deserve you,' she said, flinging her arms round him. 'You are such a sweetheart. Are you absolutely sure you don't mind?'

'Quite sure.' He certainly was; he thought he might

have overdone it just now by seeming to be so opposed to the idea that she was about to turn the job down, which was the last thing he wanted. It suited him very well for her to be away for a while but it wouldn't do to let her know that because she would almost certainly become suspicious. 'You go and get all this countryside lark out of your system once and for all before we settle down together.'

'Thanks, Arnold,' she said gratefully.

'You're welcome,' he said, feeling pleased with himself. Things were definitely going his way these days.

Chapter Eight

'How are you getting on up there?' Charlie called. Clara was busy in the upper branches of an apple tree examining the shoots for signs of disease and spraying any suspect ones to prevent the foliage from curling.

Dressed in trousers and a white cotton blouse, she looked down and brushed her hair from her face, shading her eyes from the dappled sunlight. 'I'm doing fine, thanks,' she replied. 'But I didn't realise the extent to which fruit growing involves such a constant battle against nature.'

'Disease is our biggest enemy,' he said, standing by the tree with his beloved Rex sniffing around nearby, the dog's shiny coat living up to the name of his breed in the golden sunshine.

'So I'm beginning to find out,' she told him. 'Before I came to work here, I hadn't thought much beyond the aesthetics of apple blossom. I certainly didn't realise it was such a magnet for destructive bugs that could potentially ruin the crop.'

'I doubt if the crowds who come to see the Kent orchards in bloom realise it either; there's no reason why they would,' he remarked. 'In our business you have to be one step ahead. Leave Mother Nature to her own devices and your crops will be ruined.' He paused. 'Anyway, it's teatime so you can take a break.'

'Is it that time already?' she said, making her way down the ladder.

'That's a good sign,' he commented. 'You must be happy in your work if you're not noticing the time.'

She looked up at him. 'I think you know that I am, don't you?' she said.

He nodded. 'The look on your face says it all.'

Why wouldn't she look happy when she was working out in the fresh air on a lovely summer's day doing a diversity of jobs? One hour she would be weeding, another mulching or tending to the grafts put on old trees earlier in the year, making sure the new shoots were protected from the wind until they were properly set on their stocks. There were also new trees to check on, and watering where necessary. Every day she learned something new and realised that her temporary stint as an apple picker had been the tiniest tip of the iceberg. Having been here now for several weeks she felt at one with the job, which she thought of as a somewhat unequal partnership with nature, the latter most definitely having the upper hand.

It wasn't all plain sailing. She still had a great deal to learn, the work was physically demanding and the weather not always as clement as it was today. But there was fulfilment for her in working the land, the feel and smell of the soil when she was digging around the young trees or clearing a new patch or simply pulling out weeds; it was all so rewarding. Life in the country invigorated her, made her feel fully alive and healthier. She ate well and slept soundly at night.

The only negative aspect had nothing to do with the work and everything to do with Charlie's wife, who blatantly exuded hostility every time Clara saw her, which was usually over dinner at the big house in the evening. Fortunately Hester wasn't around the orchard much during the day. Her job was exclusively to look after her home and her husband, apparently.

Clara knew instinctively that Hester's affair with Vincent was still in progress. She could see it in their body language and almost feel the chemistry between them. But everyone else seemed so oblivious that she sometimes wondered if perhaps she could see something that wasn't there because of what she knew.

'Tomorrow you can do something a little less strenuous as it's a Saturday, if you like,' Charlie was saying.

'And what might that be?' she enquired.

'We've got some early fruit that can be sold very cheaply at the roadside,' he explained. 'Windfalls that can only be used for cooking because they're not ripe. Do you fancy setting up a stall outside the orchard?'

'I'd be happy to,' she said, thinking yet again what a variety of tasks were included in this job as they walked towards the house for tea. 'That will make a nice change.'

'Good,' he said. 'We'll set you up with a table and stool so you can have a sit down between customers.'

'Lovely!'

The road that ran alongside Brierley on the far side of the orchard was a main thoroughfare to the coast and plenty of motor cars passed along it carrying day trippers and people who could afford to take a holiday by the sea. Most of the cars were open topped and carried well-dressed people of the upper classes, though there were a few small Austin family cars owned by professional and business people. Clara was used to seeing motorised traffic around in London but no one in her usual circles had a car of any sort. Her ex-employer at the tea rooms and the Fenners were the only car owners she knew personally.

But she was speaking to plenty of them today because she was the only source of refreshment in the area, so passers-by were buying fruit to eat on their day out, sour or not. Many stopped just to make enquiries.

'Is there anywhere around here where we can get a cup of tea and a cake, miss?' asked one young man wearing goggles in an open-topped car, his female companion in the full motoring regalia complete with a yellow silk scarf over her hat to keep her hair in place.

'I'm afraid there isn't,' replied Clara. 'Not in the immediate vicinity anyway. There isn't even a café in the village. Perhaps there might be somewhere nearer to the coast.'

'That isn't very good, is it?' he said as though she was personally to blame. 'Someone should open a tea shop. People need food and drink when they're out for the day.'

'I'm sure they do.'

'Why has provision not been made, then?' he demanded, in a manner to suggest that he had a right to such facilities.

'I've no idea,' replied Clara coolly.

'You country bumpkin types don't see an opportunity when it's staring you in the face,' he said rudely.

'I doubt if there was any need for a tea shop until so many motorists started coming along here,' she pointed out. 'There wouldn't have been much custom about before.'

He muttered something to his companion that Clara

guessed was detrimental to country people, then drove away without another word to her.

She was inwardly fuming at his ignorance when she was distracted by the appearance of a woman of middle years whom she recognised from the village. The woman held the lead of a dog that was sniffing round the grass verge.

'They've got you out selling today then,' she observed in a pleasant manner. 'I expect it makes a change.'

Clara nodded, smiling. 'I'm really enjoying myself out here, and selling lots of apples.'

'I'll have some too, please, dear,' she said. 'Four big ones if you will.'

'None of them are very big because they're early, so they're a bit sour because they aren't properly ripe,' Clara explained. 'They'll need cooking.'

'With plenty of sugar they'll be just right for an apple pie,' she said. 'I like a bit of sharpness in fruit.'

The woman was clearly in the mood for conversation so Clara asked politely, 'Are you just out for a stroll or going visiting?'

'Just taking my dog for a nice long walk to give him some exercise,' she replied. 'Time was when he could run free along here, but now there are so many danged motor cars on this road I have to keep him on the lead.'

'Shame,' Clara sympathised. 'But I suppose we can't stand in the way of progress.'

'Of course you'll be used to lots of traffic, I suppose, coming from London.'

'There are plenty of cars and motor buses where I live,' she said. 'I must say the buses are useful.'

'It must be a complete contrast for you here,' said the woman. 'How are you liking it?'

'I love it,' she replied without hesitation.

'You don't miss all the entertainments they have in London, then?'

'Not so far,' she said. 'But I do enjoy that sort of thing so I suppose I would miss them if I was here long enough.'

The woman looked in the direction of Brierley. 'Nice family, the Fenners,' she said in a confidential manner, as though she was hoping for a spot of gossip.

'Yes, I get on well with them.'

'I expect you find Mabel a bit difficult though.' The woman frowned, her eyes glazing over in thought. 'She's never been the same since they lost their little girl. A shocking tragedy, the poor little mite.'

Clara nodded.

'Mabel used to be quite a bright spark before that happened; she was involved in all sorts of village affairs, but we very rarely see her now and she never speaks to anyone if she does show her face. A nod is the best you can hope for these days.' She paused thoughtfully. 'She never used to be so sour-faced. I don't think I've seen her smile in all the years since it happened.'

Clara nodded, careful to keep a diplomatic silence but finding it hard to imagine this other Mabel Fenner who was once cheerful and sociable.

'They say her other daughter has left home now too,' the woman went on.

'Yes, that's right.'

'Nice girl, Eva,' the woman remarked. 'A bit of a handful, so they say, but she was always very polite to me.'

'Yes. I like Eva,' said Clara. 'We're good friends, actually.'

'Good. I'm glad she's got a friend.' She paused. 'Well, I

reckon I've walked too far,' she said, sounding weary. 'I could do with a sit down and a cup of tea.'

'Have a seat here for a while to rest before you walk back,' Clara suggested, offering her the stool.

'How kind you are,' said the woman, sitting down. 'I think the Fenners were very lucky when they found you.'

'I don't know about that,' said Clara. 'I think I'm the lucky one to be here.'

And she did; she really did.

Over dinner Charlie and his father told Clara how pleased they were with the way she'd shifted the apples.

'I think perhaps I have something of a market trader in me,' she said jokingly.

'Among all your other talents,' joshed Charlie. 'An experienced waitress and a trainee fruit grower.'

'Don't forget apple picking,' she laughed. 'Oh, and by the way, I had an idea while I was out there. Lots of people asked if there was anywhere they could get a cup of tea and a bite to eat round here. Why don't you open a little tea shop?'

There was a stunned silence.

'Where would we do that?' asked John Fenner at last.

'I haven't thought that far, but maybe you could convert one of the small barns,' she suggested with enthusiasm. 'It would do well with the passing traffic. There isn't anything like that round here at all. It would be another string to your bow and the demand will grow as more people get motor cars and take to the open road.'

'It would be a big project.' John Fenner was cautious.

'Not the sort of thing I have in mind,' said Clara. 'Some minor alterations to one of the barns and a few tables and chairs, that's all you would need. The catering could be done here at the house; nothing elaborate, just tea and cakes.' She looked towards Mabel. 'Mrs Fenner's lovely cakes would go down a storm.'

'It's a good idea, Clara,' said Charlie thoughtfully. 'Definitely worth some consideration.'

'Yes, I can see that there are possibilities for something like that,' his father added.

Mabel knew better than to enter into business discussions and stayed silent, but Hester felt the need to have her say, as usual. 'It would just create extra work. Someone would have to look after it and do the serving,' she said.

'Mm, that is a point,' her father-in-law agreed.

'You could just open during the summer when people are out and about going to and from the coast,' suggested Clara. 'Perhaps get some temporary help.'

'We'll give it more thought, and maybe do some costings,' said Charlie. 'Thanks for suggesting it, Clara.'

'It was just an idea,' she said, flinching under the withering look that Hester was throwing in her direction.

After dinner, when she'd helped Mabel with the washing up, Clara usually went to her room for the rest of the evening, rather than sit downstairs with Mabel and John, and Vincent if he was in. She generally read a book, or wrote letters; sometimes she went downstairs again and went out for a walk. That evening she was sitting on the bed replying to a letter from Eva, who had written recently full of news about her new boyfriend with whom she was 'desperately in love', when there was a knock on the door. She opened it to find Hester standing there.

Without waiting for an invitation, she pushed her way

past Clara into the room and said aggressively, 'I think you need a reminder about your status here, madam.'

'Really?'

'Yes really. You are an unskilled worker, not a business adviser to my husband and father-in-law,' she informed her. 'How dare you suggest they open a tea shop?'

'What's so bad about opening a tea shop?' asked the stunned Clara. 'It would complement the business perfectly.'

'That isn't the point,' Hester ranted, obviously furious. 'The running of this business has nothing to do with you. You've no right to suggest anything at all about the place.'

'It was only a casual comment.'

'Well, keep your thoughts to yourself in future.'

'Are you put out because you're afraid they might ask you to work in the tea shop?' suggested Clara. 'Is that why you are so much against it? I notice that you don't lift a finger anywhere in the business at the moment.'

'I'm against you poking your nose into this family's business,' Hester stated baldly. 'And what I do with my time is none of your business. It's between my husband and me.'

'What have I done to upset you, Hester?' Clara asked in an even tone, managing to hang on to her temper.

'I've never said I was upset.'

'You don't need to say anything,' she told her. 'It's all there in your attitude. Your hostility flows towards me every night at dinner. It was the same when I was here before. Yet, to my knowledge, I have never done anything to you to warrant such dislike.'

'If you want to know the truth, I don't like the way you push your way in, persuading them all to like you.'

'I do no such thing,' she denied hotly. 'Whether they like me or not is up to them.'

'What are you after, anyway? That's what I want to know.'

Clara was puzzled by the question. 'I'm not after anything. Why would I be?'

'That's what I'd like to know.'

'I was offered a job here and I took it; that's all there is to it.' She narrowed her eyes on her. 'What is it about me that frightens you? You can't be worried that I might steal your husband, since you're having an affair with his brother.'

Hester turned crimson, then the blood drained from her face. 'You mouthy cow,' she rasped. 'How dare you come out with such wicked lies?'

'I was out for a walk one night when I was here last year and saw the two of you together. I also heard what you were saying, so there's no point in denying it. But you've no need to panic. Your secret is safe with me.'

Hester lunged towards her with her arms outstretched and put her hands round Clara's throat. 'You filthy liar,' she raged, her voice distorted with fury as she increased the pressure until Clara was choking helplessly. 'You're nothing but a troublemaker, a rotten stinking trouble-maker.'

Clara finally managed to secure her release by kicking Hester in the leg until the pain forced her to let go. 'You little savage,' she rasped, grabbing Clara's hair and pulling it so hard she cried out. 'Why don't you go back to London where you belong?'

Struggling for breath after being half strangled and almost having her hair pulled out by the roots, Clara couldn't speak for a moment. 'I will go back to London when I'm good and ready, and that will be when my employment here is finished,' she said when she'd recovered.

Malice exuded from Hester's every pore but there was fear in her eyes too, Clara saw.

'You've no need to look so worried. I've said I won't tell anyone.'

'There's nothing to tell, you silly bitch.'

'We both know that there is, but you're quite safe; not because I give a damn about you or Vincent but because I don't want Charlie to be hurt. The affair will undoubtedly run its course – from what I heard Vincent isn't too keen to commit himself – and Charlie will never have to know. Ignorance is bliss in this particular case.' She paused, looking at Hester. 'That doesn't mean I approve. I think what you're doing is unspeakable and Charlie doesn't deserve it.'

'You're after him yourself, you schemer.'

'Don't be stupid. Charlie is a friend as well as my boss, and none of us want to see our friends hurt. Not that you would know anything about that because I doubt if you have any friends. Now get out of here before I scream for help and bring your in-laws up here to find out what's going on.'

After one more look of undiluted hatred, Hester left the room and Clara sat down on her bed. Her hands were trembling as she resumed her letter to Eva.

'She knows about us, Vincent,' announced Hester later that same night when the two of them were having their usual rendezvous. 'That danged woman from London. She knows.'

'How can she? We've always been very discreet.'

'Apparently, she was out for a walk one night and she saw us together. She heard what we were saying too. She was skulking out there in the dark, watching and listening.'

'Bloody hell,' he exclaimed.

'You'll have to get rid of her,' said Hester. 'The sooner she's gone from here the better.'

'She'll still know though, won't she, wherever she is,' he pointed out. 'So she'll still be a threat.'

'You'll have to make sure that she isn't,' she told him in a shrill panicky voice. 'I don't know how you're going to do it but you'll have to think of something. We need her gone from here because I can't bear the thought of her snooping around. She'll probably forget all about it once she's back in London. Either that or we do a bunk together to avoid taking the flak. Everyone will know then so it won't matter.'

'You know we can't do that, Hester,' he said for the umpteenth time. 'We've far too much to lose, both of us.'

'So you are always telling me.'

'If you didn't keep on about it I wouldn't have to tell you again and again, would I?' he said irritably.

'All right. There's no need to get niggled.'

'It's that woman from London I'm niggled with, not you,' he said, which wasn't entirely true. 'But don't worry about it. I'll fix it.'

Clara was sitting alone on the grass in the orchard enjoying the sunshine with a cup of tea and a cake in her break the following afternoon when Vincent came to join her.

'I won't beat about the bush,' he said, squatting down beside her and speaking in a low voice. 'I understand that you know about my . . . er, friendship with Hester.'

'The affair, you mean; the one she denies having,' she said pointedly. 'Yes, I know all about it.'

'She's just trying to protect herself, the same as anyone would. But there's no point in us lying about it as you actually saw and heard us.'

'You're not exactly full of remorse, are you?'

'No, not really,' he said breezily. 'This sort of thing happens. It's human nature. Anyway, it's only a bit of fun; nothing serious. As long as no one gets to find out about it, no one gets hurt.'

'She's your brother's wife, for goodness' sake,' she reminded him. 'I doubt if Charlie would see much fun in the situation.'

'I didn't come here for a lecture,' he said superciliously. 'What Hester and I do is our business and nothing to do with you.'

'Why have you come to see me, then?'

'To offer you a proposition.'

'Oh yeah, and what might that be?'

'You leave here tomorrow and promise you will never tell anyone what you know and I will give you fifty pounds.'

'No thanks.'

'It's a lot of money.'

'Maybe, but I don't want it.'

'Think how pleased your boyfriend would be if you were to go home with a nice little wad,' he coaxed. 'You'd be able to bring the wedding forward.'

'Absolutely not,' she said. 'You could offer me a thousand pounds and I wouldn't take it.'

'Why, for God's sake?' he demanded. 'Surely the job isn't that important to you.'

'I am committed to four months' work here and I won't

leave until it's finished,' she said. 'I agreed with your father and brother to stay that long and I won't let them down.'

'They can easily get someone else,' he pointed out. 'People who can do your job are ten a penny.'

'Maybe they are. But it's me they want and I won't be driven out because you can't behave yourself,' she said flatly. 'Anyway, I'll still know about your nasty little secret wherever I am so you will never feel quite safe. There is a postal system and even public telephones for people like me to use these days.'

'But I suspect that you're one of those principled people who won't go back on your word. My bet is that if I'd paid for your silence, I'd get it.'

'As I have said to Hester, I have no intention of spilling the beans.' She paused, looking at him thoughtfully. 'But you can never be absolutely sure of that, can you?'

'Exactly, and I don't want you around here reminding me,' he said. 'I am not going to lose my inheritance because some cockney tart is a nosy parker who spies on people.'

Ignoring the insult, she said calmly, 'The best way you can protect your inheritance is to behave decently and not betray one of your own family.'

'Oh, give over preaching, will you,' he said peevishly. 'You'll be leaving here sooner than you intend, I can promise you that. In fact you've done me a favour by refusing the money because you've forced me to think of another, better way of getting you out that won't cost me a penny. You won't go with money in your pocket as you could have done. But you *will* leave and you can tell anyone you like about Hester and me and not a soul will believe you, I shall make damned sure of that. You chose not to co-operate so you'll have to take the consequences.'

And with that he got up and marched towards the house, leaving Clara feeling very uneasy. She knew instinctively that his weren't just empty threats.

'I still say we should go away together,' Hester said to Vincent the following morning when she waylaid him at the far end of one of the apple fields and he told her of his plans. 'It's got to come out in the open sometime, so why not now?'

Vincent had no intention of letting their affair become known now or at any time in the future. In fact he was sick to death of the whole thing. Hester used to be good company, full of laughter and sexuality. Now she was just a nag, always pestering him for commitment and to hell with his inheritance. He was bored stiff with her. But he had to be careful how he handled it or he would have her making trouble as well as Clara Tripp. Hester was a very volatile woman, completely driven by her feelings of the moment; she could blurt the whole thing out to the family in a fit of temper.

'Now isn't the right time, sweetheart,' he said, forcing a pleasant manner. 'I have to wait until I can get hold of some decent money first. I've decided to fiddle some dough out of the business somehow so that we can live decently if it takes me a while to get a job. I just have to work out a way of doing it.'

'You promise it won't be long?'

'I promise,' he lied smoothly. 'But I think it would be a good idea to cool things down for the moment; at least until we get rid of Clara Tripp.'

'What exactly do you mean by that?' she demanded, sounding frightened.

'I think we should stop meeting for a while.'

'Are you chucking me?' she asked, her voice trembling.

Oh, God, she was so damned clingy, he thought, but he said, 'Of course not.'

'Are you sure?'

Her constant need for reassurance was testing his patience to the point where he felt like strangling her. 'Quite sure!' he said through gritted teeth. 'We don't want to take any chances with things as they are, do we? If Clara Tripp does decide to open her big mouth we need to be in a position to deny it and have them all believe us. Because we are jumpy we could get careless and someone else might see us. If Clara did, so could others.'

'Mm, I suppose so.' She sighed miserably. Looking at her down-turned mouth and slouching shoulders, he wondered what he had ever seen in her.

After Vincent's threats Clara was wary, expecting something untoward to happen at any moment. But day followed day and life went on as before, filled with hard work and increasing understanding of the management of an orchard. Although there were no more confrontations with the guilty couple, Hester still made her dislike of Clara obvious, and Vincent more or less ignored her, saying the occasional word to her over dinner presumably so that the family wouldn't suspect that there was bad feeling between them.

Clara guessed that Vincent was just biding his time. She didn't know when it would come but she was certain that something unpleasant lay ahead of her. She could just leave; that would be her most sensible course. But her spirit wouldn't allow her to be bullied out of Brierley.

* * *

Mabel Fenner was a plainly dressed woman who wore her best on Sundays and never made any effort apart from that. The only social event of her year was the annual dinner of a fruit growers' association that her husband belonged to. Socialising wasn't for her and she hated going, but the other wives would be there so she felt duty bound to go along and support him.

She had a few suitable dresses, which she rotated, and rarely bought anything new. This year she dragged out a black taffeta floor-length gown and spent more time than usual doing her hair in the dressing-table mirror. This was the only occasion on which she wore jewellery apart from her wedding ring, and when she was satisfied with her appearance she reached for her jewellery box to add the finishing touches. She didn't have a great deal in there but what she did have were very expensive diamond pieces that she had inherited from her mother.

Staring into the opened box, she couldn't believe her eyes. It was empty! Not a single item of jewellery lay there; just a few shirt buttons. In a state of shock, she got up and rushed from the room and down the stairs into the sitting room where her husband, smartly dressed in a dark suit, was waiting for her.

'My jewellery has gone,' she burst out emotionally. 'Every single bit. Oh, John. We must have been burgled.'

'How can we have been burgled when the place hasn't been left empty?' he asked, rising from his chair and going over to her in concern. 'You must have put the jewellery away somewhere else the last time you wore it.'

'I haven't had it out of the box since last time we went to the dinner,' she told him. 'Someone has taken it, John.'

'When did you last look in the box?'

'Last week when I was looking for some pins,' she told him. 'I keep a few odds and ends in there as well as the jewellery. Everything was there then.'

'It's valuable stuff, too,' he said, worried now.

'It has sentimental value too.'

'Yes, of course,' he said kindly. 'Let's go upstairs and look for it together.'

'We can do but it isn't there,' she told him. 'There's nothing wrong with my eyesight and I know what I saw.'

The instant Clara heard about Mabel's missing jewellery, she knew that Vincent had made his move and the blame was going to be placed firmly on her shoulders.

She had been asked to go downstairs where the family was gathered, the Fenners senior having cancelled their night out. 'We wanted you to join us because we wondered if you had seen anything suspicious,' said John Fenner gravely, having explained the situation to her. 'Someone must have got in without us knowing and taken the jewellery.'

'No, I haven't seen anything unusual at all,' she told him, feeling so tense that she suspected she sounded guilty.

'I don't see how anyone could have got in,' said Charlie. 'Mum hardly ever goes out so the house isn't left un-occupied.'

'That's true. The thief must have slipped upstairs while we were outside working and your mother was busy in the kitchen,' said John. 'The doors are left open at this time of the year.' He paused thoughtfully. 'It's possible one of the delivery people somehow managed to get in without your mother noticing; the grocery boy for instance.'

'Nobody from that shop would do such a thing,' claimed

Mabel, aghast at the suggestion. 'I've been dealing with them for years and trust them completely.'

'In that case it must have been someone who was already here,' said Hester, choosing her moment carefully and throwing an accusing look in Clara's direction.

All eyes turned to Clara and she felt her face burn because their thoughts were almost tangible.

'Don't be so ridiculous,' said Charlie angrily. 'That's a terrible thing to suggest.'

'Not so terrible,' Vincent put in. 'She is the only non-family member living in the house.'

'Take that back,' snapped Charlie. 'Can't you see you're embarrassing the girl?'

'I don't like what you're suggesting either, Vincent,' added his father. 'It really isn't on.'

'I'm only pointing out the facts,' said Vincent. 'Think about it. We are all family so obviously can be trusted. Clara is virtually a stranger and from a poor background. She'd get a very good price in London for your sparklers, Mum.'

'Yeah,' Hester agreed. 'She's trying to get the money together to get married. That's why she's taken the jewellery.'

'Shut up, Hester.' Charlie looked at Clara. 'I'm so sorry about this. I'm ashamed of them for saying such things.'

'It isn't your fault, Charlie,' she assured him, then looked at the others. 'I'd rather you didn't talk about me as if I wasn't here. I can assure you that I have not taken Mrs Fenner's jewellery. I am not a thief. But why not search my room if there's any doubt about it.'

In her heart she knew that the jewellery was going to be found there. But when they all trooped upstairs and it was

discovered in her suitcase under the bed, she was quite unpre-
pared for the intensity of her reaction. She wanted to shout
the truth and physically attack Hester and Vincent. But this
would hurt and humiliate Charlie, and Vincent would make
sure she wasn't believed. He was no fool; he would have
made provision for that eventuality. She was, as far as the
others were concerned, an outsider here.

'I knew she'd done it,' said Hester victoriously, 'the dirty
rotten thief. We should call the police right away.'

'No, there'll be no need for that,' said Vincent, who
didn't want it taken further for fear of recriminations if
the professionals became involved. 'So long as she's
dismissed and sent packing, that will be enough.'

'At least give her the chance to defend herself,' said
Charlie furiously.

'Go on then, Clara, talk yourself out of this one,' invited
Hester in a mocking tone.

'Yeah, what have you to say for yourself?' added Vincent.

Managing to hang on to her composure and her dignity,
Clara looked at Mabel and said, 'I didn't take your jewellery,
Mrs Fenner. I wouldn't do a thing like that and if you
knew me better you would know that. But I realise that
the evidence against me is damning so I will leave first
thing in the morning.'

'Yes, I think that will be the best thing,' she said
brusquely.

'I am very disappointed in you, Clara,' said John, looking
sad. 'It's the last thing I expected of you.'

'The bare-faced cheek of it,' Hester ranted convinc-
ingly, looking at Clara. 'Coming into decent people's homes
and stealing from them. You obviously stashed the jewellery
away in your case to take with you next time you went

home for the weekend. If Mabel hadn't happened to be going out tonight none of us would have been any the wiser.'

'Stop it, Hester, for goodness' sake,' said Charlie, his voice rising. 'Just leave her alone.'

'Why are you sticking up for her?' Hester demanded. 'Fancy her yourself, do you?'

'Stop it, all of you,' intervened John Fenner. 'Clara has told us she will leave in the morning so there is nothing more to be said. Don't make her feel worse than she already does.'

'Thank you, Mr Fenner,' said Clara politely. 'If you'll all go now I'll start packing ready for the morning.'

And with a grateful smile towards Charlie for his support, she closed the door on them. Tears were burning at the back of her eyes but she was far too angry to cry.

'Did you have anything to do with Mum's jewellery being found in Clara's suitcase, Hester?' Charlie asked back at the cottage.

'What on earth makes you say that?' she demanded, terrified he had somehow discovered the truth. 'Why would I do a thing like that?

'I'm not quite sure,' he said slowly, giving her a long look. 'Maybe because you've never had a good word to say for Clara the whole time we have known her. You've either ignored her or sniped at her and you didn't want her to come here this time. Possibly you're afraid that I might start to fancy her if she's here any longer so you decided to get rid of her.'

She was so relieved he was barking up the wrong tree that it was a few moments before she retaliated. 'Your imagination is running away with you if you think I give a damn about who you might fancy,' she said at last. 'The woman took your mother's jewellery, so get used to it and stop making up silly stories to feed your vanity.'

He stared at her, seeing the glint in her eyes and the slight smile on her full lips that belied her look of outrage. He had a strong suspicion that she was somehow involved in the jewellery theft but knew she would never admit it. One thing he was certain of was that Clara Tripp had been set up.

Much to Clara's amazement Charlie knocked on her door early the next morning to say that he was going to drive her to the station and there was to be no argument about it.

'You're not going to be popular with the rest of your family for driving a thief to the station,' she said to him as he waited with her on the damp platform at Tunbridge Wells. 'They would have preferred me to walk, especially as it's raining cats and dogs. A three-mile walk in a down-pour might go some way towards the punishment they think I deserve.'

'I don't believe you did it,' he said. 'I don't know how or why the jewellery got into your suitcase but I know that you didn't put it there.'

'That means a lot to me, Charlie,' she said, realising at that moment that none of the rest of it mattered as long as he believed in her. She was outraged at being blamed for something she didn't do, of course, and disappointed not to be able to finish her stint at Brierley doing work she enjoyed, but it was Charlie's opinion that mattered. All else was incidental, compared to his friendship and respect.

'I'm glad,' he said, looking at her searchingly. 'I'm sorry to lose you. You're a natural for our sort of work. I would shout the others down and insist that you stay, but they'd make your life such a misery you're probably better off going back to London.'

'I wouldn't want to stay anyway, not now,' she said. 'It's all been ruined. At the moment I feel as if I never want to go back to Brierley again.'

'That's understandable,' he said. 'It makes me feel ashamed of my family.'

'What else could they do in the light of the evidence?' she pointed out.

'Why didn't you fight back?'

'What could I have said except that I didn't do it?'

'I suppose you're right,' he said sadly.

'Anyway, it's all in the past now,' she said, looking down the line to see the train on its way in. 'I'll go back home and get on with my real life.'

'I hope you'll be able to get a job,' he said.

'I'll get something, don't worry.'

The noise of the steam engine was deafening as it drew in and came to a halt, the doors banging all along the train as people alighted and others got on. He lifted her suitcase on to the train.

'Goodbye, Clara,' he said, giving her a gentle hug and kissing her on the cheek. 'You take care of yourself now, and give my love to Eva.'

'Will do,' she said, looking at him and seeing her own tears reflected in his eyes. 'You do the same.'

Neither of them said any more. She turned and got on to the train and went to the far side of the compartment so as not to have to wave to him out of the window. It felt wrong that she was leaving. She belonged here with Charlie; not in London with Arnold. As the train drew out of the station she knew she must be strong and face up to life as it was, not how she wished it could be.

What Charlie was still trying to come to terms with as he walked back to the car in the rain was why he had ever let Clara go. Yes, he had been traumatised after the war and had had no idea of her address, but he could have found her instead of letting himself be persuaded into marriage with Hester. It was one of those mistakes that came back to haunt him every day of his life.

He stood in the heavy rain for a few moments, so deeply immersed in thought that he hardly noticed he was getting soaked. After a while, he got into the car and drove back to Brierley and a marriage he regretted more with every day that passed.

Chapter Nine

'Come on, Clara, let's have all the details. We're waiting to hear all about it,' urged Frank Tripp when the family were gathered round the table for the evening meal. 'Your mother tells me that you're home for good. What brought you back to us so soon?'

'It just didn't work out, Dad,' she replied, having already been quizzed individually by the other family members about her early return. Their deep concern for each other overruled any prompting of tact and meant that privacy was all but impossible in this house. 'I didn't find the work as enjoyable as I expected so it was mutually agreed that I quit.' She forced a smile and made a joke of it. 'I was missing you lot too much, that's the truth of it. Why wouldn't I when all you do is fire questions at me?'

'As long as you're all right, that's what matters.' Flo cast her eye round the table. 'So leave her alone, all of you, and stop giving her the third degree.'

Lies didn't come easily to Clara but were necessary in this particular instance. If she were to tell the family the truth about her departure from Brierley, an angry deputation would head for Kent with all guns blazing to seek justice for her. Even if she were to omit the part about Hester and Vincent's affair her family was still likely to accuse the Fenners of unfair dismissal or even gross defamation of character, in which they would be correct. Besides, there were Eva's feelings to consider. So she deemed it wise to give them a fictional version and put the whole thing behind her.

'Anyway, what's been going on here while I've been away?' she enquired brightly. 'Anything exciting?'

'Cuddy is singing a solo in front of the whole school at assembly one day next week,' Flo announced.

'Well done!' Clara smiled at her brother. 'I'm so proud of you.'

'We're getting him a pretty frock to wear for the occasion,' said Frank with a wry grin.

'Da-ad,' objected the young boy, colouring up.

'Now Frank, let's have none of that sort of silly teasing,' Flo said sternly.

'No, let's not,' agreed Clara firmly. 'Now that I'm back you'd better watch yourself. Any mickey taking aimed in my little brother's direction will be severely dealt with by me personally.'

All eyes were on Cuddy, who diverted attention from himself by making an announcement. 'The really big news around here is that Eva is in love,' he said.

'Yes, she said something about that in her last letter.' Clara looked at Eva. 'Still going strong then?'

Flo answered for her, smiling towards the radiant Eva. 'We've got love's young dream here. She's on cloud nine and hardly knows what day of the week it is.'

'So, tell me more, Eva,' Clara urged.

194

'His name is Gordon. He's nineteen, nice natured and very good looking.'

'Is that right, everybody?' asked Clara, looking round at them all. 'Is he as handsome as she says?'

'He seems a nice enough young man, and yes, he is rather easy on the eye,' said Flo.

'Never mind what he looks like, he's got a steady job; that's the important thing,' said Frank, typically down to earth.

'What does he do?'

'He works in one of those new menswear shops that have opened in the West End,' replied her father. 'Cheap off-the-peg suits are their speciality. Ordinary working men are buying suits these days so it isn't a bad line of business to be in. Regular money and good prospects for Gordon; that counts for a lot, especially these days with so many men out of work.'

'I take it you all approve, then?' said Clara, looking round.

Sydney shrugged. 'He's just a bloke,' he said, sounding disinterested.

'He seems all right,' added Cuddy. 'We hardly know him, though. As soon as he comes to call for Eva she whisks him off so that they can start kissing and cuddling. They're really soppy. Ugh, it's 'orrible.'

'Oh, Cuddy,' said Eva, blushing. 'Don't be so awful.'

'Take no notice of him, Eva,' said Flo. 'He'll be doing the same thing himself before very long.'

'Never *ever*,' declared Cuddy.

Before the conversation could develop further, Sydney said, 'Are you going to leave that potato, Cuddy?'

'No.'

'Oh, go on,' he coaxed. 'You're only a sprat. You don't need as much food as I do.'

'Leave your brother's food alone, Sydney,' Flo ordered. 'If you're still hungry you'll have to fill up on bread.'

'All right, Mum,' said Sydney. 'Don't get your knickers in a twist.'

Clara was still desperately hurt and angry about what had happened at Brierley, but she thanked God for the love and honesty here at home. Any sort of betrayal within this family was unthinkable.

'So, how is everybody at Brierley?' Eva asked later that evening. They were in the bedroom, Clara finishing her unpacking while Eva put on some lipstick ready to go out with her boyfriend.

'They're all fine.'

'I guessed you didn't give them the whole story downstairs,' said Eva. 'Was it Hester who made you quit? I know what a nasty cow she can be.'

'No, it was nothing like that.' Clara didn't want to spoil things for Eva while she was so happy. 'Charlie sends his love, by the way.' She worried suddenly that Charlie might tell his sister what had happened in his next letter, but comforted herself with the thought that he too would try to spare Eva's feelings as much as he could.

Eva smiled. 'Dear Charlie. He's the only decent one out of the lot of them. Except for Dad, of course.'

'So tell me more about this romance of yours,' said Clara, changing the subject.

'Oh, it's wonderful and a bit agonising too at times,' she sighed, too full of her own affairs to be overly curious about Clara's untimely departure from Brierley. 'I want to be with him all the time and I can't stop thinking about him. When I'm with him I'm so happy I never want it to end, and I always feel sad when it does.'

'You *have* got it bad.'

She nodded. 'Oh, yeah, absolutely head over heels. I ache to be with him so much when he isn't around, it's like a physical pain.' She looked at Clara. 'Still, I suppose you know all about that sort of thing. You must feel the same way about Arnold.'

The remark set Clara thinking. She couldn't remember ever feeling that way about Arnold, even at the beginning. It had been pleasant enough and a relief to have a boyfriend because no one wants to be on the shelf; she had looked forward to seeing him with pleasurable anticipation. She couldn't recall the intensity of emotion that Eva described but she said, 'Yes, of course.'

'It almost makes you feel ill at times, doesn't it?' Eva went on. 'You know, when you have to leave them.'

'Arnold and I have been together for a long time,' Clara reminded her. 'Obviously the excitement lessens when you get more used to each other.'

'I can't imagine that ever happening to Gordon and me.'

'No, I don't suppose you can at this stage.' Clara suddenly felt afraid for her friend. In losing her heart so completely she had made herself acutely vulnerable.

'He'll be coming to call for me in a minute and butter-flies are fluttering like mad in my stomach,' said Eva, combing her blond hair in the dressing-table mirror.

'Be careful, Eva.'

Eva looked at her, turning pink. 'Oh, Clara, really! Are you suggesting . . . ?'

'No! Not that . . . well, not that in particular. Just be careful in general, that's all.'

'Of course I will,' said Eva breezily. Clara knew she wasn't going to take the slightest bit of notice.

'It's lucky for me that it didn't work out, isn't it?' Arnold said the following evening. She had given him the same version of events that she had presented to her family. 'It's selfish, I know, but I get to have you back and that suits me fine.'

'You are sweet,' she said. 'I think I shall have to finally rid myself of the idea that country life is for me and stay at home.'

'Good idea,' he agreed. 'Let's hope you've got the wanderlust out of your system now.'

Her words had been uttered lightly to please Arnold, but she knew she would always have rural leanings. A part of her, also, couldn't let Brierley go because Charlie was there. But this was her life; here with Arnold. 'Yeah, let's hope so,' she said.

'Don't worry if you have trouble finding a job,' he told her. 'I'll help you out financially so that you can pay your way at home until you get fixed up.'

She was instinctively opposed to the idea, but it was very considerate of him to offer. 'It's really good of you, Arnold, but I'm hoping it won't take me too long to find work, especially as I'm prepared to do anything that's going. I shall go out cleaning again if I have to, but I'm going to the West End tomorrow to see if there are any waitresses' jobs about.'

'Well, you only have to ask if you need money, or anything at all,' he told her.

'Thank you.' He really was being very good to her, which only increased her longing for escape. 'So how have you been keeping while I was away?'

'Not so dusty, though I missed you, of course.'

'I should think so too,' she said, smiling. 'Not working too hard, I hope?'

'I'm still doing overtime when it's there,' he told her. 'But I'm young and strong. I can take it.'

She nodded, trying to look interested. Far from aching to be with him, as Eva so eloquently put it, she couldn't wait to get away.

'Do you fancy going out somewhere tonight, sweetheart?' he asked. 'We could go to the flicks if you like.'

'That would be nice. Thank you, Arnold.'

He really was bending over backwards to be nice to her and he was a thoroughly decent man. She was very fortunate to have him, she reminded herself yet again.

Clara really was the loveliest girl, thought Arnold, with her dark eyes and shiny hair, and he was lucky to have her. Despite his assertions to the contrary, her coming back early from Kent had made things a bit awkward for him. But he'd just have to keep his wits about him. Fortunately she wasn't a demanding or possessive woman and it would never occur to her to doubt his word, so he should be able to work things out without too much trouble. He really did love her, in his way, and would hate to lose her.

'If you are so unhappy being married to me, why don't you just pack your bags and leave?' suggested Charlie impulsively, after Hester had finished another tirade of abuse.

'Leave?'

'That's what I said.'

'You mean go for good?' It was the first time Charlie had ever suggested such a thing and it made Hester realise with something of a shock that she needed to soften towards him or she could find herself without a home and a meal ticket if she couldn't persuade Vincent – who was really dragging his feet – to do right by her.

'Yes, for good. No one is forcing you to stay, though you'd think so to hear you talk. You never stop complaining about me, so why don't you get out of here and give us both some peace? You won't get any resistance from me, I can promise you that.'

'Oh, Charlie,' she said with feigned contrition. 'Have I really been so bad that you want to throw me out?'

'Don't twist my words, Hester. I would never throw you out,' he said sharply. 'But if you wanted to go I wouldn't try to stop you, put it that way. I would, however, consider all obligations towards you at an end the minute you walked out of the door.'

Hester was really worried now. Maybe she had pushed her luck too far with him. 'Perhaps I have been a bit difficult lately,' she admitted, trying to sound remorseful.

'Difficult,' he exploded. 'You've been downright unbearable.'

'Have I really? Oh, dear, I'm sorry,' she said meekly. 'I'll try to make it up to you, I promise.'

He stared at her in disbelief, having expected a vicious outburst from her. *Sorry* wasn't a word he normally associated with Hester. But he didn't want her to make amends. He just wanted her out of his life for ever. He couldn't have Clara but he certainly didn't want Hester. But it wouldn't be right to make her leave against her will. As her husband he had a duty towards her.

'There'll be no need for any grand gestures,' he said. 'If you don't want to be here then leave; if you want to stay, do so, but stop moaning and being so critical of me. Enough is enough, and I've reached my limit.'

'I'll be good in future,' she said seductively, coming over to where he was sitting in an armchair and leaning over as though wanting to put her arms round him.

'Not now, Hester,' he said quickly, pushing her away. 'I said there was no need for any grand gestures and I meant it. I just want an end to all this complaining and bickering.'

'Oh.' She moved back, her mouth open ready to emit some strong words in return for his rejection of her. But she held back, mindful of what she had to lose if she acted too hastily. Yes, she did want to leave, but when she was ready and not a minute before. She would save her energy for Vincent, who had to be persuaded to get the money they needed to get away from here. 'Shall I make us some tea?' she suggested sweetly.

'Good idea,' he said and continued reading his newspaper, ostensibly calm despite the turmoil within him.

'How are things at home with that girl Eva now?' enquired Tub when he and Sydney were queuing up for chips at the fish shop. 'Is she still going out with that Gordon bloke?'

'I'll say she is; she's mad about him. Anyone would think he was a bloomin' film star to hear her talk. He's only an ordinary feller . . . well, I suppose a girl might think he's good-looking but I can't see anything special about him at all.'

Tub laughed. 'I'd worry about you if you did,' he quipped.

'I suppose you would,' said Sydney, far too intent on the subject to see the joke. 'He's got this poncy job in the West End in a menswear shop. The way they all go on about it at home you'd think he was the Prime Minister.'

'Still, I suppose as she's out more, she's not under your feet so much in the house,' suggested Tub.

'There is that, but then there's all the worry of her coming home late,' said Sydney.

'How is that a problem for you?'

'How can you help worrying when an innocent girl like her is out late in London?'

'Lover boy brings her home to the door, though, doesn't he?'

'Of course.'

'What have you got to worry about then?' Tub asked. 'She isn't your responsibility; you don't even like her.'

'I dunno what it is, mate, but I can't get to sleep until I've heard her come in; probably because you can hear her close the door and come up the stairs and I know that that will wake me up so I'm too on edge to sleep. It's a bloomin' nuisance – it means I'm tired when it's time to get up in the morning, and all because of her. Flamin' women. It was bad enough with Clara's wet stockings hanging up in the kitchen to dry and getting in your way every time you went by; now we've got Eva's there as well.'

'Talking about girls,' said Tub, 'we've got a cracker just started at work at the factory, in the office.'

'Oh yeah?' said Sydney, looking at his pal with interest, his attention diverted from his own problems. 'So what are you gonna do about it then?'

'Nothin', of course.'

'Why not?'

'I would have thought that was obvious. She wouldn't look at someone like me.'

'Stop doing yourself down,' said Sydney. 'I've told you before about that. You're in with as much chance as the next man.'

'I'm fat.'

'So what?'

'Girls don't go for fat boys.'

'You're far too sensitive,' said Sydney as the queue moved up so that they were actually in the shop and surrounded by the tantalising aroma of frying. 'I'm not fat and I don't have a girlfriend, do I?'

'Only because you're not bothered,' said Tub.

'There is that, I suppose,' Sydney admitted.

The assistant called out, 'Next please?'

And they both forgot about the non-existence of their love lives and wallowed in their glorious treat smothered in salt and vinegar.

Unable to find employment in the West End, Clara managed to secure a position as a waitress in a local café. It was much less grand than Taylor's: just a basic workmen's café. The job was more that of an all-round assistant, serving at the counter as well as waiting at table and a certain amount of cleaning. It was hard work but that was no problem for Clara, and at least she had a wage coming in.

As summer passed and the glorious autumn colours darkened towards winter and frosts and fogs abounded, the memory of the events at Brierley began to hurt less as she determinedly engrossed herself in the routine of her London life. She and Arnold set their wedding date for August, which gave everybody plenty of time to get things arranged. They booked the church and her mother reserved the hall for the reception. Clara hoped that by the time the date came round she would be feeling more enthusiastic.

In early December Clara was distracted from her own affairs when Eva came home one night in tears saying that it was all over between her and Gordon.

'What happened?' asked Clara in their bedroom, where Eva had fled as soon as she got in. 'Did you have a tiff?'

'No, there was nothing like that at all,' she sobbed. 'I thought he seemed a bit offhand with me all evening but wasn't too worried; then when he brought me home and we were outside he told me, out of the blue, that he was very sorry but he'd met someone else and didn't want to see me again. I begged him over and over to change his mind. I was crying and everything but he just left.'

'Oh, that's awful,' said Clara sympathetically. 'I'm so sorry.'

'What's wrong with me, Clara, that he doesn't want to see me again?' Eva wept.

'There's nothing wrong with you at all, Eva, I promise,' Clara said gently.

'There must be,' she sobbed. 'I must have done something wrong. It must be my fault.'

'It isn't your fault,' Clara tried to assure her. 'These things happen, especially when you're young. It's just the way life is. I've heard that some men like to play the field before they settle down. Gordon is still young and immature. He's probably not ready to settle down.'

'I can't bear it, Clara,' Eva cried. 'I hurt so much inside. I can't imagine life without him.'

Clara cradled her in her arms and let her have her cry out. Her own feelings for Charlie meant she knew a little of what Eva was going through, but she lacked the experience that might have helped her to advise and comfort her friend. 'I don't know any more about these things than you do,' she said. 'But I'm sure the pain will pass after a while. Nothing lasts for ever.'

But Eva was inconsolable. She cried herself dry then lay awake for most of the night, dozing then waking and remembering and starting to cry again. Clara didn't sleep much either. She was far too upset on Eva's behalf. Her instinct was to go and find Gordon and give him a thorough trouncing, but what good would it do? Nothing she or anyone could do would make him feel for Eva as she felt for him. Clara suspected that her friend might have read too much into the romance too early and her intensity had frightened him off. Healing was just a question of time. All Clara could do was to offer her wholehearted comfort and support.

Christmas and New Year passed and still Eva showed no sign of recovery.

'She doesn't seem to be getting any better at all, does she?' said Flo in concern, one evening in early January when Eva had left most of her meal and gone straight to bed yet again. 'She'll waste away altogether if she doesn't start eating properly soon. She barely ate a mouthful tonight.'

'She is looking very drawn,' agreed Clara, drying the dishes as her mother washed them. 'I've tried everything I know to bring her out of it. I've encouraged her to talk if she wants to, I've let her be quiet; I've even suggested we go to the flicks to take her mind off it for a while, but she just wants to go to bed and cry.'

'Her eyes are almost black underneath.'

'I know, and I'm at a loss to know how to help, I really am, Mum.'

'We all are, love,' said Flo. 'I was wondering if we should contact her family. What do you think?'

'Apart from her father there's only Charlie who gives a damn about her and I don't want to worry him unless it's absolutely necessary,' Clara said. 'If she doesn't soon pick up I suppose we ought to let him know, but I don't think there's anything he can do to help her at the moment. She doesn't seem to want anyone with her. She wants to be on her own all the time.'

'And that can't be good for her,' Flo fretted. 'Too much solitude causes morbidity, so they say.'

'I think that's probably true,' agreed Clara. 'She was so happy here in London too, until this.'

'She was such a chatty little thing; now she barely says a word when she's at home.'

'As if she hasn't had enough rejection in her life from that mother of hers. This is the last thing she needs. I suppose it was one knock too many and she just can't cope.'

'The poor girl; it's such a shame,' said Flo sadly. 'I only wish there was something we could do to help.'

'How's that Eva girl now?' asked Tub. 'Is she getting over her broken heart?'

'No, not at all; in fact she's in a shocking state,' Sydney told him, sipping his half-pint of bitter. The two young men had recently turned eighteen so were able to go to the pub for a chat now. 'She's in bed before eight o'clock every night. Hardly eats enough to keep a fly alive. Everybody at home is very worried about her.'

'Poor thing.'

'Yeah, she is a poor thing at the moment.'

'Still, at least she isn't keeping you awake now that she isn't out late,' said Tub helpfully.

'I'd sooner that than see her like this,' confided Sydney. 'I hate to see her so miserable.'

'Why should you care? She isn't even your sister.'

'I don't know why, mate. It's strange,' he said thoughtfully. 'There's something very sort of delicate about her that makes you feel sorry for her. I'd like to go and sort that Gordon out for what he's done to her, but we don't know where he lives.'

'I reckon you're sweet on her; that's what all this is about,' Tub said with a grin.

'How can you be sweet on someone who lives in the same house and is one of the family?' Sydney demanded. 'It would be like fancying your sister.'

'She isn't your sister though, is she?'

'No, but she might as well be,' Sydney insisted, his voice rising. 'She's just a girl who lives with us. If someone in the house is miserable, it affects everybody. That's all there is to it.'

'All right, don't get narked. I was only making a suggestion.'

'Well, don't talk out of your backside,' said Sydney hotly. 'You shouldn't come out with such disgusting suggestions.'

'I'll get us another half, shall I?' said Tub diplomatically, and got up to walk over to the bar.

★　★　★

It had just turned eight o'clock and Eva was curled up in bed sobbing her heart out. She simply didn't seem able to stop. Since Gordon had jilted her she had been plunged into a new dark world. She was used to emotional pain; to feeling worthless and rejected. But this was worse than anything she had ever experienced before. Growing up at Brierley she had often felt isolated, distanced from everything and everyone around her. But losing Gordon was almost physical; she felt grazed inside and wanted him back more than she had ever wanted anything, even her mother's approval. If she knew where he lived she would go round there and beg him to take her back – never mind her pride – but he'd never given her his address.

To make things worse, her trauma had caused her to make mistakes at work and she'd been in trouble there. There was a tight feeling in her stomach that interfered with her concentration and made her feel as though even the smallest task was beyond her; when that eased up she was too exhausted to function properly.

Vaguely, she was aware that people were trying to help her but she couldn't reach them. They were on the other side of a grey, impenetrable fog which surrounded her and cut them off. All she wanted was to go to sleep and never wake up.

'So, Arnold, this time next year you'll be one of the family,' said Flo. He had come to call for Clara and the two of them were sitting in the parlour with the family. Sydney was out with Tub and Cuddy was reading a comic.

'He's already one of us,' Frank reminded her.

'I know, but it will be legal then.'

'And very honoured I'll be too,' said Arnold.

'We've got the church and the hall booked, that's the main thing,' Flo went on. 'It's a little bit too early to do anything else.'

'Getting the wedding dress will be the best part,' said Clara, entering into the spirit of things.

'I think you're supposed to say that becoming my wife is the best bit,' Arnold chortled.

'I was referring to the preparations,' she said, flustered.

He grinned. 'Only joking.'

'There'll be a lot to do when it gets a bit nearer,' said Flo, looking delighted at the prospect.

'You're not going to be one of those mothers of the bride who drives everyone mad, I hope, Mum,' said Clara.

'I shall want everything to be done just right if that's what you mean,' her mother made clear. 'I want every detail to be perfect for my only daughter's wedding day and Gawd help anyone who stands in my way.'

'Heaven help us all,' said Clara.

'Hear, hear,' chuckled Frank.

'I won't have to be one of those pageboy things, will I?' asked Cuddy worriedly.

'No, we'll spare you that,' Clara assured him. 'You're a bit too old for that job.'

'You'll have Eva as a bridesmaid, though, won't you, dear?' said Flo.

'Oh, yes. She'll definitely be one of them,' Clara replied. 'I haven't decided on the others yet.'

'How is Eva now?' Arnold enquired. 'Clara tells me she still isn't over that business with Gordon.'

'No, I'm afraid she isn't,' said Flo gravely. 'She isn't herself at all and we're very worried about her.'

'Blimey, that's a bit of a swine,' he said sympathetically.

'If you want me to go and give that Gordon bloke a kicking, I'll do it right away, no trouble.'

'Sydney has already offered to do that several times,' said Flo. 'But that sort of thing won't help. Anyway, we don't know where he lives.'

'Oh well, anything else you need just give me a shout. I'm always ready to help.'

'Thank you, Arnold. You're a good lad.'

'I'm almost one of the family now,' he said. 'So your problems are mine too.'

'You've got a good 'un there, Clara,' her father said. 'He's really one of us.'

'Pity young Eva wasn't so lucky in her choice,' added her mother.

Arnold was being exceptionally helpful and co-operative lately, Clara observed. He'd always been easy-going but not as kind and attentive as this; it was strange. Never the romantic type, he used to sometimes take her for granted but now he couldn't seem to do enough for her, especially since they had set the date for the wedding. It must be because he wanted them to be married so much. The thought should have filled her with pleasure, so why did she feel so oppressed?

Eva woke up with a start and knew from the silence in the house that it was early. The room was in darkness and Clara was still sleeping. Waking up for Eva was agony every day. After an initial blank second without pain, she remembered and blackness engulfed her. Today she felt particularly hopeless. She wanted to cry out for someone to help her but no one could, except Gordon, and he didn't want her. The thought was torture but she couldn't stop doing it to herself. How could she get through another day feeling like this?

In a sudden moment of clarity she made a decision and immediately felt better. She got out of bed quietly, careful not to wake Clara, pulled on her clothes, took some coins from her purse and crept downstairs and out of the silent house, closing the front door carefully behind her.

Barely aware of the bitter cold eating into her bones, she walked along the frosty street towards the Green, passed the silent shops around it – the closed coffee house, the bicycle shop, the laundry, the general store – and headed for the Underground station.

There weren't many people about at this time of the morning but the ticket office was open for the workers on early shifts so she bought a ticket and walked to the edge of the platform to wait for a train to come in. It didn't matter which; any one would do. With her hands in her pockets and her head down, she stood motionless until at last she heard the sound she was waiting for and looked towards the approaching train. Thank God. Just seconds now and the pain would be gone. As the noise of the engine grew louder she knew it was time . . .

'Where's Eva, Mum?' asked Clara, hurrying downstairs.

'She's not up yet.'

'She's not in her bed so she must be.'

'I haven't seen her or heard her come down,' said Flo, looking puzzled.

'She must be in the lav then.'

'No, your father's out there.'

'In that case she must have gone somewhere while we were all asleep.'

'At this time of day? Why would she do a thing like that?'

'I've no idea, but she isn't herself at the moment, is she?'

'But where would she have gone at such an hour?'

'Who knows, Mum?'

'Home to Kent perhaps?'

'No, she might be traumatised but she wouldn't go there. I'm absolutely certain of that,' declared Clara. 'I'll go upstairs and see if her clothes have gone.'

She tore up the stairs and was down almost at once.

'No, her clothes are still there; just the things she was wearing yesterday and her coat from the hallstand have gone.'

'Woss goin' on?' enquired Sydney, coming into the room bleary-eyed in his pyjamas with his hair standing on end from bed. 'All this noise. People rushing up and down the stairs.'

'Eva's missing.'

'What do you mean? How can she be missing in a small house like this?'

'She isn't in the house,' said Clara sharply.

'Blimey,' gasped Sydney, wide awake now. 'I'd better go and look for her.'

'Put some clothes on first,' advised his mother as he headed for the front door in his pyjamas.

'Oh yeah, of course,' he said distractedly, and turned round and made his way towards the stairs.

'I'll come with you to look for her,' said Clara, following him upstairs to get dressed. 'In the state she's been in lately, who knows what she might do?'

★ ★ ★

'Any luck?' asked Flo when Clara and Sydney returned.

'Not a sign,' said Sydney. 'We've looked all over but she's vanished into thin air.'

'We've been to the police station to report her missing. The officer told us that they'll make some inquiries but because she's free to come and go as she pleases they can't give it priority, not until she's been gone for longer,' Clara explained. 'He seemed to think that she'll probably turn up; people usually do, he said.'

'The copper we spoke to had only just come on duty,' added Sydney, sounding peeved, 'and he seemed more interested in doing his paperwork than getting a search organised.'

'She's only been gone for a matter of hours, Sydney,' his sister reminded him. 'You can't expect the police to drop everything and put on a massive search when they have other perhaps more serious things to deal with.'

'But people don't go out in the middle of the night if they're in their right mind. Which to me means this is very serious.'

'We don't know that it was the middle of the night when she went, do we?' Clara pointed out. 'She could have gone out just before I woke up.'

'It's still a very strange thing to do.'

'It certainly is,' agreed his mother. 'How would it help to go out in the cold, that's what I want to know?'

'I suppose she could have woken up, felt a bit depressed and gone out for some fresh air to clear her head,' suggested Clara, trying hard not to panic.

'I suppose that's possible.' Flo wasn't convinced.

'Why hasn't she come back then if that's all it was?' Sydney wanted to know.

'I admit it isn't looking good,' Clara conceded. 'Anyway, Mum, the policeman took Eva's details and our address in case they hear anything.'

'Well, there's nothing you can do here, so the two of you had better have some breakfast and get off to work,' suggested Flo sensibly. 'You're late as it is. I had a hell of a job getting Cuddy off to school. He didn't want to go until Eva had been found.'

'He's very fond of her,' said Clara. 'But he'll be better off at school rather than moping around here.' She gave Sydney a shrewd look. 'And that goes for you too.'

'I'd rather carry on looking.'

'We don't know where else to look,' his sister reminded him. 'We've been all over the place. Anyway, she could be anywhere by now. It's better that we leave it to the police.'

'Go to work, son,' Flo urged, 'or you'll be in trouble with the boss. Eva will be very upset if you lose your job because of her.'

'She certainly will,' agreed Clara, but she didn't know how she herself was going to do her job with Eva's disappearance on her mind. Where on earth could the girl have gone to? Given the state of her friend's mood lately, the whole thing had a very ominous feel to it indeed.

Chapter Ten

Dismally clad in a dark green smock – standard dress for every patient in this south London mental hospital – Eva was being forcibly detained in a grim ward whose occupants were frighteningly troubled.

'Please let me go home, nurse,' she begged for the umpteenth time. 'There's been a terrible mistake. I shouldn't be here at all. I'm not like the others.'

'How many more times must I tell you to stop pestering me?' snapped the nurse, a burly disciplinarian who was accustomed to dealing with seriously disturbed patients and had very little compassion for attempted suicides like Eva, whom she considered to be nothing more than time wasters. 'I have far more needy people to deal with at the moment than a selfish girl like you.'

'I wasn't going to do it, not in the end,' Eva claimed pleadingly. 'Honest, I really wasn't.'

'Don't tell such lies. A railway worker had to drag you back from the path of an oncoming train,' said the nurse. 'If he hadn't been on the platform and acted with such speed and efficiency, you'd have been splattered all over the railway line now, upsetting a lot of people. You've no right to try and take your own life. God decides when our time comes, not you or I. It's downright disgraceful. And you should be very ashamed of yourself for causing such trouble.'

'I am, very,' she said, genuinely contrite. 'I realised at the last minute that what I was going to do was really bad and I was about to move away from the edge of the platform when the man pulled me back.'

'That's your story,' the nurse sniffed. 'Anyway, it's sinful to even consider such an idea.'

'I'm very sorry.'

'And so you should be.'

'Please can I go home?' Eva asked again. 'Then I'd be out of your way and you wouldn't have me bothering you.'

'If it was up to me, you'd never have been brought here in the first place. I'd have left you to walk the streets after what you tried to do, but people who try to kill themselves are considered to be a danger to themselves and are taken into places like this as a matter of course.'

Just then one of the other patients in the ward emitted a scream of terror; another wandered past Eva's bed and stared at her with wide insane eyes. It was very alarming.

'I shouldn't be here,' declared Eva, her eyes brimming with tears. 'Please let me go.'

'Think you're better than these other poor souls, do you?'

'No, of course not. It's just that I'm not as sick as they are.'

'It isn't for you to be the judge of that,' the nurse informed her briskly. 'That's for the doctor to decide.'

'Can I see him then, to ask him . . . please?'

The nurse opened her wide mouth and emitted a raucous laugh, displaying large yellow teeth. 'So you think the doctors are at your beck and call, do you?'

'No, but—'

'All the doctors here are very busy and one of them will see you when he has the time,' she told her sharply. 'He will decide what is to be done with you. Until then you stay where you are in bed and stop bothering staff who have far more deserving patients than you to attend to.' She took her by the arms and shook her roughly. 'Do you understand?'

'Yes,' she said meekly.

'Yes *nurse*, if you please.'

'Yes nurse,' Eva echoed.

'That's better,' said the woman and turned and marched off down the cheerless ward.

Eva was imbued with fear, shame and a feeling of desolation. The memory of the approaching train terrified her. She had been so close to taking her own life. The blackness that had consumed her and driven her to such an action had been replaced – partly due to her current situation – by a longing for normality; to get out of this place where she felt so alien and be at home with Clara and her family. How could she have been so stupid as to think of throwing herself under a train?

Something she couldn't quite identify had happened to her as her life had hung in the balance. It was as though the terrible realisation of what she was about to do had somehow brought her to her senses. It wasn't that she had lost her nerve on the platform; it was more that she had realised the enormity of her actions.

What happened after someone had dragged her back

from disaster was something of a blur because she'd been so traumatised, weeping so hard her muscles hurt. She remembered being taken into the station office from where she was eventually bundled into an ambulance and brought here, where she had been given a cold bath and ordered to put on this hideous hospital garment.

It was an old, cold, forbidding building and she ached with a feeling of alienation. Of course, it was entirely her own fault that she had ended up here with no way of contacting the Tripps and little chance of being discharged. A sickly smell of urine and carbolic soap hung over the ward. Some of the patients were up and about. An elderly woman shuffled by, leaving a sour-smelling puddle behind her. Another patient then assaulted the poor soul, saying she was a filthy old hag and should be taken away. 'You shouldn't be living among decent people, you stinking old bugger.' She grabbed her and shook her hard. 'Ugh, you make me feel sick.'

'Hey, don't do that,' Eva protested, instinctively getting out of bed and going to the old woman's aid.

'Who asked you to interfere?' demanded the attacker.

'She's old and frail,' Eva pointed out. 'She can't help her personal weaknesses. The nurses should do something to help her.'

The aggressor then turned on Eva, pulling her hair and punching her in the stomach, whereupon Eva screamed and the nurse rushed on to the scene.

'Oh, not you again,' she said to Eva, pulling the other woman away from her. 'I thought I told you to stay in bed until after the doctor has seen you. Instead of that you're out of bed and causing trouble at the first opportunity.'

'I didn't cause—'

'If you carry on like this we'll have to put you into a straitjacket to quieten you down.'

'Oh, no, please . . .'

'Behave yourself then. Go back to bed and stay there until your condition had been assessed.'

'Yes nurse,' she said obediently.

Back in bed she suppressed her tears, beginning to realise that the more emotional she appeared to be, the less chance she had of getting out of there. She felt so desperately alone, she began to wonder if it might have been better if she had gone under the train.

A few days after Eva's disappearance, two policemen came to the Tripps' front door while the family were having breakfast.

'Oh my good Gawd,' gasped Flo, clutching her throat at the sight of them.

'Don't panic, Mum. It might not be bad news,' said Clara, putting a supportive arm round her.

'Are you Clara Tripp?' one of the officers asked.

She nodded.

'We've been making inquiries and have news of the person you reported missing.'

'Oh yes?' She could barely breathe for fear of what they were about to tell her.

'She's safe in south London,' he informed her. 'She's a patient in a mental institution.'

The blow the information might have caused was softened by the relief that Eva was alive. 'Oh, thank you, officer,' said Clara. 'Thank you very much indeed.'

Having explained the circumstances that had led to Eva's confinement, the two men left.

'Oh, the poor thing,' said Flo, with tears in her eyes.

'Yeah, it's awful for her,' agreed Clara. 'I'll go to the hospital as soon as I can.'

'I'll come with you,' said Sydney.

The absolute joy in Eva's eyes when she saw Clara and Sydney helped Clara to come to terms with the terrible sadness of her surroundings: a room full of mental patients sitting around staring ahead of them, some mumbling, others shouting at some unseen enemy, an air of hope-lessness pervading everything. Clara and Sydney were the only visitors even though it was the official visiting time.

'Eva!' said Clara, wrapping her arms around her. 'We've been so worried about you.'

'Sorry I've caused you such trouble,' Eva sobbed, tears streaming down her pallid face. 'Don't let the nurses see me crying. It will go against my being allowed to leave.'

Sydney stepped forward with a clean handkerchief. 'There don't seem to be any nurses about at the moment,' he said, handing it to her, 'so wipe your eyes quickly and no one will be any the wiser.'

'Thank you, Sydney.' She smiled at him. 'It is so good of you to come, both of you.'

He shrugged, colour rising in his cheeks. 'What else would we do when we finally found out where you were? You seemed to have disappeared into thin air.'

'I had no way of letting you know where I was because they won't let me out and I have no writing paper or stamps,' Eva explained. 'I'm so sorry about everything.'

'Coming here was no bother at all, but we were frantic when you went missing,' Clara told her.

Eva bent her head. 'I'm so ashamed,' she confessed, over-burdened with remorse.

'As long as you're all right, that's the important thing.'

'You would have been spared the worry if they'd let me go home from the Tube station instead of bringing me here. But now I'm stuck here until they're sure I won't try anything like that again. I keep telling them that I wasn't going to jump off the platform but they don't seem to believe me.'

'You must have been feeling desperate to have even considered it.'

'Yes, I was.' Eva's lips were dry and sore, her eyes deeply shadowed. 'I wanted to die for a while back then. Now all I want to do is come home with you. Please will you ask them if I can leave with you?'

'We'll certainly do our best,' Clara assured her. 'But are you sure that you're ready? It was a pretty drastic thing you almost did and you have been very depressed for a while.'

'I won't be considering it again. I don't know exactly what has happened to me but it seems as though the shock of what I nearly did cleared my mind somehow, especially when I landed up here.'

'It's enough to frighten the life out of anyone,' said Clara, glancing round the morbid room.

'I'll go and find a nurse right away and get you discharged,' said Sydney, becoming heated. 'We are not leaving you in this miserable old dump.'

'Calm down,' said Clara. 'It might not be as easy as that. We know nothing about this sort of thing.'

Before he had a chance to do anything further there was an interruption. An elderly lady shuffled up to Eva and looked at her pleadingly.

'All right, Ada,' responded Eva, understanding the wordless plea immediately. She stood up and took her arm. 'Try to hang on till we get there if you can.' She gazed at Clara as though fearing she might disappear, and turned her head away from Ada so that the old woman wouldn't hear what was being said. 'I'll have to take her to the toilet, the poor love, or she'll be in dead trouble with nurses and patients alike. The staff beat her if she does it on the floor and the other patients are horrid to her. Will you wait for me while I take her down there? She's a sweet old thing really; she's just old and a bit batty and her family don't want to be bothered with her so she's stuck in here.'

'Of course, we'll wait,' said Clara, impressed by the fact that Eva was making herself useful. Best of all, she was showing compassion for someone the rest of society had rejected, which must mean that her all-consuming preoccupation with Gordon's rejection of herself was fading at last.

Getting Eva discharged from the hospital proved to be more difficult than they expected.

'She seems quite well to me, doctor, and perfectly compos mentis,' declared Clara when, after a lengthy wait and a lot of persuasion, she and Sydney were finally allowed to see a doctor, a thin, serious man with spectacles and a colourless complexion. 'She seems to have learned her lesson and she's only depressed now because she's here and not at home with us. I don't think she'll try anything like that again.'

'Do you have medical qualifications?' he asked with withering sarcasm.

'Of course not . . .'

'Perhaps you'll allow me to be the judge of your friend's condition then,' he said scathingly.

'Yes, I'm sorry,' she responded, duly reprimanded.

'We'll look after her, doctor,' put in Sydney eagerly, 'and keep a close eye on her to make sure she doesn't get so low as to think about suicide again.'

'Your friend's condition isn't something that disappears overnight, you know,' the doctor pointed out. 'We need to get her stabilised before we can think of letting her leave here.'

'You mean you'll keep her sedated so that she's no trouble and leave her to sit about all day with all the other poor souls in there until her spirit is destroyed completely,' said Clara.

He rested his elbows on the desk, his forefingers on his chin. 'We have plenty of people needing the beds so I can assure you that we don't keep patients here unless we have to,' he told her. 'Attempted suicide is a very serious matter.'

'But she didn't attempt it,' Clara pointed out. 'She changed her mind before she was dragged away.'

'We only have her word for that.'

'Look, doctor . . . she had her heart broken by some unfeeling man and that's why she's been depressed; it was her first love,' Clara explained. 'These things take time, but she'll get over it.'

'Yes, I've heard all about the love affair from Eva herself,' he said. 'She has also had a very troubled past and still has a difficult relationship with her mother.'

'But with our family she's happier than she's ever been; she was, that is, until Gordon let her down,' Clara pointed out. 'She wants to be at home with us.'

'I wouldn't recommend a discharge to anyone but a close relative anyway.'

'We're closer to her than her family.'

'I'm sorry, but we have rules to abide by,' he said firmly. 'She was brought in here in a very distressed state and it's my job to make sure that all suicidal tendencies are under control before I can recommend a discharge.'

'We won't let her do anything silly,' said Clara.

'You can't be with her twenty-four hours a day.'

'No, I realise that, but we'll be very diligent when we are with her and look out for any warning signs.'

'It will be my reputation on the line if I make an error of judgement over this. I won't discharge her unless she has some family to go to.'

'Is that why those poor souls out in the ward are trapped in here?' asked Clara, her voice rising. 'Because their families don't want to know about them; because mental illness has such a stigma attached to it and they are ashamed?'

'Sadly, that is true in many cases,' he said, showing a fleeting moment of compassion. 'The behaviour of the mentally ill is difficult to deal with and people outside the medical profession find it hard to cope. All members of our nursing staff are properly trained for every eventuality and there is always a doctor on hand for emergencies. We might seem harsh to people on the outside but a firm hand is needed in a place like this. Without strict discipline the patients would run riot and there would be chaos.'

'So are you saying that we definitely can't take Eva home?' asked Clara, eager to bring the matter to a conclusion.

'I'm saying that I won't let her go at this moment,' he

said. 'You come back with a member of her family and, depending on her condition between then and now, I will reconsider the matter.' He stacked the papers he had been referring to and turned them over to indicate that the interview was at an end. 'Now, if you'll excuse me I have things to attend to.'

'Yes, of course,' said Clara politely, rising to leave. 'Thank you for seeing us.'

'So I shall have to go down to Kent and ask one of the Fenner family to come to London to get Eva out of that place,' Clara told Arnold, having explained Eva's situation to him. 'I can't just leave her there feeling so miserable. I don't want to write or send a telegram – it will be better if I explain the situation personally as it's such a delicate matter.'

'Would you like me to go with you?'

'Oh no,' she said quickly, recalling how economical she had been with the truth about her sudden departure from Brierley. 'Sydney offered to come with me but there's no point in paying for two train fares just to deliver a message.'

'If you're sure, then.'

'I am, but thanks for offering.'

'That's all right,' he said. 'When are you going?'

'Tomorrow. If I go early I won't be too late back. As it's Sunday, I won't have to get time off work but it means I won't be able to see you as usual. Sorry about that.'

'Don't worry about me, sweetheart,' he said, dipping into his pocket for his wallet. 'How much do you need for the train fare?'

'Don't be silly, Arnold. I don't expect you to pay for something like that.'

'I know you don't, but I insist and I don't want any argument about it.'

She looked at him, thinking that he seemed more eager to please her every time she saw him. For some reason it made her uneasy, but it would be ungracious to refuse his offer. 'It's very good of you. You've been really spoiling me lately.' She laughed and added in a light-hearted manner, 'If I didn't know you better I might suspect that you had a guilty conscience.'

'It's a good job you do know me so well then, isn't it?' he said, laughing.

'It is indeed,' she said, her mind moving on to the trip to Kent, too busy with her thoughts to notice the uneasy look behind his smile. 'Thanks for paying the fare.'

'You're welcome,' he said, breathing a sigh of relief as he handed her some money. The problem with an uneasy conscience was that it led to overcompensating and he'd gone too far with the generosity again. One of these days his luck was going to run out if he wasn't very careful.

When Clara came out of Tunbridge Wells station, everywhere was white with a light dusting of snow. Most of the passengers who had got off the train with her headed for the taxis, but such extravagance was beyond her means. She set off down the lanes, catching her breath at the beauty of the bleak winter landscape visible through the hedgerows. Her reason for being here was a sad one but her feelings were of joy because she so loved the countryside.

As she neared Brierley, it started to snow and the cold penetrated through to her bones so it was a relief when she reached her destination. Opening the big wooden gate, she walked across the yard to the house and knocked at the door, hearing the dog barking on the other side. She had been so anxious about Eva, she hadn't given much thought to the reception she would receive until now. It occurred to her that she could hardly expect a warm welcome.

It was Mabel Fenner who answered the door. Holding Rex back by his collar, she scowled. 'You. I didn't think you would ever have the nerve to show your face here again. How dare you come to this door?'

'I need to speak to you, Mrs Fenner.'

'There's nothing you could say that anyone here would want to listen to, so be on your way.'

'Please, Mrs Fenner,' begged Clara, shivering from the cold, snowflakes glistening on her clothes. 'I've come a long way and it's very important.'

'I suppose you've come here looking for work,' she said accusingly. 'There's nothing here for you.'

'No, I haven't come looking for work. It's about Eva and it's very urgent.'

'Eva ceased to exist the day she left here,' Mabel said coldly. 'So go back where you came from.'

As she went to shut the door, Clara darted forward and put her weight against it.

'For goodness' sake, Mrs Fenner,' she burst out, 'Eva is your daughter and she's in trouble. Do you have no heart at all?'

A voice came from inside the house. 'Who is it, Mum? Is there a problem?'

Charlie appeared and the pleasure in his eyes when he saw Clara melted her heart. 'Clara!' he said. 'What are you doing outside in this weather? Come in out of the cold.'

'She's not welcome here,' declared his mother.

'I've come about Eva,' Clara said to him.

'Come on in before you freeze to death,' he said. 'Move aside, Ma, and let the lady in.'

Giving Clara a look of undiluted hostility, Mabel moved back and Clara went inside.

'Poor Eva; the poor girl,' was Charlie's sympathetic re-action when Clara had finished explaining the situation to the family. Everyone was sitting around the wooden table in the kitchen, a fire glowing in the stove, except Hester, who was, apparently, at home at the cottage. 'I'll come back to London with you and go to the hospital. I'll soon get her out of there.'

'That would be a great help. Thank you,' said Clara.

'More trouble,' snapped Mabel. 'That's all that girl ever brings to this family.'

'That's a bit harsh, dear,' said her husband. 'Eva has obvi-ously been very badly hurt and it's made her sick.'

'Sick,' exploded Mabel. 'You call attempted suicide sick. I call it downright sinful.'

'Yes, I expect there are some people who might agree with you about that, but she must have been very disturbed to have tried it,' suggested John in his usual mild manner.

'She didn't try it, though,' Clara said quickly. 'She changed her mind at the last minute; the shock of real-ising what she was about to do brought her to her senses. Had the railway worker not intervened she would have come back home to us and nothing more would have been said about it. But as it is, she's stuck in a mental hospital and very unhappy.'

'Lunatic asylum, you mean.' This was Mabel.

'If you like,' Clara conceded. 'What you call it makes no difference to the fact that she needs family support to obtain a discharge; and the sooner the better.'

'Surely the doctors know what they're doing,' put in Vincent. 'They'll release her when she's better, won't they?'

'No, they'll release her when the rules allow them to and that means covering their backs and keeping her longer than they need,' she explained. 'This's why someone from the family has to step in. She could be there for months otherwise. For some people it might be the best thing but not for Eva. She's in a ward with very sick people and the regime is harsh. It could be very damaging to her if she's left there for too long.'

'Oh, dear,' said John worriedly. 'The sooner you go to London and get her out the better, Charlie.'

'Don't bring her back here,' Mabel warned. 'She's caused enough gossip in the past already. We don't want people saying we have a lunatic in the family.'

Clara gasped at her blatant cruelty while Charlie said, 'She's your daughter, Mum. How can you turn your back on her?'

'You are being rather hard, Mabel,' added John.

'She's always been a loose cannon,' Vincent put in. 'She doesn't like country life anyway.'

'With respect, I don't think she'll want to come back here,' said Clara. 'She's very happy living with us.'

'Sounds like it,' said Vincent with a mocking grin. 'So happy she considered the idea of doing herself in.'

'I've explained to you why that was,' said Clara briskly. 'Anyway, I've done what I came here to do so I'll be on my way.'

'Not until you've warmed up and had something to eat and drink,' said Charlie. 'Then we'll go to London together.' He turned to his brother. 'Vincent will drive us to the station, won't you? Then you can bring the car back here in case it's needed while I'm away.'

'Well, yeah, I suppose so.' Vincent didn't sound willing. 'So long as the snow isn't too deep.'

'Mum will fix you up with some food, Clara, won't you, Ma?' said Charlie, giving his mother an insistent look. 'I'll go home to the cottage to put Hester in the picture and pack an overnight bag. I'll get a room in a hotel if I need to stay over. You sit by the fire while you're waiting, Clara. I won't be long.'

The last thing Clara wanted was to accept hospitality from Mabel Fenner, but it was a long time since she'd eaten the sandwiches her mother had made her for the train and she was feeling hungry. It wouldn't be sensible to refuse as she had a long journey in cold weather ahead of her.

'Just some bread will do, thank you, Mrs Fenner,' she said courteously.

Without replying, Mabel Fenner got up and went to the larder while her husband invited Clara to sit closer to the stove. Smiling kindly at her, he left the room, saying he was going to the office. Apart from Mabel no one had mentioned the distressing circumstances of Clara's dismissal from Brierley last year. She assumed that they were all too busy thinking about Eva.

Clara's intention was to leave as soon as Charlie was ready without entering into any sort of discussion. But when Vincent followed his father to the office and Charlie had gone to the cottage leaving Mabel and Clara alone, Mabel launched into a vicious attack on her.

'You had no right to come here bothering us with Eva's problems,' she said furiously. 'Now poor Charlie has got to go rushing off to London and my husband is upset. Neither of those two could ever see how selfish and manipulative Eva was. She always managed to fool them somehow, the danged girl.'

Clara bit into the bread and cheese she had been given, trying not to retaliate.

'They both seem to see good in her for some unknown reason,' Mabel went on.

'Perhaps that is because there is so much good in Eva,' Clara was unable to stop herself from pointing out. 'She's no more selfish than any other young person and she really wouldn't know how to be manipulative.'

'I think I know my own daughter better than someone who has only known her for five minutes, thank you very much.'

'You ruined her life,' Clara blurted out without any prior intention, her cheeks flaming. 'You made her what she was when she was here; loud and attention-seeking, which she isn't when she's with us. The poor girl was made to feel worthless every time you opened your mouth to her. It's no wonder she was difficult.'

'I did no such thing.'

'Think on, Mrs Fenner. I saw the way you treated her when I was here; and all because you blame her for something that wasn't her fault. Worse than that, you made her believe she was to blame and that is unforgivable.'

'What are you talking about?'

'It was not her fault your other daughter died. Eva was four years old and shouldn't have been left in charge of a toddler.'

'Oh, she's told you about that, has she? Trust her to discuss private family matter with outsiders.'

'She needed to talk to someone,' said Clara heatedly. 'The girl was broken by the rejection you gave her on a daily basis. When Gordon let her down it was just one blow too many. No wonder she was disturbed enough to consider suicide.'

'You can't lay the blame for that at my door,' Mabel declared loudly.

Clara gave her a long look, having detected something like bewilderment in her eyes.

'Words can be dangerous weapons,' she said. 'Maybe you forgot them the instant they'd rolled off your tongue, without realising the effect they had, but Eva didn't. They hurt her more deeply than you knew. She wanted love from you and all she ever got was hatred.'

'That just isn't true.'

'That's the way Eva sees it, and it was what I saw when I watched the two of you together.'

'Her sister died! How do you think that made me feel?'

'Terrible, I should imagine, but you still shouldn't have blamed Eva. She was just a little girl; far too young to be responsible for a baby sibling. Both children were your responsibility. If you need to blame someone look no further than yourself. But in my opinion you should accept the fact that the child has gone and thank God you have other children, including a daughter who has never had a kind word from you.'

'Get out of this house,' Mabel ordered, her voice rising

to a shriek. 'Just go and never come back.' She flapped her hands towards the door. 'Be gone with you.'

'I'm going, don't worry,' Clara assured her, walking across the room towards the hall to get her coat.

Just then Charlie came in the back door carrying a small bag.

'You wait in the car, Clara,' he called to her, unaware of the tension between the two women. 'I just have to speak to Dad and Vincent in the office. Won't be long.'

'Yes, all right,' she said. Putting her coat on, she went back out into the bitter weather.

She was walking across the yard towards the car when Hester approached her.

'Here to make trouble again, are you?' she said accusingly.

'Why would I do that?'

'Because of you my husband has got to rush off to London to see his batty sister.'

Clara wasn't normally a violent person but it was as much as she could do to keep her hands off this awful woman. Instead, she said, 'His sister isn't batty. Not in the slightest. She's been badly let down, that's all.'

'She's in some loony bin so she must be mad.'

'Oh, go away, Hester,' said Clara wearily; she was tired of the ignorance of the two Fenner women.

'You're the one who needs to go away and never come back.'

'I came because I needed to, not because I wanted to,' she said. 'You must be very lacking in common sense if you imagine I would ever want to come here after the dreadful way I was treated the last time.'

'You can't keep away from the place,' Hester carried on. 'Any excuse and you're on the train.'

Clara turned to look at her and noticed a difference. Hester's face looked pale and strained, her greenish eyes shadowed.

'What's the matter, Hester?' she asked. 'You're looking a bit peaky today. Not your usual self at all. Aren't things going too well with you and Vincent? Can't you persuade him to go away with you?'

'How dare you!'

'I thought the two of you would have been well away from here by now. I dare say if it was up to you, you would be.'

Hester looked guarded. 'I don't know what on earth you mean,' she said.

'Don't tell me it's all over between you,' Clara mocked. 'Not that I'd be surprised, given Vincent's attitude.'

'No, of course it isn't over,' she responded. 'Vincent loves me, and I hope you haven't got any ideas about telling my husband on the way to London.'

'Who knows?' said Clara, who didn't think it would do Hester any harm to worry a little.

'You wouldn't!'

'You can't be sure of that, though, can you?' Clara told her. 'The only way to have peace of mind is not to mis-behave in the first place. It takes quite a while to get to London. There'll be plenty of time for a nice friendly chat, and it'll just be the two of us; nice and private, if you know what I mean.'

'You bitch.'

'Now now, Hester. That's not a very nice thing to say to someone who has come on a mercy mission,' said

Charlie, appearing on the scene with Vincent behind him.

'How long have you been there?' asked Hester, her eyes wide with alarm.

'Long enough to hear you calling Clara a bitch,' he replied, opening the car door. 'You really should be more polite to visitors. Clara has come all this way for our sakes, not hers.'

'It was only a bit of fun,' his wife lied, relieved that he hadn't heard more. 'I was just larking about.'

'I very much doubt that, but there's no time to go into it now,' said Charlie, eager to be on his way. 'I probably won't be back until tomorrow. It depends what happens at the hospital, so expect me when you see me.'

'All right.' Without looking at Clara, Hester turned on her heel and hurried towards the cottage. The other three got into the car and drove slowly across the snow-covered yard en route for the station.

'I'm sorry the women of the family are always so hostile towards you, Clara,' said Charlie when they were settled in their seats in the train. 'It makes me feel embarrassed and ashamed when they treat you so badly.'

'It's like water off a duck's back to me,' she fibbed to put him at his ease, though in truth she was terribly affected by so much enmity. 'So don't give it another thought.'

He couldn't tell her that it was almost a physical pain to hear her being verbally abused. Neither could he tell her that seeing her again was like a burst of winter sunshine. He was a married man and Clara was here because his sister was in trouble. It was no time for romantic confessions.

'As long as you know that the fault lies with them and

not you,' he went on. 'Mum is still angry about that business last summer and Hester . . . well, I've no idea why she has such a down on you.'

Clara could have told him the truth there and then. In fact it was the perfect moment. But she wouldn't hurt him simply to make herself feel better so she said, 'It's probably just a female thing. Hester is used to being the only young woman around the place and maybe she doesn't like what she considers to be competition. So I should forget all about it if I were you. It really doesn't matter.'

'The female mind has always been something of a mystery to me,' he said lightly.

'And long may it stay that way for all men,' she said jokingly.

'How have you been, Clara?' he asked more seriously, turning to her, his face just inches away.

She moved her head to meet his eyes and was moved by the warmth in them. 'Not so dusty,' she replied.

'Not married yet then?' He'd been quick to notice the lack of a wedding ring.

'No, not yet. We've set the date for August, though, so we're getting there.'

'You must be very excited about it. It's meant to be the happiest day of a person's life.'

'Naturally I'm looking forward to it.'

'How is Arnold?'

'He's fine, the same as ever,' she replied. 'He's very good to me, I must admit.'

'I'm glad,' he said, with mixed emotions. He was glad that she had someone who was treating her well, because she deserved it, but he was very envious that that someone wasn't him.

'How about you, Charlie?'

'Oh, just jogging along the same as usual,' he said, because he wouldn't burden her with the misery of being married to the wrong woman. 'We're busy checking the apples in store and getting the healthy fruit off to market. Our outside jobs are held up until the weather improves.' He grinned. 'I bet you're not so keen on country life now that you've seen it in the depths of winter.'

She smiled and he really thought he would lay down his life for her if it was ever necessary. 'I was in the Land Army, remember, so I'm not put off by a bit of cold weather and a few snowflakes,' she told him. 'In fact I found the bleak landscape very beautiful.'

'Yes, I thought you might say something like that, knowing what a romantic you are about the country.' He looked away and a silence fell between them. 'How is Cuddy?' he asked, moving the conversation on to more neutral ground. 'Is he still singing?'

'Oh, yes, all the time.'

'Even when your dad and Sydney are around?'

'Until they tell him to shut up,' she said and they both laughed, easing the tension that was never more than a whisper away because of the strength of their unspoken feelings.

Later that day Mabel Fenner was making pastry at the kitchen table. Normally an expert at the job, on this occasion she'd added too much water to the mixture so had to counteract that with more flour, and the whole thing had ended up in such a mess she had had to start again. All because her mind wasn't on the job, thanks to that wretched Tripp woman coming here and upsetting her with drivel about her relationship with her daughter.

How dare she accuse her of rejecting Eva for most of her life? Mabel had done no such thing. Of course she had had to keep Eva in order because she was so wilful but she hadn't rejected her. Well . . . maybe she'd been a little cold towards her immediately after the death of her sister, because it hurt so much. But rejection! Never! She wouldn't do that to one of her own.

Usually a most particular and light-fingered pastrycook, she kneaded her second attempt vigorously, thinking back. Eva had always been an extremely difficult child. Mabel had had to be firm with her to keep her in order. Had she become hard to manage after her little sister's death, or had she always been like it? Mabel honestly couldn't remember. Snatches of conversation came into her mind, making her wince. Had she really said those awful things to Eva? If she were brutally honest with herself, she knew that she had. Maybe she had been looking for someone to blame because her own pain had been so unbearable. Perhaps that Tripp woman was right, and she herself was culpable for her daughter's death. Barely aware of what she was doing, she worked the pastry harder, unconscious of the fact that it was already entirely ruined.

Clara Tripp had even had the audacity to suggest that Mabel herself had contributed to Eva's current plight. No, she couldn't accept that; she refused to. Maybe she'd not been the most loving of mothers but it wasn't her fault that Eva had got involved with some undesirable Londoner. It would be just like her to fall into the arms of the first man who gave her a second glance.

On reflection, she could feel again the uncontrollable

force of the irritation Eva had aroused in her, which had made her lash out almost without realising it. The girl had never seemed to do a thing right, so Mabel had had to reprimand her as any mother would. Children needed discipline. It was essential to the building of their character.

Had she really made her feel rejected, though? No, that line of thought was too painful so she wasn't going to pursue it any further. Eva had only herself to blame for leaving home and getting involved in an unsavoury love affair. Mabel wasn't going to give it another thought. Recalled to the present and the fact that the pastry was spoiled yet again, she emptied it into the bin and started over. That dratted Tripp woman had a lot to answer for, coming here and making outrageous accusations. Damn and blast her!

Chapter Eleven

Deciding that the family was in need of a little light relief, Flo made a suggestion one breakfast time in February. 'How about we all have a night out together at the Shepherd's Bush Empire on Saturday? You as well, Cuddy,' she said. 'George Robey is on so it will be a bit of fun.'

'I'm all for that, love,' her husband said approvingly. 'I could do with a good laugh. Anyone else fancy it?' He looked at Clara. 'I know you usually see Arnold on a Saturday night, so naturally he's included if you want to come.'

'Arnold never says no to a night out, so count us in,' she responded.

'What about you, Eva?' asked Flo, somewhat warily. Eva was still emotionally fragile and hadn't been out for an evening since she'd been home from hospital.

The girl made a face. 'I'm not sure that I want to go,' she said predictably.

'Oh, go on. Come along and keep me company,' urged Sydney, smiling at her warmly. 'It will be nice to have someone of my own age there. Otherwise I'll be stuck with this boring lot.'

'Thanks very much,' said his mother.

'Yeah, keep the compliments coming, brother dear,' added Clara.

'See what I have to put up with?' Sydney laughed. 'So please say you'll come.'

'I don't think . . .'

'You'd be doing me a favour,' Sydney persisted.

Eva mulled it over for a while longer, then said with some reluctance, 'All right then, since you put it like that, I'll come.'

'Good.' Flo loved family outings. 'I'll pop into the theatre and get some tickets when I'm out shopping.'

'I suppose you'll all go to the pub in the interval and leave me standing outside in the street on my own, as usual,' grumbled Cuddy. 'You're always in there for ages, too, even though you say you won't be long.'

'I'll stay outside with you,' offered Eva.

'Would you?' said Cuddy, smiling at her. 'That would be smashing, Eva.'

She had been out of hospital for three weeks. After a persuasive conversation with the doctor, Charlie had managed to get her discharged by taking full responsibility for her. As she wouldn't even consider the idea of going home to Brierley, Clara and her family had promised him they would look after her and let him know immediately at the first sign of a problem with her health. Her obvious joy at being back with them had almost brought tears to the eyes of the whole Tripp family, even the men.

'I won't get any more silly ideas and have you all tearing your hair out about me,' she had promised. 'I don't want to end up in that place again. I'm so pleased to be home.'

241

No one, not even Charlie, had pointed out that her home was in Kent. She had adopted the Tripps and they welcomed her with open arms, though Clara wished the problems between Eva and her mother could be resolved. A great deal of damage had been done but it was never too late to make things better, even if they couldn't be mended altogether. But Mrs Fenner, being as she was, probably didn't even realise the enormity of what she'd done. Eva had admitted to Clara that she missed Charlie and her father but wouldn't visit them because of her mother's hostility towards her. She just didn't feel strong enough to take it.

The doctor had said it was important for her to keep occupied, so Eva had gone to the laundry to try to persuade them to take her on again. Fortunately they were more lenient than she had expected and she was allowed back to work, but she never wanted to go out anywhere else. Clara had suggested a night at the pictures but she seemed dead set against it. The only time she set foot outside the house, apart from her job, was to go for an occasional walk in the park with Sydney or Clara, so persuading her to go to the Empire with them was a real breakthrough.

Obviously, she would have to go to places where she would meet men again eventually, but there was no hurry. She needed to regain her confidence first. Until then she preferred to stay at home playing cards with Sydney, who was very sweet to her. He was barely recognisable as the arrogant lout who'd hung around with Shoulders' gang. Thank goodness it had been just a phase, Clara thought. He seemed to have got over his awkwardness around Eva too, and they were good friends now.

She was recalled to the present by the fact that people were leaving the table.

'Don't worry about the clearing up,' said Flo as Clara and Eva started to take the crockery off the table. 'We've talked longer than usual this morning and you need to get off to work.'

'I sometimes think you're a saint, Mum, the way you look after us all,' said Clara.

'That isn't what you say when my cooking isn't up to much or when I'm behind with the laundry and you can't find anything clean to wear,' Flo reminded her laughingly.

'I'm not talking about efficiency,' said Clara. 'I'm talking about caring.'

'What else would I do?' she said. 'You lot are my life.'

Clara saw a look of sadness come into Eva's eyes and guessed that she was making the obvious comparison.

Going to the pub in the interval was as much a tradition as the show itself for the Tripp family. Cuddy palled up with another young boy whose parents had the same idea, so all the adults in the Tripp party went inside the pub.

'Are you all right, Eva?' Sydney asked. The place was packed to the doors, and he knew she was still vulnerable.

'I'm fine.'

'I was wondering if the crowd might be a bit too much for you.'

'No. Funnily enough, I'm enjoying myself. I'm looking forward to the second half,' she told him. 'Though I admit I didn't want to come.'

'The second half is always the best. Especially the top of the bill.'

She smiled at him. 'I'm lucky to have a friend like you, Sydney,' she said.

'Likewise.'

'At one time I used to think you didn't like me,' she told him. 'You weren't friendly to me like the rest of the family, until I got myself into a state over Gordon. Then you changed and you've been wonderful to me ever since.'

He shrugged, but his cheeks were burning.

'Don't tell me you were shy,' she suggested, teasing him.

He gave a wry grin. 'I suppose I did find it a bit awkward having a strange girl in the house at first.'

'But you've got used to me now.'

He nodded. 'Oh, yeah,' he said to reassure her. 'There's no problem now.'

It wasn't entirely true. He still fled from the room if she was washing at the sink in her petticoat. But he was much easier in her company now so long as she was fully dressed. He loved being with her; enjoyed her smile, the way she looked, the sweet scent of her and the sound of her voice. She made him feel special because she'd been relying on him for company since she split up with Gordon.

'That's good,' she said. 'I would hate to think I made you feel uncomfortable.'

He handed her a glass of shandy that had been passed to him by Arnold, who was getting the drinks at the bar. Then he took a pint of beer for himself and raised his glass to Arnold. A multitude of voices created a warm, sociable roar, laughing, talking and singing, and a piano was playing in the background. A pea-souper of cigarette smoke hung in the air, barely noticed as it was a normal part of pub atmosphere.

Sydney knew that the time would come when Eva

wouldn't need his company and would want to go out dancing again to meet other boys. He dreaded it because he guessed he would lose her. Tub and his other mates thought he was mad to waste his time hanging around the house with her when he should be out with them having fun and sowing his wild oats, but that was because they thought of girls only in carnal terms. They couldn't know how very special Eva was to him, as a friend. Well, yes, the other thing was there as well. He could deny it no longer; she was a very pretty girl and he was a normal young man. But he would never lay a finger on her in that way unless she wanted him to, which she never would because she thought of him only as a pal.

'Penny for them,' she was saying now.

'I was just thinking what a good night it is, all of us out together.'

'It's time we finished our drinks and left, I think,' she suggested. 'I promised Cuddy we would get back to the theatre before the second half starts. He reckons that your mum and dad always stay too long in the pub and make them all late back. He gets embarrassed because everyone in the row has to get up to let them get by and no one is very pleased about it as the show has started again.'

'Yeah, they do have a reputation for that sort of thing,' he said, finishing his beer. 'So let's go and round them up and get them back in their seats.'

Together they pushed their way through the crowds to the other family members.

The instant the top of the bill, one of Britain's funniest comedians, appeared on stage in his black frock coat, squashed bowler hat, and blackened eyebrows, the audience was laughing. Just a look or the smallest gesture had them in fits. The more he demanded that they 'desist' the more they laughed. It was all part of the act, of course, but the audience were in the palm of his hand and loving every minute.

At the end of the show the auditorium was a riot of appreciation; people were clapping, cheering, whistling, stamping their feet and shouting for more.

'Well, did you enjoy yourself, Clara?' asked Arnold as they made their way out with the still smiling crowds.

'I certainly did. You'd have to be a real misery guts not to with George Robey on stage, wouldn't you?'

'And that's one thing that could never be said of you.' He brushed her cheeks with his lips. 'You're the most cheerful person I know.'

'I'm sure that isn't true.'

'It is,' he insisted. 'I think you're wonderful the way you keep it up no matter what.'

She hated it when he lavished flattery on her but she gritted her teeth and said, 'It's all in the genes, I suppose. I come from a cheerful sort of family.'

When they reached the foyer and waited for the other members of the group to appear, he put his arm round her and kissed her cheek, urging her with his actions to turn towards him. Instinctively, she tensed and moved away from him.

'Why am I getting the cold shoulder?' he asked.

'Don't be silly, Arnold.'

'You don't seem to want me to touch you.'

'You're imagining things.'

'You couldn't be making it more obvious.'

'I was just looking for the others,' she said, peering through the crowds. 'Anyway, we can't be lovey-dovey all the time, can we? Especially not when we're out for an evening with a group. So stop worrying and enjoy yourself.'

'I thought perhaps you'd gone off me.'

'There they are,' she said as though she hadn't heard him, waving to her parents as they came out of the auditorium. 'Coo-ee. We're over here.'

She was very well aware of what she was doing, even though she feigned an innocent air. Most of the time she could respond in a normal loving way towards Arnold but at other times, especially when he was fawning over her, she didn't want him near her – and was then consumed with compunction as she was now. To help assuage her guilt, she linked her arm through his in a friendly manner and they crossed the road to the Green and began the walk home with the others, all talking about the show.

Arnold was becoming seriously concerned about Clara's behaviour towards him. She was very offhand at times lately. Did she know something, he wondered fearfully? No, it couldn't possibly be that. There was absolutely no way; he was always so cautious. Anyway, she was the sort of person who would come straight out and say so if she did. She didn't have an artful bone in her body.

He still felt uneasy though because he couldn't bear to lose her. He turned towards her and thought how beautiful she was; so young and fresh and pretty. She was lovely inside and out and he was a lucky man to have her. He would have to make damned sure he didn't get careless and risk losing her. So he would continue to be careful; very careful indeed.

* * *

'It was nice to see you enjoying yourself tonight, Eva,' remarked Clara as she got undressed.

'I didn't want to go but I had a really good time,' said Eva, who was already in bed.

'Me too. It does you good to have a laugh.' She yawned. 'I'm dead beat, though. Thank God it's Sunday tomorrow and we can have a lie-in. G'night. Sleep well.'

'G'night, Clara.'

Eva lay on her back staring into the dark, the street light shining through a gap in the curtains and making a pattern on the wall. How different it was from the inky blackness of the countryside when there was no moon. She couldn't imagine ever wanting to return to Brierley. In a way her mother had done her a favour by driving her away because she was much more suited to town life. She enjoyed the lights, the shops, the buzz of activity and the sense of people around her. Having lived in London for a while now, she realised that there was a certain melancholy in the countryside; at least that was the case at Brierley, a feeling of guilt about enjoyment. Here, in the Tripp household anyway, there were few things in life that couldn't be helped by a good night out or a bit of fun indoors. She enjoyed the banter enormously. The family had their disagreements, of course, but there was never any Brierley-style venom.

Eva still had her dark times, usually when she was in bed with nothing to distract her from her thoughts. Times when she remembered Gordon and how she'd felt when he'd said, 'You're a lovely girl, Eva, and I've enjoyed going out with you. But I've met someone else so I won't be seeing you again. Sorry.'

No matter how hard she tried to erase them from her

memory, those words came back to haunt her whenever she was off her guard, and with them came the pain she had experienced then. It couldn't have hurt more if he'd stabbed her with a knife. It was a physical ache that dragged her down and wouldn't go away.

After she'd been shocked out of her trough by finding herself in a mental hospital, and her subsequent release, she had begun to have glimpses of normality, mainly thanks to the Tripp family who were her comfort and salvation, especially Sydney who had turned out to be such a dear friend, and Clara of course. Now the glimpses lasted longer but she still wanted to cry whenever the memories of Gordon's betrayal came flooding back. But she knew she had a lot to be grateful for and her life in general was much better than it had been at Brierley with the daily trouncing from her mother.

She missed Charlie, though, and her father. The others had never had any time for her, so she was better off away from them. She couldn't help wondering if her mother ever missed her, even if only because she had no one to torment. Still, she was well away from there, whatever her mother's feelings, and she would like to put her old life behind her. But a mother wasn't an easy person to forget. She was too deeply embedded in your soul no matter how bad she'd been. Oh, those awful mealtimes and the pain of her mother's constant criticism and Hester never losing a chance to have a go. Vincent had never been kind to her either. Oh well, it was all over now, she thought, as she drifted off to sleep. She would write to dear Charlie soon, though.

'Psst, Vincent.' It was a day in March and Hester had found Vincent in one of the storage buildings.

'What on earth are you doing here, Hester?' he asked, frowning. 'It's the middle of a working day. Anyone could come in and find us together.'

'How else can I get to speak to you? You refuse to meet me after dark like you used to.'

'You know why that is.'

'I know what you've told me, but I don't see why it's suddenly more dangerous than it was before,' she said, her voice fraught with accusation. 'Anyway, no one will come in here. Charlie's busy spraying the trees to protect them against some bug or other.'

'Moth eggs,' he informed her.

'Yeah, something like that,' she said without interest. 'And your dad's doing something in the office.'

'You're still taking a risk,' he said, removing an apple from one of the barrels and examining it. 'One of the hands could easily come in and start a rumour that would spread like wildfire in a place like this.'

'We're not doing anything wrong.'

'Even so, everyone knows that you don't work in the orchard so there would be speculation as to why you are in here with me.'

'Maybe there would, but so what?'

'You know what,' he said, putting the apple in a basket for marketing.

'You're just making excuses.'

He emitted an exasperated sigh. 'You're a grown woman and you know the score, Hester,' he pointed out coolly. 'I just can't afford to lose everything.'

'How much longer must I wait?'

'I don't know,' he said brusquely. 'Nor do I know why you're in such a hurry to leave your comfortable lifestyle to go off with a penniless man, which is what I will be if we leave before I've made provision. Do you really think we'd last if I had very little money?' He looked at her. 'I think not.'

'I've been hard up before.'

'Exactly, and you wouldn't want to go back to that, would you? If you're honest you know you wouldn't. You're far too fond of your comfort.'

She had to admit that she didn't fancy the idea of being broke, but there would be no need if Vincent pulled his socks up and arranged the finance as he'd promised. 'But you said you would arrange to get money out of the business,' she reminded him.

'Yes, I'm fully aware of that, but these things take time,' he said, his irritation growing by the second. 'You're not dim-witted, so use your head. I can't embezzle money out of the business just like that. I have to plan it carefully and do it gradually.'

'So why can't we carry on as before while we're waiting,' she demanded sulkily.

'Because it's too risky,' he said. 'How many more times must I tell you?'

'We kept it going before and no one suspected anything.'

'Yes, we were lucky. And you know what happens if you push your luck too far. It has a nasty habit of running out.'

'I hope you're not just stringing me along.'

'You know I'm not,' he told her wearily, having had this conversation with her many times before.

'Only I could make life very difficult for you, you know,' she said in a threatening manner. 'I could claim you've been pestering me in an improper way. I don't think your parents would be very impressed by that.'

'That wouldn't do you any good at all,' he pointed out. 'Because if by any chance they were to believe you, they would throw me out with nothing and you'd have to stay with Charlie if you wanted three decent meals a day. I'm not daft enough to believe you would give it all up for me. Look, Hester,' he said more gently. She was so volatile there was no telling what she'd do on impulse if he upset her. 'Just be patient for a while longer if you can. We'll be together, I promise.'

'Do you really mean that?' she said, brightening.

'I mean it,' he lied. 'Now be a good girl and leave me to get on with my work. We'll arrange to meet sometime soon when I think it'll be safe.'

'Promise?'

'I promise.'

'All right then,' she said, moving forward and kissing him full on the lips. 'That's just a starter. Make sure you don't leave it too long for the rest.'

She walked towards the barn door swinging her hips in the way she had of trying to make even an old jumper and trousers look provocative.

Vincent sat down on a wooden crate and bit into one of the apples out of the basket. Something was going to have to be done about Hester, who had become a real nuisance. She would have nothing to gain by spilling the beans about their affair, but who could tell what she might do for revenge when she realised that he had no intention of going away with her now or at any time in the future?

Hester was impetuous and didn't think things through properly. She wanted what she wanted in the moment, without a thought to other people or the consequences of her actions. It was as though she had to prove to herself that she could get her own way whatever the cost. He was bored stiff with her, and could hardly bear to look at her when they met at the house over supper. He dreaded being with her on his own so studiously avoided it. But she would go to any lengths to get to him, as she had done just now.

He would like to tell her the truth: that it had been nice but never serious and now it was over. She was an adult and a married woman; she ought to understand that. But he daren't risk it because she would probably fly into a rage and more than likely go rushing off to tell the family what had been going on, no doubt putting all the blame on him. She was dangerous and he needed to get rid of her. How he was going to do that he had no idea, but he would have to find a way because he couldn't bear the sight of her. He finished his apple and went back to work sorting and checking the apples, mulling over his dilemma and searching for a solution.

'Oh no, you're not reading that danged letter from your sister again, are you, Charlie?' demanded Hester disapprovingly. It was after supper the same day and they were back at the cottage. She was still feeling peeved by Vincent's increasing lack of interest in her and was taking it out on her husband. She wasn't convinced by the promises Vincent had made that morning but she wasn't going to give up because she was determined to have her own way.

'Yes I am as it happens,' replied Charlie. 'Why? Do you have any objection to that?'

'Not an objection as such,' she said. 'I just can't see why you bother with her.'

'No . . . I don't suppose you would.'

'What do you mean by that exactly?'

'You know what I mean because we've been through it all many times before,' he sighed. 'You don't give a damn about your relatives but my sister means a lot to me. No matter how much that upsets you, it's a fact of life.'

'The girl is off her head,' she stated categorically.

'Leave it, Hester,' he urged wearily. 'Find yourself something to do and leave me alone.'

'What would I find to do in this godforsaken hole,' she asked.

'If country life doesn't suit you, there are plenty of towns you could go and live in,' he said, managing to keep his voice even though irritation was welling up inside him.

'You'd like that, wouldn't you? You'd like me out of the way.'

'When you behave like this you're not the most charming company, so yes, a bit of peace would be nice.'

'One of these days I'll go and you'll realise how much I do for you,' she said.

He looked up slowly, brows raised. 'Oh yeah, and what would that be exactly?' he asked.

'I cook and clean for you,' she reminded him. 'I wash your dirty clothes and darn your socks.'

'And I provide for you in return; that's how the institution of marriage works,' he said. 'Anyway, you don't darn my socks. I take them up to the house and Mum does them for me. The washing and ironing you do isn't up to much either.'

'I can't help it if I'm no good at that sort of thing,' she said defiantly. 'Anyway, your mother likes darning and washing. The poor cow actually gets pleasure from domestic work. I've no intention of being a slave like her.'

'Mum enjoys looking after her family and I can see nothing wrong with that,' he told her. 'I think most mothers do, don't they? Isn't it part of the maternal instinct?'

'How would I know?' she replied in an offhand manner. 'Not being a mother myself or having any intention of ever being one.'

He gave a humourless laugh. 'You're making damned sure of that, too,' he said. That side of their marriage had been non-existent for some time.

'You'd enjoy that, wouldn't you?' she said with a sneer in her voice. 'You'd love to see me up to my eyes in kids and all the work and worry that come with them.'

He certainly would love to have children, but not with Hester; not now. In the early days of their marriage she used to say she didn't want a family too soon and he had respected that and taken the necessary measures. Thank God there hadn't been any accidents. His life wouldn't have been worth living if she'd got pregnant.

'I would like to have children and have never made any secret of it,' he reminded her. 'And I suppose work and worry come with them as well as joy. But don't panic. I gave up on the idea ages ago.'

'I'm glad to hear it.'

He went back to his letter while she walked about the room restlessly. 'Find something to do, for goodness' sake,' he said. 'You're setting my nerves on edge.'

'Such as?'

'You could read a book,' he suggested. 'Don't women usually do embroidery and knitting in the evenings? Mum always does.'

'Just because your mother has allowed herself to become a drudge with nothing better to do than mend bloody socks or knit jumpers all evening doesn't mean that I have to.'

'Perhaps you miss the company you used to have working at the pub before we got married,' he suggested, genuinely trying to be helpful.

'It was a darned sight more lively than sitting here with you of an evening,' she said.

The constant criticism did have an effect on him even though he was accustomed to it. It made him feel like a man who couldn't satisfy his wife in any way whatsoever. He knew that there was nothing he could do to alter that since he himself was the problem. She really didn't want to be with him and vice versa.

'We don't have to stay together, you know, Hester,' he said in a reasonable tone. 'I know divorce is considered scandalous but some couples separate without actually divorcing.'

'What?' she screamed, coming at him, ripping the letter out of his hands and staring at him. 'Are you trying to get rid of me? Is that what you're after?'

'Not necessarily,' he said. 'But you seem to hate being married to me and we're both unhappy. I'm just suggesting that there is a way out.'

This incensed her even more.

'You don't get shot of me that easily,' she hissed, hitting him round the head then drawing her nails across his cheek; she was completely out of control.

'Hey, that's enough,' he said, managing to push her away and get to his feet, tasting the blood that was running down his face and into his mouth. 'Calm down. There's no need for any of this. Just take it easy, Hester.' He took hold of her arms to protect himself.

'Take your hands off me,' she screeched.

'Only if you promise to calm down,' he said. 'Lord knows what you'll do while you're in this state.'

'Yes, yes, all right,' she said. 'I'll try.'

He let go of her warily. She was like a wild cat that would dig its claws into him at any minute. 'Right then. How about we sit down and discuss this thing in a civilised manner,' he suggested. 'Get it sorted once and for all.'

'Go to hell,' she came back at him. Talk of a separation was the last thing she needed just now. That would finish things with Vincent completely. 'I'm going for a walk and don't you dare to suggest coming with me to talk things over because I don't want to talk about it and I want to be on my own.'

'All right,' he said, relieved that some of the fire seemed to have gone out of her. 'I'll see you later then.'

'Mm,' she muttered, heading for the coat pegs on the wall by the back door.

She put on her coat and wellington boots and left the house, slamming the door after her and making Rex bark.

Charlie was trembling in the aftermath of the argument. He went to the mirror on the wall in the kitchen and dabbed his gouged face with a handkerchief. Hester certainly had a temper and she was getting worse by the day.

Something would have to be done about their marriage. He'd reached the stage where he didn't think he could take any more of the sheer misery of it. They couldn't get along, so separation seemed to be the only answer.

The only reason she didn't want it was because she was afraid of losing her meal ticket. But something could be arranged about that. He wouldn't allow her to be destitute. It was his duty as her husband to provide for her and he would, regardless of whether they were living together.

But he couldn't bear to have her in his life any longer. He wanted out at the earliest possible moment. Holding a handkerchief to his torn face, he went to the sideboard in the parlour and took out a bottle of whisky left over from Christmas. He needed something strong to steady his nerves.

He woke up the next morning with hammers beating the living daylights out of his brain to find that he was fully dressed and in the armchair with Rex sitting on the floor beside him. He must have had a few too many glasses of whisky last night and not got round to going to bed. It was daylight and way past his usual rising time.

It was very quiet in the cottage and there didn't seem to be any sign of Hester or breakfast. With his head aching so much he could barely function, he put some fresh water down for the dog and let him out, then made his way upstairs to find that Hester wasn't there and the bed hadn't been slept in. It occurred to him that this was odd but he was too hungover to react fully. He assumed she must be at the big house and made his way there.

'Is Hester here?' he asked the family, who were having breakfast.

'No, of course not,' his mother replied. 'Why would she be?'

'She isn't at the cottage, so I naturally assumed she must have popped over here for some reason.'

'Probably gone for a walk,' suggested Vincent.

'What happened to your face?' enquired his mother, looking at him questioningly.

'Oh, er . . . I cut it shaving,' he fibbed, instinctively loyal to his wife.

'Funny place to have stubble,' said his mother. The wound was high up on his cheek. 'You look a bit peaky this morning, son. Are you all right?'

'Just a bit of a headache,' he replied. 'I had a drop too much to drink last night.'

'That isn't like you.'

'No it isn't. But we'd had words and I needed something to calm me down,' he explained. 'Hester stormed out and when I got up this morning she hadn't come back.'

'She'll want you to worry, I expect,' said Mabel, 'as a punishment for quarrelling with her. She'll be back when she thinks you've been punished enough.'

'Perhaps she's left you,' added Vincent lightly.

'Without taking her clothes?' Charlie came back at him. 'I don't think so.'

'She'll come back when it suits her,' said Mabel. 'Isn't that right, John?'

'Yes, dear, I'm sure she will.'

'I'd better go and have a look for her further afield,' said Charlie, beginning to worry.

The irony of it was that Charlie couldn't enjoy her absence because he was too worried about her. She was neurotic and unpredictable but she wouldn't stay out all night. Hester was far too fond of her comfort for that, and she didn't have any friends she could stay with. He didn't love her but, as her husband, he was responsible for her. So where the hell was she?

'So, you and your wife had an argument last night and she stormed out,' said the policeman behind the desk. Charlie hadn't been able to find Hester anywhere. No one in the village had seen her.

'That's right.'

'And she hasn't been seen since?' continued the policeman, writing the details down.

Charlie nodded.

'Unpredictable things, women,' remarked the officer. 'Don't you think she'll come back when she's ready?'

'She wouldn't have stayed away this long if she was all right,' Charlie told him.

'Mm, I see. Well, if you can let me have a description of your wife and the full details, I'll pass the information on and they'll get a search under way.'

'Thank you,' said Charlie miserably.

'Trust Hester to have us all worrying,' said Mabel later that day. Charlie was pacing the kitchen at the big house, the men having come in for tea. 'Look at the state you've got yourself into.'

'It's getting late,' he pointed out. 'It'll be dark soon.'

'Which is why we need to get back to work,' said Vincent. 'We need to finish mulching the young trees today.'

'Work will help to take your mind off it, anyway,' suggested his father.

'Let him finish his tea,' said Mabel.

'Dad's right, Mum,' said Charlie. 'I need to keep busy.'

'Aye aye,' observed Vincent, looking out of the window. 'The boys in blue are here.'

'Thank goodness for that,' said Mabel as Charlie hurried from the room to the front door. 'They must have found her. Now we can all have some peace.'

'Mr Fenner?' said one of the policemen. 'Mr Charlie Fenner?'

'Yes, that's me,' he replied. 'Have you found her? Have you found my wife?'

'Can we come in, sir?' said the policeman.

'You want more details, I suppose,' said Charlie in exasperation. 'You should be out looking for her, not here asking me a load more questions.'

'I think we'd better come in, if you don't mind, sir,' insisted the officer.

Charlie ushered them inside and took them into the kitchen, where they suggested that he sit down.

'You've got news, haven't you?' Charlie said, suddenly feeling very frightened.

'Have you found her?' asked Mabel. 'I shall give her a piece of my mind when I see her, putting us all through this worry, the selfish young madam.'

The policeman cleared his throat a few times, seeming extremely ill at ease. 'A body has been found at the bottom of the ridge,' he announced, directing his speech to Charlie and sending a deathly hush over the room.

'A body.' Charlie sounded puzzled, as though this had no relevance to his wife's disappearance.

'That's right, sir. It matches the description you gave us of your wife.'

'It can't be her. Absolutely not!' He was still bemused by the suggestion.

'Maybe not, sir,' said the policeman. 'But we do need you to come and do a formal identification for us, if you will.'

'But how can it be Hester?' he said, almost to himself. 'She only went out for a walk.'

'Of course it isn't Hester,' said his mother. 'Don't even think about it.'

'Perhaps you would come with us now, sir,' the policeman said to Charlie in a reasonable but firm tone. 'Then we will know one way or the other.'

Leaving the family dumbstruck, Charlie followed the men from the house.

Chapter Twelve

'Are all you young people rushing off out tonight?' asked Flo Tripp when the family settled down in the parlour after their evening meal. 'Or am I having my chickens at home this evening?'

'This chicken is staying home,' responded Clara, opening her knitting bag and taking out the half-finished pullover she was making for Arnold.

'Me too,' added Sydney.

'Shall we have a game of cards later on, Sydney?' suggested Eva who was looking through a well-thumbed copy of *Vogue* magazine given to her by a workmate.

'Yeah, sure, as long as you don't mind being beaten,' Sydney joshed.

'You're the one who needs to worry about losing,' she came back at him, grinning.

'You two must be experts at Snap,' Clara teased them. 'The number of times you slope off to the kitchen table to play it.'

'Snap might suit your level of skill,' countered Sydney, 'but if you were to join us sometime for a game of Newmarket, you'd get beaten hollow.'

'I shall go out every night when I'm older,' announced Cuddy. 'I certainly won't stay at home playing cards.'

'Oh yeah?' said Sydney. 'And where are you planning on going?'

'Picture houses, theatres, dance halls,' Cuddy replied. 'Maybe even concerts.'

'You're a bit ambitious, aren't you, mate? You'll need to get a good job to pay for that sort of thing.'

'You used to go out every night of the week at one time,' Cuddy reminded his brother. 'You never stayed home of an evening.'

'In my wild days, yeah, I did go out all the time,' Sydney conceded. 'But I didn't go anywhere that cost much money.'

'Where did you go then?' said Eva.

'Nowhere really. Just hanging around the streets with some mates who turned out not to be mates after all.'

'That doesn't sound very nice.'

'I can see that it wasn't now, but I thought it was fun at the time.'

'Nice was the last thing it was,' put in his mother. 'He was a right little rebel for a while but he's a reformed character now, thank goodness.' She glanced at her husband, who was reading the paper and seemed very engrossed. 'Isn't that right, Frank? . . . Frank, are you listening?' There was no response. 'Oh well, Flo, talk to yourself, why don't you?'

'Oi, Dad, Mum's talking to you,' Clara put in, smiling. 'You'll be well and truly in the doghouse if you don't pay attention to her.'

He seemed to have to shake himself back to the present. 'Oh, sorry, Flo. What is it, love?'

'Just saying about Sydney . . . oh, never mind, go back

to your paper,' she said as he was so obviously preoccupied.

They all carried on chatting but after a few minutes Frank got up, clutching the paper, and walked across the room. At the door he turned to Clara. 'Can you spare me a minute?' he asked. 'There's something I think you should see.'

'Yeah, o' course,' she said, putting her knitting down and following him out of the room.

'So, what have you got to show me that's so interesting?' she asked. 'I hope it isn't just an advertisement for some lovely household item for my bottom drawer that I can't possibly afford.'

'No, nothing like that,' he said, handing her the folded paper and pointing to one of the items. 'I thought you ought to see this because we need to decide what to tell Eva.'

The first thing that leapt out at Clara was a photograph of Charlie and Hester on their wedding day. When she read the headline she felt her legs turn to jelly. *Husband main suspect in the Kent apple orchard murder.*

'Are you all right?' asked her father in concern as Clara sank down as white as a sheet on to a chair at the kitchen table, the newspaper in front of her as she read on about Charlie helping the police with their inquiries into the suspicious death of his wife; an arrest was expected to be made soon.

'He didn't do it, Dad,' she said, her voice trembling with emotion. 'Charlie would never do a thing like that. I'll have to go to Kent right away. There are things the police need to know.'

'All right, dear, don't upset yourself,' he urged, too worried about his daughter to pay attention to what she had just blurted out. 'It's Fenner family business and nothing to do with us. I'm only concerned because of Eva. Should we tell her about it, given what she's already been through?'

'Of course we must tell her,' she replied without hesitation. 'She adores Charlie and will want to do anything she can to help him. It sounds as though he needs it.'

'Her family haven't been in touch to let her know, have they?' he pointed out.

'No, that's true.' She mulled it over. 'That's probably down to Charlie. He wouldn't want her to be worried as she's had such a bad time recently. But something as important as this, of course she must know. She'll soon find out anyway if it's going to be splashed all over the papers. It's best if I break the news to her.'

'I'll leave it to you, then.'

She nodded.

'Clara love,' he said, touching her arm in a fatherly gesture, 'I realise that the news must be a shock to you. But the Fenners are only people you worked for, not personal friends, so try not to upset yourself too much. You never know what goes on behind closed doors. Charlie seems a nice enough bloke, the little I know of him, but the police must have their reasons for suspecting him.'

'The closest relative is always the first suspect in murder cases, that's all,' she told him. 'I remember reading that somewhere.'

'And if he's innocent he won't be charged,' said her father in an effort to reassure her.

'You know as well as I do that that isn't true,' she

returned. 'Many an innocent person has gone to the gallows.'

In all honesty he couldn't deny it. 'All I'm saying is try not to get too worried about it. It really isn't our business.'

He couldn't know how emotionally involved she already was, and she wasn't going to complicate matters at this stage by telling him about the transgressions of Vincent, who was much more likely to be guilty of murder than his brother. Neither would she tell him that the thought of Charlie in this kind of trouble made her feel physically ill and she would do anything to help him.

'I'll have a chat with Eva on her own,' she told him. 'She'll be shocked, of course. Hester was her sister-in-law, after all, but I think she'll cope. Having someone else's problem to worry about might even take her mind off her own broken heart.'

'You do as you see fit and the rest of us will be on hand when you've told her,' he said.

'Thanks, Dad,' she said warmly.

Eva was stunned by the news. 'Vincent and Hester,' she said in a bemused tone after Clara had taken her upstairs to the bedroom and told her about Hester's death and everything else that had been going on at Brierley, including her own unfair dismissal. 'I should have spotted it. Looking back I can see that there was always a spark between those two. I suppose I was always too busy defending myself to pay much attention. But why didn't you tell me about it when you got back from Brierley that last time?'

'I knew it would upset you and I couldn't risk my family finding out the real reason I had come home early,' she explained. 'Dad and Sydney would have got on the first train to Kent ready to do battle on my behalf. I didn't want it all coming out for Charlie's sake. He still doesn't know.'

'It must have been awful for you, especially not being able to talk about it to anyone,' Eva said sympathetically.

'I was hurt more than angry, but Charlie didn't believe I was guilty, and that meant a lot. Anyway, I tried to forget all about it and get on with my life here. But now I shall have to go to Kent and tell the police what I know. It might make a difference to Charlie's defence. He'll have to know the truth now.'

'I'll go with you. I want to say something to the police in Charlie's favour,' said Eva. 'Whether my mother wants me there or not, I'm going. I shall have a few words to say to the family about the way you were treated too.'

'We'll get an early train tomorrow then. They won't be pleased at work when we don't turn up but we can't help that. This is an emergency.'

'Exactly,' said Eva. 'When we get to Tunbridge Wells I'll go to Brierley and tell them a few home truths and you can go straight to the police station. I shall tell them at the orchard where you are and why you're there.'

'I think it'll be best if we keep the goings on at Brierley from my family, just for the moment,' said Clara. 'At least until Charlie is in the picture. But now we'd better go downstairs and see them. Dad will have shown them the newspaper by now and they'll be worried about how you've taken it.'

'Oh,' said Eva appreciatively. 'It's so good of them to worry about me.'

Clara found it rather sad that Eva should be so surprised that people actually cared for her.

'So let's go over this again, Mr Fenner,' said the detective who was interviewing Charlie. 'You and your wife had a fight during which she caused that injury to your face; then she left the house.'

'That's right.'

'You say you didn't go after her.'

'No, I didn't.'

The officer looked at him closely. 'Didn't you feel duty bound to follow her to try and put things right?'

'She specifically told me not to. She wanted to be on her own and my wife wasn't a person you defied lightly.'

'Weren't you worried about her being out on her own afer dark?' the detective asked.

'No. Not at all. She often goes walking at night. It wasn't very late and it's quiet round our way. Not the sort of place you expect trouble, being miles from anywhere.'

'Weren't you worried when she didn't come back?'

'My client has already answered that question several times,' the duty solicitor said sharply. 'May I remind you that no charge has been made?'

The detective drew hard on his cigarette, then said to Charlie, 'All right. You say you fell asleep and didn't realise she was missing until the next morning.'

'That's right.'

Leaning back slightly with his hands clasped and his chin resting on his forefingers, the officer looked at Charlie meditatively. 'So, you had a bust-up with your wife, a violent one as we can see from your face, and yet you were able to sleep.'

'As I have already told you, I had some whisky to calm me down and one led to another and I had too much,' explained Charlie, weary of answering the same questions over and over again. 'I have admitted to you that my wife and I didn't get on and I wanted to discuss some sort of separation with her. But I did not kill her.'

'Is it really necessary to keep going over the same ground, inspector?' said the solicitor.

The detective glanced at him and continued with the interview unperturbed. 'You see, Mr Fenner, we think that your wife died as a result of a blow to her head caused by hitting it on a boulder in a deep ditch, and we believe that someone pushed her into the ditch with the intention of killing her.'

'It wasn't me.'

'Mm.' The other man stubbed his cigarette out in the ashtray. 'I'm puzzled, because you strike me as a decent sort of a chap. The sort of man who wouldn't want his wife to be out on her own at night; the sort of man who wouldn't overdo it with the booze.'

'I don't normally drink too much . . . and I've explained why I wasn't worried about Hester being out at night.'

At that moment they were interrupted. The door opened and a uniformed officer beckoned to the inspector, who got up and went to the door to listen to what the policeman had to say. When he came back to the table, he said, 'It seems that some new information has come to light, so that will be all for now, Mr Fenner. Interview ended at three p.m.'

Charlie wasn't sure how to take this. 'What does that mean exactly?'

'You are free to go, but don't leave the area, as we will need to speak to you again.'

As the stenographer finished her notes, Charlie got up and walked from the room, feeling somewhat bewildered.

In a tea room in Tunbridge Wells a shocked Charlie faced Clara across a table in the corner among the potted palms.

'That explains a lot of things,' he said, when Clara had finished telling him what she had told the police.

'I'm sorry to have brought it all out into the open when you must be hurting so much already. But I thought the police should know in view of the circumstances.'

'Thank you for coming forward,' he said. 'I don't know if it will help my case because I've already admitted to the police that our marriage was on the rocks and they seem determined to put me in the frame. But thanks anyway.'

'Surely Vincent is the much more likely suspect in the light of the new information,' she suggested. 'I've told the police that from what I heard Hester was keeping the affair from you while putting pressure on him for commitment, which he seemed reluctant to give.'

'Mm.'

'I was thinking that if she was making a nuisance of herself, he could have lost his temper and pushed her into the ditch.'

'It's all supposition, though, isn't it? None of us knows what happened.'

On impulse she reached across and put her hand on his in a comforting gesture. 'It must be awful for you; the shock of her dying in such terrible circumstances, then being suspected of her murder, and on top of all that, finding out she'd been unfaithful.'

He gave her a bleak smile and clasped her hand impulsively. 'I have had better times,' he confessed. 'But life has been pretty awful for some time because things were so bad between Hester and me. The marriage was impossible after a few happy times at the beginning. The awful thing is, I had grown to hate her by the end, and that makes it worse somehow. Having someone die when there's so much bitterness between you; knowing that it can never be made better now. We didn't get along, but I never wanted her dead. It's tragic to think of anyone dying so young. Even Hester didn't deserve that.'

'No, she didn't.' She drew her hand back and gave him a wry grin. 'We don't want anyone getting the wrong idea, do we? The way things are for you at the moment.'

'I'm past caring what people think about me.' He looked at her tenderly. 'I wouldn't want you to get a bad repu-tation, though. Holding hands with a murder suspect; that could get you involved in this rotten mess.'

'I'll risk it. So what is the actual situation with you and the police now?'

'I'm not sure. They haven't charged me so that's a good sign. But I think they might have let me go while they build a case against me. They obviously haven't got sufficient evidence at the moment or they would have done so already.'

'Perhaps they'll rule you out after they've questioned Vincent,' she suggested.

He shrugged. 'Vincent's always been wild and selfish, and having an affair with your brother's wife is the lowest of the low. But I don't see him as a murderer.'

'It does seem extreme, I must say,' she said. 'We'll just have to wait and see what happens.'

'The whole thing seems unreal to me,' he confessed. 'I just can't believe it's happening. Hester dead; murdered!' He held his head. 'God almighty!'

'You don't expect it to happen to your own family, do you?' she said. 'Murder is something you just read about in the paper.'

'Exactly.' He looked at her. 'It's very good of you to come all this way in my defence.'

'No trouble at all.'

'What are your plans now?'

'I shall go to Brierley to see how Eva got on and, you never know, I might get an apology from your parents now they know the truth about why your mother's jewellery was found in my suitcase,' she said. 'Then I shall get a train back to London. I don't know if Eva will come with me or if she'll stay on to give the family some support. I suppose it all depends what sort of a reception she gets from her mother.'

'Why don't you stay overnight?'

She gave a wry grin. 'Can you imagine your mother offering me hospitality?'

'She might do, as a peace offering,' he suggested lightly. 'But there's a spare room at the cottage anyway.'

'I don't think that would do your reputation much good,' she said. 'A woman staying at your place just days after your wife has been murdered.'

'The police have made their minds up about me so I doubt if it will make any difference,' he said. 'Anyway, you'd be in the spare room, of course.' He looked at her thoughtfully. 'Oughtn't you to stay around anyway, though, in case the police want to speak to you again?'

'They've told me that they probably will,' she replied. 'I've given them my home address and the phone number of the café where I work. They'll contact me if they need me and I'll get the first train.'

'It's a long way for you to keep coming to and fro,' he pointed out, 'so you're very welcome to stay at the cottage if you change your mind. Meanwhile, when you've finished your tea, we might as well make our way to Brierley together.'

'Good idea.' Despite the miserable circumstances, she was very pleased to be with him.

Clara's hopes of an apology were dashed as soon as she entered the Brierley house and was confronted by Mabel Fenner.

'Don't you think we've got enough trouble without you coming here and upsetting us even more by telling the police a pack of lies?'

'Eva has told you, then.'

'She's told us all right,' said Mabel angrily. 'And I've never heard such a fairy story in my life.'

'It's no fairy story, believe me.'

'She's telling the truth, Mum,' said Eva.

'The police have been here and taken Vincent away for questioning, probably as a direct result of what you've told them,' Mabel went on as though Eva hadn't spoken. 'I hope that makes you happy, Miss Troublemaker Tripp.'

'Of course it doesn't make me happy.' Clara was irritated by the woman's refusal to face the facts. 'I had to tell them, given the circumstances.'

'Lay off her, will you, Mum,' said Charlie. 'What she told the police is true. She couldn't just stand back and say nothing when it might affect the case.'

'You would say that, wouldn't you?' Mabel snapped. 'The police have let you go and taken Vincent now.'

'They gave me the impression that they haven't finished with me.'

'Oh, for goodness' sake, I know Vincent is your favourite, Mum, but surely you're pleased to have Charlie back,' said Eva, disgusted by her mother's attitude. 'He is your son as well, you know.'

'Of course I'm pleased he's back, but they've taken my other son now,' she said and Clara could see that she was so distressed she hardly knew what she was saying. 'What's happened to my family? Everything is falling apart around us.'

'A murder,' said Charlie. 'That's what's happened.'

The Fenner family had been in a state of collapse long before Hester's death, thought Clara, but she stayed silent.

'So how did you get on at the police station, Charlie?' Mabel enquired, seeming to soften a little. 'Did they treat you well?'

It had taken her long enough to ask him, thought Clara, but he just said, 'They were all right. But they have their job to do and they seem convinced that I am responsible for Hester's death.'

'Perhaps that'll change now that they know about Hester and Vincent,' suggested Eva.

'There *is* no Hester and Vincent,' insisted Mabel. 'Vincent has been brought up properly and he wouldn't do a thing like that. We don't have those sorts of carryings-on in this family.' She turned on Clara again. 'It's all just your lies, a filthy pack of lies.'

'Why would I lie about it?' asked Clara, remaining outwardly calm though her nerves were stretched almost to breaking point. 'Do you think I have nothing better to do with my time than to come down here making trouble?'

'Frankly I think you owe her an apology,' said Charlie

in a firm tone. 'For dismissing her from her job for something she didn't do and being rude to her in the process.'

'Apologise?' snorted Mabel. 'I've nothing to apologise for. I don't believe a word she says. I've told you, we don't have adultery in this family.'

'But we do, Mum. It's been going on under our noses,' said Eva. 'Hester and Vincent set Clara up to get her dismissed because she knew about them. You'll have to accept it, and at least have the decency to apologise to Clara. You owe her that much.'

'Oh, do be quiet, Eva,' said Mabel irritably. 'Vincent did nothing of the sort. The last thing he would ever do is carry on with his brother's wife.'

'I'm afraid he did, Mabel,' said her husband suddenly. He had been sitting quietly listening to the conversation from his seat by the stove.

'What are you talking about, John?' she demanded in annoyance. 'You know nothing about it.'

'I do, as it happens. I know all about their seedy little affair,' he said. 'In fact I was there when Hester died.'

A communal gasp went up throughout the room, all eyes on John Fenner.

'You?' said Mabel. '*You* murdered her?'

'There was no murder,' he said, as everyone stared at him spellbound. 'Hester's death was an accident. An accident brought about by her own bad temper.'

'I'd known they were carrying on for some time,' he said. 'I saw them together one night when I was out for a stroll and I could see it in them every time I looked at them after that; the knowing looks, the whispering in the yard and so on.' He looked at Clara. 'I didn't know by the time you were dismissed, though. That would never have happened if I had. Please accept my belated apologies.'

'Never mind all that. Just get on with it, man, for good-ness' sake,' snapped Mabel.

'I became increasingly worried about it as time went on,' he continued. 'I could tell that neither Charlie nor Vincent was happy and Hester was obviously the cause. I originally thought that the hanky-panky would run its course but there didn't seem to be any let-up in either of my sons' misery. So I decided I should at least try to do something about it.'

'Why didn't you tell me?' Mabel demanded.

'For the same reason that Clara didn't tell Charlie. I didn't want to hurt you.'

'You're hurting me now.'

'Yes, I'm sorry about that. But it's become unavoidable. I can't protect you any longer. It has to come out now or one of our sons could hang for murder.'

'And now you might be the one who goes to the gallows,' said his wife. 'If you were there when she died, the police might think you did it.'

'Let him finish, Mum,' intervened Charlie. 'So what happened that night, Dad?'

'I was out taking the air when I saw Hester slam out of the cottage and march across the fields so I went after her in the hope of having a chat with her to try to make her see reason and end her association with Vincent,' he explained. 'She was in a foul temper and told me in the most colourful language to go away, which I didn't. We walked across the fields towards the ridge. I told her I knew what was going on between her and Vincent and begged her to end it. She said she had no intention of doing so and that I was to mind my own business. She admitted that Vincent was trying to end things between them and she wasn't having it. She said that she was going to leave Charlie and go away with Vincent no matter whose feelings were hurt; she seemed absolutely determined. When I pointed out that it was a very unkind thing to do to Charlie and something that should never have been going on at all, she suddenly flew into a rage and came at me punching and scratching.'

'I can imagine,' muttered Charlie. 'She'd done the same thing to me earlier. That's how I got the scratch on my face. She could be very violent when she couldn't get her own way.'

'Anyway, she pushed me so hard I lost my balance and fell down on the ground with a hell of a bump. I was dazed and couldn't get up for a few minutes. I could hear her cursing and shouting at me and then there was a scream and silence. I eventually managed to get to my feet and looked around with the lamp until I saw her in the ditch. I climbed down there and tried unsuccessfully to find a pulse. I guessed she must have hit her head on a rock or something.'

'So why didn't you go and get help?' asked Eva.

'It was too late,' he said, his voice barely audible as he remembered. 'She was dead. I'm not sure what happened then. I know I was violently sick; then I think I just stood there for a while, unable to move. I know I should have gone straight to the police but for some reason I'm not sure of I didn't. I don't think it was even panic. It was more a feeling of confusion; it didn't seem real. I suppose I must have been scared stiff. I knew it would look as though I was responsible. Once I hadn't told anyone straight away it got harder to do so all the time.'

'It's only been a few days, Dad,' Eva pointed out.

'A few days too long,' he said. 'Anyway, now with my sons under suspicion I must go to the police without further delay.' He lowered his eyes. 'Better late than never, eh? I'm very sorry, everyone, for causing such trouble.'

'You didn't kill her, Dad,' said Eva. 'So don't make it seem as if you did.'

'No, I didn't kill her. But I've caused a lot of trouble by not speaking up sooner, especially to my sons,' he said, sounding weary, his face pale and strained. 'And made things worse for myself with the police, who will probably think I pushed her over.'

'I'll come with you to the police station, Dad,' said Charlie. 'Let's get it over with.'

'I'll come too,' said Eva.

'No, I think you'd be more useful staying with Mum,' said her brother.

'Sorry, Mabel,' said John in a broken voice, turning towards his wife sadly.

Ashen-faced, Mabel was silent and remained so as the two men left the room. There was not so much as an encouraging word or a gesture of reassurance for her poor suffering husband. But somehow Clara didn't think the omission was because of malice in this particular instance. It was more as though she was incapacitated by the shock. Much as Clara despised the woman for what she'd done to Eva, she couldn't help feeling sorry for her as her world collapsed around her.

As this was very much a private family occasion, Clara said, 'I'll make us some tea, shall I?' and made a diplomatic exit. Despite the fact that the two other women didn't get on, Clara thought this moment belonged to mother and daughter.

'I'm sure it'll be all right, Mum,' said Eva gently, sensitive to the fact that her mother must be frantic with worry. 'The police will soon realise that Dad didn't kill Hester.'

'He'll be in trouble for withholding information though, won't he?' said Mabel dismally. 'He should have gone to the police right away, the stupid man.'

'He knows what he did wasn't the wisest thing,' Eva pointed out defensively. 'At least we know that it was an accident and not murder now.'

'He could have saved us all a lot of worry by being honest from the start.'

'Dad would never deliberately hurt anyone, you must know that. I think he was probably shocked and frightened and his judgement was impaired. It must have been a terrible experience. It would have frightened me to death, I know that.'

'Yes, I suppose it must have been awful for him,' Mabel conceded at last. Eva had never seen her mother so subdued. She had been her usual spiteful self when Eva had arrived and had almost gone berserk when Eva had told her why Clara had gone to the police station. But now there was a terrible sadness about her. The anger that had always been a part of her character as far back as Eva could remember seemed to have finally burned out. For the first time in her life Eva was not tensed waiting for the next insult.

'What you said just now about Vincent being my favourite,' said Mabel, in a slow, weary voice.

'Yes?'

'Why did you say it?'

'Because it's true, of course. But Charlie and I are so used to it that we barely notice.'

'But I've never favoured any one of you.'

Eva gave a dry laugh. 'Oh, come on. Vincent has never been able to do any wrong in your eyes. If there was ever just enough for one of anything a bit special, Vincent had it. It didn't matter how rude he was to you or how many times he stepped out of line, he was still the favourite child.'

'I didn't realise . . .'

'How could you not realise? You must feel something special for him for some reason.'

'No. I don't think so.' Mabel seemed bewildered.

'Oh, come on, Mum; in a minute you're going to tell me that you haven't always hated me.'

'Hated you?'

'That's right. Please don't insult me by pretending that you don't.'

'I have never hated you.'

Even in the midst of a crisis, Eva couldn't allow her mother's remarks to go unchallenged.

'You blamed me for Rosie's death and gave me a dog's life. If that isn't hating someone I don't know what is.'

'I may have said things . . .'

'I'll say you did,' Eva came back at her. 'You practically destroyed me. But now I'm away from here that's all over now.'

She expected her mother to retaliate, but Mabel just sat with her hands clasped in front of her, her eyes lowered.

'I hear you've been ill,' she said suddenly, looking up.

'Yes.'

The two women looked at each other for a moment and Eva thought she caught a moment of warmth in her mother's cold grey eyes. But she just said in her normal brusque tone, 'You look perfectly all right to me.'

'I'm fine.'

'Some sort of mental problem, wasn't it?' Mabel obviously had difficulty acknowledging the nature of the illness.

'It was an emotional thing,' Eva told her. 'Something you wouldn't understand.'

Whether her remark hit home or not Eva didn't know, because her mother just said, 'As long as you're better now, that's the important thing.'

Needing some sort of reaction from this woman who didn't seem to have an iota of goodwill in her, Eva said, 'The Tripps have been wonderful to me. I honestly don't know what I would have done without them.'

'I'm sure you would have managed somehow,' her mother said tartly.

The tension drew tight. Eva was annoyed with herself for still being hurt by her mother's attitude, which had changed from loud and spiteful to quiet and indifferent.

'Here we are,' said Clara, entering the room, 'a nice cup of tea. I bet you can both do with one.'

'We certainly can,' responded Eva giving Clara a grateful look; another few seconds alone with her mother and she thought she would have either exploded into a fit of rage or burst into tears. The only way to survive her mother was to keep well away from her. She planned to do just that once the current crisis was over.

Sipping her tea and watching the two young women talking together, Mabel felt a burning sensation at the back of her eyes and knew she was close to tears, something she hadn't resorted to since she had stopped weeping for Rosie.

What was happening to her family? All the men were currently at the police station and all because of Vincent, who had behaved despicably in a way that went against everything he had been brought up to believe in. She didn't want to accept that he had done what he was accused of, but she knew in her heart that it was true. If he hadn't carried on in such a disgusting way, Hester would still be alive today. The thought of what he'd done made Mabel feel physically sick.

Then there was Eva, who hated her and said she'd almost destroyed her. Had she really been that bad a mother to her? Snippets of things she'd said came rushing into her mind as though out of a long forgotten dream: *stupid girl; wicked girl; you were to blame for your little sister's death.*

Had she really said such things? Surely not! But it was her own voice she could hear inside her head. It was her own pain from the past that was filling her again now. Her hands shook and the cup rattled in the saucer so violently that the hot tea spilled into her lap. The liquid was burning but it was as though she couldn't feel it.

'Oh dear, Mrs Fenner,' said Clara. 'Here, let me take the cup and saucer and I'll get a cloth.'

'Are you all right, Mum?' asked Eva. It didn't matter how much her mother hurt her, she still cared about her, even though she didn't want to.

'Yes, it's nothing to fuss about,' she said, as Clara took her cup and wiped her down with a tea towel. 'I'd better go upstairs and change my skirt, though.'

After she'd left the room, Clara said, 'Are you all right, Eva?'

'Sort of. But mothers, eh? You're never really free of them, are you?'

Clara decided to stay overnight in Kent. Eva asked her to do so to give her some support, and Mabel had agreed in an indifferent manner. A house guest was nothing to her compared to the current troubles. As for Clara, her own personal affairs had to take second place in the light of the dire events in the dysfunctional Fenner family.

As it happened Vincent came home from the police station on his own soon after the tea-spilling episode. Clara and Eva were still in the parlour. Mabel had gone to the kitchen but came scurrying into the other room when she heard Vincent's voice.

'Oh, you're on your own,' she said wildly. 'What's happening at the police station?'

'They're still questioning Dad, and Charlie is staying there to be on hand for him.'

'Don't you think you should have stayed there to give your father some support?' she said.

'It doesn't need two of us to wait around,' he said carelessly. 'After the grilling I've been given I was glad to get out of that place.'

'As it's your fault that your father is at the police station, I would have thought the very least you could do for him was wait there and see if there was anything you could do to help him.'

'My fault?' He stared at her in disbelief. 'It's Dad's fault for not coming forward earlier. He's made it worse for himself; worse for all of us.'

'Don't you dare speak about your father in that way,' she said harshly.

Vincent looked at her in a puzzled manner. Such criticism of him was unprecedented. 'What's the matter, Ma?' he asked. 'What's got into you?'

'You are what the matter is,' she spat out. 'You have brought disgrace and worry on this family with your sordid carryings-on and I want you out of here first thing tomorrow morning.'

A nerve-shattering silence shot through the room. Eva's eyes were bulging with shock.

'What?' asked Vincent at last.

'You heard.'

'You want me to leave here, for good?'

'That's right.'

'Why am I being blamed for something I didn't do?' he asked. 'Dad was the one who was with Hester when she died, not me. I had nothing to do with it. Anyway, her death was an accident.'

'Which only came about because your father tried to put a stop to your filthy affair. The accident wouldn't have happened if you'd not betrayed your brother. Hester would still be alive if it wasn't for you making her discontented with her marriage and getting into such a temper she had to go out at night to walk it off.'

Vincent emitted a dry laugh. 'Hester a victim?' he said with a cynical smile. 'That's a good one. Hester wouldn't know how to be put upon. She instigated the affair, not me. If anyone was a victim it was me. Talk about clingy; she was like a limpet.'

'Don't make things worse by trying to talk your way out of it,' his mother warned him, her voice shaky with emotion. 'You betrayed your brother and brought big trouble on this family. What if your father is accused of murder? Who knows what the police will make of it?'

'Now you're just being over-dramatic,' said Vincent.

'Maybe I am, but I still want you out of here,' she told him. 'Out of the house and out of the business. As far as I'm concerned you're no longer a son of mine.'

'But I've got nowhere to go!'

'You should have thought of that when you embarked on an affair with another man's wife,' she said. 'You know that your father and I don't approve of such things.'

'I'd finished with her. Hester was the one who wanted to keep it going.'

'That is irrelevant. It should never have started in the first place. You've been deceiving us all and I cannot condone such behaviour, so you will have to go. You can stay here tonight but I want you gone by the morning.'

'All right, Ma,' he said in a patronising manner. 'You've made your point and I've taken it. Now let's be realistic.'

'I've never been more realistic or seen things more clearly than I do at this moment,' she told him. 'Tomorrow morning I want no sign of you in this house.' She got to her feet. 'Now I'm going to cook supper. You can eat here tonight but I don't want you to sit at the same table as us. So you can go and start packing and have your meal in your room. I don't want to see your face again, ever!'

'Dad won't be pleased; neither will Charlie,' said Vincent. 'They need me in the business.'

'No one is indispensable,' she reminded him. 'They'll get help from outside.'

'You wait until they hear about it,' he said. 'They'll soon talk some sense into you.'

'I doubt it,' she retorted. 'But let's wait and see what happens at the police station and pray that your father doesn't have to sleep in a cell tonight.' And with that parting comment she turned and left the room.

'Well,' said Vincent, looking at his sister. 'What on earth's got into her?'

'I should have thought that was obvious,' said Eva coldly.

'Oh, don't tell me you're taking her side,' he complained. 'She's never had any time for you.'

'You're quite right, she hasn't, whereas you were always the golden boy.'

'Jealous?'

'I have been, many times,' Eva admitted, 'but not now. That's all in the past. I have a different life now.'

'Why are you siding with her after the way she's treated you?'

'Because she's right in this instance. The whole thing is your fault. It all stems from your affair with Hester. Surely even you must know that it's stooping a bit low to sleep with your brother's wife.'

'It was her fault.'

'Oh, please, don't try that one again. As far as I'm concerned you have broken all the rules of decency, and as for what you and Hester did to Clara here, that was absolutely despicable,' she told him. 'In my opinion you've got what you deserve and I hope Mum sticks to her guns and makes you go.'

'She won't do that, not to me,' he said with confidence. 'She'll have relented by the morning.'

'You arrogant pig!'

'Oh, I'm getting out of here,' he said. 'I don't have to listen to some loony fresh out of the madhouse.'

Eva stepped forward and brought her hand across his face with a whack.

He stared at her in disbelief, holding his cheek, and for a moment Clara thought he was going to retaliate. But he turned and left the room.

'Well done,' said Clara. 'He deserved that.'

'Why do I feel so awful, though?' asked Eva shakily.

'It's a bad time for all of you,' said Clara, putting her arm round her. 'It'll pass. Everything does eventually.'

In the kitchen, Mabel was stirring the mutton stew on the stove through a blur of tears. Telling Vincent to go had all but crippled her. The thought of not having him around made her feel bereft, but most of all she was leaden with disappointment to know that he could go against the principles she had brought him up to believe in. She'd had to tell him to leave. She couldn't have him living under her roof, knowing that he had committed such a transgression.

Her family was growing smaller so quickly. She had driven Eva away and now she'd been forced to send Vincent packing. And of course she had lost Rosie long ago. There was only Charlie left. Poor Charlie! Since Rosie's death, Mabel had lost the ability to empathise but she did find herself wondering now how Charlie must be feeling. To lose his wife was bad enough, but to find out she'd been deceiving him as well must be a terrible blow.

She and her elder son hadn't always seen eye to eye. He'd never been slow to speak his mind to her, and he'd always taken Eva's side against her. For some reason he had never been able to see how difficult it was for Mabel to forgive her for causing Rosie's death. In fact, he didn't think it was Eva's fault at all. Neither did Clara Tripp, who'd even had the audacity to suggest that it was Mabel's own fault.

Troubling thoughts were beginning to insinuate themselves into her mind. No, she couldn't bear them. She must somehow push them away; they were too painful and she couldn't cope with them at this awful time. Not on top of everything else that had happened. She wanted John to come home safe and free from the police; that was all that mattered now.

She brushed her tears away with the back of her hand and added the dumplings to the stew.

It was late when Charlie and his father finally got home from the police station. John had been released without charge, though warned that there would be further questions and a strong possibility of his being charged with perverting the course of justice.

Both men looked strained and exhausted, and neither wanted to talk much. Mabel insisted that they sit down and eat the mutton stew she had saved for them, and then the Fenners senior went to bed, obviously wanting to be on their own to talk. Eva brought Charlie up to date on the subject of Vincent.

'Well, well. Mum must be really rattled to have done a thing like that to the son who can do no wrong,' he said. 'I wonder if she'll actually go through with it.'

'Vincent thinks not. He reckons she'll back down, probably because she's always been soft with him and also because you and Dad need him in the business.'

'We can employ someone to do what he does,' said Charlie. 'I can't say I'll be sorry if he goes. He never pulled his weight in the orchard and he and I didn't really get on, even before his latest piece of mischief. So I won't be backing Dad up if he wants him to stay on here. I doubt if he will after what's happened. He and Mum are very strict about that sort of thing.'

'I'll back you up, Charlie,' said Eva, yawning. 'I don't know about you two, but I'm dead beat. I think I'll go to bed.'

'Yeah, I must head home too,' he said, heaving himself wearily to his feet. 'Goodnight, girls.'

As Clara went upstairs to bed she was very aware of the fact that Charlie needed her. He might not have said so or even been aware of it himself, but she'd seen it in his eyes every time he'd looked at her since he'd come back from the police station. Regardless of the circumstances or the fact that his marriage had been on the rocks, the man had just lost his wife. He would be needing a friend as never before; someone outside his family. She had to go to him.

Chapter Thirteen

'You've come like the answer to a prayer,' said Charlie when he opened the cottage door.

'I'm probably breaking every law of decency there is and my name will be mud with your mother if she ever finds out I've been here, but I sensed that you needed a friend,' Clara said as he ushered her inside. 'I couldn't bear the thought of you here alone at such a time.'

He led her into a small, oil-lit sitting room bursting with the chintz upholstery, abundant ornaments, extravagantly frilled curtains and trimmings that were typical of Hester. 'I'm not exactly full of the joys of spring at the moment, as you can imagine.'

'It might get easier after the funeral; the time in between is bound to be difficult,' she suggested. 'Do you know when it is yet?'

'No. The police won't release her, er . . .' he cleared his throat, 'her body while they're still pursuing their inquiries.'

'I'm sure your father will be cleared of any wrongdoing.'

'If he isn't it will be a travesty of justice,' he said. 'Everyone knows that Dad wouldn't hurt a fly. He got caught in the crossfire of my wife's bad temper, that's all.'

'Did you really have no idea of what was going on between Hester and Vincent?'

'None at all. It should have occurred to me. She was so discontented with me that I should have guessed there was another man, but such a thing just didn't enter my head. I suppose things were so difficult between us I just concentrated on getting through each day with as little bad feeling as possible. Anyway, can I get you a drink of something? I'm going to have a stiff whisky. I've got some cider if you'd rather.'

'That will be lovely, but just a small glass, please,' she said. 'It will remind me of the time I first came to Brierley as a picker and all us workers used to have a glass or two of cider in the evenings around the campfire.'

'Happy days, eh?' he said, getting up.

'Very,' she said, smiling at the memory.

'I bet you didn't think then that you'd become so embroiled in the Fenner family problems.'

'I certainly did not.' She paused thoughtfully. 'It's strange how my life seems to be intertwined with you and your clan. Circumstances keep pulling me back.'

'It's a wonder you want to bother with us after the way the family have treated you.'

'I came here today for you as an individual, not your family,' she told him. 'I knew Eva needed my support, of course, but it was you who brought me here. As soon as I heard what had happened I knew I had to come.'

'I'll get you that cider,' he said, sounding emotional, and disappeared into the kitchen.

'I hope I haven't embarrassed you,' she said when he returned and handed her her drink.

'Not embarrassed, no,' he responded, pouring himself a

small glass of whisky from a tray on the sideboard. 'Touched is more the way I would describe it. You are the only good thing in my life at the moment and I don't deserve you.' He sat down and took a large swallow of whisky. 'Not that you are in my life, of course. But you came today and that means a lot to me. It's a pity I let you go all those years ago.'

'As you said before, it wasn't the time,' she said. 'People's lives go in different directions, especially during and after a war.'

'They needn't have if I'd had any sense.'

'I'd be lying if I said I wasn't disappointed and surprised at the time not to have heard from you after that night,' she confessed.

'I was going into action in France for the second time a couple of days later,' he said. 'We all knew what the odds were against surviving a second stretch in the trenches. If it's any consolation, I've regretted it ever since. I never forgot you and when fate brought us together again I just couldn't believe my good luck, even though I wasn't free to do anything about it.'

'We were strangers, though,' she pointed out. 'It was just one evening.'

'But since then I've got to know you better,' he said, 'and although this is the very least appropriate time to say something like this, I knew I was in love with you the minute I set eyes on you again in the tea rooms. Those feelings aren't going to go away.'

'Charlie, don't . . .'

'Sorry. Poor Hester isn't even buried yet and this must be the height of bad taste, but I need you to know how I feel.'

'It wasn't the right time back then and the timing is worse now,' she said. 'Even apart from your circumstances, I'm engaged to Arnold and we'll be getting married in a few months' time.'

'I know,' he said. 'I'm deeply ashamed for speaking this way. I'm the one who's broken all the laws of decency. Forgive me. I should have kept my feelings to myself.'

'Don't be sorry,' she said, her attitude changing with the strength of her emotions. 'Because I love you too.'

'I've made such a mess of everything . . .'

'Shh,' she said, throwing caution to the wind and going over to him and putting her arms round him, feeling again the magic of that night at the dance all those years ago. She'd never forgotten how it felt to be close to him. 'No more words. Not now.'

As he reciprocated she knew that, no matter how wrong this was, it was right. So very right!

'I have to go back to the house,' she said later, 'and hope that no one notices that I've been gone.'

'Must you?'

'I'm afraid so.'

'I want you with me.'

'Me too, but we can't have that yet,' she said, ensconced in his arms on the sofa. 'We'll need to let some time pass before we can be together openly.'

'Not too long.'

'The sooner the better for me, but it's much too early at the moment. That really would tarnish your reputation and in turn that of your family,' she pointed out. 'I think the idea of her newly bereaved son being with another woman this quickly on top of everything else would just about finish your mother off.'

'The gossip would be upsetting for you too,' he pointed out. 'My back is broad but it would be horrible for you. We don't want to have the world against us to start with.'

'No we don't, though I'm going to get plenty of bad feeling when I break off my engagement to Arnold; and not all of it from him. Mum and Dad will be very disappointed in me for letting Arnold down. He's almost like one of the family.'

'Is there anything I can do to help?'

'No. That part is down to me,' she said. 'Though I'm dreading telling poor Arnold that I can't marry him, especially as he's been so good to me.'

'Perhaps it would be best if you got it over with as soon as you get back,' he suggested. 'There's no point in letting him continue to think you're going to marry him.'

'I wouldn't want to do that.'

'Clara,' he said, stroking her hair.

'Yes?'

'Despite all the complications I'm glad we're together at last,' he whispered tenderly. 'Even if we do have to wait a while.'

'Me too,' she said softly. 'Now give me your spare key so that I can creep back into the big house.'

'Where did you get to last night?' asked Eva in a friendly manner the next morning, when she came to the guest room with a cup of tea for her friend.

'Er . . . what do you mean?' Clara's guard was up.

'I mean that I came in here for a chat before settling down for the night and you weren't here,' she explained, sitting on the edge of the bed, 'or anywhere else in the house for that matter. You didn't say anything about going out for a walk.'

'I wasn't out walking.' Clara could feel her face burning and turned away from Eva, ostensibly to drink her tea.

'Where were you, then?'

'Actually, I popped over to the cottage to make sure that Charlie was all right. I thought he needed some company.'

'Oh, that was nice of you. I expect he was grateful, wasn't he?'

'Yes, I think he was,' she said sheepishly.

Eva looked at her. 'Clara, what's the matter?' she asked. 'Why are you looking so peculiar?'

'Am I?'

'You know you are.'

Clara made a face.

'What! You and Charlie?' Eva burst out after a moment.

'Shh,' Clara warned. 'No one must know.'

'But Hester's only just died . . . how . . . I mean it's so quick!'

'I know, it's positively disgusting,' Clara admitted, looking shamefaced, 'but it isn't sudden. I fell in love with your brother a long time ago.'

'When you met him at the dance?'

She nodded. 'When we happened to meet again four years later, the feelings were still there for both of us. But neither of us said anything – not until last night.'

Fortunately Eva had the grace not to ask exactly what had happened at the cottage. 'But what about Arnold?' she said.

'I shall have to tell him that I can't marry him.'

'Oh, dear. That won't be easy. Poor Arnold.'

'Yeah, I know. It's terrible and I feel awful about it, but I can't marry the wrong man.'

'Of course not.'

'You mustn't breathe a word to anyone about Charlie and me just yet,' Clara urged her. 'It's much too soon after Hester's death. The gossip would hurt your mother terribly and I think she's got quite enough to cope with at the moment.'

'I won't say anything.' She paused, looking at Clara and seeing the radiance she was unable to hide. 'My best friend and my brother. How lovely! I reckon he deserves someone like you after what he's been through with Hester.'

'I'm so glad you're pleased.'

Eva flung her arms round her. 'I'm absolutely delighted. You and I will become related. The sooner the better.'

'It won't be for a while,' Clara told her. 'Meanwhile, not a word to anyone. Promise?'

'Mum's the word.' She looked at her. 'Just to bring you up to date, Vincent has gone.'

'Oh, your mum kept to her word then.'

'Amazingly, yes, she did.'

Spring was in full flow and Clara noticed it with added sensitivity the next day when Charlie drove her to the station. Everything registered with dazzling clarity because Charlie was in her life: the sky was a brilliant sapphire sea with white wispy clouds sailing across it; the new shoots burgeoning on the trees and hedgerows were of the palest green enhanced by the patches of yellow daffodils swaying in the breeze on the grass verges.

Eva was staying on at Brierley until they knew more

about what was going to happen to her father; possibly until after the funeral. Clara had to go home because of her job, but anyway it would have been inappropriate for her to stay longer since she wasn't family.

'I had to tell Eva about us,' she told Charlie in the car. 'I couldn't lie to her when she asked me where I was last night. But I'm sure she won't say anything.'

'I don't mind who knows,' he confessed. 'But the gossip wouldn't be pleasant for you. And there is Mum to consider.'

'Exactly.'

'So you'll tell Arnold right away, will you?'

She made a face. 'As soon as I can pluck up the courage, but I feel really awful about it,' she confessed. 'The poor thing. He doesn't deserve it.'

'Don't back out and break my heart because you feel sorry for him, will you?' he urged her, only half teasing.

'Of course not.'

They drove up outside the station and joined the orderly gathering of motor cars, taxis and pedestrians heading for the entrance. 'Don't come on to the platform, Charlie,' she said when he stopped the car. 'I only have a small bag to carry, which I can easily manage myself, and I'd rather say goodbye here. I don't want to get on the train in tears.'

'As you wish.'

He leaned towards her and she backed away. 'Don't kiss me,' she said. 'There are too many people about and someone is bound to see us. It might be someone who knows your family. You know how close-knit they are round here.'

'Now you're being paranoid.'

'I'd sooner that than cause yet another scandal for the Fenner family.'

'I suppose you're right,' he sighed. 'We'll keep in touch by letter and I'll try to slip up to London to see you when things have calmed down here.'

'Not until after I've broken off my engagement to Arnold, though,' she said worriedly. 'I don't want to hurt him any more than I have to.'

'If you deal with it as soon as you see him it will be over and done with.'

'Yeah, yeah, I know.'

'It's going to be very busy at Brierley anyway now that the weather has broken. So I probably wouldn't be able to get away for a while, especially as Vincent won't be around.'

'We'll be together as soon as we can.'

He got out and hurried round to the passenger door and opened it for her.

'Bye, Charlie,' she said, looking at him with infinite tenderness. 'Take good care of yourself and keep me up to date with what's happening when you can.'

He nodded. 'Love you, Clara,' he whispered.

'And I love you, Charlie Fenner.'

She turned and went into the station, turning to wave before she disappeared. She and Charlie had challenges to overcome before they could be together. She was anxious about what lay ahead with Arnold and hated herself for what she was about to do. But her overriding emotion was of happiness; the sheer joy of being in love.

Mabel couldn't sleep that night. For the first time since her youngest daughter's death, she was taking an honest look into her memory. Maybe the shock of Hester's demise and the ensuing problems had opened some door in her mind; perhaps it was simply the passing of time that had unlocked it. Whatever the cause, the result was agonising. Looking back she could hear her own voice, feel again the spite she had needed to emit, see the bewildered, pleading look in the child Eva's eyes, and later the sullen, rebellious young woman as she began to dare to retaliate. There was the shouting, the accusations, the need to hurt as she herself was hurting. And now the searing compunction as she allowed herself to see the truth of her own wickedness and finally admit that she had been to blame for her daughter's death.

Careful not to wake her sleeping husband she got out of bed, put on her slippers and dressing gown and headed along the landing.

'What do you want?' asked Eva, when her mother came into her room.

'Just thought we could have a chat,' Mabel replied.

'What about exactly?'

This wasn't easy for Mabel and she struggled to find the courage to say what must be said. 'I just wanted to say that it's good of you to stay on here and I very much appreciate it,' she said, perching nervously on the edge of the bed.

'I'm not doing it for you,' Eva responded coolly, feeling the need to protect herself as always. 'I'm doing it for Dad and Charlie. The least I can do is stay on until after the funeral, so long as we don't have to wait too long for it.'

'For whatever reason, it's good of you.'

'What are you after?' asked Eva, eyeing her mother with suspicion.

'Why would I be after anything?'

'Because you are never nice to me, so there must be an ulterior motive.'

'What's going to happen about your work? Do your employers know why you have taken time off?' asked Mabel, avoiding the question because she was afraid to give an honest answer.

'Mrs Tripp is looking after things for me. She said she'd call in at the laundry and tell them that I had to come to Kent on urgent family business. So I should still have a job to go back to on my return.'

'The Tripps are very good to you.' Mabel sounded subdued.

'Very much so, and I love them all to pieces.'

'Yes, I expect you do.' Mabel stared at her hands.

'So why are you here?' asked Eva again.

Mabel cleared her throat. 'I think I might have been a bit hard on you over the years,' she began hesitantly.

'Yes, I think you can safely say that you have,' said Eva with a brittle laugh, 'though hard is one of the biggest understatements I have ever heard. Downright evil is more the way I would describe it.'

'I'm sorry.'

'It's a bit late for that now, Mum.' Eva had been so deeply hurt that sympathy for her mother wasn't possible. 'I can never have my childhood back; a childhood that was made a misery by you.'

'Oh.' Mabel had her head down, staring at the floor.

'It's all right though,' Eva went on in a brisk manner. 'I'm happy now. I'm far more suited to life in London. I never was cut out for the country. In fact I hated the whole thing. The boredom, the lack of any sort of fun, just endless drudgery and tongue-lashings from you every single day.'

'At least things are better now,' Mabel said lamely. She picked at her fingernails. 'I suppose the Tripps looked after you well when you were ill, too.'

'Very well indeed, thank you. Unlike you, who never even bothered to come and see how I was.'

'Charlie came on my behalf.'

'No. Charlie came because he wanted to; because he cares about me,' she said vehemently. 'Knowing you, you were embarrassed by the fact that your daughter was in a mental hospital.'

Her mother looked up but didn't say anything.

'I knew it,' said Eva. 'I can see it in your eyes.'

Mabel didn't even try to deny it. She realised that Eva was now a force to reckon with. Gone were the days when her mother could intimidate her. 'I'm sorry about everything.' The words came out almost of their own volition. 'The way I was with you. Looking back I can see that I was just in a rage the whole time. I had to blame someone for Rosie's death, you see. I realise now that I need have looked no further than myself.'

'Blame, guilt, regret,' said Eva, close to tears. 'It was an accident. So why not just accept that and give everyone some peace, including yourself?'

'It isn't that easy.'

'It can't be that difficult to accept the facts.'

'One day you'll have a better understanding of these things, when you have a little one of your own.'

'Look . . . we are all dreadfully sad about Rosie and wish she was still here with us even now, but you can't live in the past for ever. On the other hand, perhaps *you* can; you seem to have done a pretty good job so far.'

'I know that everything you say is true,' said Mabel. 'Can you ever forgive me?'

Her daughter gave a dry laugh. 'And make it all right for you just like that?' she blurted out. 'Not likely!'

'I really am very sorry.'

'So am I.'

'I know it will take time, but I was hoping we might be friends eventually.'

'Now you really are living in a fantasy world,' said Eva, wiping away her tears with the back of her hand. 'All those years of hell and you want us to be friends. No thank you very much.'

'I suppose I should have expected that.'

'Of course you should. I don't know how you've got the cheek to even suggest it.'

'I had to try to put things right . . .'

'Look, Mum, the only way you and I can get on is with lots of miles between us. Let's leave it at that, shall we? I would never come back to Brierley anyway. My life is in London now.'

'You could come to visit sometimes.'

'And I will, to see Charlie and Dad.'

'Do you want me to grovel?'

'No, I don't want you to do anything except leave me alone.' Eva was sobbing now. 'I don't want to be hurt again, Mum, and you've hurt me all my life.'

'Oh, Eva,' said Mabel. 'I just didn't realise . . . all those years, I just didn't know . . .'

'Look at me, Mum.' Eva stared at her mother through her tears. 'I'm in pieces again, because I'm with you and you sap all my confidence in a way no one else can. All those years can't just be wiped out because your world is falling apart. That's what this is all about. Vincent has gone, Hester is dead and Dad could be facing a prison sentence. That's why you want to make things up with me, because all your other options are disappearing.'

'That isn't the reason . . .'

'Oh, come on,' wept Eva. 'I'm not a complete idiot.'

'Maybe those things have made me think back and take an honest look at myself,' said Mabel. 'But I want to put things right for you as well as for me.'

'Yeah, well I want to forget the past and live my life in my own way. So go back to bed and leave me be. I'll be back in London soon, and that's the way I like it. You get on with your life and I'll get on with mine. While I'm here we'll tolerate each other for the sake of the others. Apart from that, nothing!'

'Is there no chance?'

'None at all. You reap what you sow and you'll just have to live with it.'

'Please give me a chance to make it up to you,' Mabel begged.

'Rejection hurts, doesn't it, when it happens to you,' said Eva through her tears. 'Now go away and shut the door on your way out please.'

As the door closed behind her mother, Eva turned off the light and pulled the covers over her head so that no one could hear her weeping. There had been no rehearsal for what had just taken place. No warning. She had reacted to her mother's attempt at an apology on instinct. But in hurting her mother she had hurt herself more and was now riddled with pain and guilt. That wasn't right. Her mother had been in the wrong; she'd admitted it. So why was Eva consumed by an ache in the pit of her stomach so strong it overwhelmed her? Would she never be free of her mother's power to hurt her? The sooner she went back to London the better.

Old habits die hard and Mabel's reaction to her daughter's rejection was to shout and scream to make her do what she wanted. But that was no longer possible. Eva was a grown woman with her own life. Mabel had lost her power over her. This Tripp woman seemed to be more of a mother to her than Mabel had ever been. She had no one to blame but herself, but that didn't stop jealousy from rearing its head.

Was there nothing she could do to put things right, she asked herself as she got back into bed, careful not to wake her husband. Eva was still a young woman with lots of years ahead of her. Surely there must be something her mother could do to add something to her life. But the damage was done, it seemed, and there was no way back.

'It's time we got on with some serious arrangements for this wedding,' said Flo Tripp one evening when Clara had been back from Kent a few days and the family was relaxing in the parlour. 'In fact I've already been busy. I called in at the hall where we're having the reception to make sure everything was still all right. I said we'd confirm the menu soon.'

'That's a bit previous, isn't it, Mum?' said Clara, perturbed by this news since there wasn't going to be a wedding.

'Just the opposite,' Flo told her. 'The wedding isn't much more than four months away. In terms of wedding preparations that's a very short time. I know I'm not normally an organised person but I am going to be over this. As the parents of the bride it's our job to put on a good show for you and Arnold, and we intend to, don't we, Frank?'

'Not half,' he replied. 'It'll be the knees-up of the year round here. Everybody will be talking about it for ages afterwards. The marriage of our only daughter is going to be the talk of the town.'

Clara was plunged into the misery of reality after the magic of Brierley and Charlie. She hadn't seen Arnold since she'd been back so she still hadn't told him the wedding was off. Obviously her parents needed to know but she couldn't tell them until after Arnold was in the picture; that would be too cruel. But she had to stop the inexorable progress of the nuptial arrangements now that her mother had clearly got wedding fever and was loving every minute.

'You'll have to make a definite decision about the bridesmaids,' Flo went on. 'I expect you'll have Eva and perhaps a couple of your other friends.'

'Probably,' said Clara.

'Don't sound so casual about it. You need to make up your mind who you're having so that we can choose the material and book a dressmaker to make the dresses. And of course you need to think about your own frock. Then there are the flowers and the cars and the photographs. I shall have to arrange a meeting with Arnold's parents, to talk things over, just in case they want to pay for anything. It's really down to us as parents of the bride but we have to be careful they don't feel left out.'

'Mum, slow down,' said Clara, seriously worried now. 'There's plenty of time.'

But there was no stopping her. 'You three will have to have new suits,' she said, casting a critical eye over Frank to Sydney and then Cuddy.

'I'm sure we don't need to go that far,' responded Frank. 'There's enough to pay for without adding unnecessary expense. My best suit is all right.'

'It's your only daughter, for goodness' sake,' Flo retorted. 'If you can't splash out for her wedding, when can you?'

Desperately in need of escape from this wedding talk, Clara said, 'I'll go and make us some tea.'

And she headed for the kitchen, leaving her mother insisting that her father go and get measured for a suit. He was objecting like mad. Suddenly the house had become infused with wedding hysteria. And all for a marriage that wasn't going to happen!

'What's up, sis?' asked Sydney, joining her in the kitchen. 'You look a bit fed up. Wedding nerves kicking in, are they?'

For a moment she was tempted to confide in him but the impulse passed as she reminded herself of her duty to Arnold. 'No, nothing like that,' she said.

'Why the long face, then?'

'I'm all right, honestly. Mum is obsessed with it all, though.'

'Isn't that normal for the mother of the bride? I think I've heard it said.'

'Probably. But she seems to have burst into a frenzy of wedding plans all of a sudden.'

'I hope we're not going to have it every day until August,' he said. 'We'll all end up in the nuthouse.'

'She'll calm down, I expect,' said Clara, putting the cups out and thinking how very much her mother's mood would change when she knew the truth.

'I thought brides were supposed to drive everyone mad by going on and on about their wedding,' he remarked. 'Yet you seem quite matter-of-fact about it.'

'I suppose it's because I've been away and my mind is still there, partly.'

His mood became serious. 'A bad business down in Kent then,' he said.

'Awful.'

'When do you think Eva will be coming back?'

'As soon as she possibly can, I should think,' replied Clara. 'Things aren't great between her and her mother. She'll probably wait until after Hester's funeral for Charlie's sake, though she might stay on even longer if her father is arrested.'

'What a family, eh?' he said. 'It's a wonder Eva and Charlie are so normal with all that stuff going on.'

'They're bound to be affected by it, though.'

'Did Eva seem upset when you were there? She's still a bit fragile.'

'She seemed to be coping.'

'Good.'

'I suppose you're missing her. The two of you are such mates now.'

'I can't wait for her to get back,' he confessed. 'But mostly I hope the whole thing hasn't upset her too much.'

'Oh, that's so sweet. You were so much against her being here when she first came, too.'

'Yeah, I was. She's grown on me,' he admitted. 'I felt really sorry for her when she was ill and I could see what a lovely person she was. She seemed so delicate then. I suppose that's when we became good friends.'

'For a kid brother, you're not a bad bloke when you put your mind to it.'

'Don't go mad with the flattery,' he joked.

'Let's hope that when she does come back she'll have good news about her father.'

'Fingers crossed.'

Meanwhile Clara had to break Arnold's heart and face the family recriminations, of which there would be plenty. Mum and Dad would heartily disapprove because they were strict about keeping promises, especially of the sort she had made to Arnold when he had slipped the engagement ring on to her finger. You just didn't break them in any circumstances whatsoever, to their way of thinking. It had all seemed so easy when she was with Charlie. Away from him and back in her own world, it felt entirely different.

'Sorry I didn't let you know that I was going away, Arnold,' Clara said the following evening when she and Arnold were in the front room having a few moments alone together. 'It came up out of the blue and I had to leave right away, so I didn't have time.'

'That's all right, sweetheart,' he said in his usual amiable way. 'Your mum and dad said something about a murder in Eva's family. Blimey, it isn't so peaceful down in Kent then.'

'It turned out not to be a murder after all. It was an accident.'

'Oh, that's better,' he said, adding with a wry grin, 'Well, not so good for the poor sod who copped it, but better than murder.'

'That's one way of putting it,' she said, smiling at the direct way he had of stating things.

'So will you be staying put now? No more rushing off to Kent.'

'I was only away one night,' she said defensively.

'Only teasing,' he said. 'You know me. I never try to stop you doing anything.'

That was very true. 'Actually, Arnold, there's something I need to tell you . . .'

'Your mum is full of the wedding, isn't she?' he cut in, seeming too excited to hold back while she finished what she was going to say. 'She was talking to me about it when I came round the night you were away. She seemed to be in her element.'

'Yes, I don't know what's brought it on all of a sudden. She's like a mad thing.'

'Could the reason be that weddings have to be organised?' he suggested with a certain look in his eyes that Clara had always found endearing and a hint of a smile.

Even though she was tense, or maybe because of it, she burst out laughing in the way she had so often laughed in Arnold's company over the years. 'I asked for that, didn't I?'

'You certainly did,' he grinned. 'But I do know what you mean. She's suddenly gone at it as if it was all happening the day after tomorrow. Mind you, I'm looking forward to it myself now that it's getting nearer. Are you?'

If there was a perfect moment to break the news, this was it. 'Er, Arnold . . .' she began, frowning.

'Well, don't overwhelm me with your enthusiasm, will you?' he cut in.

'Arnold, I . . .'

'Oh no, don't tell me you've got last-minute nerves.'

'I'd have a job as it's still more than four months away,' she pointed out.

'You are a case, Clara,' he said, guffawing with laughter. 'No one makes me laugh like you do.'

At that moment there was a strong feeling of unity between them and she was very aware of the fact that Arnold was part of the world she knew; all the rest suddenly seemed like fantasy. 'I only said . . .'

'It's the way you say things that tickles me.'

Caught up in his light-hearted mood, she found herself smiling even though she was full of dread about what she had to do.

'Anyway, do you fancy a walk as it's still light?' he suggested.

'Yeah, that would be nice.'

'What was it you wanted to tell me?'

'Nothing important,' she heard herself say.

Chapter Fourteen

Eva frowned at Clara. 'So you still haven't told anyone that the wedding is off?' It was two weeks later and she and Clara were in their bedroom. Eva was unpacking her clothes, having just returned from Kent after Hester's funeral with the good news that the police had taken all the circumstances into consideration and were not going to bring a case against John Fenner for interfering with the course of justice.

'No, I haven't, I'm ashamed to say,' replied Clara sheepishly. 'I still can't bring myself to tell Arnold and he has to know before I can tell anyone else.'

'You're leaving it a bit late, aren't you? If you don't mind my saying.'

'Yes I am,' she admitted. 'I knew it wouldn't be easy, but it's proving to be even harder than I expected. Arnold is such a nice bloke and I've known him a long time. I just can't seem to bring myself to tell him that it's over between us.'

'It isn't like you to shy away from anything.'

'I don't usually, but this is so painfully personal.'

'Don't you need to tell him before the wedding preparations progress any further?' suggested Eva. 'Your parents might lose money otherwise.'

'They probably will anyway,' said Clara dismally. 'They paid the deposit on the hall ages ago when they booked it. I don't know if they will get the money back when they cancel. I shall reimburse them for anything they lose. It might take me a while, but I'll pay it back eventually.'

'Are you absolutely sure that you want to end it with Arnold?'

'Of course. What makes you ask?'

'Because you obviously still have strong feelings for him,' Eva replied gravely. 'You must do if you can't bear to hurt him.'

'It's only natural that I would feel that way,' Clara said, on the defensive. 'We've been together a long time. I'm not going to stop caring about him because I've fallen in love with someone else.'

'I suppose not. Anyway, I'm a fine one to advise anyone as I've only ever had one serious boyfriend, and I got that all wrong,' Eva admitted.

'These things are more traumatic than they might appear. It all seemed so simple when I was with Charlie. Anything seemed possible then.' Clara paused wistfully. 'Now that I'm back here it's all very different.'

'But Charlie needs to know where he stands, Clara,' Eva pointed out firmly. 'You can't string him along.'

'I wouldn't dream of doing so. Surely you don't think as badly of me as that.'

'Of course I don't. I'm just saying that you'll have to make your mind up one way or the other.'

Clara stared at her. 'There is no one way or the other,' she said categorically. 'You know how I feel about Charlie.

There isn't a decision to be made. It's only the breaking it off with Arnold that I'm finding so difficult.'

'I think you need to be absolutely certain, though.' There was an edge to Eva's voice. 'Charlie has been through enough bad times with Hester. It would be crippling for him if it all went wrong again. Better he's hurt now, before anything has really got started, than later on.'

Clara knew that she was being warned. Naturally Eva would feel protective towards her brother and she didn't blame her. 'I never want to hurt Charlie and there is no confusion about my feelings,' she said. 'I'm finding it hard to do the right thing at the moment, that's all.'

The sound of Cuddy singing somewhere in the house drifted in and lifted the tension that had crept between the two women. 'Oh, I'm so glad to be back,' exclaimed Eva, in a swift change of subject. 'What's been happening here? What have I missed?'

'Nothing very exciting. Mum's got an acute case of weddingitis, the men of the family are objecting because she's insisting they get measured for new suits, and Sydney has been missing you like mad.'

'Dear Syd. I've missed him too.' Eva gave Clara a meaningful look. 'As for your mother's weddingitis, you know what you have to do to cure her of that.'

'I do indeed.'

'Get on and do it then,' said Eva forcefully.

Another week passed and another and still Clara didn't break off her engagement to Arnold. The more time that elapsed since she'd been with Charlie at Brierley the less real that night seemed. What made it even more difficult was that Arnold was being particularly attentive; he'd insisted on giving her money for the fare to Kent and called round to see her more often than usual. It wasn't that she was impressed by these things but it seemed too cruel to just discard him when he was making such an effort.

Spring turned to early summer and she was still living a lie and hating herself for it. Her mother became increasingly absorbed in the wedding plans, and when she arranged an appointment for Clara to see a dressmaker about her wedding dress Clara knew that time had finally run out and she couldn't put off what must be done any longer.

It was the most glorious morning in late May and the orchards of Brierley were abundant with apple blossom, promising a bumper crop. In excellent spirits, Charlie had rolled up his sleeves and was working on the soil around the newly planted trees, stirring and pulverising to stop it cracking in the dry weather, the sun feeling warm on his bare forearms.

This was the part of the job he enjoyed most: actually working on the land. The other things had to be done, of course – the managing, the marketing and so on – but it was when he spent time out here in the orchard that he knew he was right for this work. It was a busy time of year and they were a man short since Vincent's departure; they had an experienced orchard man starting next week.

He had wondered if his mother might weaken and let his brother stay on when she'd calmed down, but she had been adamant and his father had supported her. Charlie knew how much it must have cost her because she adored Vincent; the fact that she had stood firm illustrated the strength of her views on morality. She'd been very subdued lately and he felt rather sorry for her. Yes, she had been cruel and spiteful to Eva, but he suspected that she might be experiencing remorse as her family got smaller. He'd been just a boy at the time of his little sister's death but he suspected it was that which had given his mother such a venomous streak, especially towards Eva. As for Vincent, he was a survivor so he would be all right. He knew fruit growing inside out so he shouldn't have too much trouble finding a job. He'd be poorer financially and less well looked after, but that wouldn't do him any harm. It might even make him appreciate what he'd had at Brierley.

At the root of Charlie's sense of well-being was his newly found relationship with Clara and he knew he would feel just as happy come storms, gales and problems at work because his joy came from within. It had been such a terrible year up until that night when he and Clara had finally declared their feelings for each other: the rows with Hester, the emptiness of his life and then the shock of his wife's death. After a decent interval he and Clara would be together and he couldn't wait. He smiled, imagining her working here with him and knowing instinctively that she would love it. Like him, she was a child of the soil.

There was a shout from the house, which meant it was time for elevenses. Having been working out here since early morning, he was ready for a break.

'I'll have mine out here, Mum,' he said at the back door, 'to save taking my boots off.'

'Right you are, son.'

She handed him a large mug of tea and a chunk of fruit cake. He took them across the yard and sat down on an upturned apple crate. His father went inside to take his break and the hands wandered off back towards the fields.

Mabel came out to the yard and headed towards him, an apron over her long skirt. 'A letter for you. It came in this morning's post,' she said, hesitating as though waiting for him to open it so he would tell her who it was from.

'Thanks, Mum,' he said, his eyes shooting to the London postmark. His heart raced as he recognised Clara's hand-writing. 'I'll open it later.'

'Oh . . . I see. Right you are then,' she said and, taking the hint, turned and went back inside.

Imbued with excitement he finished his tea and cake and headed off back to work with Rex at his heels. He and Clara had agreed early on not to write to each other too often since regular correspondence would arouse curiosity in both families. She must be missing him and have thought it was worth the risk.

Finding a quiet corner in the field where he was working, he sat on the grass in the shade of the apple blossom and opened the envelope.

Dearest Charlie,

I hardly know how to tell you this because my heart is breaking and I'm sure yours will be too, but I have decided to go ahead with my marriage to Arnold.

This doesn't mean that I don't love you because I do, more than anything, but I was brought up to always honour a promise and I find that I can't break the one I made to Arnold when I became engaged to him.

Initially I put it down to cowardice. I have certainly been unable to pluck up the courage to break it off with him. But as time has gone on and I have turned it over and over in my mind I have realised that there is more to it than that. I think it's more about commitment and trust. Arnold has been good to me over a long period and I don't feel able to let him down. It's true that he doesn't make me feel the way you do but he's a decent man and doesn't deserve such shabby treatment. I was also brought up to believe that you can't always have what you want in life and so I feel I must make this sacrifice.

I'm so sorry, Charlie. I know you will hate me for doing this to you and I don't blame you. I loathe myself for doing it to you after all you've already been through. But I do love you and always will. Please don't contact me to try to make me change my mind. That would only make matters worse.

So sorry,

Clara.

The letter fluttered to the ground from Charlie's trembling grasp. The pain, disappointment and sheer powerlessness of the situation culminated in fury. Every word of the letter was mere drivel. She was discarding him and wrapping it up in fancy words to make herself feel better. He couldn't believe she would be so shallow. This just shows how little you know her, he told himself. You've been taken for a fool, mate, an absolute idiot. He stuffed the letter in his trouser pocket and got to his feet, his emotions so raw he didn't know how to contain them.

Work is the only answer to this, he told himself, so he

went back down on his knees to finish the job in progress. He felt physically ill with the pain and there was a lump in his throat that was making his eyes smart. Men don't cry, he reminded himself. Don't let a woman make you lose your dignity. But he had difficulty holding himself together as he worked the soil around the tree.

Rex must have sensed that something was wrong because he padded over and nuzzled against him.

'It's all right, boy,' he said hoarsely, patting the animal's head. 'I'm not going to let another bloody woman nearly destroy me, so settle down while I get on with my work.'

The dog pattered off and sat down in the shade while his master struggled with his emotions.

Clara hadn't thought she would hear from Charlie after what she'd told him in that awful letter she'd wept over in the writing, so she was surprised and apprehensive to receive a reply from him. She sat on her bed to read it.

Clara,

If you loved me you would have ended it with Arnold so I am drawing my own conclusions. I wish you had been honest with me about it instead of making up fancy excuses. You owe me nothing and are entitled to be with whoever you choose but please don't insult my intelligence by pretending that you are staying with Arnold as a matter of principle, thereby making yourself some sort of a martyr. You are staying with him because you want to. No one would marry someone just because they don't want to hurt them.

Your letter was pathetic in the extreme and I am

very disappointed in you. However, as I have just said, you owe me nothing and I will ask nothing of you except that you stay away from me.

Unfortunately our paths may cross again at some point in the future because of Eva, but as far as I am concerned anything that happened between us is eliminated from my memory and will never be mentioned again so you need have no fear of embarrassment or upset to your wedding plans. From now you are just some friend of Eva's who means nothing at all to me.

Charlie.

The anger and pain he must have been feeling when he put his thoughts down on paper leapt out at her almost as if he was there with her. She could hear his deep voice saying the words and they hurt unbearably. She was physically aching with the trauma. Nothing had ever affected her as profoundly as this. She had tried to be honest in her letter to him but maybe he was right. Perhaps she was just making excuses. But in her heart she knew that wasn't true. Whatever Charlie thought of her, she had to have the courage of her convictions and go through with the marriage to Arnold. And yes, it was a matter of principle, no matter what Charlie thought.

The bedroom door opened and Eva came in, just home from work in her laundry overall.

'Whatever's the matter?' she asked, seeing her friend whey-faced and close to tears.

'I heard back from Charlie.' Clara had told Eva of her decision before she sent her letter. 'I don't think he likes me very much any more.'

'You can hardly blame him, can you?' was Eva's blunt response.

'No, and I don't. It's just hurting me so much to know how upset he is, and not to have him in my life. Believe it or not, Eva, I feel as bad about it as he does.'

'At least you told him sooner rather than later,' Eva pointed out. 'It would have been worse for him further down the road. He knows where he stands now and can get on with his life without you.'

'Yeah,' said Clara sadly. 'I suppose you hate me too for letting your brother down.'

'I could never hate you, Clara. I'm far too fond of you for that; anyway you've been a very good friend to me. But I am upset for Charlie. I'm disappointed for you both too. For what it's worth, I think you are making the biggest mistake of your life by going ahead with this wedding to Arnold. But only you know how you feel and it's your business not mine.'

'Yes, it is,' agreed Clara, standing her ground but feeling very much alone.

'You coming downstairs?' asked Eva in a casual manner to lift the mood between them. 'Your mum told me to tell you that supper is ready.'

'Tell her I'll be down in a minute,' said Clara. She needed to be on her own with her thoughts for a while.

Mabel Fenner was on the London train and she had never felt more frightened in her life. She was so nervous; she was sweating, nauseous and inwardly trembling. The capital was unknown territory to her and she found the whole thing terrifying.

Charlie and John had been surprised to hear of her

trip, especially as she hadn't fully explained its purpose. Her husband had offered to go with her but she had told him it was something she had to do alone. Mabel knew it mustn't be easy. The ultimate effort on her part must be put into it. She had known she would hate it but that was the whole point. She needed to suffer.

So she had left the meals for the day ready for the men, allowed John to drive her to Tunbridge Wells station, and boarded a train which was now about to arrive at Charing Cross station. The train began slowing down and came to a juddering halt. Someone shouted 'London Charing Cross' and the other people in the carriage stood up and prepared themselves to alight.

Mabel's legs felt so weak, she daren't get up. Doors were slamming all along the train and the noise coming from the station was a loud nerve-jangling roar.

'The train stops here, luv,' said a guard, coming on board.

'Yes, I know,' she said nervously.

'Are you all right?'

She nodded and forced herself up, expecting her legs to buckle, but surprisingly they didn't.

Stepping down from the train on to the platform she was immediately swept along by the crowds. Charlie had given her some directions, all forgotten now in the terror of the moment. She had never seen so many people in one place at the same time and moving so quickly. Tunbridge Wells station had seemed busy enough on the odd occasion she'd been there. But this was hell on earth. Somehow, she managed to put one foot in front of the other and followed the stream to the ticket collector. She handed him her ticket, feeling weak almost to the point of collapse.

'If in doubt ask someone,' Charlie had told her, so she went up to a man in uniform and said, 'Can you tell me how to get to Shepherd's Bush, please?'

'The Underground is over there,' he said, indicating some distant point at the other side of the station. 'Go to Oxford Circus and change on to the Central Line.'

'Thank you,' she said and tottered off on weak, trembling legs in the direction he had indicated.

Having managed to get herself to Shepherd's Bush and then to Green Street, despite jelly legs and heart palpitations for most of the way, Mabel was feeling a little stronger until a ball hit her in the face, and then a child on roller skates bumped into her, almost knocking her to the ground. It was a Saturday and the street was a riotous playground: dozens of children in groups, playing hopscotch, skipping, jumping off walls; there even seemed to be a game of rounders in progress. Mabel had never seen anything like it in her life. How could people live like this, all crowded together in the narrow street, children yelling and shouting all day long? She comforted herself with the thought that the children had actually said 'Sorry, missus' to her just now so they were taught manners. Recovering from these rather alarming incidents, she found the house she was looking for and knocked at the door.

'Yes?' said the woman who answered it.

'Is Eva in, please?'

'No, not at the moment. Sorry.'

'Will she be long?'

'I can't really say, dear,' replied Flo. 'She's gone into town with my daughter and you know what girls are like when they're at the shops.'

Mabel didn't actually, having always lived in the country, but she said, 'Can I come back later on?'

'Certainly. Who shall I say is looking for her?'

'I'm her mother.'

'Oh!' A shadow fell across Flo's face. Clara had told her how cruel Eva's mother had been to the girl, though she had never heard a word about it from Eva herself. Still, the least Flo could do was make her welcome. 'Would you like to come in and wait?'

'That would be very helpful. Thank you.'

'Would you like a cup of tea? I'm in on my own as it happens. My husband's taken the boys to a football match. It's only a friendly as it's out of season but you know what men are like about football.'

Mabel didn't, but she said, 'Yes indeed.'

'You sit down and make yourself comfortable, luv,' said Flo, ushering her into the parlour and pointing to a rather shabby sofa. 'I'll go and put the kettle on.'

The room seemed extremely cluttered to the house-proud Mabel. There was a pile of comics in one of the armchairs, a heap of ironing in another, cigarette packets, ashtrays and sundry other items on the mantelpiece, photographs all over the top of the sideboard and various books and magazines strewn about.

'Here we are,' said Flo, bringing in some tea and biscuits. 'Did you travel up from Kent today?'

Mabel nodded.

'Going back today?'

'Yes.'

'Must be something important then,' said Flo, a questioning lift to her brows.

'It is. Very,' replied Mabel, without enlarging on the subject.

Sipping her tea, Flo decided to chance her arm. 'Eva is very happy here with us, you know,' she said.

'So I understand,' responded Mabel. 'I know you've been very good to her.' She gave Flo a shrewd look. 'I suppose she's told you all about her wicked mother.'

'No. Eva has said nothing to me at all, but Clara did mention that you and Eva don't exactly hit it off.'

'We don't,' muttered Mabel. Then, suddenly, the guilt that had plagued her for weeks, the strain of the journey and the anxiety about trying to make her peace with Eva took their toll and she burst into tears.

'Oh, lor,' said Flo, taking the other woman's teacup from her trembling hand and putting it down while Mabel dug into her pocket for a handkerchief. 'Whatever is the matter?'

And without any prior intention, Mabel poured out the whole story, about Rosie's death and the terrible rage it had left her with, which she had taken out on Eva.

'I couldn't seem to stop myself,' she sobbed. 'All those years of her life ruined by me. I don't think I knew I was doing it half the time, it got to be such a habit.'

'And now you want to make it up to her,' surmised Flo.

'Yes, but she doesn't want anything to do with me.'

Not surprising, thought Flo, but said kindly, 'Might it not be best to leave her to herself for the moment? Maybe when she's a bit older she might be more able to understand.'

'I'm not going to interfere in her life, if that's what you're thinking,' Mabel said defensively. 'I know she will never come back to Brierley to live. I just want her to know how sorry I am and ask if there is anything I can do to make it up to her.'

'You want forgiveness?'

'Oh no. I've accepted that that isn't possible. I just want to be able to see her occasionally. Perhaps do something to make things better between us.'

Flo mulled the situation over. She couldn't even begin to imagine how terrible it must be to lose a child so she wasn't going to judge the other woman, who did seem genuinely sorry and keen to put things right. She had undoubtedly damaged Eva but, with care, damage could sometimes be lessened even if it couldn't be healed altogether. Flo couldn't help feeling rather sorry for the woman. She was a large, imposing character, out of place here in her country clothes, and she seemed lost and lonely somehow. The journey had obviously unnerved her. And as Flo's own mother used to tell her when she needed reminding: 'You can have friends, lovers and children but you only have one mother.'

'In that case you'll have to keep trying,' she said at last. 'A relationship with your daughter is worth fighting for.'

'I want nothing from her, just to hear from her now and again; to know how she's getting on.'

'I know, dear,' said the warm-hearted Flo. 'I know.'

'Why are you being kind to me after what I've done?'

'Because you genuinely want to put things right and the friendship between a mother and daughter is a wonderful thing when it works. Or at least that is my experience. I value mine with Clara enormously.' She paused. 'Mind you, I can't answer for what I'll do to you if you hurt Eva again. I certainly won't be kind to you then. We picked up the pieces when she came here; and again when Gordon let her down.'

At that moment the house became flooded with noise as the family trooped in all at the same time.

'Ooh, biscuits; smashing,' said Cuddy, bounding into the room. 'Can I have one, Mum?'

'My favourite,' said Sydney, helping himself without asking.

'Where are your manners, boys?' admonished their father, following them into the room. 'Can't you see we have a visitor?'

'Oh, sorry,' said Cuddy, who was so used to people coming in and out of the house that he usually took no notice. He looked at Mabel in surprise. 'Hello, Mrs Fenner.'

'This is Eva's mum,' said Flo for the benefit of those who hadn't met her. 'This is my husband Frank and my elder son Sydney.'

Frank offered his hand, but Sydney had no intention of speaking to the dragon who had been so mean to his friend Eva. As it happened he had no need to rebuff her because at that moment Clara and Eva came into the room.

'*You*,' said Eva, staring at her mother, her face and neck suddenly suffused with pink. 'What are you doing here?'

The room resonated with silence, all eyes on the two Fenner women, Mabel seemingly cowed and apologetic, Eva's eyes blazing with fury.

'Come on, chickens,' said Flo after a moment, walking to the door and indicating to her family to do the same. 'We're going.'

'Where to?' asked Cuddy.

'In the other room, down the park, anywhere. Now just do as you're told without asking questions for once,' she said, ushering the Tripps out of the room, leaving Eva and her mother alone.

★　★　★

'Did you come on your own?' asked Eva.

Mabel nodded.

'Blimey, you're getting a bit adventurous in your old age, aren't you?' Eva said coolly. 'I thought a very occasional trip to Tunbridge Wells was about your limit.'

'I was very nervous,' Mabel admitted. 'London is a foreign country to me.'

'But you wanted me to know you'd made an effort; put yourself out for me,' said Eva perceptively. 'Is that it?'

'Yes, that's it exactly.'

'So now that you're here . . . what do you want?'

'I want to make my peace with you,' Mabel said bluntly.

Eva gave a dry laugh. 'You could walk barefoot to Scotland and back to impress me and it would make no difference.'

'You're being very hard.'

'Yeah, well, I had a good teacher, didn't I?'

The two women were standing either side of the fireplace, unlit at this time of the year. 'Look, I can't change what happened in the past, much as I would like to,' Mabel blurted out. 'But surely there must be a way back for us.'

'No, absolutely not.'

'I don't want anything from you.'

'Yes, you do. You want me back in your life so that you can make me miserable again.'

'No . . .'

'You might be nice for a while,' said Eva, 'then you'd be feeling a bit moody one day and you'd revert to your old ways. I don't want that in my life any more. I can't take that sort of pain.'

'I wouldn't do that.'

'You wouldn't be able to help yourself. Making me

suffer is second nature to you. I don't think you even know you're doing it.'

'I'm sorry . . .'

Eva sat down in an armchair across the hearth from her mother. 'I only have to think of you and I feel worthless,' she told her. 'When I was out in town this afternoon with Clara, I felt happy and good about myself. All right, so working in a laundry isn't much of a job compared to being the daughter of orchard owners. But I earn my money and pay my way. I have friends at work who seem to like me and the Tripps who couldn't do more for me if I was their own. Then I came in and saw you and I was an unwanted child fit for nothing again.'

'You were never unwanted.'

'Oh no, not much.'

'Never that, Eva; I promise you.'

'That's what it felt like.'

'The fault was never with you,' Mabel tried to explain. 'It was with me. I realise that now. I was taking my grief out on you. I've already told you that. There was never anything wrong with you.' She looked misty-eyed. 'You were a beautiful child.'

'But not as beautiful as Rosie, obviously . . . you wished I'd died instead of her.'

'That really isn't true.' Mabel was genuinely shocked at the suggestion. 'I didn't want either of my daughters to die. Of course not. I'm no saint, but not that much of a monster, Eva.'

'That's debatable.'

Mabel flinched. 'All right, you win,' she said thickly, getting to her feet, red blotches standing out on her face, her eyes wet with tears. 'I can see that I'm upsetting you just by being here so I'll be on my way.' She walked heavily to the door, then turned. 'Please thank Mrs Tripp for her hospitality, and offer her my apologies for being so rude as to leave without saying goodbye. I won't bother you again, Eva, I can promise you that.'

She closed the parlour door behind her and Eva watched from the window as she walked down the street, every inch the country bumpkin in her long skirt and black straw hat.

Eva was physically shaking as she stared through the net curtains, and the salty lump in her throat was almost choking her. This was why she couldn't have her mother in her life. This was what Mabel did to her: made her nervous and unsure of herself just by being there. But was it entirely her mother's fault this time? Could she herself be partly to blame? Was it the cruel hostility she had shown to her mother that was upsetting her so much now? The things she had said were a bit strong by anyone's standards.

She was recalled to the present by Flo, who had come into the room and was saying, 'Has your mother gone already, love? We heard the door go.'

'Yes, she's gone.'

'Oh, I see. Well, it's about time we had our tea,' said Flo diplomatically. 'I got some nice fresh buns from the baker's this morning.'

'Did I hear something about buns?' said Cuddy, appearing behind her.

'Don't you ever think about anything but your stomach, boy?' said his mother.

He grinned. 'No, not often. I'm a growing boy.'

'Are you all right, Eva?' asked Sydney, coming into the room.

'Yes, are you?' added Clara, seeing from her friend's face that all was not well.

'Sit yourself down, Eva, and I'll bring the tea in,' said Flo, because Eva was prone to help out every time anything was being done in the kitchen.

'I have to go out,' Eva heard herself say. 'I won't be long,' and she ran from the house.

Clara made as if to go after her but Flo said, 'Leave her, love. She'll have gone after her mother. She needs to work things out without any of us around.'

Eva found Mabel sitting on a bench in the sunshine on Shepherd's Bush Green.

'What are you doing here?' she asked. 'Shouldn't you be getting the train?'

'I'm a lot earlier than I expected and I've got time to kill before I need to get to Charing Cross, so I thought I'd have a break and watch London folk go about their business,' Mabel replied, her voice still ragged with emotion. 'There are so danged many of 'em, like ants around cake crumbs. In and out of the shops, staring in the windows, groups of 'em standing about talking on the pavements.'

'There are always plenty of people around on a Saturday afternoon,' said Eva, sitting down beside her. 'Everyone is out and about.'

'What do they get out of it, I wonder, just wandering from shop to shop and back again?'

'Town people like shops and enjoy having a look to see what's on offer even if they don't have money to spend. I'm the same. I love looking around the shops, especially on a Saturday. There's something special about it.'

'Why have you come after me?' asked Mabel, without turning to look at her daughter.

'I'm not really sure.'

'There must be a reason.'

'I think perhaps I might have been a bit hard on you,' Eva confessed. 'Some of the things I said.'

'That's the trouble with words,' said her mother, still not looking at her. 'Once they've been uttered it's too late. The damage is already done.'

'I shouldn't have said that you wanted me dead,' said Eva. 'That was uncalled for.'

'Yes, it was indeed,' Mabel agreed. 'But I think you've a long way to go before you catch up with me on the subject of cruel and hurtful talk.'

'That's true. But look, Mum,' Eva began thoughtfully, looking into her mother's scrubbed countrywoman's face as she turned towards her, her small grey eyes full of regret.

'Yes?' Mabel cut in hopefully.

'It might take a long time and I can't promise ever to like you, but I am willing to try to get to know you better,' she said.

'Oh, Eva. Thank you.'

'We'll have to take it slowly and it might not work; we could be completely incompatible even with effort on both sides. There is also the fact that I'll be living in London so won't see you all that often.'

'I'll do my best to be patient.'

Knowing how lacking in patience her mother was, Eva said, 'The first time you turn nasty on me could be the last. Leastways don't expect me to just sit back and take it.'

'You never did that,' Mabel reminded her. 'You always

had something to say for yourself. But whatever you want
I'll go along with it.'

'For starters why not come back to the house for a
little while and have a cup of tea and get to know the
Tripp family better. Then I'll go with you to Charing
Cross and see you on to the train. It'll be a start, anyway.'

They both knew that it was too soon for any sort of
physical embrace so they walked back to Green Street in
the sunshine, each keeping her distance. Despite all Eva's
prior intentions, she found herself with a warm feeling
inside.

Chapter Fifteen

The cars and photographer were booked, the flowers ordered, the dresses made, and every arrangement was in place with nothing left to chance. The normally haphazard Flo had excelled herself in the case of her only daughter's wedding. Now, with just a month to go until the big day, Arnold had found them somewhere to live: two unfurnished rooms and a shared kitchen and lavatory, but it was in a convenient location just a few streets from the Tripps.

'Well, what do you think?' he asked when he took Clara along to see it. 'It'll be a little palace when we get all our stuff in here, don't you think?'

'I'm sure we can make it nice,' she responded, casting a critical eye around. It was probably the best they would get for the rent they could afford, but it was undeniably shabby and sour-smelling, with yellowing patterned wallpaper and worn lino on the floor. 'Once I've given it a thoroughly good clean.'

'The first thing we need is a bed, and we've enough money saved for that,' he said with enthusiasm.

'Mum and Dad are giving us a few bits and pieces of furniture so we should be able to make it cosy.' She was trying her hardest to match his keenness. 'You did well to find this, Arnold.'

'I'm glad you're happy with it,' he said, beaming.

If only he wasn't so eager to please her. All it did was increase her longing for escape.

'Now that we've found a place we can go out on Saturday and buy a bed to put in it,' he suggested.

'You and the flippin' bed,' she said, because he talked about it ad nauseam. 'You're obsessed.'

'Not half,' he conceded cheerfully. 'It's the best bit. Any man will tell you that.'

Quite how she was going to cope with that side of things, she had no idea. They hadn't yet. Arnold knew that a well-brought-up girl like her didn't until after she was married; except that she already had, which was something else Arnold would know when it finally happened.

But worrying as the idea of sleeping with Arnold was, it wasn't half as bad as the prospect of being with him every day for the rest of her life. Two or three nights a week was one thing but just the two of them all the time was quite another, and seeing the place that would be their home really made her realise the serious trouble she was in, especially as there was no way out. Even apart from Arnold's feelings, arrangements had been made, presents bought, new clothes purchased.

She'd tried every way she knew to love Arnold since she'd cast Charlie out of her life, but the feelings didn't come so she faked them. She'd gone along with the whole wedding charade by constantly reminding herself that she was doing the right thing and trying not to feel as though she was on the road to hell. And now tonight, seeing her future home, she was desolate.

'So, as you're pleased with it, I'll go and see the land-lord on my way home from your place and give him a month's rent in advance to keep it secure,' Arnold was saying. 'At least it's a place of our own and will do until we can afford something better. We won't be cooped up with parents like a lot of young couples. We need to be by ourselves, don't we?'

'Mm.'

'You want me to go ahead then?' he said, pressing the point as though he was uncertain of her. 'Is that all right?'

'That's fine, Arnold,' she assured him. 'You go and see the landlord and I'll plan where to put the furniture.'

It was going to be all right, she told herself. She would be a good wife and mother to his children. She was absolutely determined. There was nothing like a spot of positive thinking to raise the spirits and she felt a whole lot better for it. Everything was going to be fine. She would make sure of it!

The weather was good and Brierley Orchard still looked set to have an excellent yield. The fruit would soon be ripe for harvesting; some of the early varieties were almost ready now. Charlie should have been on top of the world, but he felt like hell.

There was a reason for this. It was Clara's wedding day; in a few hours from now she would be Arnold's wife. Charlie was kept up to date with events in the Tripp household by Eva, who wrote to him regularly and had been to Brierley for the weekend recently.

He was glad that she and their mother were getting along better now. Eva had told him in confidence that she was still very wary and suffered a huge loss of confidence whenever she and her mother were together. But she was willing to give Mabel a chance and hoping their relationship would improve with time. Apparently she still lived in fear of a barrage of abuse, which was only natural given what had happened in the past. But Mum really did seem to be making an effort; even he had noticed a change in her attitude towards Eva and life in general.

The departure of Vincent from the family circle had left its mark on her. She'd been a whole lot quieter since he left. Vincent had written to his parents to let them know he had got a job in an orchard in Somerset, obviously making sure they knew where he was in the hope that they might change their minds and invite him back into the family at some point. Whether or not that would ever happen Charlie had no idea. Mum and Dad were very strait-laced, so it would certainly take time for them to forgive him.

But the person most on his mind today was Clara and he wished ardently that her marriage wasn't happening. Having calmed down since he'd written that dreadful letter to her, he thought he might have been too callous in the emotion of the moment but had let it stand. Nothing could change the fact that she had chosen Arnold over him.

The wedding was apparently at twelve noon so perhaps when that time had passed he might feel better. At least it would bring definite closure.

He continued on through the orchard, inspecting the trees for any sign of damage or disease, thinking how Clara would have loved Brierley at this time of the year with everything so green and abundant.

★   ★   ★

There was a gathering of neighbours outside the house when Clara emerged in her wedding finery with her father.

'Aah, don't she look lovely,' said someone.

'An absolute picture,' agreed another.

'Good luck, luv.'

'All the best, dear.'

In the back of the ribbon-bedecked wedding car, her father said, 'I am so proud of you today, Clara. You look a real treat. Arnold is a lucky man.'

'Thanks, Dad.'

'Are you nervous?'

'I am a bit.'

'You'll be all right.' He paused. 'You are quite sure about this, aren't you?'

She tensed. Had he noticed something? 'What makes you say that, Dad?'

'It's traditional for the father of the bride to make certain his daughter is sure she wants to go through with it,' he told her. 'Us dads are a protective lot when it comes to our daughters.' He cleared his throat. 'I'm not a man of fancy words and I don't often get to speak to you on your own, but I want to take this opportunity to say what a joy you've brought to our lives, me and your mum. You were such a dear little thing when you were a child, and since you've grown up you've always been a strong support and a stabilising influence to the rest of us. When your mother has needed help in the house you've given it without complaint, and when we've had trouble – like when Sydney went off the rails – you did everything you could to help.'

Hearing the emotion in his voice, she lifted her veil and turned to him and saw tears in his eyes.

338

'Oh, Dad,' she said, putting her hand on his. 'Don't be sad.'

'I'm giving you away,' he reminded her, 'handing you over to another man. How can I help but be sad?'

'You're making me cry now,' she said with a nervous laugh, 'and it will ruin my make-up.'

He laughed then and blew his nose. The car drew up outside the church. 'Be happy, love,' he said. 'That's all me and your mum want for you.'

'Thanks, Dad,' she said thickly.

The bridesmaids – Eva and two of Clara's school friends in pale blue taffeta – were waiting at the back of the church when Clara and her father arrived. There was a brief pause while the group checked their dresses and arranged themselves; then, to the traditional wedding music, Clara walked elegantly down the aisle on her father's arm, a vision in a white floor-length dress with a fitted bodice and lace-edged sleeves, her veil over her face.

Arnold was waiting for her at the altar with his best man, both looking very smart in dark suits with white carnation buttonholes. Arnold looked very handsome, she noticed, as he turned to her and gave her a nervous smile.

'Dearly beloved,' the vicar began, and the service got under way.

Clara was becoming increasingly worried with every word he uttered. She felt unreal, as though this wasn't happening to her. It shouldn't be happening to her! It was wrong! The whole thing was a farce. Her heart thumped as panic consumed her. What was she to do? She had to get away.

They had reached the vows. 'Do you Clara Lily Tripp take this man to be your . . .'

She couldn't go through with it. This charade must end right now! She opened her mouth to put a stop to this travesty, but the words were not uttered because there was a sudden interruption at the back of the church. Clara couldn't see what was happening but there was shouting and what sounded like a scuffle.

'Let me get my hands on him,' said a gruff male voice and a man of about thirty appeared at the altar, grabbed Arnold roughly and punched him on the jaw so hard that he staggered. Then the interloper pulled him towards him by his lapels. 'You've got the cheek to stand here in a house of God after what you've been doing for the past two years with my wife?' He turned to Clara. 'He's been sleeping with my wife during the week, while I've been away working. I don't know what he's told you but whatever it was it was lies. When he wasn't seeing you, he was with her.'

There was a collective gasp from the guests. Sydney and his father rushed to escort the man from the scene but he struggled free.

'It's him you want to remove from the church, not me,' he protested. 'He's the one who's been doing wrong. I'm the victim here.'

A dishevelled woman with a kind of dubious glamour about her appeared and tried to grab the man but he wouldn't let her near him. 'Leave me alone, you disgusting tart,' he growled.

Arnold looked at Clara. 'It isn't true,' he said sheepishly. 'He's making it up to cause trouble for me.'

'Why would I want to cause trouble for you if there

wasn't a reason?' said the man. He turned to Clara. 'Sorry to spoil your wedding, love. But you're better off without him, believe me.'

'I tell you it's all lies,' protested Arnold.

'Oh, do us all a favour, for goodness' sake, Arnold,' said the woman, who looked to be in her thirties. 'You've been found out so at least have the grace to admit it.'

Arnold stood there visibly squirming.

'People have seen you coming to the house and there's been gossip,' the woman went on. 'A neighbour blurted it out to my ol' man and he confronted me with it. I told him it wasn't serious and that you were getting married today anyway so he had nothing to worry about, but he forced me to tell him which church.'

There wasn't much Arnold could say after that, so he just looked helplessly at Clara. He couldn't know how grateful she was to him for giving her a means of escape.

Even in the chaos and embarrassment of the moment she could see the irony, in that she had agonised for months over her doubts and her one indiscretion with Charlie, and Arnold had been betraying her on a regular basis for two years. The sly old dog. Despite everything, it was a shock to know that he was capable of such deceit. She'd never really known him at all.

The awful thing was the misplaced pity. Everyone was sorry for Clara, not knowing that she had been spared, not destroyed. To tell the truth would only be seen as a pathetic attempt to save her pride, so she had to let them all carry on seeing her as the wronged woman, whilst assuring everybody that she was fine and having them think she was just being brave.

Her only confidante was Eva. 'It came like a gift from heaven,' she told her that night in the privacy of their bedroom. 'I was just about to say that I couldn't go through with it when all hell broke loose and I didn't have to.'

'Honest?' asked Eva. 'You're not just saying that because you've been humiliated?'

'No, honestly I'm not, though I could tell the others that until I'm blue in the face and they wouldn't believe me.'

'Is it because of Charlie?' she asked.

'It was Charlie who made me realise that there was something more than what I felt for Arnold out there,' she replied. 'But in the church today when I was going to say no to marriage with Arnold, it was because I knew for certain that he wasn't the man for me and I could never make it work, regardless of Charlie. As it happens, it seems as though I've had a lucky escape.'

'Yeah, who would have believed it of Arnold?' said Eva. 'He always seemed so devoted to you.'

'He was still claiming to love me when Dad and Sydney dragged him away from me; he said that it was me he loved and the thing with that woman was just sex and meant nothing.'

'What a day, eh?' said Eva. 'We had an unfinished wedding ceremony and a reception without the bride and groom.'

'Mum had to let it go ahead or all the food would have been wasted,' she said. 'It would have embarrassed everyone to have me there so I stayed away.'

'I don't blame you.'

'I feel bad about all the money Mum and Dad wasted. I shall try to get some extra shifts at the café to pay at least some of it back.'

'I'm sure they don't blame you.'

'If Arnold's misdeeds hadn't come out I would have stopped the wedding anyway,' she said. 'So I'm just as much to blame as Arnold. I should have broken it off ages ago. But this is all just between you and me, Eva. If you tell people they'll think I'm just trying to save my pride. Best to leave things as they are. The fuss and gossip will die down eventually.'

'I won't say anything,' she assured her.

Arnold came into the café one day the following week and asked if he could see Clara when she finished work. She could see no harm in it so she agreed and they walked across the road and sat on a bench on the Green.

'So what exactly do you want to see me about, Arnold?' she asked coolly.

'I wanted to say how sorry I am about everything. Especially for ruining your day,' he said. 'What happened with that woman meant nothing. It's you I love.'

'You said all that at the church,' she reminded him. 'I don't think we need to go over it all again.'

He smiled, misunderstanding her. 'Oh, so you are going to give me another chance then?'

'Oh, no,' she said in manner that defied argument. 'You and I aren't right for each other so let's just go our separate ways.'

'You're punishing me?'

'No, Arnold. I just don't want to marry you.'

'Look, I'm really sorry,' he said. 'She was an older, experienced woman and she was all over me. I was weak but it was only ever a bit of fun.'

'Two years is a long time for a bit of fun to last, isn't it?'

'I mean it was never serious.'

'It wouldn't have happened if you and I were right for each other,' she said, troubled by her own conscience. 'I don't feel malice towards you but I don't want to see you again. I think it would be best.'

'I've done wrong and I'm ashamed,' he said, his voice rising. 'Do you want me to go down on my knees?'

She heaved a weary sigh. 'No, of course not. I just want you to accept that there is no way back for us. It's over. Truth be told, you're probably relieved.'

'Of course I'm not!'

'You'll soon find someone else,' she said. 'If you can manage two women at the same time, I'm sure you won't be on your own for long.'

'It's you I want.'

'Please don't try to see me again, Arnold.'

She walked across the Green in a homeward direction without looking back, but she knew that he wasn't following her. There was a sense of finality in the air and he had felt it. She knew, somehow, that Arnold wouldn't pursue her again.

As September arrived with golden days and cool hazy nights, Clara did some evening shifts at the café and worked on her Saturday off to get extra money to pay some of the cash back to her parents. They protested but she insisted and was glad to do it.

She also did something she had wanted to do for a long time. She joined a course of evening classes at a local school. Everyone assumed it was her way of healing a heart broken by Arnold and all attempts to disabuse them failed, so she had to leave it be. The subject she had chosen to study caused an element of surprise.

'Basic horticulture,' exclaimed Flo. 'What earthly good will that do you?'

'There's nothing wrong with improving your mind, Mum,' she said. 'It's a subject that interests me, so knowing more about it will give me pleasure.'

'I could understand you doing a typing course; something that would give you a chance to get a better job, in an office. But horticulture? What can you do with that round here?'

'She could get a job in the park as a gardener,' suggested Sydney with a wry grin.

'What's wrong with learning about something that interests me?'

'Well, nothing, I suppose,' said Flo. 'It just seems a bit peculiar. Working-class people like us usually take lessons with the express purpose of bettering ourselves.'

'I will be, because I'll be learning something new,' said Clara, knowing that they would never understand. 'And I'll practise by doing something with that scruffy little patch of green in the backyard. There will be something other than weeds growing there in the spring, I promise you.'

'That will be nice, Clara,' said Cuddy in his usual enthusiastic way. 'I'll help you.'

'If it's what you want to do then good luck to you,' said her father. 'I wish you well with it. It seems a bit of a strange thing for a girl to want to learn but if it's what you want, why not?'

'I blame the Land Army,' said Flo.

'I thank them,' said Clara, 'for doing me a favour and showing me something outside my own environment.'

'Oh well, if you want to spend one night a week in

the classroom that's your business,' said Flo. 'If it makes you happy that's all that matters.'

'I've had a letter from Eva,' said Mabel Fenner to the family over lunch in the kitchen. 'You'll never guess what's been happening up there in London.'

'No, we can't guess,' responded Charlie. 'But I'm sure you're going to tell us.'

'Clara Tripp didn't get married after all.'

'Oh?' said Charlie, with feigned disinterest. 'How did that come about?'

'There was a hell of a to-do at the altar apparently when the couple were about to make their vows,' his mother explained. 'The bridegroom had been carrying on with another woman for ages and her husband arrived at the church and tried to beat the living daylights out of him. Clara's had a lucky escape if you ask me.'

'What a shame,' said John. 'She's such a nice young woman, too.'

Charlie had mixed emotions. He felt sorry for Clara and angry with Arnold for betraying her. But he also felt a sense of jubilation that Clara was free and had to remind himself that nothing had changed. As far as he and Clara having a future together went, it wasn't going to happen, not now, not ever! Whatever had happened at the church on her wedding day, she had chosen Arnold over him. The only reason she wasn't married to him now was of Arnold's doing, not hers. That was where the matter ended. He couldn't help feeling for her, though, and hoped she was bearing up.

★　★　★

The autumn flew by for Clara as her course got under way, and she worked long hours at the café. In the classroom it gave her a thrill to learn the basics about planting, different soils, and nature's hazards in terms of growing of which there were plenty, the two main ones being disease and unseasonable weather. Every week she had homework to do and she did it willingly, finding herself with a voracious appetite for the subject.

The wedding drama gradually slipped into the background. At first Clara had guessed that she was the main topic of conversation when she wasn't around; she saw the pitying looks, noticed a room go quiet when she entered it. But other things soon happened for people to gossip about.

The big news in the Tripp family was that Cuddy was singing solo in the school carol concert in front of a large audience of parents and friends.

'We're all going to the concert,' stated Flo to her husband when they were out of earshot of Cuddy. 'And that means you and Sydney as well.'

'It'll be all women there,' he protested. 'The dads don't go to that sort of thing.'

'Yes, they do. I've mentioned it to you before when I've been to the children's school plays and concerts over the years,' she told him. 'And this one is special, with Cuddy doing a couple of solos, so you're coming and you'll pretend to want to within Cuddy's hearing. You will also tell him he did well whether you enjoyed it or not.'

'Seems I don't have a choice then,' he said.

'None at all.'

*　　*　　*

On the day of the concert Cuddy awoke in the early hours feeling awful. He'd been feeling off colour for a few days but had kept it to himself, hoping it would pass because he didn't want to miss the concert. Now, as he thrashed about in the sheets, he knew he was in trouble because his whole body ached, he was shivering then burning, and he felt sick. The only saving grace was that his throat wasn't sore, so it was still possible for him to sing.

Normally when he wasn't well, he would tell his mother and she would give him something to make him feel better. She would also insist that he stay in bed and miss school, so this time he couldn't tell her. Somehow he had to get through the day and do the concert tonight. He longed for the comfort she would have given him, bringing him drinks and making a fuss of him, but he couldn't let the music teacher down any more than he could let himself down. He would have to brave it through the day. If only his legs and head would stop aching.

The hall was packed, the performers singing their hearts out in 'O Come, all ye Faithful' on stage and the Tripp family plus Eva was sitting near the front.

Flo swelled with pride to see her boy up there, clean and smart in a white shirt and school blazer. He looked very flushed, she thought, and guessed it was excitement. Was it her imagination or did he look funny around the eyes? She did hope he wasn't going down with anything.

It was time for Cuddy's first solo and never had she heard 'Silent Night' sung so beautifully. His pure voice filled the hall and there was no other sound to be heard.

Tears filled her eyes and out of the corner of her eye she saw Clara dig a handkerchief out of her bag.

Frank Tripp was feeling most peculiar. The atmosphere here this evening had raised his spirits and made him feel emotional. Now, as he listened to his boy singing up there on stage, he felt tears come into his eyes. How could his son sing so beautifully? There was nothing like that in the family. He was so damned good. Pitch and word perfect. He was always singing around the house, of course, which could be irritating. But he would never tell him to shut up again, or tease him about singing not being for boys; not after hearing this.

He reached for his wife's hand, wanting to share this moment of pride with her.

It was nearly time for Cuddy's second solo. How he had got through the first he would never know, but it seemed to have gone quite well and the audience had given him a standing ovation. But he was feeling so ill it seemed impossible to stand for another moment on this stage.

But when the music teacher, who was also the choir mistress, indicated to him, he stepped forward, waited for the pianist to finish the introduction, then launched into the carol. 'O Little Town of Bethlehem'. Oh, if only he didn't feel so bad!

Clara was so proud of her brother, she almost ached with it. He had such a beautiful voice. He looked very hot up there, which wasn't surprising as he was putting his all into this. She could listen to him singing all night, but the carol had come to an end and the hall resounded with applause. And then she watched in horror as Cuddy turned very pale suddenly and crumpled to the floor.

There were gasps from the audience and Clara got up and rushed up to the stage, followed by the rest of the family. Cuddy was lying still on the floor.

'He's fainted,' said the music teacher. 'I must have been working him too hard.'

As the headmaster came on to the stage and told the audience that the concert would continue in a few minutes, Frank and Sydney lifted Cuddy between them and took him off the stage.

'But how could it have come on so suddenly, to knock him out like that?' Flo asked later after Cuddy, now in bed with a high fever, had been examined by the doctor.

'It didn't, Mrs Tripp,' he replied. 'I suspect he hasn't been feeling well for a few days.'

'But he would have said,' she told him. 'My family aren't ones to suffer in silence when they're ill.'

'Well, this family member did. Probably because of the concert you told me about,' he suggested. 'He wouldn't have wanted to miss it or let anyone down. Albeit ill judged from a medical point of view, it was very brave of him to have kept going like that.'

'Oh, dear, I should have noticed,' said Flo, biting her lip anxiously. 'What sort of mother doesn't know when her child is unwell? I can always smell it on them when they're ill.'

'Cuddy is growing up, Mum,' said Clara. 'He's smart enough to hide things if he needs to now.'

'He had a very high temperature and should have been in bed,' the doctor continued. 'The strain of doing the concert was too much. That's why he fainted.'

'So what's actually the matter with him?' asked Clara fearfully.

'I can't say for sure at this point, but I think he may have rheumatic fever.'

'Oh, my good Gawd,' gasped Flo emotionally. 'Isn't that the thing that affects the heart?'

'It can,' the doctor confirmed.

A silence fell over the room. 'What can we do to help him?' asked Clara, trying to stay calm for her mother's sake.

'Keep his temperature down as much as you can by bathing his face with a cool flannel and make sure he drinks plenty,' he said. 'Aspirin will give him some relief too. I'll be back to see him tomorrow but if you're worried during the night send someone for me.'

Tears were running down Flo's cheeks and Clara put a comforting arm round her. She was alarmed by the real-isation of how tragedy could strike at any time. It had been such a perfect evening, then in a second it had been shattered. People had been very kind. The father of one of the other boys had a car and had brought them home, then gone to fetch the doctor.

'Try not to worry too much, Mrs Tripp,' the latter was saying kindly. 'I won't lie to you. Your boy is very sick, but he does have a good chance of recovery.'

'I'll look after her, doctor,' said Frank, moving towards his distraught wife.

Noticing Eva placing a hand on Sydney's arm to comfort him, Clara suddenly felt very alone. Miserably, she went to the kitchen to put the kettle on.

Cuddy was very sick for several days. He did eventually come through the fever, but he was very emaciated and weak because he hadn't been able to eat. Having confirmed his original diagnosis of rheumatic fever, the doctor said out of Cuddy's hearing, 'It could have weakened his heart; only time will tell. It might not show up until later on in life, if at all. There isn't anything we can do about it at this point, I'm afraid. But there is something we can do for him in the present to help him back on his feet. I recommend a period of convalescence when he's well enough to travel. Do you have any relatives who live by the sea or in the country where he could go for a few weeks?'

'No.'

'In that case, you will have to make sure he takes it very easy for a considerable time. There will be no going back to school until I say so and it will be quite a while. Keep him in bed until I call again in a couple of days, then provided he is still progressing we will see about him getting up for a few hours a day.'

Flo looked worried and the doctor knew there was something else on her mind besides her son's health. He came across it all the time in his job. 'Don't worry, Mrs Tripp. I won't charge you beyond your means.'

'Thank you, doctor; you're very kind.'

'Just doing my job,' he told her. 'You look after that boy of yours; that's your job.'

She nodded and saw him to the door.

Christmas was quieter than usual because Cuddy was still in bed for part of the day. He was well enough to be up and dressed for Christmas dinner and the afternoon, though. Eva had gone home to Brierley as a gesture of goodwill towards her mother who, she knew, would miss Vincent terribly over the holiday.

The Tripps' numbers were also depleted by Arnold's absence. He always used to spend most of the holiday with them.

'It's like old times with just the five of us,' said Flo on Christmas afternoon when they were all sitting round eating sweets. 'Seems funny without Eva about the place.'

'I miss her,' said Clara.

'Not as much as Sydney does, I bet,' said Cuddy, teasing his brother. 'He's really sweet on her.'

'Don't listen to him.' Sydney looked at his brother. 'You're only getting cheeky because you're ill and you know I can't talk back to you or give you a clout.'

'That's right,' admitted Cuddy. 'There aren't many perks to being ill but that's one of 'em.'

'Uh-oh,' said Sydney, grinning. 'He's getting lippy again. So look out everyone.'

'Anyone fancy a game of cards?' asked Cuddy.

'No,' said Sydney. 'But I suppose I'll have to because you're ill.'

'I'll play too,' said Clara. 'Mum and Dad can have a snooze.'

Cuddy laughed. 'I'll make the most of this, because once I'm better I won't have you all in the palm of my hand.'

'I'll say you won't,' said Sydney. 'In fact, I can feel a bout of ordinariness coming on right now.'

'It's too soon,' Cuddy joked. 'I'm still officially ill, remember.'

'As if any of us could forget,' Sydney came back at him.

But Clara knew that Sydney was just as proud of their brother as she was. To have kept going through the concert when he was so ill showed a huge amount of courage.

And although he was playing on his illness now just for fun, not once had she heard him complain about not feeling well. She'd always loved him but she had a new respect for him now and she knew this was something she shared with Sydney and her father.

'Come on then, Sydney, let's get the cards out,' she said cheerfully.

The Fenner family Christmas was depleted too without Vincent or Hester. It was just Eva and Charlie and their parents. It seemed very quiet to Eva, who had got used to the noisy rough and tumble of the Tripp household. She felt so at home with them it was as though she had lived in London a long time, when in fact she had only spent one Christmas with the Tripps.

Still, this Christmas was a whole lot better than the last one she had spent at Brierley with her mother getting at her the whole time. Now Eva didn't know what to make of Mabel. On the face of it she was a changed woman, but Eva found it hard to believe that anyone could undergo such a transformation and thought that her claws must still be there hidden under a near desperation to please. On the other hand, if she could have had a change of personality once before in her life – when she lost her youngest child – maybe it was possible to reverse the procedure. But Eva wasn't sure who the real Mabel Fenner was. She was wary, still expecting her to fly into a rage the instant she said something that displeased her. So although things were better between them, they weren't spontaneous because Eva was always on her guard.

But she was glad she had come, for Charlie's sake. He'd been through a lot this past year and although he was his usual cheery self, she guessed he was happy to see her. To give her mother due credit she had made a huge effort with all the Christmas food, and Christmas dinner had been a positive banquet.

Now it was late Christmas afternoon and the light was fading. Eva, Charlie and their parents, still replete from their meal, were lazing around in the sitting room.

'So how's everything with the Tripps?' asked Mabel, who had made a real effort to be friendly that day back in the summer when she'd gone to London to make her peace with Eva and they had gone back to Green Street before she'd caught her train to Kent. She'd even sent them a Christmas card.

'We've had a big drama because Cuddy's been ill,' she said, and went on to tell them the whole story of his collapse on stage.

'Oh, the poor lad,' said Charlie with real concern. 'It just shows how much his music means to him, to soldier on like that.'

'You should have let us know, Eva,' said her father.

'I didn't think there was much point as I was coming for Christmas,' she explained. 'Anyway, there was nothing you could have done.'

'We'd have liked to know just the same,' said John. 'He did spend some time here, after all, and we all liked him.'

'So how is he now?' asked Mabel.

'Recovering slowly, but it will be a long time before he's properly well again,' she told them. 'He's still very weak. It could have affected his heart, the doctor said.'

'Oh, dear,' gasped Mabel. 'His mother must have been out of her mind.'

'It all happened so fast,' said Eva. 'But yes, she was

very worried. Still is, I should think. It will be ages before he goes back to school so he'll be bored stiff, especially when he's up and about all the time. At the moment he still has to spend part of the day in bed. The doctor recommended a period of convalescence by the sea or in the country when he's strong enough, but the Tripps don't have anywhere for him to go outside London.'

'He can come here,' suggested Charlie impulsively. 'He loved it when he was here before.'

'It's the middle of winter, Charlie, and this is a working orchard, not a convalescent home with nursing care on hand,' his sister reminded him.

'It's warm inside the house,' John said enthusiastically. 'We'll make sure all the fires are lit, and it would be a change of scene for him.'

'And when we get some dry winter days he can come out in the fields with me for a short time,' said Charlie, fervour rising with every syllable. 'It would be something different for him and some fresh air. Good clean country air. It'll do him the world of good.'

'It's a really kind suggestion, but you'll be working during the day and Cuddy has been very ill,' said Eva anxiously. 'He'll need someone to look after him.'

'That's where I come in,' said Mabel in a surprisingly willing tone. 'I'll look after him.'

They all stared at her. Eva was extremely wary of this unexpected offer because of the nasty streak she suspected her mother still had hidden away inside her. If it emerged in Cuddy's direction it would be miserable for a young boy, especially as he wasn't on top form.

'It's good of you to offer, but he's a sensitive boy, Mum,' she said.

'And you think I might not be kind to him?'

'I think you might get cross with him if the mood takes you,' said Eva honestly, because she daren't put Cuddy at risk of her mother's sharp tongue. 'You're not the most patient of people.'

'I'm sure your mother would be very nice to the boy,' said John defensively.

'I would,' she said, looking downhearted. 'But if you don't trust me you'd better not let him come.'

'Mum will be fine,' said Charlie lightly, making a joke of it to ease the rising tension. 'Dad and I will be here to keep her in order, won't we, Dad? One cross word and she'll have us to contend with.'

'Honestly,' protested Mabel. 'Anyone would think I was some sort of witch.' She looked down at her hands and spoke quietly. 'I know I've been very short-tempered in the past, especially with Eva, but I'm doing my best to change and I feel as though I'm doing rather well. Do I have to spend the rest of my life proving that I can be better?'

'No, of course not,' said Eva, softening. Her mother did seem to be sincere. 'But are you sure you won't find a young boy too much for you?'

A withering look came Eva's way. 'I'm not in my dotage, you know,' Mabel said.

'I mean because you're not used to kids now that we are all grown up.'

'He's not a baby,' her mother pointed out. 'It isn't as though he'll need his nose wiping every five minutes. What is he, about twelve?'

'Thirteen.'

'It will take more than a boy of that age to be too much for me,' Mabel declared.

'If you're sure, I'll see what the Tripps think about it when I get back, and find out if Cuddy wants to come.' Eva paused thoughtfully. 'Then there's the journey to be considered. It's cold and draughty on the trains in winter. I'm not sure if he'll be up to it.'

'I'll go and get him in the car to save him travelling by train,' said Charlie. 'I'll take plenty of blankets to keep him warm, and a pillow for his head.'

'That's very good of you, Charlie. I'll discuss it with them as soon as I get back,' said Eva, glad that her family were willing to help the people who had come to mean so much to her. 'I'll write and let you know what they say. After that, if they agree, we can get it arranged.'

'How's young Clara now?' enquired her father. 'Has she got over that awful business on her wedding day?'

'I don't know, because she doesn't talk about it,' said Eva. 'But she's certainly too busy to mope.' She went on to tell them about the extra hours Clara was working, and the evening classes.

'Not many girls would worry about paying back the wedding expenses,' said John. 'They'd just agree to have something small the next time.'

'I don't think Clara's got a next time in mind at the moment,' said Eva. 'Once bitten twice shy as far as she's concerned.'

'That's only natural,' said her father. 'But I expect she'll change her mind in time when some nice young man comes along.'

'Who knows?' said Eva casually.

Charlie kept a diplomatic silence on this subject. It was far too personal a matter for him to comment.

Chapter Sixteen

1923

'Hello, Clara,' he said guardedly.

'Hello, Charlie,' she responded nervously. 'Come on in. He's all ready and waiting for you.'

As the visitor entered the hallway he was greeted by a welcoming committee, led by Flo.

'You're a real good 'un to come all this way to collect him, Charlie,' she said warmly. 'We're ever so grateful.'

'No trouble at all,' he assured her.

'Wotcha, Charlie,' said Cuddy, still rather pale but not as fragile as he had been. 'Thanks for comin'.'

Charlie shook him by the hand. 'I hear you've been a bit under the weather, young man.'

'Just a bit.'

'The country air will soon have you fit and thriving,' said Charlie, smiling at him affectionately.

'Have you got time for a hot drink and a bite to eat before you go?' Flo enquired.

'Of course he has,' her husband cut in. 'He's got a long drive ahead of him. He needs something to sustain him on the journey.'

'Mum made me some sandwiches and I ate them on the way, but a cup of tea would be nice,' Charlie said.

'Come on into the parlour in the warm,' Flo said. He followed her, greeting his sister and Sydney on the way.

It had previously occurred to Clara – when the idea of Cuddy's going to Brierley for a recuperative break had arisen – that the two drastically diverse families of Fenner and Tripp were destined to be connected in one way or another. Now, watching Charlie in the bosom of her family, so obviously at ease, the thought drifted back into her mind.

On the face of it they could have nothing in common, one a sedate dynasty of country people with a thriving orchard of their own, the other a rough and ready family of Londoners living in a rented house with no financial assets whatsoever. But fate seemed to want to bring them together: Eva and Sydney, herself and Charlie, Cuddy and Charlie. It was strange.

'Tell your mother not to be afraid to tell him off if he misbehaves,' Flo was saying.

'He wouldn't do a thing like that, would you, Cuddy?' Charlie said, smiling.

'Don't be fooled by that angelic face,' Flo advised lightly. 'He can be a wicked little so and so when he's in the mood, like any other boy of his age.'

'I thought there was a ban on telling him off because he's ill,' said Sydney.

'There is up to a point, but he's getting better now.'

'Does that mean I can have a go at him?'

'No, it most definitely does not. You leave him alone.'

'You wait till the next time I get ill,' said Sydney, laughing. 'I'm going to milk it for all it's worth.'

'And your mother will spoil you like she does all of us when we're ill, grown up or not,' said Frank.

And so it went on; chirpy surface conversation until Charlie said that he and Cuddy should be on their way. Out they all trooped to the car, Charlie carrying Cuddy's suitcase, Flo with her arm around her youngest boy, the neighbours twitching their curtains because a motor car was virtually unknown in this street.

'Look after him, won't you, Charlie? He's delicate at the moment,' said Flo emotionally.

'Don't fuss, Mum,' responded Cuddy predictably.

'Don't worry, Mrs Tripp; we'll take good care of him,' Charlie assured her.

Then they were gone and the family went back inside. Clara hadn't had a chance to speak to Charlie alone. She couldn't help but feel bitterly disappointed.

'So, how are things going with you and Eva now?' asked Tub when he and Sydney were having a drink and a chat in the local pub.

'They're not going anywhere, mate. Not in the way you mean, anyway. We're still just pals.'

'But you admitted to me that you fancy her,' said Tub.

'Of course I do. What bloke wouldn't? You've seen her; you know how gorgeous she is.'

'So why haven't things moved on?'

'Because I'm Sydney Tripp and she's who she is. Why would a girl like her be interested in someone like me, an assistant in some grotty little grocer's shop?'

'But she works in a laundry, which is even lower down the scale,' Tub objected.

'Yeah, but only because she left home. Her family have

money,' Sydney reminded him. 'I'm not saying that they're rolling in dough or anything like that; they are hard-working country people from what I've heard. But they must be worth a good few quid if they've got an orchard and a ruddy great house. So they wouldn't want their daughter getting involved with a shop boy.'

'Eva strikes me as the sort of girl who would make up her own mind about things, especially something like that. Anyway, didn't you have a promotion recently?'

'Only to senior assistant. It just means that I don't have to go out on the delivery bike any more because they've taken on a boy, and I do get a little bit of extra pay each week.'

'There you are then; that's progress,' Tub said encouragingly. 'Play your cards right and you'll get to be manager eventually.'

'Fat chance. Not for years, anyway.' He paused thoughtfully, sipping his beer. 'The thing is, Tub, it isn't easy to change the way you are with a girl when you've been mates. She sees me as a brother, I think.'

'You'll have to try to alter that then, won't you . . .' His voice tailed off and his eyes widened as something attracted his attention by the door. 'Uh-oh,' he said, sounding worried. 'Look what the cat's dragged in.'

Sydney didn't recognise their old adversary at first glance because it had been two years since they had seen Shoulders and his appearance had changed dramatically. No longer a youth, he had matured into a tall, thickset man.

'Blimey,' exclaimed Sydney. 'He looks different.'

'Oh, Gawd, he's seen us,' said Tub, frowning. 'He's coming over.'

Sydney had known that this moment would eventually arrive because Shoulders couldn't stay locked up for ever. He gritted his teeth. He hadn't forgotten the last beating he'd taken from this pig's lackeys.

'Wotcha, boys,' said Shoulders with a slow smile. 'Still grassing people up, are yer?'

'We haven't needed to,' replied Sydney boldly. 'We don't mix in that sort of company now.'

The other man shrugged. 'Oo-er. Gone up in the world, 'ave yer?'

'No. But we have grown up.'

'Haven't we all.' He looked towards the bar. 'What are you 'aving, boys?'

'Not for me, thanks,' said Sydney, making a stand. It was important that Shoulders was left in no doubt that there was to be no association between them whatsoever.

'I don't want another one either,' added Tub.

Sydney held his breath in anticipation of the threats he felt sure the snub would produce. But Shoulders just said, 'Suit yerselves,' and moved away along the bar.

People like Shoulders would always be a threat, Sydney knew that, and maybe one of these days when he had mates with him he might come after himself and Tub looking for revenge. But Sydney wasn't going to waste so much as a minute thinking about it. He had stood up to him before and would do so again if it was ever necessary. But somehow he didn't think it would be. Shoulders and his kind preferred to bully those less able to defend themselves.

'So what were we saying before we were interrupted?' he asked.

'I think we were talking about your love life,' Tub replied.

'You mean my non-existent love life, don't you?'

'That's the one.'

They both laughed with relief. Although they would be unlikely to admit it, they had been more than a little unnerved by the reappearance of their old enemy.

It was one of those rare January days when the bleak countryside was lit with a wintry sunshine, lifting the gloom and making everything seem gloriously alive. The leafless trees were etched against the pale blue sky, a light coating of frost making them glisten. It was Charlie's lunch break and he and Cuddy were out for a walk. Cuddy's health was improving daily as the fresh air agreed with him.

'Are you very rich, Charlie?' the teenager asked suddenly, with a youthful lack of tact.

'It depends what you mean by rich,' Charlie replied. 'I have good health, a job I enjoy doing and enough food on the table to eat, if that's what you mean.'

'No. I mean rich in the usual sense, like having lots of money,' he explained.

'Oh, that's a good one,' Charlie said, laughing heartily. 'Whatever has given you that idea?'

'Because you seem to have so much,' Cuddy explained. 'A big house, a car, lots of land; things like that.'

'But all the money is tied up in those things and our income is uncertain.' Charlie halted in his step and pointed towards the skeletal orchard. 'Our fortune is in the trees, Cuddy,' he said. 'They have to be carefully nurtured and protected from disease and damage. We do that well because we know what we're doing after years of experience. But Mother Nature is an awesome opponent and sometimes we lose out to her. If the trees are damaged and our yield isn't good then we have cause to worry. We work all year for the harvest and if it's poor or ruined we have to work for another whole year for the next one.' As he was explaining it to Cuddy, Charlie realised what a struggle the whole business of fruit growing was. 'So, to answer your question, we make a reasonable living but we are not rich. Everything is tied up in the land.'

'So the only way you'd be rich is if you sold it all.'

'We wouldn't be wealthy even then, but I suppose we'd be able to get by.'

'But you would never sell up.'

'Not unless we were forced to for some reason.'

'Thank goodness for that.'

Charlie looked at him. 'Why the sudden interest in money anyway?' he asked.

'I was just wondering how things worked,' Cuddy explained. 'I mean, you and your family are different from us but you're not posh. You're the only people outside Shepherd's Bush that I know. I always thought people outside the Bush would be peculiar.'

'I take it that us Fenners are quite normal then,' Charlie said light-heartedly.

'You're different but not peculiar,' Cuddy said bluntly.

Charlie laughed. 'That's a relief. But we'd better get you back now. My mother will have my guts for garters if I keep you out too long in the cold. Our accountant is coming over to see us about business at two o'clock so I have to be back for that anyway.'

'All right.'

'Shall we have some fun with the piano tonight?' Charlie was giving the boy a few basic lessons and they had been enjoying themselves playing easy duets together.

'Yes, please.'

The thing that was so delightful about Cuddy, Charlie thought, was his enthusiasm for everything. He was keen to know and learn about anything that came his way. He had thrived in the orchard environment and they would all be sad when it was time for him to go home. Even Mabel seemed to enjoy having him around. The boy chatted to her while she was working in the kitchen, helping out where he could and always very appreciative of the fact that they had invited him here. He wiped the dishes and laid the table. Charlie hadn't seen his mother so happy in a very long time.

'Right, boots off,' he said in the lobby just inside the kitchen door, 'or we'll be in dead trouble for putting muddy footprints all over the floor.'

'I know the rules,' said Cuddy, smiling. Something about that smile reminded Charlie so vividly of Clara that he caught his breath.

Mr Parker, the Fenners' accountant, had a furrowed brow.

'I won't lie to you,' he said. 'As you requested I've been looking through your accounts in view of the fact that you want to have a new storage unit built. Frankly, gentlemen, I think you'll have to delay spending such a large sum of money.'

'But we need more and better storage,' Charlie pointed out. 'You know how important it is in our business. We're out there doing the job, not adding up figures. We know what we need.'

'The profit just isn't there at the moment, Charlie,' sighed Mr Parker, who had known the family for many years. 'The rising costs of materials and the fact that your selling agent is taking such a large chunk of your profit means funds just aren't available to cover any special expenditure this year. Next year maybe, if you have a good harvest in the autumn. We'll just have to wait and see.'

'But we've been losing stock because we haven't enough decent storage,' Charlie said. 'The fruit isn't marketable if it's stored for too long in conditions that aren't top notch.'

'That's right,' said his father, who was looking pale and worried. 'Throwing fruit away doesn't help our profits.'

'I know all about that, but I'm just your accountant,' said Mr Parker, 'not your managing director. I can only do what you ask me to and report what I see on paper.'

'Mm,' said John, stroking his chin. Stress made him feel quite ill now that he was getting older. 'So, what actually is the situation?'

'The truth is, it is absolutely imperative that you have a good yield this year or you'll be in trouble.'

'As bad as that?' said Charlie.

'It isn't bad at the moment but I have known better times at Brierley. Times when you have had more behind you,' he told them gravely. 'In my opinion you should put any large spending on hold for the moment.'

'It's very disappointing,' Charlie grumbled. 'We work hard and we expect to be able to invest in the business.'

'Of course, if the yield is good this year you've nothing to worry about,' the accountant said, 'and you can go ahead and get your new storage unit built.' He pushed his spectacles down his nose and looked at them over the top. 'There is nothing to stop you ignoring my advice and approaching the bank for finance; it is your business, not mine. But in my professional capacity I can't advise it because I think it would cause trouble later on. It wouldn't be a good idea to get too deeply into debt at the moment. Speaking as a long-term friend as well as your accountant, I strongly suggest you wait until after the harvest and see how things look then.'

'Perhaps I should do more on the marketing side so that at least some of the profits don't get eaten up in agent's commission,' said Charlie. 'But there is always so much to do here.'

'There's no need to go rushing out trying to find new buyers at the moment,' said Mr Parker. 'Just leave things as they are and wait and see what sort of harvest you have and no big purchases until then. I think that will be best.'

'Mm,' said Charlie.

'I hate to put a damper on things but we accountants are cautious fellows. It's part of our job to keep our clients' feet on the ground.'

'Oh, well, it looks as though we'll have to wait for our new storage space, then,' said Charlie.

Mr Parker smiled. 'Cheer up. It isn't as though you can't afford to eat or anything. We have to count our blessings, with so many men unemployed.'

'Yes, there is that,' said Charlie, feeling guilty.

There was a knock on the door and Mabel appeared with a tray of tea and homemade biscuits.

'There's something to cheer you up,' said Mr Parker. 'Mrs Fenner's delicious biscuits.'

'We don't have much to complain about while we have those,' Charlie concurred, trying to brighten the mood.

His father nodded in agreement but he was sick with worry. The orchard had been in his family for three generations through good times and bad. You could never feel entirely safe with fruit growing because there were too many hazards involved. As John got older he didn't have the same stamina for it as he'd had when he was young. He seemed to have lost his appetite for struggle and always felt tired lately.

The way he was feeling at the moment, he would cheerfully hand the whole shooting match over to Charlie, and help out only when he was needed. But he wasn't even sixty yet so that sort of luxury would have to wait. He would have to soldier on.

He took a biscuit and dipped it in his tea. 'Thank you, Mabel,' he said; 'just what the doctor ordered.'

'You're welcome,' she said, and hurried back to the comfort of her own domain.

Mabel was busy making bread at the kitchen table. Cuddy was sitting at the other end of it writing a letter home. He finished it and put it into an envelope.

'Can I go to the village to post my letter, please, Mrs Fenner?'

'Oh, no, dear,' she said, kneading the dough with vigour. 'It's too far for you to walk in your delicate condition. I'll ask Charlie to take you down to the village in the car as soon as he can spare the time,' she told him. 'An outing will do you good.'

'Thank you, Mrs Fenner,' he said politely.

'It's a bit quiet for you here with us after London, I reckon.'

'Yeah, it is. I like it here though,' he told her. 'I'm not allowed to play in the street until I'm properly better so I wouldn't see much of my mates anyway if I was at home. I miss Mum and the others, but I don't miss Mum fussing over me since I took ill.'

'It's only because she cares about you.'

'I know. But it does get a bit much when you're thirteen,' he sighed. 'But Mum's lovely. She's the best.'

Mabel felt a lump gather in her throat on hearing the evidence of such devotion. Much to her amazement she was thoroughly enjoying having the boy here. He was an absolute joy and breathed new life into a house that had been racked with sadness lately. Although she had offered to have him to stay, she'd suspected that she might find him a nuisance and had been afraid she wouldn't be able to stop herself from getting impatient with him as she had with Eva.

Instead, she enjoyed doing things for him, loved hearing him singing around the house and was very impressed by his readiness to accept whatever came his way. Whether or not he was merely filling a gap left in her life by Vincent, she didn't know and wasn't going to worry about. She was merely going to embrace each day as it came. As the thought struck her, she realised that it had been so long since she'd really enjoyed anything, she'd almost forgotten how good it felt.

The time for Cuddy to go back to London came towards the end of February. His health was so much better now, there was no need for him to stay any longer. The Tripps were eager to have him home, especially his mother whose letters were full of longing to have her boy back.

Mabel was sad to see him go, though, and the place felt empty for a while without him around. She even shed a few secret tears after his departure.

It was March before the doctor decided it was time for Cuddy to go back to school.

'Don't forget, son, tell the teacher straight away if you don't feel well,' said Flo, seeing him off at the door. 'Even if it's just that you feel a bit more tired than usual.'

He emitted an eloquent sigh. 'Yes, Mum.'

'Have you got your lunch?'

He nodded.

'Would you like me to walk with you to the school gate?'

'Mu-um, of course not,' he said, cringing. 'I'm going with the other kids.'

'Yeah, course you are. Sorry, love.'

'Bye, Mum,' he said as some of his mates appeared.

'Bye,' she said, managing not to embarrass him by kissing him in front of his friends but unable to stop herself from watching him as he walked down the street with the others until he was out of sight, before going back inside.

It was very difficult not to show how worried she was about her youngest child. It was the uncertainty of the condition that was so hard to deal with. There was no way of knowing for sure if his heart had been permanently damaged by the illness. If it had it could give out on him at any time, or at some point later in life. On the other hand, he could have a normal lifespan. The doctor had advised her to let him lead an ordinary life but to let him know if he seemed excessively tired or had breathing problems.

Sending him to school this morning had been very stressful for her and she was already having visions of him dropping dead in the playground from the strain of the rough and tumble. She hoped her confidence would grow as she got used to him going out and about with no disastrous consequences. This was the price of being a mother.

It meant that you were always vulnerable, she thought, as she went to the kitchen to wash the breakfast things.

'Egg and chips twice, bread and butter and two cups of tea, please, miss,' said one of the two young men who had come into the café where Clara worked. They were good-looking, well-built types of about her age and were dressed in working clothes and caps worn at a jaunty angle, which they removed when they sat down. 'And my friend 'ere wants to know if you're doing anything tonight.'

'Why can't he speak for himself?'

'He's shy,' said the dark-eyed one and the two of them laughed raucously.

They were obviously in the mood for some fun at her expense, but Clara had been waiting at table for long enough to be more than able to deal with this sort of thing.

'Tell him I'm busy tonight,' she said.

'Busy doing what?'

She pointed to her nose, wrote down their order and took it to the kitchen through a door behind the counter, where a few people were waiting to buy some of the cakes and pastries on display. By the time she had dealt with them, the lads' meal was ready, so she took it over and said their tea was just coming.

'I thought you'd rather wait until you had your food in case the tea went cold,' she said.

'Thoughtful girl,' said Dark Eyes. 'We like that in a woman, don't we, Baz?'

When she returned to the table with their tea, Baz must have recovered from his 'shyness' because he said to her, 'So how about coming to the pictures with me tonight?'

'I've told you I'm busy.'

'You're courtin' then?'

'There are other things in life besides courting.'

'Such as?'

'If you must know I'm going to my evening class.'

'Evening class,' exclaimed Dark Eyes, astounded. 'A waitress going to school at night. Well, that's a turn-up for the books. What are you learning, how to wash up?'

'Horticulture,' she said, standing her ground.

'What's that, lessons in dirty looks,' chortled Baz. 'Haughty culture . . . get it?'

'Enjoy your meal,' she said briskly and moved to another table to take an order.

Such bawdy mockery would never have come her way from the clientele of Taylor's Tea rooms. Here the customers were mostly working men wanting large meals that would sustain them in their labours rather than the dainty menu offered at a classy tea room. But even so, she had learned early on in the first term of her evening classes that, apart from her fellow students on the course, no one would understand why anyone would take the trouble to study something that, as far as they could see, had no practical value.

In the world in which she moved you had your place; she was a waitress, so she waited at table and wasn't expected to have any other aspirations. It didn't worry her that Dark Eyes and his friend mocked her, or that people couldn't understand the pleasure of learning, but she did wish she had some way of putting her newly found knowledge to good use. She had transformed the rough patch of ground in the back yard into a showcase of daffodils and tulips and planned a display of summer flowers right through the season. But she was hungry for more scope for her talents. She knew that to work with the soil was what she was meant to be doing.

But now she had people to serve, so she finished taking their order and headed for the kitchen.

'Do you think Sydney likes me?' Eva asked Clara as they got undressed for bed one night in May.

'He absolutely adores you,' Clara replied.

'If that is the case, why hasn't he asked me to go out with him?'

'Oh, it's like that, is it? I didn't realise. I thought the two of you were just good friends.'

'We were at first . . . well, we still are,' Eva tried to explain. 'He was awkward with me at first so it was difficult, then it got better but I was afraid to get involved with anyone after Gordon. But Sydney has sort of grown on me and I like him a lot. He hasn't shown any sign of wanting anything more but I think he likes me . . . really likes me, I mean.'

'Why don't you ask him out?' Clara suggested.

'How can I?'

'Open your mouth and let the words come out; that's the best way.'

'Oh, Clara, you know what I mean,' said Eva. 'It has to be the boy who makes the first move.'

'Rubbish,' said Clara. 'Just because it's the done thing doesn't mean that everyone has to stick to those rules. Knowing my brother, he probably thinks he isn't good enough for you or some daft thing like that. The only way you're ever going to find out is to ask him if he'd like to go out with you.'

'You really think it would be all right?'

'Listen to me, Eva. I've stuck to the rules all my life, and what has it got me? Humiliation at the altar because I felt I had to marry a man I didn't love because it was the right thing, and losing the man I really wanted to be with. Women have the vote now – at least those over thirty do – thanks largely to the Pankhursts and their like. Where would we be today if they'd been ruled by convention? Why shouldn't a woman take the initiative if the man won't do it? The worst that can happen is that he'll say no, but I'm absolutely certain that he won't.'

'I'm not so sure.'

'You had the courage to leave home and make a new life for yourself here; I'm sure you can cope with this.'

'You're right,' she said with a sudden surge of spirit. 'I'll do it at the first opportunity.'

'Good girl.'

Clara lay awake for a long time mulling things over, her pep talk to Eva reminding her of her own situation. She was a fine one to advise anyone. She had no man in her life and a job that bored her to tears. There wasn't much she could do about the former, because she'd lost the man she loved through her own fault and no one could replace him. There wasn't a great deal she could do about the latter either because unemployment was still rising and all the interesting jobs went to the men, especially any that included any form of horticulture.

Maybe her mother had been right and she should have taken a typing class instead of something that wouldn't be a practical asset. But she couldn't regret her choice because it gave her so much pleasure, even if its only worth was giving her an understanding of the family's tiny green patch.

'What are you doing out here, Sydney?' asked Eva, finding him sitting on a kitchen chair in the garden the following evening.

'Enjoying the nice weather,' he replied. 'It's as warm as in high summer. Lovely flowers too, thanks to Clara.'

'Nice weather for a walk,' she suggested.

'I suppose it is.'

'Are you going for one then?'

'One of what?'

'A walk.'

'No. I'm enjoying myself sitting here. Would you like me to get you a chair so that you can join me?'

'No thanks,' she said sharply.

He looked up at her quickly, sensitive to her change of mood. 'What's the matter? Was it something I said?'

'No,' she said, her voice rising. 'That's the trouble, you never say anything.'

'Oh, come on, Eva, we have loads of long discussions. We talk about everything, you and me.'

'Except about you and me. We never talk about that subject.'

'Oh.' He coloured up. 'Is there . . . Do you mean, er, you and me, as in . . . us?'

'Of course I do, and I'm not going to beat about the bush any longer,' she said. 'Do you want to go out with me or not?'

A smile lit his face. 'I never dared hope . . .'

'And I never dared say.'

He got up and moved towards her, taking her hand. 'So will you be my girl, Eva?'

'Course I will,' she said. 'Now can we go for that walk I suggested? There are always too many people around here who might appear at any moment. Let's go off on our own for half an hour.'

'Try stopping me,' he said and they went down the garden and out of the back-garden gate, holding hands.

Watching from the bedroom window, Clara smiled. If ever a couple were meant to be together, it was Sydney and Eva, and she was happy for them.

She made her way downstairs and out into the back yard to weed and water her little patch of garden, enjoying the balmy evening air. The long spell of warm weather had brought everything on and the bed was a riot of colour, with orange marigolds, purple pansies and budding geraniums in a variety of hues.

'It looks lovely,' said her mother, coming into the yard to the dustbin. 'It's cheered the place up no end. Well done, Clara! I enjoy watching the flowers come on when I'm washing up at the sink. I think we all enjoy the results of your efforts. So your course hasn't been a waste of time.'

'Thanks, Mum,' she said, glowing with pride. Some things you couldn't put a price on and her newly acquired gardening skill was one of them.

Chapter Seventeen

'We've pulled it off then, Dad,' said Charlie in buoyant mood as he and his father walked through the flourishing orchard. 'We've looked after our precious babies and done everything we could to protect them from all possible hazards and this is our reward, fields of glorious blossom that will become healthy fruit for marketing come the autumn as long as we continue to take care. We'll be able to have our new storage unit and money left over.'

'The trees are a sight for sore eyes and that's a fact,' agreed John happily, 'and it's all your doing, son. You do all the hard work and organisation these days.'

'You do your share,' Charlie told him.

'Which is nowhere near as much as I used to do as a young man,' his father pointed out.

'That's how it should be too. You're not expected to work as hard when you get older. That's what sons are for,' Charlie suggested lightly. 'To take the burden off their dads as time goes by.'

The other man nodded. 'I suppose you're right. None of us can stop age slowing us down. Anyway, our trees really are magnificent this year.' He looked across at them, lush and green and topped with blossom like marshmallow for as far as the eye could see. 'It's a load off my mind, given what Mr Parker had to say.'

They were always thorough in their work at Brierley but since the accountant's warning they had been even more meticulous and had left nothing to chance with this year's crop. Charlie and his team had been painstaking in their inspections and had made sure to spray at exactly the right time, making it nigh on impossible for even the most determined bug to damage the blossom.

'So, how about we go down the local for a drink tonight to celebrate,' Charlie suggested.

'Good idea, son. I'll check with your mother first; make sure she doesn't mind.'

Charlie thought of suggesting that they invite his mother along, as a good harvest affected them all, but the village pub was almost exclusively male territory, apart from the bar staff, and she would consider it most improper to be there.

The pub was full of fruit growers, the area being in the heart of England's orchard country. The conversation ranged from the best spraying methods and equipment to fertilisation and storage but rarely moved away from work, though there was a darts game in progress and some old men were playing dominoes at a table in the corner.

'Nice to see you, Charlie,' said the landlord when Charlie went up to the bar. 'We don't see so much of you in here these days.'

'No, I haven't been out a lot lately.' Probably because he didn't have Hester to drive him out, he thought. 'I don't seem to get round to it.'

'It's hard when you lose someone,' remarked the landlord sympathetically. 'It must be a year or more now since . . .'

'Yes, it is,' he cut in quickly, not wishing to linger on the subject. 'But I'm doing all right.'

As he uttered the words he realised with surprise that it was almost as though the Hester period of his life had never happened; maybe because it had been such a miserable time he had subconsciously blotted it out. Or possibly because he had fallen in love with someone else.

'Oi, Charlie, fancy helping us out over here?' called one of the darts players. 'Someone's dropped out and you used to be quite nifty with an arrow.'

'Why not?'

After a few pints Charlie really began to enjoy himself. He liked the robust, sometimes crude camaraderie of male company and the game was fun.

'A good night, eh, Dad?' he remarked as they left the pub, both a little worse for wear.

'Yeah. Enjoyed myself, son. All the more so for knowing that things are on the up for us.'

Then he broke into an out of tune version of 'Nellie Dean' and the two men walked home, somewhat unsteadily, along the deserted country lane, singing drunkenly.

The women of the Tripp household had also had a night out. Flo had been in such a state of stress about Cuddy since his illness, the family thought that a break from the house might take her mind off it. So Clara, Flo and Eva had been to the Cinema on the Green to see a comedy film called *Safety Last* starring the famous comedian

Harold Lloyd, who carried out several daring stunts.

'Good picture, wasn't it?' said Clara on the way home. 'What about the bit when he was dangling off the side of that tall building.'

'I was scared stiff for him,' Eva confessed.

'My favourite was when he was hanging off the hands of that clock,' Flo put in. 'My heart was beating so fast I thought it would burst.'

'I've heard that he does all those dangerous stunts himself,' said Clara. 'He doesn't have someone else to do them for him like some film stars.'

'Brave man, and all to keep us entertained.'

'Oh, it seems to have turned a bit chilly,' said Clara, shivering suddenly. 'I'd got used to that lovely warm weather.' She thought for a moment. 'I hope my plants will be all right.'

'You and your plants,' her mother joshed as they reached their front door. 'Anyone would think they were your children the way you fuss over them.'

'They're the nearest thing I've got to children at the moment,' she responded, chuckling.

'They're a darned sight less worry than kids, and that's a fact,'

'Don't forget you promised to try not to worry about Cuddy so much.'

'Let's get inside and make some cocoa to warm us up,' suggested Eva, changing the subject. 'You're right, the weather has turned much cooler. In fact it's flippin' freezing.'

Charlie woke the next morning with his head hurting so much, he could hardly open his eyes. But as he gradually came to, cursing the indulgence of the night before which had left him with such a hangover, he observed one salient fact. He was cold.

'God almighty,' he mumbled, instantly awake as he scrambled from bed, threw on some clothes and tore out to the orchard. His father was already there.

'All our grand expectations gone,' John said simply. 'The frost has taken the lot.'

'It might not have,' said Charlie, not wanting to accept it. 'Some of the trees might be all right.'

But he knew they were just empty words as he walked with his father from tree to tree and saw all the precious blossom coated with frost. When he turned to John, for the first time in his life he saw his father weeping.

Knowing John would consider his tears to be a shameful sign of weakness, he just said, 'We'll be all right, Dad.' He put his hand on his shoulder in the most intimate gesture he dared. 'We'll manage somehow.'

'We both know that isn't true,' John responded thickly. 'There is no way we can come back from this. All the blossom is ruined; there will be no harvest. Brierley is finished as a working orchard. We should have been prepared.'

'For frost this late in May?' exclaimed Charlie. 'No one could have predicted such a thing and we won't be the only ones to be caught out by it. There will be fruit growers all over the county in the same boat as us.'

'It's never happened in my time as an orchard man, I must admit.'

'Because it's a freak of nature, that's why.'

'We'll have to sell up.'

'Not so fast, Dad. We don't know the extent of the damage yet.'

'I think we do.'

Charlie couldn't deny that things were looking dire. Without the income from the bumper crop they were expecting, they couldn't continue in business because they had nothing to fall back on. Glancing at his father, he noticed how very pale and drawn he looked. He'd been worried for a while about the business and this was the final straw.

'Try not to worry too much, Dad,' he said gently. 'We'll sort something out between us.'

But he really didn't know how they were going to get out of this one.

Cuddy came in from the street one evening in late May with a black eye and a bloody nose.

'Oh, my good Gawd,' exclaimed his mother, pale with fear. 'What have I told you about fighting? You're not to do it, Cuddy. Not since you've been so ill.'

'You can't expect me to stand back and take it if someone picks on me,' he declared as his mother dabbed the blood from his nose with a wet flannel.

'That's quite true, Flo,' agreed his father. 'Boys will always scrap. It's in their nature.'

'They'd give him a hell of a life out there if he didn't stick up for himself, Mum,' added Sydney.

'But he's been ill.'

'And he's better now,' her husband pointed out.

'Yeah I am, Mum,' Cuddy assured her. 'So, if you've finished slapping that wet cloth all over me, can I go back out?'

'After what's just happened?'

'Yeah, o' course. I've got friends out there as well as

enemies. Anyway, I only came in for a drink of water.'

'Go on then,' said his mother worriedly. 'But no more fighting, now.'

All the adults were in the parlour relaxing after their evening meal. As soon as Cuddy was out of earshot, Flo said to her husband, 'You know what the doctor said.'

'Yeah, he said that there's a chance Cuddy's heart was affected by his illness. It's just a possibility, Flo. Not a fact. You can't risk spoiling the boy's life because of something that might not even be there.'

'You shouldn't be encouraging him to fight.'

'He's got to stand up for himself, Mum,' said Sydney, who was sitting next to Eva. 'He's a boy and they have to. It's a matter of principle.'

'Don't get on to her,' admonished Clara, fiercely defensive of her mother. 'Mum is the best and she would never spoil anyone's life, Dad. She's only looking out for him.'

'I know that,' said Frank. 'Sorry I was a bit hard on you, Flo, but you must learn to stand back a bit, for your own sake as well as Cuddy's.'

Just then there was a knock at the front door.

'Oh, no,' said Flo, rising and heading for the door. 'What's happened to that boy of ours now?'

When she returned she was holding a telegram. 'It's for you, Eva,' she said shakily, handing her the yellow envelope.

'Oh.' Eva turned scarlet before her face became bloodless after she'd read it. 'I have to go to Kent right away. It's my father; he's ill. He's had a heart attack.'

There was a general outpouring of sympathy. 'I'll come too,' offered Sydney, his arm round her supportively. 'You need someone with you at a time like this.'

'No, no, you don't want to take time off work,' she said. 'This is family business. I have to do this on my own. I'll try to get a train tonight.' She brushed her hand across her damp brow anxiously. 'Oh, dear, I do hope I won't be too late to see Dad . . . if the worst happens.'

'You'll let me come to the station with you though, won't you?' said Sydney.

'Yeah, of course,' she replied. 'I'd like that. Thank you.'

Seeing her father unconscious in the hospital bed was the most frightening thing that had ever happened to Eva. It was the utter powerlessness that affected her so profoundly. His life hung in the balance and there wasn't a thing she could do about it. Her mother seemed to look older and frail too, sitting beside his bed holding his hand. Eva felt frighteningly grown up suddenly.

'I'll stay here if you want to go for a break, Mum,' she suggested.

'No, I'm not leaving him.'

'Shall I go and see if I can get you a cup of tea?'

'That would be nice. Your brothers are outside. Perhaps they might like one too.'

'Won't be long, then.'

Eva hated to admit it but it was a relief to be out of that room, staring at her father and dreading that his next breath would be his last. He had apparently collapsed in the orchard and Charlie and one of the hands had got him indoors. The doctor had been called and immediately sent for an ambulance.

There was no sign of her brothers anywhere in the corridor but she could hear men's voices in a waiting area at the end so she headed towards them.

'If the old man pops off, don't think you can cheat me out of my share of what I'm entitled to just because I got chucked out of the family home,' Vincent was saying, and his words stopped Eva in her tracks out of sight round the corner.

'Dad isn't dead yet so show some respect, you callous bugger.' That was Charlie.

'He's on his way out,' Vincent predicted callously. 'No doubt about it.'

'Not necessarily,' Charlie disagreed hotly. 'He isn't an old man; he's still only in his fifties. It's worry about the business that's brought this on, not age. I'm hoping and praying he'll get better and you should be doing the same.'

'If his time has come—'

'I refuse to think it has,' Charlie cut in. 'He'll have to take things a lot easier, of course, but while there's life there's hope.'

'He's a goner, so get used to it.'

'My God, you're evil.'

'Never mind all that holier than thou stuff,' said Vincent. 'I want my share.'

'If Dad were to die, and I'm still hoping that he'll come through this, the orchard – for what it's worth – will go to Mum, I should imagine. Everything will go to her.'

'What do you mean, "for what it's worth"?'

'The business is in big trouble and whatever happens to Dad, Brierley is going to have to be sold,' said Charlie. 'And by the time everything is paid and accommodation found for Mum and Dad, there won't be anything left for you to fight over.'

'Why is the business in trouble?'

'The frost got at the blossom and this year's crop is ruined.'

'You let the frost get at the trees? How the hell did you manage to be that incompetent?'

'No one expected such a heavy frost so late in the year.'

'Nothing like that happened when I was still working there.'

'A frost heavy enough to ruin the crops this late in the year hasn't happened before in living memory, that's why. Growers all over the county have been affected.'

'I don't know, I get thrown out of my home and the business and you manage to wreck it.'

'The frost wrecked it. Anyway, what loyalty did you have to the family or the business when you were sleeping with my wife?'

'Oh, not that boring old chestnut again,' Vincent said. 'Let it go, for God's sake!'

Eva had heard enough. She turned the corner and faced her brothers.

'You should never have sent for Vincent, Charlie,' she declared. 'He doesn't give a toss about Dad. He's only here for what he can get. He's practically willing our father to die.'

'I felt I had to let him know, sis. Dad is his father too.'

'He doesn't deserve to be here with us. He's a disgrace to this family and I'm ashamed to have him as my brother.'

A sudden interruption halted the conversation. 'Excuse me, Mr Fenner,' said a nurse to Charlie. 'You're wanted in the ward.'

'Oh, no,' exclaimed Charlie, the colour draining from his face. 'Has he . . . is he . . .'

'He's come round,' she informed them. 'So perhaps you'd like to join your mother at his bed.'

Charlie and Eva practically ran down the corridor. Vincent merely sauntered.

It was still early days and nothing could be guaranteed, but the doctor at the hospital was cautiously optimistic about a full recovery for John Fenner, though he warned the family that he would have to take things very much easier in future. To carry on working was completely out of the question.

'So what will happen then, Charlie?' asked Eva when they were alone together at Brierley a few nights later. Vincent had gone back to Somerset, Mabel was in bed and John was still in hospital. 'I heard you telling Vincent that Brierley has to be sold. Is that definite?'

'I'm afraid so. Dad and I knew that when we saw what had happened to this year's blossom. He collapsed soon afterwards. It must have been the shock.' He went on to tell her about the meeting with the accountant and how vital it had been for the harvest to be good this year.

'So sad for you both,' she sympathised. 'I know what this place means to you.'

'It's a blow, I can't pretend otherwise, but it's just one of those things. Anyway, Dad is going to have to retire because of his health so I'll get myself a job and we'll sell the orchard, lock, stock and barrel; house, cottage, the lot. I think there will be enough money to set Mum and Dad up in a nice little place with enough money left to last them. If there isn't I shall have to support them from what I earn. As the eldest son, it's up to me.'

'Oh, Charlie, I'd like to help, but I barely earn enough to pay my way as it is.'

'I wouldn't dream of letting you help,' he assured her.

'Anyway, there should be no need to supplement them as long as we get a reasonable price for Brierley.'

'Is there no other way?' she asked. 'Brierley is in your blood, yours and Dad's. You'll be miserable without it.'

He shrugged. 'Maybe. But I won't miss all the headaches that go with it, that's for sure. Fruit growing is such a worry, the same as anything that is so reliant on nature.'

Something about his tone made her narrow her eyes on him. 'You're not thinking of getting out of the growing business altogether, are you?' she asked.

'I'd certainly have an easier life if I did.'

'You always used to say that fruit growing was working with nature and that's what you loved about it,' she reminded him.

'I probably thought that at one time, but things happen that change your opinion,' he said. 'This last blow has knocked the stuffing out of me, and look what it did to Dad. He keeled over just after we'd seen what the frost had done to the blossom.'

'But what else would you do, Charlie? Fruit growing is in your blood. It's all you know.'

'I was thinking of going into the marketing side of it, as a matter of fact.'

'A salesman?'

'A freelance sales agent, perhaps. Those chaps earn a decent living. We've paid enough commission to them over the years so I know what I'm talking about.'

'You would hate it. Oh, please think about this some more, Charlie.'

'Who says that I would hate it?'

'I do.'

'A change is as good as a rest, they say, so maybe it's

time I had a new challenge. I know these sales people work hard for their money but it's a different sort of thing altogether and would be a piece of cake compared to running an orchard.'

Eva was deeply worried. 'I've never heard you speak like this before,' she said. 'It isn't like you at all.'

'A lot has happened, hasn't it?' he pointed out. 'We're all victims of circumstance. I've had enough of such an uncertain way of earning a living. I think it's time I tried something else. Maybe I could actually succeed at something.'

'You've been very successful as a fruit grower,' she said ardently. 'You've practically run this place for the last few years. This recent blow was not your fault. It was an unforeseen circumstance. Take no notice of what Vincent says. All he cares about is getting something for nothing. He's never done anything for this family except make trouble.'

'I know,' he agreed. 'But whatever happens to me, the main thing is that Dad is on the mend. Nothing matters except that, as far as I'm concerned.'

'Me too,' she said. 'How does Dad feel about selling up? He's lived here all his life.'

'He accepted the inevitable when we saw the frost, I think. It made him ill but now that's over, I think he'll be glad to be shot of all the problems, though he will miss it like mad, of course. I think he always had the dream of retiring and handing the responsibility over to me, but being on hand to help out when he felt like it. That isn't going to happen now. Still, he needs plenty of relaxation.'

'Relaxation, yes, but not complete inactivity and being cut off from a world he knows.'

'What else can I do, sis?' he asked, spreading his hands in a helpless gesture.

'I don't know, Charlie. Are you sure there is no way you can keep Brierley?'

'Not in its present form. So you'll just have to leave it to me.' He paused, looking at her. 'I'm sorry, kid. I know this is your home too.'

'Don't worry about me,' she told him. 'I never liked it here and I'm not planning on coming back to live, ever. It's you I'm worried about. I know you'll be miserable away from Brierley and the way of life you're used to.'

'It's just one of those things. The good news is that we have someone interested in the place even before it's gone on the market. We're expecting an offer any day.'

'Oh, Charlie. I didn't realise it was quite as imminent as that.'

'I had a preliminary chat with an estate agent in Tunbridge Wells and he just happened to have someone on his books who was looking for somewhere like Brierley. We're lucky.'

'If you can call it that.'

'Under the circumstances it is. Look, sis, don't worry about it. I'll be all right and Dad is on the mend. That's what you've got to keep in mind. Go back to London and enjoy your life there. You've got Sydney now so things are even better.'

'For me, yes,' she said. 'But what about you?'

'I'll be fine,' he assured her. 'So you can go back to London with an easy mind.'

'Oh, Charlie, I'm so lucky to have you as a brother.'

'Give over with the soft soap and go and put the kettle on,' he said affectionately, managing a smile which faded as soon as his sister left the room.

★　★　★

It was a warm evening in June and the Tripp family – except for Cuddy who was outside in the street – were gathered in the parlour with all the doors and windows open. Flo was reading a magazine for film fans called *The Picturegoer*, Sydney had his head in the sports pages of the newspaper, Clara – who had just finished watering the plants – was mending the hem on a dress, Eva has just washed her hair and was towelling it dry and Frank was talking about the latest invention, the wireless.

'We'll all have one before very long, they reckon,' he enthused. 'Everyone will be able to afford them eventually. Bert down the pub has got one and he thinks it's marvellous. He can hear the football results on it. You don't have to wait for the paper to come out to find out how your team got on.'

'What? Sound coming into your house, voices and that?' said Flo, looking up from her magazine. 'That seems a bit creepy. How can they do that?'

'They pick up signals by tickling crystals with "cat's whiskers" wires then listen on earphones,' explained Frank. 'Bert says you sometimes have to fiddle about with it for ages before you get a result, but you get one in the end.'

'Fancy being able to hear the football results in your own house,' said Sydney. 'Oh, yeah, I like that idea.'

'What will they think of next,' Flo wondered.

Sydney rose. 'Phew, it's warm in here. I'm going outside to get some fresh air.'

He went out through the back kitchen door while Frank continued to wax lyrical about the wonders of the up and coming wireless set. 'There's going to be a programme for women called *Woman's Hour* and there's even a magazine thing that tells you what's on. It's called the *Radio Times*.'

'I like the sound of that,' said Flo, impressed. 'It would be exciting to have a set.'

'Most people make their own,' her husband informed her. 'You can buy the parts in special shops or order them from *Practical Wireless* magazine.'

'Do you think you can make one for us?' she asked excitedly.

'I don't know, but I'll certainly find out more about it because I'm as keen as you are.'

Sydney came rushing back into the room.

'Cuddy's lying on the ground in the yard,' he panted. 'He must have had a turn.'

'Oh, lor,' said Flo, dropping her magazine and rushing out through the kitchen door, followed by the rest. In the yard they found Cuddy lying on his back with his eyes closed.

Filled with terror, his mother got down on her knees. 'Cuddy, come on, love, open your eyes.' Her voice was shaking. 'Get 'elp, someone, get the doctor. Oh, I knew something like this would happen. I should have been more careful with him.'

'I'll go for the doctor,' said Frank, heading back to the house.

Clara felt for a pulse and found one. 'He's alive, anyway,' she said. 'Try not to worry, Mum. He's probably just fainted because of the warm weather.'

'Oh, please wake up, Cuddy,' wept Flo. 'Please, please don't die. I'll never go on at you again if you'll only open your eyes.'

The boy's eyes shot open and he grinned. 'Can I have that in writing?' he asked.

'Cuddy, you young heathen,' Flo said, holding her chest. 'You frightened me half to death.'

'Just pretending,' he said, scrambling to his feet.

'That was a wicked thing to do, Cuddy,' Clara said. 'Frightening us all like that.'

His father swept back on to the scene having been told by Sydney – who was in on the joke – that medical help wouldn't be necessary. 'It was a very bad thing to do, Cuddy,' he said sternly. 'Now apologise to your mother at once.'

'Sorry, Mum,' he said, looking contrite. 'It was just a joke.'

'Whatever made you do such a silly thing?' Flo asked. 'It isn't like you at all.'

'You're always expecting me to pass out or die or some-thin' so I thought if I played a trick it would make you laugh and stop you worrying so much.'

'How, exactly, would a stunt like that stop Mum from worrying?' Clara demanded.

'It was only a bit of fun,' he said lamely.

'You've got a very weird sense of humour,' said Clara, worried on her mother's behalf.

'I didn't realise it would give you all the flippin' hump,' said Cuddy defensively.

'You're no better, Sydney, for putting him up to it,' said Flo.

'Who says I put him up to it?'

'I can tell by the look on your face.'

'I don't know how you do it, but you always know everything,' he said.

'It's what mothers do,' she told him.

'It was just a bit of a laugh,' Sydney explained. 'We didn't expect another war to break out over it.'

Warm with relief, Flo started to laugh in the sheer joy

of the fact that her son hadn't fallen ill after all. She was suddenly aware of the effect her constant observation had been having on him. 'You little perisher,' she warned Cuddy, when she managed to stop giggling. 'Don't you ever do anything like that again.'

'And have you all go barmy? Not likely!' he said.

The laughter was infectious and soon the whole lot of them were in fits, except for Eva, who, Clara noticed, although enjoying the fun, seemed more than a little preoccupied. Come to think of it, she had been rather quiet ever since she got back from Kent a few weeks ago. Clara did hope she wasn't still worrying about her father. She would have a chat with her later to find out if she could do anything to help.

'Is everything all right, Eva?' she asked that night when her friend came into the bedroom after saying her usual prolonged goodnight to Sydney. Clara was already in bed.

'Yeah. Sydney and I are getting along just fine,' she replied, misunderstanding.

'That wasn't what I meant. I couldn't help noticing that you've been a bit quieter than usual since you got back from Kent and I wondered if everything was still all right with your dad.'

She nodded. 'I rang from the telephone box near the station on the way home from work and he's coming along fine, apparently,' she said.

'I haven't wanted to intrude but I can tell that something is bothering you,' Clara said. 'If I can help in any way . . .'

Eva sighed. 'I haven't said anything because I didn't want to put a damper on things here, and also because it's

Fenner family business. But you might as well know. Brierley is being sold and the sale will be finalised any time now. It could even be sold as we speak.'

'What! Oh, Eva, how terrible,' Clara gasped. 'Brierley not in your family. I can't believe it!'

'It's taken a bit of getting used to for me as well and I still keep hoping that by some miracle they manage to keep it.' Eva told Clara about the frost and its effect on Brierley and Charlie's plans for the future. 'It's my brother I'm more worried about than anything. It'll be hard for Dad, of course, but at least he'll be retired and he'll have Mum's company and support. Whatever her faults she's always been a very good wife to Dad. But what about Charlie? He'll be lost without the orchard. I mean, can you imagine him as a sales agent, working with figures rather than on the land?'

'No, I certainly can't. Surely something can be done to save Brierley?'

'He says not, and the facts don't look good. But he seems to have lost heart. It isn't like him to be defeated. Maybe he's had enough of things going wrong; a bad marriage and Hester's death, and then things didn't work out for you and him. He hasn't spoken to me about it because it's personal, but I suppose he must have been hurt. And then the unexpected frost and Dad's illness. I suppose you can't blame him for wanting to distance himself from it all.'

'No, of course not.'

'Of course, he could look for a job managing someone else's orchard but that wouldn't be easy for him, having worked in the family business for so long,' Eva went on. 'That's why he's talking about going into the marketing side. But he'll be miserable in a job like that, I know he will, and I don't know what to do to help because there isn't anything I *can* do.'

In a defining moment Clara decided to do something she should have done a long time ago. She was going to act on her instincts, and she hadn't a moment to lose.

'There may not be anything you can do, Eva,' she said. 'But there's nothing to stop me trying.'

When Clara arrived at Brierley the next day, Charlie was in the yard talking to a man she hadn't seen before. When she opened the gate Charlie looked over and saw her, said something to the man and came across to her.

'Clara,' he said, looking puzzled. 'What are you doing here? Has something happened to Eva?'

'No, Eva's fine. I'm here to see you urgently and in private.'

'I'm busy as the moment, as you can see,' he said, pulling the gate open to let her in. 'If you'd like to wait in the house I'll see you later on.'

'No, Charlie, I'm sorry but it can't wait. It's really important and it has to be now.'

'I've told you I'm busy,' he said sharply. 'I'm in the middle of some important business.'

'Charlie,' she almost shouted. 'I have to speak to you right away. Please just hear me out.'

He looked at her long and hard, then walked back across the yard to the man.

'So what is so important I had to cut short my business?' he asked, as they walked down the lane at Clara's suggestion; she wanted to make sure they weren't interrupted. 'And why the urgency?'

'Eva has told me what's going on here and I suspect you were talking to that man about selling Brierley.'

'Yes I was. He's buying the place and we were clearing up a few final points. So say what you have to say and make it brief. I've sent him into the house and promised I won't be more than half an hour. God knows what he must think of me, just walking off like that.'

'Please don't do it,' she urged him. 'Don't sell Brierley. It would be wrong, and I think you know that.'

He halted in his step and looked at her. 'You've come all this way, uninvited, just to tell me that?' he said, astounded.

'Yes, that's right.'

'You've got some nerve, I'll give you that. But just so that you know the situation, I have to sell the place whether I like it or not. It's no longer economically viable for us to keep it. Surely my sister told you that, as she's obviously been discussing our private family business with all and sundry.'

'She hasn't told anyone else, and she only told me yesterday,' Clara said quickly. 'I think she's so worried about it, she needed a friend to confide in.'

'And you think I'm not worried? Do you think I want my parents to have to leave their family home and go and live somewhere strange? Do you think I want to have to work for someone else? Of course I don't, but there is no choice.'

'Couldn't you just sell some of the land to raise enough money to keep you going and keep the rest as a working orchard?'

'It wouldn't be feasible,' he said dismissively. 'It wouldn't make enough to keep us and pay the workers' wages.'

'If you had a smaller area you wouldn't need as many hands, so you would save money there. And you could diversify; make the cottage into a tea room, which wouldn't cost much to set up as you already have the building and a kitchen. I'm sure your mother would be pleased to do the baking now that she has less family at home to look after. People would come for miles for her cakes once the word got around. And you would still have enough fruit trees to keep you busy and earn money, especially if you cut your costs by doing your own marketing. If you're thinking of going into marketing anyway, be a sales agent for yourself and save on commission. You could even offer bed and breakfast accommodation in the summer to bring in more money if you needed to. There are extra rooms at the big house as well as the cottage now that Vincent and Eva aren't there.'

He looked completely bewildered. 'Where did all this come from?' he asked.

'As soon as Eva told me what was happening here, my brain started working overtime. I just can't accept that there isn't a solution other than all of you moving out of Brierley.'

'It's all very well in theory, but—'

'Please just think about it, Charlie,' she implored him. 'That's all I ask.'

'There's no point—'

'I'll come here and work for you without pay until you get back on your feet,' she interrupted, driven by enthusiasm. 'All I would need is my keep and a few coppers for sundries. I could run the tea rooms and help in the orchard. I'm doing a course at night school so I know a bit more than I did when I was here before.

Perhaps there is a class in Tunbridge Wells I could go to to learn more about running a business. Anything I can do to help, I'll do, willingly. I'll work all hours if necessary.'

'Why would you give up your life in London and come here to work for nothing?'

'Because I care about Brierley and your family, because I think you will be miserable away from here, but most of all because I'm in love with you and would do anything to help you,' she blurted out.

His eyes widened and there was a stunned silence.

'That's why you chose Arnold over me, is it?' he said after a moment, an edge to his voice. 'Because you're in love with me.'

'I didn't marry Arnold.'

'Only because he let you down at the altar.'

'No, that isn't how it was. I wouldn't have gone through with it anyway. You can believe this or not and I have no way of proving it but I can promise you it's the truth. I knew I couldn't marry Arnold and I was about to say so when there was a hullabaloo and the wedding was off anyway.'

'So why didn't you let me know?'

'Because I thought you wouldn't believe that I was about to say no to the vows. I wouldn't have blamed you either. I'd already hurt you; I didn't want to disrupt your life again and have you think I was using you. So I stayed away and let everyone else think I was the one who was let down, because they all saw me as the victim and if I'd tried to tell the truth it would just have looked like a bid to save my pride.'

'So why should I believe you now?'

'You don't have to. Just let me help you. I want nothing from you, only that you give my ideas some thought. Or at least take another look at the situation and maybe have another chat with your accountant before you sign the place over. Obviously I don't know how bad things are, but if there's even so much as a glimmer of hope, please don't give up on something that means so much to you without a fight.'

'These fancy ideas are all very well, but I have serious responsibilities. Dad has been forced to retire, so it's up to me to do what's best for Mum and Dad.'

'I know, Charlie,' she said gently, 'but I'm sure your father would rather have a smaller orchard than no orchard at all, even if you'd have to do other things as well to make it pay.' She paused, looking at him and seeing the strain etched into his face, the dark shadows under his eyes, the tightness of his mouth, and knew how worried he was. 'Surely it's worth a little more thought.'

There was a long pause; then he said, 'I'll have to be getting back now.'

'To finalise things?'

'Yes, that's right,' he confirmed briskly. 'Verbally, at least, and I'm a man of my word. Once I've shaken hands on something I won't go back on it, even though I haven't signed anything.'

'I see,' she sighed. 'I'd better make my way back to the station then.'

'You'll call into the house to see my father, though, won't you? He'll be very hurt to know you've come all this way and not bothered to say hello.'

'Of course,' she said. 'I didn't suggest it because I don't want to impose.'

'You won't be. He'll be glad of some fresh company,' he assured her. 'Now that he's getting better he gets very bored just sitting about all day.'

'I'll pop in for a few minutes then,' she agreed. 'Then I'll be on my way. I've said my piece; there's nothing more I can do.'

'No, there isn't,' he confirmed coolly. 'It was good of you to come but I have to face facts.'

'Of course.'

They walked back towards the house in silence.

Was there anything more she could have done, Clara asked herself as she stood on the station platform waiting for the London train. She couldn't have been pushier without insulting him. He was an intelligent man and an experienced fruit grower while she was just a waitress whose love for him made her concerned. She had told him how she felt about him and his response had been negative.

What had she expected? That he would say her ideas were the saviour of Brierley and fall into her arms after her declaration of love for him? The truth was, she had been so fired up with the idea of saving Brierley and making things right for him, she hadn't got as far as bracing herself for rejection. But that was what she had got and she was still reeling from it.

When they had got back to the house, Charlie had gone straight off with the buyer. She'd spent an hour or so with his parents, then left and walked to the station while Charlie was still in the office with the buyer, presumably shaking hands on the deal.

She was bitterly disappointed, humiliated and genuinely worried for him. The sooner she was back home in London the better. She was hurting badly and needed to be away from here. Where was that wretched train?

'So are we agreed on the final points then, Mr Fenner?' said the buyer. 'You are quite happy to deduct the cost of repairs that need doing to the property from the price?'

Charlie's head was spinning. He couldn't stop thinking about Clara and the fact that she had come all the way to Kent to tell him she would give up her life in London and work for nothing to help him keep Brierley. That was some commitment!

'Mr Fenner,' said the man again, looking at his pocket watch. 'Can we get this last point settled, please? I have things to do and need to be on my way.'

'Yes. Of course,' Charlie said, recalled to the present. 'Now where were we?'

At last the train was coming in. Clara could see it in the distance, snaking its way towards the station heralded by clouds of steam. About time too! It was late due to some problem on the line.

There was a tap on her shoulder and, turning, she found herself face to face with Charlie.

'Did you mean what you said?' he asked.

'About working for nothing?'

'No, the other thing.'

She looked at him, thinking back over their conversation. 'The main reason I want to help, you mean?'

'That's the one.'

She smiled and melted his heart. 'Yes, I meant it,' she said. 'Very much so.'

The train came and went without Clara on board.

Epilogue

A year later Clara walked to the altar in her local church on her father's arm for the second time. But on this occasion there were no interruptions and the wedding of Clara Tripp and Charlie Fenner came to a happy conclusion.

There were church bells, confetti, and a reception at the same hall they had booked before. The only difference was that this time Clara was marrying the right man.

Everyone who mattered was there. All Clara's London friends and relations and quite a crowd from Kent. Even John Fenner was well enough to travel to London with his wife for the event. It was a real family occasion with Eva as the bridesmaid and Sydney – to whom she had recently become engaged – the best man.

But now they were at the reception and Charlie was coming to the end of his speech.

'Clara and I have had a few hiccups on the way but we finally made it,' he said, looking at her tenderly. 'And this lady who has honoured me by becoming my wife has also done a lot for my family as well as for me personally. She dropped everything in London to come to Kent to help me hang on to our orchard. It's smaller now and busier because we don't employ many staff and we have more irons in the fire, but it's still ours. Clara runs the tea room, helps in the orchard and organises the bed and breakfast side of our business. Mum has a new lease of life baking for the café customers and Dad is able to do his bit in the orchard which we would have lost had it not been for Clara.' He looked towards Flo and Frank. 'The only thing is, I have taken her away from her family.'

'Not to mention stealing another of my brood,' Flo cut in laughingly because Cuddy, no longer a schoolboy, had decided to go to Brierley and learn the business because he thrived in the country environment. 'But he's happy, that's the main thing, and he does come back home when he can. Anyway, we have Eva who will be marrying our boy Sydney next year and she's planning on staying in London, so you could call it a fair swap.'

There were gales of laughter. Mabel was pink-cheeked and happy. Her life had been transformed by having the tea room and the bed and breakfast visitors to cook for. The house had seemed empty with two of her brood gone, so providing delicious food for paying customers had helped to fill the gap.

'Anyway, may I just say in conclusion,' continued Charlie, 'that I am happy and honoured to be married to such a beautiful lady. Please raise your glasses to my wife Clara.'

As they all stood and drank the toast, Clara thought that nothing in her life could ever compete with how good she felt now. But then, as she turned to her husband and smiled, she realised that there would be many more moments to equal and even surpass this one as she and Charlie headed along life's path together. They had so very much to look forward to.